# School of Dreams

# School of Dreams

Book One of The School of Dreams Series

**Julia Sutton**

# Acknowledgements

I would like to thank all at Next Chapter and especially Miika Hannila, for giving me this opportunity and for the help, support and advice.

Thank you to my husband Stephen and two children Jack and Issy, for their encouragement and for listening to me read parts of the book.

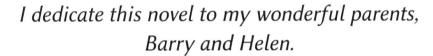

*I dedicate this novel to my wonderful parents, Barry and Helen.*

*Nefelibata:* '*Cloud Walker*', *one who lives in the clouds of their own imagination or dreams or one who does not obey the conventions of society; an unconventional, unorthodox person.*

*Welcome to the City of Chattlesbury, England*
*In this, our fair city, learning is the key. We can open minds and hearts. Learning enables us to be free.*

# Chapter One

**Sophie**

"Kids, breakfast is nearly ready." Sophie stood at the bottom of the winding staircase and yelled. Hopefully her voice would carry into their bedrooms and over the hum and drone of TVs and X-Boxes. A few minutes later there was a clatter from upstairs, doors opening, feet stomping, and then twin boys tore into the kitchen swinging their school bags high above their heads.

"What's for breakfast Mom?" Asked eight-year-old Jake.

"Can I have orange juice?" Josh demanded at the same time.

"Eggs and soldiers Jake and yes Josh, there's orange on the table." Sophie pulled her silk dressing gown tighter around her, then continued flicking the egg yolks with bubbling water.

"Is your dad up yet?" She asked, without looking around.

"Dunno," said Josh as he poured juice into a Monsters Inc. plastic beaker. Sophie sighed. Ryan O'Neill, her husband of ten years, was a lazy good for nothing, she thought sourly. Last night he had promised he would be the one to get up this morning and see to the boys, so she could have a lie in. Yet here she was, in the kitchen again. Thank god the cleaner was coming in half an hour. *She* could tidy up the breakfast things and put the washing in, plus there was a mountain of ironing to be done. Sophie yawned, it had been a heavy night last night. They had entertained friends and after a three-course meal, courtesy of 'Spice of India', they had partied until two o'clock.

That's when Ryan had promised to do more with the boys, a drunken declaration in front of friends. Sophie knew she had been nagging him a lot these past couple of weeks, but sometimes she felt like a single parent. Today was no exception. The eggs hissed in the pan and Sophie transferred them to slices of overcooked toast, then set them down in front of the boys. She shuffled into the large utility room searching around in the medicine cabinet for Alka-Seltzer; she needed something to settle her stomach sharpish. Her mouth felt dry and her head was pounding. Too many bottles of Chardonnay were overturned in the sink; she looked at them with a grimace. Hadn't that been her New Year's resolution, to cut down on the booze? January seemed a long time ago now though. It was July, warm and sticky already and it was only seven thirty in the morning. Sophie thought about what she could wear today. It was the twin's sports day, she wanted to be cool but classy. She swallowed down the Alka-Seltzer, then padded back into the kitchen. Josh had turned on the TV; Cartoon Network blared out, making her pounding head feel even worse.

"Mom, can I have jam sandwiches?" Asked Jake, between mouthfuls of runny egg. Sophie nodded and grunted a reply. She peered into the cupboard and extracted a half open loaf of bread. Food shopping was also on the agenda today, a trip to Waitrose was required to replenish the fridge. Although she herself ate little and was currently on the cabbage water diet, where she had successfully lost seven pounds off her petite, size ten frame, Josh, Jake and Ryan however, were forever snacking. Sophie opened the huge American style fridge, taking out margarine and a large pot of supermarket best brand jam. She smeared it on the bread, generously thick, then searched in the cupboard for lunchtime snacks.

"Boys, have you done your homework?" No reply, eyes were fixated on the TV

"Boys," Sophie yelled. They turned to look at her quizzically, so she had to repeat the question. Still no reply.

"So you haven't then," she paused, while two heads shook in unison.

"Well what's Miss Marshall going to say now," Sophie sighed. That would be another phone call home from the head teacher. She ran through a list of excuses and couldn't think of any that were plausible. She could try flirting with the Head; she had learnt from experience that men were suckers for flattery and a whiny voice. But Miss Marshall, well she was a different kettle of fish. At the last parents evening, Sophie had been intimidated by the older woman with the stern voice and the piercing eyes. God knows how the kids found her. Although Sophie had to admit that her twin's boisterous behaviour had certainly calmed down since they had been in her class.

"You both need to read now," Sophie decided. Josh and Jake pulled faces at their mother but obediently rummaged in sturdy school bags for their reading books. Thank god it was nearly the end of term, Sophie thought as she scribbled her signature in their reading diaries.

While they read above the din of the TV, Sophie listened distractedly, rubbing her head with one hand and her stomach with the other. Truthfully, she felt awful and wanted nothing more than to climb back into bed and shove Ryan O'Neill out.

"Okay, that's enough boys," she snapped irritably. Their attention was immediately back on the gigantic screen and Sophie felt a pang of guilt. Hangovers and young children were not a good combination; they made her bad tempered for the whole day and tested her patience considerably. No more drinking, she thought firmly as she fetched the dirty plates, plonking them in the sink with a clatter, and then made her way sluggishly up the winding staircase, to her bedroom. On the way she caught sight of herself in the mirror and grimaced. God, she looked awful. Her normally immaculate straight hair had balled into a fluffy mess and last night's make up was crusting on her eyes and cheeks. Spots! She thought with a silent wail. She could hear the sound of heavy breathing and snoring emanating from the bedroom. Her darling husband was lying in the bed, sprawled on his back, with his face turned up towards the ceiling. Sophie snapped on the light, then pulled the wardrobe doors open with a bang. There was a rustling and squeaking from the bed. As she searched through her hanging clothes, he sat up.

"Huh, what time is it?" Ryan O'Neill croaked.

"Seven thirty," Sophie snapped, without turning around. Finally, she decided on something to wear, a polka dot playsuit, which would look good when teamed with her new blue wedges. She laid it on the bed, then searched in her dresser for suitable matching underwear.

"Got a bad head have ya?" Sophie asked, then without waiting for a response continued, "I told you not to start on the whisky."

Ryan groaned and fell back on plump, feather pillows.

"How many bottles of wine did you and Clara polish off then?" He retaliated.

"Well I can take my alcohol, unlike some," she sniffed, "and it doesn't stop me having to get up at seven o'clock with the boys. Angrily, she flung lacy bra and pants on the bed, then stormed into their en suite, to turn on the power shower. It rumbled to life, spraying her arm with cold water, making her jump. Sophie flung her dressing gown on the floor in a heap, then stepped gingerly into the shower cubicle. As she exfoliated, she could hear Ryan's deep snores again. Unbelievable that he could sleep so easily. Sophie herself, suffered from bouts of insomnia, which improved with the help of alcohol. Maybe she shouldn't cut out alcohol completely, she surmised. She washed her hair quickly. She would be taking the kids to school in about forty minutes which meant no time to straighten it; another reason to heighten her bad mood! Sophie snapped off the water and then wrapped herself in a luxurious, fluffy bath sheet before brushing her teeth. She examined her mouth in the steamy mirror. Her teeth were looking a bit off colour, even though she used whitening toothpaste. Maybe she should have them professionally whitened. Mentally, she added this to her to do list.

"What's for breakfast?" A voice behind startled her. She watched Ryan's reflection as he staggered to the toilet.

"Whatever you want to make yourself," she replied crisply, "there's eggs, sausage, cereal, toast…"

Ryan flushed the chain, "What time is Helga coming?"

"She should be here for nine, why?"

"I'll ask her to rustle me up a cooked breakfast."

Sophie tutted, shook her head and spat out the minty toothpaste. Helga was their fifty-four-year-old housekeeper, cum general dogsbody. Although it wasn't in her job description to cook for the O'Neill clan exactly, Sophie doubted that she would be able to resist the Irish charm. Ryan knew exactly how to turn it on, to his advantage and there were not many people who were immune to it; herself included. He wound strong arms around his wife and nuzzled her neck. Sophie sighed and stifled a giggle. She was supposed to be mad at her husband, but it was hard to be, when he knew, from years of exploration, where her erogenous zone was!

She playfully slapped his hands away, "have you got footy practise today?" Ryan groaned and nodded.

"Do I have to go?"

"Well you'd better if you don't want Coach Jones on your case."

Ryan was a professional football player. As a young boy he had been football crazy, spending all his spare time with a ball at his feet. Academically he flagged behind his peers, but at sports he excelled. He found school overall to be boring and unstimulating. He was happiest having a kick about with friends in the park. At the tender age of twelve, he had been scouted by a large, well known Midlands football team. He had joined the academy and had never looked back since. Now he was twenty-eight, in his prime and adored by thousands. Men and women jostled for his autograph as soon as he stepped out of the front door, he had his own aftershave range and a calendar shoot, which had been extremely popular, resulting in millions of pounds' worth of sales. He was certainly riding the crest of a wave in the popularity stakes at the moment, and Sophie hoped and prayed that it may continue.

She had known him since school. At the age of sixteen, after months of wooing, she had succumbed to his Irish charm and dark, Gaelic good looks. Over the years, they had dated and she had fallen deeply in love with him. When they were nineteen, they had splashed out on a trip to Hawaii, where surrounded by friends and family, they had married. Twelve months later, the twins had blessed their life. Now, here they were in a sprawling eight-bedroom mansion, with two dogs and three cats to add to their entourage. Sophie struggled into her expensive underwear. It had been a Christmas present from Ryan. Although the pants fit snugly, the bra was a cup size too tight. Since when had she been a 'C' cup she thought with a flicker of annoyance? – maybe before the twins had been born when she was skinny – but that had been years ago. These days, pregnancy and breast feeding had accentuated her curves to a 'D' cup much to her delight.

"Can you make sports day?" Sophie asked expectantly.

Ryan shook his head, "no can do babe," he retorted, as he clambered back into bed, "footy practise, physio and then team lunch. I won't be home until later this afternoon."

Sophie sighed, "okay fine, I'll go alone...again." She stepped into her cotton playsuit, pulling it up quickly, then searched in her wardrobe for her wedges. A quick blast of the hairdryer and she was nearly ready. She perched at her dressing room table and smothered on her makeup.

"Mom's coming for dinner tonight."

She heard Ryan groan in response, "and don't wind her up!" She snapped.

"I'll be on my best behaviour for sure," Ryan replied cheekily, as he pulled back the duvet slightly to reveal a large erection. "Sure you can't come back for a bit?"

Sophie grinned and peered at his naked frame. As well as being footy mad, Ryan was also sex mad. Her friends thought that she was dead lucky, but sometimes Ryan's pestering became tiresome. Just lately she had been more tired than usual after a day running around after the kids and the animals. Her libido was in sleep mode. And some nights, even Irish charm could not kick start it. Sophie worried about refusing him though, especially as there was a plethora of eyelash fluttering groupies hanging around at the club. She knew that being a footballer also bought attention from hordes of females who would be only too happy to jump into bed with her charming, handsome husband.

"Maybe later," she said with a sultry smile. She grabbed her Gucci handbag and blew him a kiss.

"See ya later honey, have a good day."

Ryan grumbled in response, burying himself back under the duvet. Sophie clattered down the stairs, calling Josh and Jake. They raced into the hallway like two whirlwinds.

"Have you got your bags and lunches?" she hollered, above their enthusiastic singing. A few minutes later, they were yelling goodbye to their dad and charging outside into the sunshine.

The school run was hectic as usual. Sophie weaved her four by four around parked cars, looking for a big enough space. She cursed as a BMW manoeuvred into a space directly in front of her. Sophie honked her horn and was answered by a rude, two fingered salute.

"We'll have to go down the side street and walk," she informed the boys, as she turned down the volume on the radio. They groaned in protest.

"Look," she said annoyed, "I had to walk everywhere when I was your age, it'll do you good."

"Get rid of some of that energy," she muttered under her breath. Josh and Jake charged up the street, pretending they were Power Rangers, swinging their lunch boxes high above their heads. Sophie lagged behind, breathless and panting. I really must stop smoking, she thought with a grimace. They reached the lollipop lady just in time, she beckoned them over with a grin and a wave.

"Hi Jill," Sophie panted.

"Hi Soph, how's your Ryan?"

"Good thanks," Sophie called, hurrying past.

The school gates were busy, teeming with children and harassed looking parents. The bell rang out shrilly, just in time! Sophie kissed her boys, waving as they skipped up the driveway. She breathed a sigh of relief, her shoulders sagging, then turned back to cross the busy main road.

Sophie had timed it just right. A flying visit to Waitrose, back home to unpack and she was back at the school gates for eleven o'clock. As she stepped outside her chilled four by four, the heat hit her with a rush. She snapped her sunglasses on, rubbed lip-gloss off her teeth and marched towards the school, swaying her hips. A dusty white van passed, slowing down to reveal two dusty looking youths who wolf whistled at her. Sophie smiled slightly, revelling in the unexpected male attention. I've still got it, she thought, tossing her hair back, even though it was so politically incorrect to admit she liked the attention of workmen.

"Woo hoo." Standing on the opposite side of the road, waving enthusiastically was Sophie's friend Amber. Amber was two years older than

Sophie, tall and elegant looking with a mane of luminous, dark brown, cascading hair. She had one child who was in the same class as Josh and Jake called Angel, who was anything but. Her husband was a bank manager and they were absolutely loaded.

"Hi Soph," she gushed, air kissing both cheeks. Sophie smiled, "hi," she replied warmly.

"Are you excited about the sports day? I am. Angel has been practising races all weekend at home, I'm exhausted." Sophie looked in surprise. Josh was too laid back to be competitive and Jake was too interested in his x-box and computer games to worry about sports day.

"It should be fun," agreed Sophie politely.

"I've got a new camcorder, so I can record Josh and Jake if you want me to." Amber waved an ultra slim, state of the art contraption.

"Oh that's a great idea," Sophie replied, trying to create a sense of enthusiasm. She doubted whether Ryan would have the time or inclination to watch hours of blurred footage of hundreds of over excited school children. They made their way through the jostling crowds onto the school field, where an army of parents had set up camp behind the partition.

"Excuse me," Amber said with a derisory curl of her lip. A windswept man in front moved a fraction to his left, giving Amber the opportunity to shove her video recorder into the gap.

"This is one of Angel's," she informed Sophie with a proud grin. Sophie stood on tiptoe so she could watch six eight year olds line up obediently with plastic eggs and shiny dessert spoons. Thank goodness Josh and Jake were not participating in this one! It would definitely be a designer hand bags at dawn saga. Sophie relaxed and popped a mint humbug in her mouth.

"Come on Angel," shouted Amber. Sophie waved in half-hearted support. Although she was fond of Amber, her daughter left a lot to be desired. Ryan called her the rich imp from over the bridge. Of course Sophie remonstrated, but secretly agreed. To look at her, she was certainly angelic; a round cherubic, rosy face, framed with golden ringlets and huge sapphire blue eyes. Her personality, however, was certainly devilish and that was being polite. During the reception and year one phase, Amber had been called by the head teacher on an almost weekly basis. 'Angel', had stolen from other children's bags, bullied her peers for money, cut two girls' ponytails off and called the chief dinner lady a fat frustrated bitch! She was certainly articulate, if nothing else, Sophie thought ruefully. She almost felt sorry for her teacher, Miss Marshall, bet she just loved inclusion!

Sophie watched the teachers, as they yelled instructions and cajoled the children into their places, their faces red and perspiring. She stared at their frumpy and flowery attire, wondering if they had ever heard of the word fashion.

Amber was shaking her head thinking the same thing. "Dearie me," she commented, peering over her sunglasses, "is that a tea dress?" Sophie giggled along with her friend.

"I love your playsuit darling; the colour is awesome." Amber gave her a thumbs up and Sophie grinned, feeling happy with her choice of outfit. The teachers looked so dowdy and frumpy, she thought with a shudder, and some of them looked as if they were going to combust through a mixture of heat exhaustion and stress. Overworked and underpaid, she decided, but there was no excuse for letting your appearance go, surely? Only last week, she had watched a TV programme on teaching in the modern era and had been shocked by the revelations of a newly qualified teacher's salary. Ryan had laughed, but Sophie had been shocked and red faced when she compared her husband's salary to that of a teacher. Although Sophie did concede that Ryan was extremely talented with a ball, his feet were made of gold. They should be insured, she thought with a happy smile, like Beyonce's bum or Cindy Crawford's legs. Anyway, millions of normal people had the ability to teach, but there were only a handful of truly exceptional foot-ballers – wasn't that right?

Although they had plenty of money, Sophie considered herself normal, down to earth even. Although just lately, she had felt restless, with a sudden inclination that there was much more to life than being a footballer's wife. She reminisced on her own school days. She had been an average pupil, not very studious at all, more interested in living it large with her friends and batting her jet black voluminous lashes at the likes of Ryan O'Neill. There were a few subjects however, in which she excelled; mainly Art and English. Sophie had subsequently left Allhallows Secondary School with a handful of GCSEs and A levels. She remembered her friends being well jealous of her. An 'A' in Art and her 'A*' in English. Sophie had been coolly overjoyed, not wanting to look like a girly swot. When she was with her circle of ultra cool friends, she had been blasé, but secretly, she had been ecstatic at her English results.

English had always been her favourite subject. Since an early age, she had been a voracious reader, devouring books at the eager rate of two per week and more during the summer holidays. Before the mid teen phase, she always had her nose stuck in a book, but by the time she was fifteen, friends and partying had taken precedence and she had forgotten her much loved tomes. They lined the walls of her bedroom, gathering cobwebs and dust.

"Whoop, whoop," Amber erupted, startling her so that she jumped. The hot and flustered head teacher stood in the middle of the field waving a white hankie in the air and bellowing "go." Sophie peered on tiptoe. She could just make out Angel's plump frame, waddling down the field, as she cast mutinous glares at her peers, who duly fell back so she could take the lead. Sophie shook her head in disbelief and glanced at the teachers to see if they had noticed, but they were too busy chattering amongst themselves, so Sophie shrugged and clapped along to Amber's exuberant encouragement. The noise on the field had grown considerably as the six children stumbled down the field, and then suddenly, there was a shriek and Angel toppled over, landing in a crumpled heap, while the egg bounced off ahead. Good job it was plastic! Amber gasped theatrically.

"Here, hold this." She shoved the camcorder into Sophie's sweaty palms, and then barged through the crowd to tug up the partition.

"I'm coming darling!" she called, running across the field to pick up a bellowing Angel. From nearby, someone sniggered. Sophie zoomed in the camcorder's lens, so that it magnified Amber's tight, skinny buttocks straining under the weight of her only daughter. She stifled a giggle. Then she felt a pang of guilt and turned off the contraption, with a soft click. The other children seized their chance of victory and galloped off ahead, to whoops and yells from the crowd. Amber supported a limping, wailing, red faced and furious looking Angel.

"Well done Angel," Sophie called feebly. The man in front and a cluster of women to her left stared at her incredulously.

"Little brat!" she heard one state, with barely concealed venom, "serves her right." Sophie blinked, moved away from the crowds and decided to linger at the back and await the return of her friend. After a quick glance at the wilting programme, she spotted Josh and Jake's names in the running races, right at the end. She wandered over to the refreshment tent, grabbing lemonade for herself and Amber. On the table there was an assortment of flavoured muffins, which looked delicious. She managed to avoid temptation, stuffing her notes back in her purse and moving away. As she sipped the cool refreshing drink, her mind wandered back to her own sports day. She remembered winning the three legged race with Darren Carruthers. They had been paired together because they were the smallest in the class. To her shame, they had been jeered and heckled by their classmates. God, kids were cruel! But, after weeks of practise on the school playground, they had triumphed and won. Sophie smiled at the memory, pushing her slippery glasses back up the bridge of her nose. The sun was high in the sky, beating down hotly; thankfully there was a slight breeze rustling the trees. This calls for a spot of sunbathing and Pimms, she thought with relish. Maybe she would invite Amber over for lunch and a good gossip.

Another group of children were being herded up to the start line. Jeez, it was like a military procedure, she thought with a sniff. The children looked very small and absolutely terrified. Sophie herself had always loved primary school, in fact her childhood had been pretty idyllic she ruminated, but nowadays, it was all SATS and stress on the poor kiddies. At their age, she had been happy and carefree, but now as an adult, she felt anything but. There was always so much to worry about. Carefree had been replaced with anxiety and true delight was something she only experienced when purchasing a new pair of Louboutin shoes; that feeling was even better then sex! A trip to the doctor six months ago had resulted in a "short" prescription of anti-depressant medication, which she was still on six months later. Some people, like her natural, organic, health mad mother, avoided prescription drugs like the plague, but Sophie was happy to take them. They calmed her jangling nerves, kept her precarious moods stable and generally perked her up. In fact, she was loath to give them up. Although she knew she really should, she couldn't keep blagging her poor, manipulated doctor forever. Also, one of the warnings of the medication was to 'avoid alcohol,' which was a big incentive to kick the meds. Sophie had therefore culminated a plan to wean herself off them and generally improve her life prospects.

She had been waiting in the doctors' surgery, on a grey, wet miserable day, when she had noticed a bright flyer advertising the city's university. A quick scan had cheered her up immensely.

Words such as 'prospects', 'achievement', 'enjoyment', 'goals' had captured her attention and she was immediately drawn in. After her consultation and re-prescription, Sophie had surreptitiously snatched one up and shoved it away. Weeks had passed and she had forgotten all about it. Then, one warm, sunny, Sunday morning while cleaning the car, she had found it crumpled in the glove compartment and stood there for a while, on their vast driveway, reading it over again, as it fluttered in the light breeze. Ryan had been away for the weekend, on a friendly football tournament to Ireland. So Sophie had fired up her laptop and had spent the rest of the morning and part of the afternoon studying the university's website. Excitement had coursed through her as she navigated to the English course structure and read over it. Then, on the spur of the moment, an impulsive madness had taken hold and she had quickly completed the online application, sending it flying off into cyberspace, with trembling fingers.

That had been about six weeks ago and since then, she had heard nothing, which spoke volumes really, she thought; they must have re-jected her application. Not enough 'A' levels maybe she pondered. Would two be sufficient, when compared with the fresh school leavers of today, who left with three and four. Or maybe they had recognised her name and had a good laugh about it. Imagine it, a footballer's wife at uni. Sophie gulped down her lemonade and pushed the negative thoughts aside. Silly dreams, that's all they were. Just then Amber came bounding over, panting and puffing. Sophie passed her the drink wordlessly and listened as she complained bitterly and loudly about the un-fairness of the egg and spoon race. She could see Josh and Jake sheltering from the fierce heat un-derneath a large oak tree, with a group of their friends. It was nearly time for their race. She pulled Amber up to the partition, with her cam-corder in tow. They were moving towards the starting point. Sophie was mortified to see Josh picking his nose and Jake looking as nonchalant as ever. They had managed to squeeze into a good position, so Sophie could clap and cheer her boys, as they ran their hearts out in the relay race, winning easily. Sophie watched in delight as they high fived their team mates. They had always been good at running, she thought proudly, although as yet, they hadn't shown much interest in footy, much to Ryan's chagrin. The other races passed quickly with her boys excelling, coming first and a very respectable second.

Sophie wiped away beads of perspiration from her brow. She felt that she herself had run the races and was relieved that another sports day was over. Another one that Ryan had missed, she thought sadly.

"You wanna watch this tonight with Ryan?" Asked Amber, waving her camcorder.

Sophie sighed, "there's no rush. You go ahead and enjoy it with Martin."

Amber shrugged, tucking it away in her designer handbag.

"Hey, do you fancy coming over for a Pimms lunch? We could walk and get the kids from school."

Amber's eyes brightened, "great idea," she replied, then wrinkled her nose. "Forget walking though, I'll get the Au Pair to pick the kids up." She fished in her bag for her mobile and began yelling instructions into the phone. Sophie smiled. What the heck, she deserved an afternoon off from motherly duties.

"Hell yes," she answered. Linking arms with her friend, they strode off in the direction of their gleaming, waiting cars, giggling like school girls.

Back at home, she searched in the fridge for the Pimms. Luckily, there was almost a full bottle, thank god! She hunted around until she found the lemonade then squashed it in, removing a bottle of cabbage water in the process and binning it. The diet was out the window for the next hour, she thought with glee. There was a sudden noise and Sophie almost jumped out of her skin, as she noticed the housekeeper hovering in the doorway, a yellow duster in her hand.

"Hello Mrs O'Neill, you back early."

Sophie glanced her way nodding, "yes," she replied.

Her mother had always warned her about becoming too friendly with the staff.

"They take advantage," she had snapped, even though she herself lived alone and had no staff to worry about. Sophie had taken heed however, although to be fair, Helga was very polite and hardworking and that was how Sophie intended it to stay. She chewed her lip thoughtfully. "Could you please make two salads for lunch Helga," she stated, rather than asked. The housekeeper's nostrils flared.

"Is Heidi mam."

Sophie batted away the correction.

"Yes, yes Heidi…erm, with extra cheese and Branston."

There was a silent pause. Sophie turned to stare icily at the housekeeper, whose face had turned pink.

"I…I, finish at twelve," she indicated at the clock.

Sophie looked up. "Well you have another five minutes yet, that's plenty of time," she snapped.

Heidi paused then nodded, "okay Mam, I make quickly, but then I go…I pick up granddaughter from how you say – nuture?"

"Nursery," Sophie corrected with a sigh. "Okay, well you see to the salad and I will slice the bread." Sophie theatrically removed a crusty loaf from its wrapper, then sliced it clumsily, placing it next to a pot of butter and Branston.

As Heidi whizzed expertly around the kitchen, Sophie instructed.

"The best Royal Doulton plates please and the crystal wine goblets." Sophie noticed the house-keeper peer at her a few times and if she wasn't mistaken, there was a definite unattractive curl to her lip. Maybe it was time she got herself a nice English housekeeper, she thought spitefully. Ryan seemed to love her though and the feeling was definitely mutual. Heidi couldn't do enough for *him*, granddaughter or not!

As Heidi was covering the food with cling film, the doorbell chimed.

"Okay, you can finish," Sophie decided crisply, "please let Mrs Lavelle in on your way out."

"Thank you mam, have a nice lunch," the housekeeper replied, with an exaggerated bow to her head. Sophie tutted crossly, but decided to leave it this once. She busied herself, covering the bread, just as Amber sauntered into the kitchen.

"Hi babe," Amber air kissed both cheeks. "This is lovely," as she motioned to the food, with one perfectly manicured finger. Sophie tried to hide her chewed nail varnish under a napkin.

"Just something nice I put together for us," she replied with a bright smile. What was a little white lie between friends!

Amber gripped her arm, "Is the dressing low-cal honey?" There was a worried look across her thin face.

"Of course," Sophie nodded, wide eyed, as if she had just been asked if the sky was blue.

"Phew," breathed Amber, "only there's a big banker's luncheon coming up and I've got my eye on this amazzzzing size six Versace dress."

The two women clattered into the garden, armed with the plates of food. When she had settled Amber at the luxurious garden furniture, Sophie meandered back inside for the booze and the ice bucket. On the way out she grabbed the mail, which was perched on the breakfast bar.

"This is amazing," Amber commented, as she hungrily devoured the salad, "the salmon is to die for."

Sophie smiled at her friend's enthusiasm. Tugging the top off the Pimms with a flourish, she poured the frothing liquid into the goblets.

"It's one of Gordon Ramsey's Cordon Bleu range," she couldn't help but brag. They ate their lunch quickly, as both were famished. Sophie looked through the mail; bills, bills, takeaway fliers, bills, more bills and oh what was this? Sophie's eyes widened at the university symbol on the white rectangle envelope. She dropped her cutlery with a clatter and with shaking hands, tore open the envelope, pulling out the single piece of paper with the elaborate crest at the top. OMG, her application had been successful! Sophie coughed and took a large swig of Pimms.

"You okay Soph?" Amber asked, peering over the rim of her Prada sunglasses. Sophie nodded, with a wide grin.

"I've been accepted onto an English degree course," she hugged the letter to her ample bosom.

"What?!" Spluttered Amber, "you never even told me you'd applied."

Sophie shook her head, "I haven't told anyone," she divulged.

Amber shook her head, "not even Ryan? Well what's he going to say?"

Sophie bristled, "he'll be happy for me of course!" She had expected Amber to be excited or happy for her at least, but her whole attitude was coming across as being very negative.

"Why on earth would you put yourself through all that stress Soph?" When there was no reply, Amber continued, "why are you doing it? You don't *need* to work!"

That was stating the obvious Sophie thought. She chewed her lip considering the question, why was she doing it? She wondered. Amber was staring at her, waiting for a reply.

"I've always wanted to..." she explained lamely.

Amber sniffed, "well, rather you than me. I don't envy you, that's for sure."

"Thanks Amber," Sophie retaliated, her voice dripping with sarcasm; she was regretting inviting her for lunch now. She could feel her excitement dissipating inside of her, like popping bubbles.

"Anyway hun," Amber carried on oblivious, "about that dress..."

# Chapter Two

**Evelyn**

The letter arrived second class post. The university must be saving on postage, Evelyn thought with a smile, as she bent forward to collect Tuesday's mail from the fraying, dull red carpet. From upstairs she could hear movement. Although it was almost midday, Nora, Evelyn's Mother was just rising. She could hear the squeak of bedsprings and then a moment later a call.

"Evelyn, Evelyn dear," her daughter placed the mail on the small telephone table, there would be plenty of time for that later.

"Coming Mam," she called. Nora was due out this afternoon, to the council run daycentre, where she passed the time playing bingo, listening to music and having copious amounts of tea with other similar pensioners. Although Evelyn doubted there was anyone quite like Mam there;

she was a real gem. Nora's weekly outing gave Evelyn some much needed respite, a chance to unwind, to catch up with housework, or do a spot of shopping and very rarely even to run a relaxing bath and read a book. Although she loved Mam dearly, it was tiring being the sole carer for a ninety-six-year-old.

She slowly climbed the stairs. Today she felt all of her fifty-four years, her back was aching and her arms felt like lead. Only last week, her doctor had suggested yet again that maybe Nora might be better suited in a residential care home. But Evelyn had rejected the idea immediately, telling the doctor that there was no way her mother would be going into a home for the elderly. Only last night there had been another documentary on the TV investigating poor care in those places. No, there was no way she would even consider it; her mind was resolutely made up. Nora had cared for her when she was a child and now she was returning the favour. Mam had been a single parent when Bert, Evelyn's Father had passed away from a sudden heart attack at the age of fifty-six. She had struggled to keep a roof over their head, holding down two jobs and also working as a seamstress in whatever little spare time she had. Now it was Nora's turn to be cared for.

Evelyn had been born as a late surprise. Nora and Bert had spent years trying to conceive. They had almost given up hope, then Evelyn had come along. She had been a happy addition to a warm and loving family. As an only child, she had been cherished, but not spoilt, no, never spoilt. Evelyn glanced at the photo frames on the wall as she passed them; her mam and dad cuddling up and laughing together, the three of them grinning like fools on a beach in Somerset. Her dad in his fishing gear, with his arms wrapped around a beaming Evelyn. So many happy memories, she thought, as she opened Nora's bedroom door with a sigh. The scent of lavender clung to the air mixed with her mam's sweet perfume. As she entered the spacious room, Evelyn thought how tiny Mam looked in the king-size bed. Nora was leaning over, trying to reach a glass of lukewarm water. Evelyn rushed over, wincing at the pain in her lower back.

"Here, let me!" She scolded, helping Nora to sit upright and fluffing the pillows behind her.

"Did you sleep well Mam?" She enquired, as she passed her the glass of water.

Nora took a sip, "too well my dear, did you?" Evelyn nodded, hoping Nora had not noticed the dark shadows below her grey eyes.

"But you look tired," Mam stated, squinting over the rim of her glasses. Evelyn sighed, there was no tricking Nora, she was still as quick witted and astute as she had been forty years ago. Doctor Dunn always asked her secret, on one of his rare home visits.

"There is no secret," Nora would reply, "just clean living and crosswords." She had winked at the doctor then, making everyone laugh.

Evelyn smiled warmly at the memory, her eyes brightening. "I wrote another chapter of my book last night," she disclosed quietly, perching on the edge of the soft bed, "I didn't sleep until gone midnight. The ideas kept coming."

Nora clapped her hands together with excitement and there was a twinkle in her eyes as she said, "you are so clever! Is it nearly finished now?"

Evelyn nodded, "another few chapters and then lots of editing."

"You must send it off Evelyn, you have a real talent and it's time you shared it with others."

"It's probably not good enough to be published," she replied, with a small shake of her head. Nora tutted and reached forward to clasp her hands.

"What you read to me so far was just brilliant. Don't put yourself down love, you have to think positive." But Evelyn found that advice so hard to listen to. She was full of self doubt. Writing was her passion, always had been, ever since she had been a child, but she lacked confidence in her ability, and constantly referred to her stories and poetry as 'just a hobby.' And now, over the past twelve months, she had written a novel, a romantic saga, bursting with love, trials and tribulations and colourful, engaging characters. Now she was nearing the end, and all the ties were binding together nicely. In spite of her insecurities, Evelyn was so excited. Most evenings, when Mam had retired to bed, she fired up her laptop and began tap, tapping away, her fingers flying over the keyboard, rushing to free all the racing thoughts and ideas inside her head. She had read the first few chapters to Nora, who had been enthusiastic and supportive, but family and friends always were Evelyn thought hesitantly. What she really needed was honest, unbiased advice, but professional proof readers were so expensive and Evelyn didn't feel that she was ready for that kind of criticism just yet.

"Let's get you up then Mam," Evelyn decided crisply, as she pulled back the warm duvet. She hoisted Nora out of the bed and together they hobbled to the en-suite bathroom.

After a fine brunch of poached eggs and warm crusty bread, they sat together in the lounge discussing the weather and the day's upcoming events.

"It's bingo today, followed by afternoon tea and scones," Nora said with a twinkle in her eye.

"Sounds good," Evelyn replied with a smile. Her mother's enthusiasm for the daycentre was touching and endearing she thought, as she cleared away the plates and cutlery.

"Will Joe be there today?"

"Sure to be," Nora replied with a chuckle, "he's won the last two weeks, bless him, he's probably hoping his luck continues."

"It might be your turn to be lucky today," Evelyn called from the kitchen, where she busied herself with the washing up. Her mother's soft laugh tinkled in the quiet stillness. The dishes were left to drain, then at twelve thirty, she helped Mam into her coat. Even though it was hot today, Nora still felt the cold. Her chilly hands brushed Evelyn's as they both made their way down the hall, to wait in the open doorway. Ten minutes later, the council bus rumbled into view. The driver jumped out spritely, a wide grin on his face.

"Hi there Nora, how's my favourite girl?"

"Tch, you say that to *all* the girls," Nora admonished, but there was a soft smile curling her lips.

"Evelyn," he tipped his cap in her direction and she felt herself blush.

"Afternoon Jacob," she mumbled, looking down slightly. Jacob had been picking Mam up and dropping her off for years now, but Evelyn still felt embarrassed in his company.

She had always been shy, but with men it was even worse. Nora often commented that Jacob was a 'lovely chap' and Evelyn would change the subject. She got the feeling that Mam was trying to match make. Although Jacob indeed was lovely: polite, friendly and charming. Evelyn had pushed aside any thoughts of romance. Her life was happy and complete; she did not need a man to complicate it.

In truth, she had ever only had one boyfriend, when she was in her twenties; Roger Salter, a work colleague that had taken a fancy to Evelyn. She had been immediately attracted to his tall, well built frame and steely blue eyes, so when they had started dating she had been smitten. When he proposed a year later, she had been overjoyed. When he had cheated on her three months before their wedding, she had been utterly devastated. There had been no one else since. Heartbreak had hardened her heart to love. She still found men attractive, indeed Jacob could be considered handsome with his sandy hair and dark eyes, but she had learnt from experience that men were not to be trusted. Apart from her dear, departed Dad of course.

Jacob was helping Nora onto the bus, making her chuckle with his amusing anecdotes. Evelyn watched as he guided her to an empty seat. Then with a toot of his horn and a wave from the window, they had gone, chugging up the street, narrowly missing a parked bicycle. Evelyn sighed and lifted her face upward, so the sun could warm it with its beaming rays. It was such a beautiful day she thought, maybe she could do a spot of gardening. Then she remembered her unopened mail and she rushed inside, her heart fluttering a little faster.

She made herself a pot of tea, before sitting down at the table with her letter. Her breath quickened as she gently opened the envelope, then caught her throat as she read the surprising news, that yes! She had been accepted onto the English degree course. Evelyn's eyes widened and the letter fell from her fingers with a flutter.

"Oh my," she said quietly.

For years she had passed the glass fronted building on the number six bus and stared up at the vast modern architecture that housed the city University.

'Gateway to learning,' a banner yelled, beckoning and enticing. And it had eventually enticed Evelyn. One rainy day, she had disembarked the bus a stop early and had wandered in front of the university, looking up at it in awe. It just so happened that this particular day was an open day. There was a small Asian lady sheltering underneath a bright brolly, giving out leaflets and chatting to passers-by.

"Everyone welcome," she had said with an encouraging smile, as she pressed a flyer into Evelyn's receptive hands. She had found herself being ushered inside, with a crowd of others and had stared about her in wonder at the plush, modern, squeaky clean surroundings. To her right stood the library.

"Come in, come in," welcomed a softly spoken librarian. The crowd of people had dispersed. Evelyn swallowed a nervous lump and followed a man with jet black, startling curls, inside. There were so many books! They were everywhere, perched on tables, propped on shelves and overflowing the reception counter.

"Feel free to look around," encouraged the librarian, before disappearing. The man with the curls had turned to Evelyn then, "impressive isn't it," he commented. Evelyn could only nod mutely. She had spent the whole afternoon there, looking around at the books, whizzing up and down floors in the vast lift. There were books on every subject; philosophy, art, history, literature even knitting! Evelyn had explored in delight, running her fingers over hard, cool covers and breathing in the smell of crisp, clean pages. Eventually parched, she had reluctantly left the library and followed the signs for the cafe, where she had sat with a polystyrene cup of English Breakfast tea and a scone, just people watching.

The cafe had been alive with the hum and drone of cookers and refrigerators. The ping of electronic tills as they opened and closed. It was full of people milling around. Many of them were young, fresh faced and noisy, although some were mature like herself. The cafe was bright, clean and airy, with a warm welcoming ambience. Evelyn had loved it immediately. She had sat sipping her tea, poring over the prospectus and the English course structure. Then she had looked at her watch and got herself into a fluster. Mam was due back from the day centre in half an hour. Carefully, she had tucked the paperwork into her bag, then rushed off to catch her bus.

On the journey home, reality had crept into her excited thoughts, putting a dampener on things. Who would look after Mam? Her conscience nagged. How on earth would she cope with studying for a full time degree? She had decided not to tell Mam. The last thing she wanted was to worry her with her silly dreams. And they were silly really, there was no way she could neglect Mam, just for fanciful ideas of 'education and empowerment,' as the advert suggested. So Evelyn had put the university prospectus and application form resolutely into her bedside drawer, covering it up with her underwear. She could not bring herself to throw it away. But she pushed it to the back of her mind well enough and concentrated on caring for Mam and writing her novel.

Then, a few weeks later, Josie, an elderly neighbour had passed away. It was at her funeral that Evelyn had a change of heart. Josie's son had spoken of her with tears in his eyes. Of her inspirational, positive character, of her steely determination and her upbeat determination to everything she did.

"If she wanted to do something, she just went right ahead and did it," he concluded proudly and the congregation had nodded in agreement. All except Evelyn, who had been unaware of her neighbour's strong character. In her memories, Josie was a sweet old lady from three doors away. It was a revelation to her and later, when her and Mam had been alone talking, Nora had commented how if you had a dream, that you should always follow it. Evelyn had been tempted to confide in Mam then about her university dreams. Instead, she had waited until Nora was on her next outing, before filling in the application form and posting it before she could change her mind.

Now she felt a fraud, as she had always told Mam everything. Where would she start with this? And who would care for Nora, while she was gallivanting around the University? Thoughts tumbled around her head as she opened the garden shed and tugged at the handles of the mower. She could feel a migraine niggling at the front of her forehead and she tensed. Well, she would just have to talk to Mam; there was no avoiding the issue. She would speak to her directly after tea. Evelyn cleared her mind and set about the arduous task of the overgrown garden.

* * *

"Mam, I need to talk to you," Evelyn said softly, as she set down two pieces of crumbly fruitcake. From the hallway, the clock chimed six o'clock and on the TV, the evening news was just beginning.

"Why yes dear, turn the TV down," Nora instructed pleasantly, looking at her daughter in anticipation, "what is it?"

"Well," she began, sinking down on the sofa and looking at Nora earnestly, "you know I love my writing and my books."

"Yes dear, go on," Nora urged, her tiny hands clasped together in her lap.

"I applied to go to University to do an English degree and I've been accepted," Evelyn gabbled breathlessly. She waited for a response, while the clock ticked loudly. There was a brief look of confusion on her mother's face and then a slow smile lit up her wrinkled features.

"University, Evelyn? Well that's just brilliant."

Evelyn breathed a sigh of relief and felt her whole body droop in relaxation.

"Really Mam, you don't mind?" She asked, surprised but relieved.

Nora shook her head, "why would I mind dear? I think it's a brilliant idea."

Evelyn grinned, "I didn't think they would accept me on the course, but they have." She paused, searching Nora's face for signs of distress, "but I just want to make sure that you're okay about me doing it. It will be hard work Mam."

Nora reached forward to pat her daughter's hand lightly. "Of course it's okay dear, you will love it I'm sure and it will help you with your writing." Evelyn felt a deep love for her mam encompass her.

"It's just, I don't know who is going to care for you while I'm at uni," she faltered. There was a pause, while both women contemplated the thought.

"I could go to the daycentre another day or two," Nora began slowly, "and maybe you could ask one of the neighbours to look in on me."

Evelyn nodded enthusiastically. "Yes I could ask Judy," she thought briefly of her kind, newly retired neighbour, and then frowned. "Are you sure it will be okay?" She asked tensely.

"Yes I'm sure," Nora replied with a laugh, "you should go for it Evelyn! Your dad would be so proud."

A tear sprang to Evelyn's eye as she nodded, "then I will."

Nora nodded, "now, tell me all about it…"

* * *

They sat together all evening, intermittently watching TV and chatting. Evelyn showed Mam the glossy prospectus and read her the course description. She told her about the open day and the impressive library.

"It's so much bigger than our local library," she explained with wide eyes, "four, no five times bigger." By eleven, they were both tired and yawning.

"Let's get you to bed Mam," Evelyn said as she helped Nora to her feet. They slowly climbed the stairs. Then when Nora was settled, eyes drooping, Evelyn locked up for the night.

"Good night Mam," she whispered, poking her head around the bedroom door.

"Good night Evelyn dear," came the sleepy response.

Evelyn smiled in the darkness and clicked the door to softly. She made her way into the chilly bathroom, changed into her warm, flannelette nightie and brushed her teeth. A happy face stared back at her, her normally pale cheeks were flushed and her grey eyes were twinkling. Evelyn combed her soft silver curls, humming to herself. As she lay in bed, waiting for sleep to claim her, she thought of the university, the thousands of books and her dreams of becoming a writer.

# Chapter Three

## Ann

"For goodness sake, I've already explained to two people before you." Ann Stokes barked into the telephone, feeling extremely irate and close to losing her temper completely.

"If you could just explain to me please…" the soothing tones of the admissions clerk infuriated Ann further.

"I sent the application months ago," Ann reiterated, "and I haven't heard a thing since. The course is due to start next week!" Out of the corner of her eye, she could see her husband Jon, hopping from foot to foot, mumbling for her to calm down, while wafting his hands in a conciliatory motion.

"I won't calm down," Ann snapped.

"Pardon me?" Replied the lady on the other end.

Ann sighed, "not you. Look, can you just find the damn application form, or do I have to waste further time filling in another."

"I don't think that will be necessary Mrs…"

"Stokes," came the sharp retort.

"Yes, Mrs Stokes, I'm sure it is in our system. Would you like me to call you back when I've searched the admissions database?"

Ann nodded wearily, "okay," she left her landline number, then cut the call abruptly, without a goodbye.

"Bloody useless," she exclaimed, as she flung the telephone down. Jon stepped forward to check the call had been properly disconnected.

"Calm down love," he soothed.

"I mean how inadequate can you get! How can my application be missing?" She lifted her fingers in mock speech marks.

"They must have been inundated with applications love, I'm sure yours will turn up."

"It better," growled Ann, as she expertly wheeled herself back into the lounge. "If I wasn't stuck in this damn thing, I would drive down there now and search the bloody database myself."

Jon sighed, "want a cup of tea?"

"Is that your answer for everything…tea!"

Her husband smiled patiently, "yes, with two custard creams?"

Ann frowned, "okay," she conceded, "but not too milky, you know how much I hate weak tea."

"Yes dear," Jon replied, as he bent to kiss her head. He went into the kitchen, leaving Ann alone to simmer. She picked up a magazine and flicked through the glossy pages, her spirits sinking further as she speed read over an article on 'depression in the modern era.' Two high fliers spoke candidly of their pressurised lifestyle and the detrimental effect it had played on their mental health.

Ann snorted. What on earth were they moaning about?, she thought in exasperation. How would they cope if they were stuck in a wheelchair twenty-four seven? At the end of the article, there was a questionnaire. Are you depressed? It enquired. Well maybe I am now, thought Ann sourly. She bent forward to reach for a pen, but it fell to the floor, rolling underneath her. Frustrated, Ann backed up her wheelchair then snatched up the pen with a grimace. She quickly ticked the boxes, then added up her score. Yes, she was definitely depressed! Something else to add to her ailments; a depressed paraplegic with hypertension and mild asthma.

Jon came back into the room carrying a flowery tray of tea and biscuits. Ann dunked her custard cream, then bit into it angrily. She searched in her pockets for her cigarettes, lit one then inhaled deeply. The cigarette calmed her slightly, but then triggered a coughing fit, so she reluctantly stubbed it out.

Jon shook his head, "those things will kill you."

"I'm not afraid to die," she retorted, "besides, I'm half dead anyway," she pointed to her legs. Thin, numb, devoid of life and feeling. That's what happened when you were involved in a car crash with a drunk driver. She closed her eyes and an image flashed before her; a dark winding road, a tight bend, flashing lights, an almighty banging and crunching, searing pain and then total blackness. Ann had woken two days later in Ambleside – a huge sprawling hospital in the middle of Chattlesbury. She had been brought in by air ambulance, air lifted through the starry skies. When she had woken, her teary parents had informed her that the doctors had worked tirelessly.

"You could have died," her mom cried, hugging her tight. Ann had felt dead inside; she was physically a mess. Her face was bloody, bruised and swollen. Her right arm was fractured and her ribs were sore and tender. It was excruciating just to inhale, but the worst was yet to come.

Pretty soon after she had woken, she noticed she had no feeling in the lower half of her body. She had screamed for her parents and they had hugged her tight, sobbing. The doctor had explained in no uncertain terms that she would never walk again. He was a small, middle aged man, with tired dark eyes, that appraised Ann sympathetically.

"You sustained a very serious injury to the middle of your spine, which has caused a complete loss of function and sensation in your legs," he explained gently but firmly. He went on to disclose medical jargon, explaining why. It made

Ann's head spin. The information was just too much to take in. Her mom had wailed, asking if there was anything to be done.

"Physio will help strengthen the muscles, but I'm afraid Ann will never walk again."

Her parents had clung to her and each other, while she cried bitter tears. She was just twenty-two, with a great job, a trendy car and a gorgeous boyfriend. Her happy, perfect life had been completely smashed like her spine and she was forced to pick up the pieces. Over the years, Ann had reluctantly adapted to life as a paraplegic. Her parents had converted the downstairs lounge into a wheelchair friendly bedroom, the bathroom had been knocked out and extended, painted a pretty blue green sea colour. But Ann's dreams of moving in with her boyfriend Allen had soon turned sour. Just months after she had left the hospital, he had ended the relationship, citing 'work commitments' and 'growing apart' as the reason. Ann knew that it was because she was disabled and that he just couldn't cope with the reality of it. She had screamed at him, crying tears of anger and frustration, flinging the jewellery he had bought her back at him. Those were her darkest days, when she lay all alone at night, thinking about the life she should have had. Ann resigned from her job at the bank. She didn't have the inclination anymore to help people with their financial future, when she thought she had no future herself.

She pushed her friends away, hating the pity and uncertainty in their eyes. How should they act around a wheelchair bound recluse? When all they wanted to do was party and plan fun filled holidays abroad. Some of them tried to include her in their plans, but Ann would reject their offers. She felt a burden to her friends and her family and spiralled down into depression. They were definitely dark days. She felt utterly despondent, like the old extrovert Ann was trapped inside a useless body. She became withdrawn, and refused to go out. Her famous temper became worse, she snapped at everyone and eventually, they drifted away, so she was left alone, with only her parents for company.

Then she had met Jon, a physio nurse fifteen years her senior. His warm, kind demeanour and abundance of patience, had slowly chipped away at her defences. They had begun tentatively dating. Slowly, Ann had begun to live life again, eating out in restaurants, attending the theatre, visiting the beautiful English countryside, where Jon would push her around and point out the different species of birds swooping overhead. Slowly, Ann had fallen for him and after a few happy years together had finally agreed to move in with him. Three years later, they had a simple wedding ceremony at the local registry office, followed by an intimate meal with close family.

On her wedding day, Ann beamed with happiness and not even her broken legs could spoil it. Jon had surprised her with a magical honeymoon to Paris, where they had cruised on the river Seine drinking champagne. They talked candidly about her disability and their future together. She told Jon hesitantly of her dreams of going to university. He had held her tight, "you can still go," he urged, "there's so much support now-a-days for disabled people." Ann wasn't completely sure. She had waited another twelve months, and then decided to apply for the BA (Hons) in English at the University of Chattlesbury. Now they had lost her application and she had taken it out on her lovely, caring husband.

"Sorry I snapped," she said quietly, as she sipped her tea. He didn't reply, just smiled at her over the rim of his mug. Ann felt a surge of guilt, "why don't you go on down the pub tonight," she suggested. "I'll be fine with the remote and a couple of magazines." He came to squat in front of her.

"I've an even better idea," he replied, his nose almost touching hers, "why don't we order a takeaway, share a bottle of wine and download a new release film?"

Ann sniffed and smiled grudgingly, "vodka and coke instead?"

He nodded and his huge grin warmed her heart. He kissed her gently, while his hands held her face.

"Love you," she gasped.

"Ditto."

Just then, the telephone rang, interrupting their romantic interlude. Jon was at the phone in a flash, "yes she's here, just a minute."

He passed her the cordless telephone. Ann cleared her throat and listened as the clerk explained that she had found her application and yes, she had been accepted onto the course! Ann gave a little yelp, punching the air with her fist.

"We will send out the dates for enrolment in a letter via the post office Mrs Stokes."

"Thank you," Ann replied, beaming up at her husband as he pranced joyfully around the room. "And I didn't mean to snap earlier." The clerk replied that she understood and that it was no problem.

"Oh my god," she erupted, after she had politely ended the call, "I've been accepted. I'm going to uni!"

"Told you babe." He hugged her hard, then spun her chair around, until she felt sick with dizziness.

"Enough!" She laughed breathlessly.

"Celebration tonight honey."

"Yay," Ann shouted, looking up at Jon. His enthusiasm was infectious and she thought again how lucky she was to have him in her life.

"Will I be alright?," she gasped uncertainly, "I mean going to uni on my own?"

Jon paused, his arms akimbo in mid air. He gazed at his wife's trembling lower lip and was touched at her sudden vulnerability.

"Course you will babe. There'll be plenty of support and I'm only a phone call away."

"You might be at work if I need you," she said quietly. The enormity of what she was about to embark on suddenly overwhelmed her and she felt a little afraid.

Jon shook his head, "you will be fine. You'll forget all about me when you're in that lecture theatre surrounded by other students."

Ann's eyes widened in excitement; they had been to the university for a look around on the open day. It was a new building, right in the centre of the city, surrounded by shops, bars and a beautiful old fashioned church. The bells had been ringing as Jon had parked the car. Ann had been acutely observant, looking for wheelchair friendly access around the campus. Everything appeared to be in order, so she allowed herself to relax and be carried along with Jon's enthusiastic tour. They had spent a lovely morning exploring the university and talking to tutors. Ignoring Ann's protestations, Jon had proudly told them of her dreams of becoming a Doctor of Literature. The small, friendly tutor had beamed.

"That's wonderful, we don't get many students with the longevity and aspirations to follow that path and the English course structure is just brilliant, with a wide range of interesting modules, from Shakespeare to 1960s Avant Garde literature. It will give you a wealth of experience and knowledge for the masters' course."

With Jon's encouragement, Ann had sat at one of the state of the art computers in the library and filled in the online application, before she could change her mind. It was strange but exhilarating to find that she was going to be a student again!

Now it had been officially confirmed, Ann felt nervous but excited. A bad combination when your stomach was already rumbling for food.

They both laughed as the sound of Ann's loud hunger pains reverberated around the room.

"Come on," said Jon, "we'll go and get your vodka, then you can order the Chinese."

As he wheeled her out of the room, "I think this calls for extra prawn crackers."

"And extra egg fried rice," Ann laughed as they opened the front door and made their way out into the warm September sunshine.

# Chapter Four

## Will

Will Bentley received his 'A' level results on a wet, muggy August day. Early in the morning, his mom had appeared in the bedroom doorway, holding a steaming mug of tea and hot buttered toast.

"Will, Will," she had called until he had raised his sleepy, teenage head off a feather down pillow.

"Ugh," he grunted, with one eye open.

"It's the day Will," she was excited as she crossed the room, to tug gently on white venetian blinds. Sunlight flooded into the room, banishing night time shadows, and bathing the walls in warm, luminous light.

"Here," she waited patiently while he scrabbled into a sitting position.

"What day?" He teased taking a large slurp of tea. His mom, Flora tutted, and busied herself picking up dirty clothes from the blue speckled floor.

"You know very well it's 'A' level results day," she smiled broadly, "we can go pick them up between eleven and twelve."

Will glanced across to his wall clock that was half hidden by posters.

"So why have you got me up so early? It's not even eight," he grumbled with a yawn.

"There's a lot to do love. Nan's coming to dinner, I need to hoover, dust, take the dog for a walk," she listed her chores on her fingers, while Will pulled the duvet back over his tousled head.

"Call me again at nine." His words were muffled by the thick cover, but Flora heard and sighed.

"Okay honey, but no later, we can't be late for your results." As the door clicked softly closed, Will was already breathing deeply, as sleep pulled him under once again.

He woke to the whirring, sucking noise of the hoover. Swinging himself out of bed, he bit into the cold toast, checking his phone for messages. There were five texts from various friends and two missed calls from his father. Will sighed, ruffled his hair, then logged onto his Facebook account. On his wall, tons of good luck messages greeted him. He scrolled down, speed reading, then paused as a message from Hema caught his eye, 'good luck' it simply read. Will smiled sleepily, thinking of his girlfriend of six months. Their fledgling relationship was surrounded by secrecy. Only their best mates knew about it and they had been sworn to silence. Will thought of Hema's jet black flowing hair, her huge, golden brown eyes, full mouth and tantalisingly curvy figure. He felt a stirring in his loins and decided he needed a cold shower.

Once he was dressed, he carefully gelled his hair into the casual, messy look that was so popular at the moment, thanks to numerous boy bands, then bounced down the stairs, taking them two at a time. Flora was packing the hoover away, singing softly to herself. Will marvelled at his mother's cheery disposition. She was always so happy! God knows why, when she was married to Dad and had no work life, or friends of her own.

"Hello," she said cheerily, as if to reinforce the fact.

Will mumbled a reply, then swung his leather jacket off the coat peg. The smile on Flora's face slipped southwards.

"Where are you going?" She asked shrilly.

"Just down to Jimmy's for a bit," he responded cagily.

"But...but, we'll be leaving soon."

"We've got another hour yet Mom." Will glanced in the mirror. "I won't be long," he said to his reflection. He heard Flora sniff and looked round. She was wringing her hands in an obvious state of panic.

"I really think we should be going soon son," she insisted, "the traffic might be busy and I bet they'll be no parking spaces left!"

"Chill Mom," Will laughed, "I'll be back in a flash." He opened the front door, and threw his mom a wink.

"Don't be long," she called, as the door closed in front of her.

The walk to the shop only took ten minutes or so. 'News Express' stood on the corner of the main road, dilapidated and run down, with bars fixed securely to the doors and windows. A dark green weather beaten canopy fluttered overhead and just outside the door, a news board advertised the day's gloomy goings on. An old lady was bending down, struggling with her dog's lead.

"Here, let me," Will said helpfully, as he quickly untied the leather strap from the lamp post.

"Thank you dear," the old lady beamed. Will smiled and shrugged, then watched as she went on her way down the street, while her Yorkshire Terrier yapped at passers-by. He pushed open the door and heard the soft tinkle of the bell above him. The shop was busy with children and harassed looking mothers. At the end of the store, a line of people waited patiently to be served at the Post Office. Will brushed past a young girl with pigtails in her hair; she was staring at the sweets on display with wide cerulean blue eyes. He searched around the shop, scanning over the top of shelves which were stacked with bread and plastic bottles of fizzy pop. Then he saw her in a corner, stacking crisps onto a buy one get one free display. He shoved his hands into his jeans pockets then cleared his throat.

Hema spun around, her arms loaded with crisps. A wide smile lit up her face at the sight of him. Will felt a warm sensation settle in the pit of his stomach.

"Hello," he whispered, grinning from ear to ear. Hema looked anxiously to the front of the shop where the till stood.

"Mom's here," she whispered back.

Will took her hand and pulled her towards him, so they were hidden behind the high shelves.

"I've missed you," he mumbled, kissing the corner of her full mouth. He heard her sigh and increased the pressure of his lips.

"Will, not here," Hema exclaimed, as she backed away slightly. A serious look his way halted his advances, so instead he took her dainty, painted hands in his own. The bracelets on her arms tinkled as he spun her around. Hema giggled, "stop," she admonished quietly, "do you want us to get caught?"

Will shrugged in defiance, "let them catch us. You are Mahila." His hands slid over her slender hips, drawing her closer to him.

Hema grinned up at him, "and you are Rupavan. But Will, you must know that if we get caught, I'll never be let out again and then we'll never see each other."

He frowned down at her pretty face, "you *are* eighteen," he argued, "they can't stop you!"

Hema shook her head with a sad smile. "You don't know my parents, they can and they will."

Will grumbled in frustration, he was beginning to tire of all the secrecy. At first it had been exciting, but now when all he wanted was to hold her in his arms, it all seemed oppressive and frustrating.

"You must understand," she pleaded, "my parents are different from yours. Their culture is different."

"Yeah, it's stuck in the 1800s," he moaned.

Hema glanced towards the front of the shop. In the round, overhead mirror, she could see her mom serving one of the regulars. She wound her arms around his neck.

"I'll see you at school later…okay?"

"Okay," he groaned, liking the warmth of her hips pressing against his. She kissed his lips chastely, then reluctantly backed away.

"Good luck with your 'A' level results," she whispered.

"And you."

The queue of people at the post office had grown and Will noticed that a few people were staring their way.

"Hema, Hema," her mother called from the front of the shop.

"Coming mom," Hema replied, smoothing her clothes and ushering Will away. As she disappeared to the front of the shop, Will lingered, looking for something to buy. The fridge door squeaked as he opened it and took out a can of Irn-Bru. He walked slowly to the till, watching Hema help load a lady's shopping trolley with groceries. Mrs Kumar was stacking bananas, bent over with her back to them. Will winked Hema's way and saw a small smile in response. He dug in his pocket for change, took out a few coins, passed them to her slowly so their hands could touch and linger. Then with a precise thank you, she had moved onto the next customer. He raised his hand a fraction in a small wave, then turned his back and left the shop and his secret girlfriend behind.

On his way home, his thoughts drifted to Hema. She had been wrong about his parents. The similarities between them were obvious to him. They both had pushy, overbearing fathers and they were both oppressed by religion. Although he acted like he didn't understand the difficult position she was in, he understood a lot more then he let on.

Hema was Hindu. On weekends she worshipped at the large temple, dressed in beautiful saris. On Sundays Will went to church, with his family, dressed smartly in a shirt and tie. Max and Flora Bentley were Roman Catholics, his mom being devout. The walls at home were covered in religious memorabilia. They prayed at mealtimes, thanking God for what they were about to receive. Will would bow his head, mumble the familiar words, but in his mind he would be thinking of Hema, wondering what she was up to. He wasn't really a believer, had lost faith during his early teenage years. How could there be a God when there was so much evil and destruction in the world? The priest talked about free will and man's failings, but Will didn't buy into that ideology. He had argued his point a few times at school, received a lukewarm response from the R.E teacher, but at home he never discussed religion. It would be pointless and his mom would just get upset – her only son, a non-believer. So Will endured the prayers and the mass, the smell of incense each Sunday, the wooden cross in his bedroom and the defiant thought that he would have none of it in his own home.

But for now, there were his results to think of. His parents were more agitated and nervous then Will, or so it seemed. They had dreams, big dreams for their son; university, a respectable and well paid career, a large house in the suburbs, grandchildren. Their ambition was driven by Will's father who was the head teacher of a large, catholic primary school. Max Bentley had been the youngest head teacher in the borough. A brilliantly clever maths graduate, with a keen sense of propriety. He had risen from teacher status to head within ten years. His impressive CV boasted prestigious qualifications and accolades and an unblemished employment history. He longed for his son to follow in his footsteps. So here he was, on the cusp of university, awaiting 'A' level results. He should be excited and happy, but inside he felt dull, confused and angry.

Angry at his parents for pushing him into university, and angry at himself for allowing them to do so. What Will wanted to do was travel around the world. That was his dream. Yet when he had suggested this to them, it had caused an uproar. Flora had been in tears and Max had raged around the house for days. In the end he had succumbed to pressure, backed down and agreed to go to university, but his heart was not in it. It was up in the sky, on a 747 plane, jetting to exotic places, swimming in bright blue seas and backpacking from one motel to the other. That's where Will's aspirations were. Instead, he was stuck on the outskirts of Chattlesbury, surrounded by factories, traffic and pollution. Hema was the only light in his boring, dreary life.

Before her, there had been other girls; he was handsome and popular. But Hema was different; special. She was gorgeous, kind, caring and feminine. She was so different to many of his female school peers, who seemed hell-bent on partying, buying cheap vodka and getting wasted. The more he saw of her, the more he liked her, he looked forward to their secret dates and spending time with her. Will turned into his street. The pavements were lined with blossom trees, the houses were opulent, and every drive had at least two / three cars parked up. As he opened the latch on the garden gate, a smile replaced his frown, painted on for his mother. He opened the door. Ruby, their border collie rushed down the hall, tail wagging furiously.

"Hello girl," Will stooped to pat her.

"Oh, you're back," Flora exclaimed, as if she were expecting someone else. Her raincoat was on and a set of keys dangled from her fingers.

Her face was a picture of excitement and expectancy.

Will stifled a sigh, "come on then, let's go get my results," he beckoned to his mom and held the door open for her, as she practically skipped towards him.

On their way to Priorsfield Catholic Academy, they listened to radio four. Flora stopped at the numerous traffic lights, checking her mirrors nervously, humming along to the music. Will knew his mom didn't like driving, she was an anxious person and a born worrier. The total opposite to his dad, who was full of confidence and self-assurance. He often wondered how he came to be conceived; his mother with her pious shyness and his father with his career driven life. The thought made him smile and lifted his mood.

"The lights are green Mom," he noted, pointing out the window. A car horn tooted from behind. Will resisted the urge to turn round and flick the v's. Flora laughed nervously, turned the key and the engine shuddered to life. He wondered why she always cut the engine at traffic lights. Will himself loved to rev the accelerator and then speed off as soon as they had changed to green. He had been having driving lessons for a month now. Unlike his mom, he loved driving, loved the feel of the steering wheel as he swung around tight corners and manoeuvred busy roundabouts. He was eager to buy his own car, although his dad grumbled regularly that the insurance would cost a bomb. He longed for a car to whizz him and Hema around in.

Flora slowed down as they turned into a narrow road. They were almost crawling as they arrived at the school gates.

"It's a good job we came when we did," Flora commented, as she followed the line of traffic down the twisting driveway. Groups of teenagers hung around on the grass verges, hugging and squealing. Will recognised most of them from his year. It was almost eleven when Flora had finally managed to find a parking space.

"Come on Mom," he said impatiently, as she tried for the third time, to reverse in between two white lines.

"There," she said, pulling up the handbrake.

Will was up out of the car. In the distance he could see a group of his mates milling around with their parents. He waited for Flora to grab her bag, then they were off, striding across the grass to the front reception of the formidable looking school.

"Yo Will," Charlie greeted him with a high five.

"Hi bro," he responded, raking a hand through his tousled hair. He noticed some of the teachers hovering with nervous smiles on their faces and the Principal standing in the doorway greeting parents and inviting them inside.

Flora tugged at his arm, "come on love," she said, barely able to control her excitement. Will rolled his eyes at his friends and followed his mom to join the throng at the entrance.

"Good luck," Mr Cuthbert, the physics teacher, slapped his shoulder and nodded at Flora.

The hallway was packed; they joined a long queue of nervous, fidgeting students. The excitement in the air was palpable. Will craned his neck to stare away from the line, where the first recipients were standing clutching results. Some were looking despondent, with tears in their eyes while many others were hugging, grinning with delight. Will swallowed nervously, rummaged in his pocket for his mobile and checked for a message from Hema. There was none. He quickly scanned the hall, and then spotted her near the front of the queue. How did she get here so quickly he wondered? Her father was standing next to her. Tall, black hair peppered with flecks of grey. His hand resting firmly on her shoulder. She looked petrified. Will's fingers flew over his phone, then he watched as she spotted the incoming message and looked down furtively. A small smile lifted the corners of her mouth, but she stayed resolutely looking forward.

Will sighed in frustration, and turned away to watch a small group of girls yelping with excitement. It seemed to take forever to reach the tables at the front of the line. By now he had lost sight of Hema. She had been swallowed up in the large volume of people commiserating or celebrating. The smiling clerk handed Will his envelope with his name on. He clutched it looking down at the bold italics. They swam in front of him and he felt a sudden dizziness. The heat in the hall was stifling. A fire exit had been propped open. With Flora in tow, he moved towards the open doorway.

"Will?" Flora questioned, looking at his hands.

"You open it," he decided, thrusting the paper at his surprised Mom.

She paused for a second, making the sign of the cross against her breastbone, then tore open the envelope with trembling fingers.

Will watched her face, saw her nervous expression alter and change to one of delight.

"I guess it's good news?"

Flora laughed, "my clever son," she beamed proudly, "two As and a B!"

He felt himself enveloped in the softest of hugs. He could smell her perfume, light and refreshing. The warmth of her cheek, as it pressed against his stubbly neck.

"Well done, Dad will be so pleased."

The mention of his father brought a frown to Will's face. His forehead crinkled but his smile remained.

"We must celebrate," Flora gabbled with excitement. In her head she was already making plans for a meal at The Bistro.

"Actually Mom, I was going out with friends," he meant Hema of course, that's if she were able to sneak out.

"Oh," Flora's face fell, "okay love, we can celebrate at the weekend."

During the journey home, Flora chattered with excitement about his results and university. If she noticed he was quiet, she didn't let on. Her enthusiasm and happiness was enough for them both. Will watched the rain running down the windscreen in rivulets. He felt trapped. Trapped and angry. Thoughts of uni weighed heavily on his mind. His spirit felt crushed and deflated. It was *their* dream, not his, not yet anyway. He longed for Hema, her warmth, beauty and kind understanding. Closing his eyes, he flew away, jetted off to a different place, while in the background, Neil Diamond crooned about lost love and his mom sang along, her voice a happy, soft tinkle.

# Chapter Five

## Juliette

"And they all lived happily ever after." Juliette Harris softly closed the fairy-tale book and leaned forward to place a gentle kiss on her daughter's cheek. Molly was fast asleep, snuggled inside the warm duvet, with red curls peeking out of the top. The clock on the bedside table flashed eight fifteen. Juliette yawned, and manoeuvred her way across a pretty pink bedroom floor that was strewn with toys and books. A plastic yellow duck squeaked in protest as she trod on it, but Molly slept on, her breathing deep and regular. In the doorway, Juliette paused to pick up a pile of clothes that looked as if they needed a wash. She threw them unceremoniously into the laundry basket then went into the small bathroom and turned on the taps. Water gushed out, filling the tub. There was a tiny bit of

Apple Blossom bubble bath left. Juliette poured some water in, shook it around and then poured it out again, so that it created a cloud of frothy bubbles. A mini orchard, she thought with a tired smile, as she grabbed clean towels out of the airing cupboard.

While she waited for the bath to fill, Juliette tapped softly on her son's bedroom door. There was no reply. She opened the door a fraction, and quickly scanned the room. Harry was propped up in bed, headphones blaring music, while he played on his Nintendo DS.

"Hi," she whispered, with a smile.

"Hello Mom," came his cheery reply, he tugged at his headphones until they were hanging loosely around his neck.

"Can I go to bed at ten tonight?"

Juliette thought about the looming weekend, "Okay," she nodded at her ten-year-old son, "but no later."

Harry gave her the thumbs up then disappeared back into his electronic, music filled world. Juliette discarded her clothes, adding them to her growing laundry pile. These days she always seemed to be washing and ironing, she thought ruefully, when she wasn't doing other household chores of course. All her time seemed to be spent running round after her kids, or working as a barmaid at the local social club; there wasn't much time for herself. Life as a single parent was busy and stressful, a soak in the bath was a luxury. But tonight she needed to relax. Her whole body was aching with tiredness, heavy arms, legs and eyes and a brain muffled by reminders, of what to do's.

She gingerly tipped one foot in the bath and gasped as the heat struck her toes. Quickly turning the cold tap on, she sloshed the water around the tub, attempting to cool it. Steam licked around her, warming her naked body as she stepped into the warmness and eased herself down into the apple scented bubbles. As the water lapped her skin she felt herself relax, felt the tension draining away. Juliette sighed, reached for a scrunchy to tie up her mass of red, corkscrew curls, then sank down so her body was immersed under the water. Thoughts raced through her mind. She had so much to do for the rest of the evening. Tomorrow was Molly's seventh birthday and in celebration, Juliette was throwing a party and inviting family and close friends. There was much to prepare, but at the moment Juliette felt lethargic, wanting nothing more than to curl up in bed with a hot drink and a good novel. She thought about the presents she had yet to wrap. Hoped her daughter liked them.

Her wages hadn't stretched to much, so unable to purchase expensive gifts, she had caught the bus into town yesterday and hunted around the shops looking for bargains. While up town, she had checked her bank account, there had been an available balance of three pounds. Her family allowance hadn't gone in yet unfortunately; she would have to use the council tax money to buy the buffet food. Luckily Iceland had some great deals on sausage rolls and gateaux at the moment. She had staggered back from town laden with carrier bags of food and toys. She couldn't afford a taxi so had to endure a packed bus journey sitting next to an elderly man who coughed and sneezed all the way home. Juliette didn't have time to be ill, so had taken a garlic tablet, washed down with a glass of vitamin c fortified juice. Summer colds were sometimes the worst, she thought with a grimace.

The fingers on her hands were beginning to pucker as she picked up the sponge and soaped herself down. The water was now cooler and she shivered slightly as she stood to pull out the plug, watching the water whirl and gurgle down the dark hole. She turned on the overhead shower and tipped her head forward to shampoo her long, thick hair. Afterwards, she wrapped herself in the fluffy dressing gown, hanging on the back of her bedroom door and headed softly into the small, but cosy living room. Toys were strewn across the floor in this room also; Barbie dolls and racing cars, scattered pieces of jigsaw. Juliette sighed, and bending down, she began the clear up. The kids were usually so good at tidying up after themselves. She would have to give them a gentle reminder tomorrow. After the floor was clear again, she grabbed the scissors and sellotape, took the bag of toys out from behind the sofa and sat cross legged on the chocolate coloured rug and set to work wrapping.

Time ticked by and soon she was finished, surrounded by bright colourful boxes. She made some bows out of scraps of glittery paper, cut out stars and sequins, stuck them on top of the presents. Molly loved anything sparkly; she was very girly thought Juliette with a smile. She was in the process of blowing up balloons when the phone rang. Juliette hunted around, and found it underneath a roll of paper.

"Hi," she said breathlessly into the mouth-piece.

"Hello Jules," it was her older sister Marie, "what time shall we come tomorrow?"

"Erm..." Juliette thought rapidly, "anytime from three onwards."

"Okay young un," Marie said with a chuckle. Juliette laughed along, she was hardly young at the age of thirty.

"Mom's bringing garlic bread, cola for the kids and I'm making a pasta salad."

Juliette frowned, the family knew she didn't like the kids having fizzy pop. "It's important to look after your teeth," she would explain to her toothless Mom. But yet again Violet Harris took no notice. Juliette decided to let it drop this once, as it was a special occasion and frustratingly, the kids *did* love cola.

"He's not coming is he?" Marie asked sharply.

Juliette knew straight away who 'he' was; Molly and Harry's Dad. Her ex-boyfriend, jail-bird Marty.

"I haven't heard anything," she replied quietly. There came an angry tut from the other end of the line.

"How long has he been outta jail?"

"About three weeks or so, I've heard."

"Has he tried contacting the kids?," Marie asked sharply.

"No, we haven't heard anything from him," Juliette sighed in relief, pulling her warm dressing gown tighter.

"Good riddance hopefully. Anyway, have you heard from the university yet?"

Juliette smiled, "no nothing," she replied, her tone light, "but I haven't checked my emails for a week, so I'm hoping they've contacted me."

"And me sis, I better go, see you tomorrow yeah? Do you want me to bring anything else?"

Juliette assured her sister that the pasta salad was fine, she had plenty of food crammed in the fridge and freezer. She cut the call, placed the phone back in its cradle to charge, then walked to the window to gaze out at the night sky. From her fifth floor maisonette, she could see into neighbour's gardens, and watch the traffic whizzing by on the darkened roads. The street lights were flickering, attracting moths and lighting the pavements around them. A group of children were making their way back home, throwing sticks into the hedgerows and laughing raucously. In the corner she could see her neighbour, Paul, struggling with a large bag of rubbish, she tapped the window to wave but she was too far up for him to hear her.

Juliette sighed, as her thoughts turned to Marty. They had been split up for years now, but as her children's father, he was still a big part of their life. Their split had been amicable at the time; Juliette was concerned of the effect on her children so had remained on friendly terms with her ex-boyfriend. But over the years, their relationship had become strained and more cordial than friendly, largely due to his shady lifestyle, which he refused to alter for anybody. He had just served a six-month jail term for petty theft and joyriding, but Juliette doubted he would feel remorse, or that it would put a halt to his criminal activity.

Marty had been in trouble with the police since he was eighteen and in his case, rehabilitation had completely failed. In fact, jail had made him worse in many ways. He had mixed with other criminals who encouraged his disreputable lifestyle, he was easily led and impressionable, wouldn't listen to sense. Juliette had tried to talk to him and help him, she had found him a job as a handyman at the social club where she worked, but he had blown it when he had become involved in a gang. He seemed to be more interested in his mates' advice so she had backed away, and tried to distance herself and the kids from him. They were her priority now and she was fiercely protective of them.

She reached to close the heavy brown curtains with one last look at the twinkling lights of the city below. It was quiet in the flat, the double glazing shut out the sounds from outside. She went into the kitchen, switched the kettle on and peered in the fridge for something to eat. It was packed full of party food but not much else, so she decided to make herself a banana sandwich. As she sank on the sofa and ate, she fired up her laptop, and waited for her login sign to appear. It seemed to take forever to install. When it was ready, she went straight to her email, watched as incoming messages flashed on the screen. Juliette searched for one in particular, and then she spotted it, from the university. Her heart beat a little faster as she double clicked the mouse. It read, 'Dear Miss Harris, we are pleased to inform you that your application for an English degree has been successful. We will be sending confirmation and enrolment dates in the post.'

Juliette let out a scream of delight. She suddenly felt wide awake and excited, extremely excited. For the past twelve months she had been attending college part time, studying for an access course which would hopefully be a stepping stone to university. After twelve months of hard work; balancing family life with work and college, she had passed with flying colours.

When she had collected her results, her tutor had hugged her tight.

"Well done Juliette!" She had said with a wide, infectious grin. Marie had been with her and on the way home had insisted on a detour via the off license, where they had gone halves on a bottle of cheap, pink fizz. She couldn't wait to tell her family, but resisted the urge to call them. The good news would wait until tomorrow. Juliette printed off the email, then stuck it to the cork notice board. As she tidied the kitchen, her eyes were repeatedly drawn to it. When she had applied a few months ago, she hadn't really expected them to say yes. This didn't happen to people like her she thought; people who struggled to live from day to day, who had to watch every single penny. She would have to ring the student finance first thing next week, to see what help she could get. Juliette took a yellow post it note, scribbled a reminder and stuck it next to the email, then added a smiley face in red marker. That overused icon definitely represented her mood at the moment. In fact, she felt ecstatic and did a little dance around the kitchen, waving a damp tea towel above her head.

All of her worries seemed to melt away at that moment, the financial burdens, the pressure of being a single parent, she forgot all of that, allowing herself to savour the realisation that yes, she would be going to university! And now she was a step nearer to her dream of becoming a primary school teacher. For years now she had worked towards that goal; academically at college and also by gaining practical experience. She had been volunteering one morning per week in her children's school, where she witnessed the pressure and stress the teachers were under, yet she still wanted to do it. If anything, it had made her more determined. She longed to have a rewarding, fulfilling and stimulating career, where she could make a difference and she absolutely loved children. She wasn't just doing it for herself either, she longed for a better future for Harry and Molly. In the future she envisaged owning a house with a garden, so they could play outside in the fresh air, instead of being cooped up in a maisonette. She wanted to be off benefits, she wanted to be earning enough money to support her family without having to rely on others. She wanted to contribute towards the economy, to shrug off the stigma of being a benefits scrounger, to help others less fortunate. She wanted to open a savings account, to show her children the value of money and how important it was not to squander it. Juliette had so many dreams. Her mom had always teased that she was a dreamer with her head in the clouds, but she was determined to succeed and make them a reality.

The remainder of the evening passed in a blur. She turned on the TV but was unable to concentrate, so tackled the mountain of ironing instead. By ten o'clock she was exhausted, decided to lock up for the night, kissed Harry goodnight, checked on Molly, who was upside down fast asleep in the bed, then curled under her own duvet with a book and a hot chocolate. Tomorrow's party niggled at her mind; she tossed and turned, unable to get much sleep. Much too soon it was six thirty and Molly was bouncing on the bed in excitement.

"Happy birthday!" Juliette gave her daughter a big hug, planting kisses on top of her warm head.

"Can I go open my presents," Molly pleaded, wide eyed and full of energy. Juliette nodded, feeling her chest constrict with love for her little girl. How did she get to be seven she wondered, as she clambered out of the bed? The time had flown by.

"Let's wake Harry first."

They tumbled into his bedroom. Molly snapped on his light, running forwards to shake her brother's uncovered arm. He turned, grumbled, then stuck his head out of the duvet.

"Come on Harry," gabbled Molly, "it's my birthday...Get up!"

"Happy birthday," ten-year-old Harry rolled sleepily out of the bed, yawning and rubbing his eyes. His hair, dark like his fathers, stuck up and outwards in odd angles, he was tall and slim, and swathed in Spiderman pyjamas. The kids raced into the living room, while Juliette trailed behind, yawning and attempting to wake herself up. Like her son, she wasn't a morning person, never had been. She needed caffeine to kick start her day and even then, she was usually lethargic until lunchtime. Molly was squealing with excitement as she tore open her presents. A cute teddy from

Harry had her jumping up and down with glee and flinging herself into her brother's arms. He looked suitably embarrassed, pretending to gag when she smothered him with kisses.

Juliette laughed, "here," she handed a small package to her son. On each other's birthday, it was traditional for her to buy the other child a present so they didn't feel left out. Molly had opened all her presents and was staring around her in awe, unsure of what to play with first.

"Thanks Mom!" She beamed, hugging her left leg.

"You are very welcome."

Molly turned her face upwards, presents momentarily forgotten.

"Is Daddy coming today?" She asked in a serious manner.

Juliette's spirits sank, but she kept the smile firmly fixed. Every birthday her daughter asked the same question. Juliette should be used to it by now, but it still felt like a knife to her heart each time she heard it. She also found it difficult to articulate an honest, yet sensitive response, without hurting a young child's feelings further.

"I don't know sweetheart," she began hesitantly, the disappointed look on her daughter's face tugged at her heartstrings, "I'm sure he will try his best."

"Okay," Molly seemed pleased with that answer, but she noticed that there was a frown on Harry's face, at the mention of his father.

While the children played with their gifts, Juliette snatched up the phone and sneaked into the kitchen. His mobile number was programmed in, so she quickly flicked through the address book until she found Marty.

"Damn," she cursed aloud as the call went to a flat, buzzing sound. He must have changed his number *again*. She fished in her bag for her address book, searching for Marty's Mom's number. The call was answered on the eighth ring.

"Hello," the greeting was muffled but Juliette could hear the annoyance in it.

"Hello Brenda," she began firmly, "it's Juliette…is Marty there please?"

"No he's not, do ya know what the time is!"

Juliette sighed, "do you know where he is? I need to speak to him."

"He's not here I told ya," came the irritated response, "he's staying with a friend, *we* don't want him here."

"Do you know who, or do you have a number for him?" Persisted Juliette.

"No!" Snapped Brenda, "I don't know an' don't care neither."

Juliette exhaled shakily, "okay," she replied, "it's just that it's Molly's birthday today…"

Buzzzz, the line went dead. Juliette's eyes welled with tears of frustration, no wonder Marty was like the way he was. Brenda obviously didn't care that it was her grand-daughter's birthday. Thank god she had her family. Juliette thought fleetingly of her mom and dad. They would be here later, she thought with relief. At least the kids had one set of grandparents who cared about them. She wiped her eyes, breathed deeply to compose herself then made her way back into the lounge.

The rest of the morning flew by. Juliette hoovered the flat then prepared the buffet food. The kitchen table groaned under the weight of sandwiches, vol au vents and quiches and in the corner was a scrumptious array of sweets; gateaux's, jelly and cheesecake. Juliette surveyed the food with satisfaction, and wiped her hands just in time to hear the doorbell ring. She glanced at the clock, two thirty, they were early. As she passed, Harry and Molly were sitting transfixed on the sofa, watching Harry Potter. That DVD had been a good buy she thought with a contented smile. The doorbell buzzed again just as she was reaching for the latch.

"Hello," she said brightly to her mom, dad and sister Marie. They trooped in, arms laden with food.

"I know you said you didn't need any more food, but I brought goodies for the kids." Her mom deposited a 'Happy Shopper' carrier on the sofa and laughed as Harry and Molly ran into her arms.

"Have you had a nice birthday princess?" She asked as Frank twirled Molly up into the air. The birthday girl nodded as she chattered away, telling them all about her presents. Marie produced more brightly coloured gifts, holding them out for her excited niece. She was soon tearing the paper off and gasping in delight at the new pink Barbie jeep. Juliette frowned slightly, she knew her mom and dad didn't have much money; they were even worse off than her. How had they afforded that? She wondered.

"Dad, it's too much," she whispered, as Frank kissed her cheek.

"Nothing's too much for my granddaughter," he retaliated proudly, "besides, your mom won a tenna on the lottery, so we splashed out a bit."

Juliette nodded, watching with an emotional lump in her throat as Marie handed her niece a square object that had to be a book. Like her mother, Molly loved books and would spend hours reading. Her teacher, Miss Daisy had commented that her reading skills were very advanced for her age; she was expected to excel in her literacy sats. As Juliette couldn't afford new books, they regularly visited their local library. She would also buy them very cheaply from car boot sales. Books were especially cheap there, and she could often barter and get them for twenty pence a go.

In her living room stood Juliette's walnut bookcase. It didn't match the decor but Juliette didn't care. It had been her nans, she had left it to her when she had died and Juliette treasured it, it was the only object in the house which she enjoyed dusting and keeping tidy. The shelves were full of all sorts of books. There was a couple of shelves of children's, the rest were an eclectic mixture of horror, chick lit, classics and crime thrillers. Now she would be able to add more, she thought with a gasp about the university.

"I'm glad I've got you all together," she began, looking around her family, "I've had some good news." All eyes turned to her expectantly, "I'm going to uni...I've been accepted onto the English degree course!" Juliette grinned and found herself being smothered in a tight embrace and surrounded by cheers and whoops of delight.

"Ah that's great news hun," big sister Marie said with a grin.

"Oh Juliette, that's grand!" Violet ruffled her daughter's hair affectionately, "we've got a clever daughter haven't we dear."

"We sure have," Frank smiled and winked.

"I might need some extra help with childcare," Juliette explained. Violet Harris was a retired cleaner, she had toiled for thirty years, cleaning for others. Last year she had hung up her apron at the age of sixty-five and now was busier than ever, looking after her brood. Juliette was one of seven children, her and Marie being the only girls. The other five were strapping lads, mostly living around the Midlands area, except for Rick who had escaped the Harris clan and now resided in Australia. Violet and Roger had twelve grandchildren of varying ages ranging from the age of two up to nineteen. They loved their family passionately, their life revolved around them.

Her dad worked in a local factory making aircraft parts. It was hard work, and he had recently asked for redundancy as his health had been deteriorating for years. Juliette noticed his limp seemed to be getting worse and he looked tired. It would be a good job when he could stop work, she thought with a frown.

"Mommy," asked Molly, from the warmth of her aunty's arms, "does that mean you're going to school like me?"

"Yes," Juliette replied, her eyes twinkling, "a big school and I'll have homework and everything."

She tweaked her daughter's nose, making her laugh.

"Cool!" Harry commented, as he looked up from his racing cars.

Just then the doorbell rang again. Juliette hurried to answer it; two of Molly's school chums tore into the room, their arms laden with presents. Juliette picked a CD, 'Pop Party' blared out of the stereo, as more children arrived, followed by three of her brothers and their families. The flat was soon full, they moved the furniture to make a dance floor, the children bopped away to Katie Perry, while the adults sat on the outskirts, chatting and laughing.

"So," Mark, her eldest brother slung his arm across Juliette's shoulders, "I hear my clever sis is off to uni."

Juliette looked up at him with a wide grin, "I sure am, I can't wait." She was explaining about the course when there was a sharp rap on the door.

"Excuse me a moment," Juliette balanced her plate of buffet food on the shelf, then edged around the dancing children to open the door.

The smile slid from her face as she looked into the eyes of Marty.

There was a pregnant pause while they surveyed each other.

"Hi Juliette," he drawled, breaking the awkward silence.

"Hi," she replied, firmly blocking the doorway. Her hand on the knob trembled slightly.

"Can I come in?" Marty asked, motioning to arms full of presents.

"I tried ringing you," she began sharply, "Molly was asking after you."

Marty ducked his head, and looked up from beneath his baseball cap.

"I'm here now," he stated, with an air of arrogance.

"Well, she wanted to speak to you this morning. Her birthday's nearly over and your mom was really rude when I rang..."

"Yeah, yeah," he interrupted, "can I see Molly or not?"

Juliette could feel hot tears threatening to overspill, but she chewed on her lip, determined not to let him see how upset she was. Do not cry damn it!

"Okay," reluctantly she opened the door, let him brush past her, then closed her eyes as she heard Molly's squeal of delight.

The atmosphere in the flat dramatically altered. The children carried on dancing and running around with sandwiches and sausage rolls in their hands, but the adults stopped talking and laughing. Juliette noticed her mom staring at Marty with open dislike and her brothers looked positively fuming.

She quickly moved forward, "what have you got there?" she asked, squatting next to Molly.

"Look Mommy," her daughter gasped in delight, "a CD player, a pink one!" Juliette smiled, and smoothed her daughter's hair out of her eyes.

"That's wonderful honey."

Molly nodded happily, "thank you Daddy." She hugged his leg then continued unwrapping dolls, tea sets, dressing up clothes, but no books. Marty had never bought his children books. She wondered where he got the money, as he was unemployed, just out of prison and always broke, best not to know she thought crisply, as she moved to stand besides Marie.

"What's he doing here?" whispered Marie, her breath was hot in Juliette's ear. She shrugged in resignation as she watched an excited Molly urging him to open the tea set.

"She is his daughter; I can't stop him."

"Maybe he could pay you maintenance then!"

"Now is not the time," Juliette replied firmly, "let's all just try to… get along."

"I suppose so…for Molly," she conceded. Her daughter was so pleased to see him that Juliette felt herself soften slightly. Harry's behaviour however, was totally different.

She noticed his reluctance to hug him and when he did, he backed away slightly with a frown creasing his young face.

"Harry, why don't you get your dad some food." She ignored the frosty look of disbelief that emanated from Marie and a few others. Marty was still kneeling on the floor beside Molly, they were laughing together as he helped her into a bright green fairy dress. She turned, made her way into the kitchen, where a miserable looking Harry was stuffing food onto a paper plate.

"Why did *he* have to come?" He looked up at Juliette with huge, angry eyes. She swallowed, her throat suddenly dry.

"He wanted to see you and Molly on her birthday," she replied brightly, slicing a small piece of quiche and balancing it on top of a wilting egg and cress sandwich.

"He'll only go away again," he mumbled. Juliette knelt in front of her son, took his small, warm hands in her own.

"Don't be angry Harry, not today, I know it's hard but let's enjoy your sister's birthday...we can talk later, OK?" He nodded grudgingly.

"Here," Juliette smiled, passing him a glass jar, "your dad loves pickled onions."

Marty didn't stay long, even his thick skin was riled by the daggers thrown by Juliette's family. After devouring the plate of food and demonstrating how the CD player worked, he rose to his feet, knees cracking loudly.

"Well, I'd best be off." No one answered.

Juliette surveyed him over her mug of coffee. He looked thin and unkempt. His hair hung in greasy strands and his clothes looked like they could do with a good iron. She felt a surge of pity and bewilderment. How had she fallen for him she wondered sadly, they were so different? But she had been young and naive, and thought that she could change him. He had been the school heart throb a long time ago; a cheeky chappy with a good heart. Now he looked a mess and *was* a mess.

"Mommy's going to school," Molly chirruped loudly. Juliette felt her cheeks burn. Marty was looking at her, waiting for an explanation.

"Erm yes, I passed the access course and have been accepted at uni."

"We're very proud of her," Violet interjected.

"I'll show you out," Juliette said with a tight smile. Molly threw herself into Marty's arms.

"Bye Daddy, will you come see us soon?"

Marty, looking uncomfortable, did not reply, but stared down at his scuffed trainers. Juliette could have slapped him then, but instead she intervened.

"Molly, show Uncle Mark your new books."

"Bye Haz," Marty held up his hand for a high five, Harry complied without enthusiasm.

"So, who is going to be looking after the kids then when you're at uni?" He sneered the last word.

Juliette spun around in the hallway to face him.

"Don't worry, I won't be asking *you*," she retorted angrily.

Marty's eyes flashed, "kids need their mom."

"They've got me – all the time!" she almost screeched at him, she was so angry. Juliette almost made a nasty reference to his own mother but bit her lip instead, "My parents have offered to help out, so *you* don't have to worry."

"Why do you wanna go there anyhow?" he asked, looking genuinely puzzled.

Juliette laughed bitterly, "you wouldn't understand."

Marty shrugged, his face a facade of indifference, "I'll be in touch."

Inside her head Juliette screamed 'don't bother' but composed herself and turned to open the door, "bye Marty."

He was gone, without a reply. She closed the door firmly and leant against it for a while, breathing shakily. "Damn him," she muttered, he wasn't going to ruin another birthday. Juliette wiped her perspiring hands down the front of her jeans then made her way back into the living room.

"Who wants to dance with me?" She beamed, as she shimmied round the children and bent over to turn Rihanna up on the stereo.

# YEAR ONE

## So it begins…

# Chapter Six

The canteen was packed full and sweltering. The perspiring cashier complained to a work colleague, as the line of students purchasing food and beverages grew longer.

"Air conditioning's broke again," she said tersely, her face was red and her hands were slippery with sweat. Evelyn stood patiently, clutching her tea and cereal bar. She herself felt hot and flustered, her stomach was somersaulting and she felt faintly nauseous. This morning she had risen early to get ready for enrolment day. Mam had caught the earlier bus to the day centre, leaving Evelyn alone in their large house to prepare. In her leather handbag she had her I.D, along with her letter of confirmation, but she had no idea what to expect, or what the day would entail.

"That'll be four pound ten please love," the harassed cashier stuck out her hand with a weary smile.

"Thank you," Evelyn replied quietly. She took her purchases and quickly scanned the room, looking for a free table. There was one left, wedged into the corner of the canteen. She walked quickly across to it, slid down onto the plastic seat and sipped her hot tea. A speaker above her rumbled loud pop music, Evelyn winced thinking, *what am I doing here?* At this moment, she felt like a fish out of water. She glanced at the doorway, tempted to up and run. *Be brave Evelyn* she told herself.

As a distraction, she looked around the canteen. At the table next to her sat a young couple. A striking Asian girl with long, black silky hair that almost touched her waist. Next to her sat a handsome boy with messy hair. He had his arm wrapped around her and she leant her head on his shoulders. Above the din of the music, she could hear their conversation. The girl seemed excited, talking animatedly while the boy seemed more subdued.

"Excuse me, is anyone sitting here?" Evelyn was startled by the voice, and looked up in surprise. A lady stood at the side of her, clutching a folder and a cup of coffee. Evelyn could smell the aroma, bitter and strong, mingling with an overpowering perfume that clung around the woman. She coughed and shook her head, "no, no," she replied, with a small smile. The woman sat opposite her, dumping her belongings on the table, and immediately began yakking on her mobile. Evelyn surreptitiously observed her. She had long, honey blonde hair, super straight it clung down her back, shiny and smooth. The woman repeatedly flicked it as she talked. Evelyn felt her own grey bob tingle with envy.

"Are you a new student?" The question hung in the air. It took a while for Evelyn to realise that she had finished her call and was talking to her.

"Oh, erm... yes," she nodded in surprise.

"What degree are you doing?"

"English." There was a silent pause until Evelyn asked, "and you?"

"English too," the woman beamed, eyes sparkling. She stuck out a hand towards Evelyn who took it politely.

"I'm Sophie...Sophie O'Neill," she paused for effect, "you might have heard of me."

Evelyn thought for a moment then shook her head, "no sorry, I'm Evelyn Cooke." The woman's pretty face became crestfallen but she continued, "just English?"

"Yes," Evelyn nodded.

"I was going to do combined art but decided against it. I'm so excited are you?"

She didn't wait for a reply, "I really didn't know what to wear today, I mean when I was younger, students were a bit out there, all Goths and Hippies." She laughed loudly, causing the boy with the messy hair to look around. Evelyn smiled feeling a little bemused, she hadn't given a thought to her attire this morning, she was more concerned about Mam. Just then Sophie's phone rang shrilly, vibrating across the table. Sophie snatched out a hand, "that's for me again."

Evelyn tried not to listen as she spoke to someone called Ryan. She sipped her tea, gazing around the heaving canteen. There were more people still flooding in. A tall man pushed a lady in a wheelchair through the open doors; she looked nervous too.

"Yes, I'll be home this afternoon!" Sophie's voice was raised, as she ended the call.

"Men!" She tutted crossly, taking a gulp of coffee, "it's just my husband, worried about who is going to do tea."

"Ah," Evelyn smiled.

"Do you like football?"

Evelyn was saved from answering, by another question.

"Hi, is anyone sitting here?" It was the tall man with the disabled lady.

"No, no," she replied, grateful for their interruption.

"Thanks," he smiled, pulled out a few of the chairs to make way for the lady in the wheelchair.

Evelyn stood to help him, "are you okay?" She asked kindly.

The lady in the wheelchair frowned, and looked annoyed.

"Yes I'm fine, never better!"

Evelyn felt her cheeks burn. Have I been condescending?, she wondered. The man with her looked embarrassed.

"I'm Jon." He nodded at her, he had a kind face and a deep melodic voice.

"I'm Evelyn," she replied brightly, then remembered her other guest, "and this is erm... Sophie."

"And this is Ann," he smiled down at his companion.

"I can speak for myself!" Ann looked irritated.

"Shush," Jon replied, looking unfazed by her rude behaviour.

"Are you here to do a degree?" Sophie asked, leaning forward in her seat.

Evelyn winced.

"No, I thought I'd just come for a coffee," came the sharp reply.

Jon held up his hands, shaking his head at Ann, "yes, Ann is here to do an English degree."

"Oh," Sophie laughed, as if she had just been told the punch line. She motioned at Evelyn.

"We are too. Isn't this going to be fun!"

"I'm not here to have fun," responded Ann, as she glanced at her watch. Sophie sniffed, turned away slightly in her chair, giving Evelyn her full attention.

"We can sit together if you like," she beamed, tossing her hair again.

Evelyn nodded, "yes, that would be nice. I don't really know where we've got to go though."

Sophie jumped up, almost sending the remnants of Evelyn's tea out of its polystyrene cup.

"I do, come on," she picked up her belongings with perfectly manicured hands and looked at Evelyn expectantly.

"Excuse me," Evelyn said to the messy haired boy and his girlfriend, as she squashed past. She heard the scrape of chairs as they obligingly pulled them in.

"Nice to meet you," Evelyn nodded at Jon and glanced at Ann, who was studying the breakfast menu.

"Nice to meet you too. Hope you enjoy your course," he said, throwing his wife an exasperated look. Evelyn nodded and hurried quickly out of the canteen, following her new friend.

* * *

"That was rude!" he stated as he watched them leaving the canteen.

"Well, how ridiculous – asking if I'm doing a degree."

"She was trying to be friendly Ann."

"Too friendly," Ann snapped, then sighed, "look, I'm not here to make friends."

"It might do you good," Jon suggested patiently, "Isn't that part of uni life; meeting new people?"

"I suppose so," Ann acquiesced grudgingly.

Jon began a spiel of his own time at uni. Ann listened distractedly. To be honest she was nervous and having second thoughts. She had dreamt last night that she had been stuck in the university lift and no one could hear her banging the doors to be let out. She had woken in the early hours sweating and unable to go back to sleep, she had lain in bed worrying about today and the impending course. Lack of sleep had resulted in bleary eyed tiredness and a grumpy mood. Jon however, the eternal optimist, was annoyingly happy and full of enthusiasm.

"Do you want anything to eat?" He asked, digging deep in his pockets for loose change.

"No thanks I'm not hungry."

"I'll just grab a bacon sandwich, then we can go get you enrolled."

"Jon, am I doing the right thing?" She asked tentatively, peering up at him with troubled blue eyes.

"Course you are! You are going to love it Ann, I guarantee it!" He smiled down at his wife, shaking his head, "but please...be nice!"

* * *

Will was enjoying sitting so close to Hema. She was warm, soft and her hair was silky, and smelt faintly of coconut. He felt a stirring in his loins and slung one leg over the other casually, to try to conceal it.

"Will I see you later tonight?" He asked, nibbling her ear. Hema giggled, and leaned closer next to him.

"Maybe," she gasped.

"Are you teasing me?" Will smirked, then grabbed her waist to tickle her. A catering assistant sniffed as she passed them, looking their way with disapproval.

"Are you going to buy anything?" She asked, "only there's customers waiting to sit down."

"Erm…we were just leaving," Will scraped back his chair with a laugh, and waited for Hema to collect all her things together.

"Can I carry anything?" He asked, giving her his full megawatt smile.

"I can manage…but thank you," she reached up on tiptoe to kiss his mouth softly.

"I'll text you later ok?"

Will nodded, already planning what they could do this evening. He had some spare cash, he wanted to take her to the cinema to see the new Bruce Willis film, followed by a Kentucky.

"I'll tell Mom and Dad I'm going to Lucy's."

"Good idea," Will nodded, "can't you pretend she's having a sleepover, so I can spend the whole night with you?"

Hema slapped his wandering hands away, "see you later handsome," she waved in the doorway.

"See you later gorgeous," he returned. Then she had disappeared up the stairs, while he followed the sign for humanities enrolment.

\* \* \*

"Bus is late again,"

Juliette nodded at the elderly woman who had just complained and looked at her phone for the time.

"Fifteen minutes," she agreed.

"Never on blasted time," said a gruff male voice from behind her, "maybe we should only pay half in protest."

"Good idea, but I don't think they'll let us get away with that," she replied with a small smile.

At that moment the bus swung into sight, chugged up to the stop, splashing puddles on the way. Juliette waited patiently for the elderly lady to hoist her shopping trolley onto the thrumming vehicle, then stepped up to rattle change into the fare machine. A smudged ticket spewed out. Juliette tore it off then took a seat near the back. The windows were filthy, dusty and smeared with fingerprints. She wiggled in her seat as a rakish teenager parked himself next to her. A beeping noise made her look down, and she fished in her rucksack for her phone. It was a message from Marie wishing her luck. Juliette smiled, and felt her stomach do a little flip of excitement. Enrolment day had arrived at last!

It was warm today. Juliette felt too hot in her woollen cardigan, so she shrugged out of it and held it loosely on her lap. As the bus rumbled its way to the city centre, she gazed out of the window, watching the world fly by. Last night she had organised her bag ready for the morning. She had purchased new stationery from the local Pound Shop: pens, pencils, highlighters and a thick notebook. She was ready! She thought with a determined smile. Marie had taken the children to school for her so she had been able to get ready in peace and also have time to cram a load of washing in.

"Drat," she said aloud as she remembered the spaghetti Bolognese she had forgotten to take out of the freezer. Looks like it would be something cheap and cheerful like chips and egg for tonight's tea. The youth next to her must have heard her exclamation for he took out one earphone, and looked at her quizzically.

"Just thinking aloud," she informed him. He shrugged, giving his music his full attention again. Juliette sighed, pulled her diary out of her bag, and scanned what was happening the following week. Parents evening was coming up.

The last one had been brilliant, and she had been extremely proud to receive glowing reports from both the kids' teachers. Thoughts of Marty occupied her. There had been no contact from him since the birthday party, but Molly was still asking after him. Should she tell him about the impending parents' consultation? Then she remembered she had no way of contacting him. Oh well, that solved that dilemma. Juliette moved in her seat, as the bus pulled round an island, then came to a shuddering stop.

"Excuse me," the boy lifted his knees so she could squeeze past.

As she walked through the busy town centre, she had a spring in her step. It was a mild day, the sun peeked from behind layers of fluffy white cloud, and birds chirruped in the trees overhead. Juliette felt happy and excited, eager to get to the university. There was a group of students milling around the entrance to the huge glass fronted building. As she approached, she gulped nervously.

"Hello love," the rotund security guard greeted her.

"Oh," Juliette rummaged in her bag for her letter. The guard waved her through with a grin. She walked down a bright corridor, passing small shops on her left. As she neared the library, she paused to peek in at the many books and people wandering around. Then she was back outside, in a tree lined courtyard, which was peppered with bins and benches. A sign advertising humanities enrolment flapped in the doorway. She paused at the entrance of the canteen, but decided against going in for she was late already. Instead, she followed the signs that took her into a huge lecture theatre. Juliette looked around in awe, there were rows of tiered blue seats and overhead lights that sparkled and shone. It smelt of fresh paint, polish and lavender air freshener. The carpet was plush, thick and at the front stood a huge projector with podiums on either side.

Juliette joined a long line of students waiting to enrol. In front of her stood a messy haired youth, with a grimace on his face.

"Hi, are you enrolling for English?" She asked, as he turned around.

"Yeah…unfortunately," he replied.

She stuck out her hand, undeterred by his negative attitude.

"I'm Juliette," she said with a smile.

He took her hand lightly, "Will... Will Bentley."

"Will we be getting our timetables today?" She wondered.

"Yeah, think so, it should all be online." He pointed to two ladies sitting behind a wooden desk, "they're giving out all the information."

Juliette nodded, "thanks," she said gratefully.

While they waited in the line, Juliette chatted to Will. She was surprised that he was only nineteen as she thought he looked older. He lived on the outskirts of the city in an affluent area. Juliette had heard of it but had never been there herself. As he spoke, she got the distinct impression that he didn't really want to be here and wondered why that was. She didn't have time to find out, for they were nearing the end of the line and Will was moving forward to speak to the clerk. Juliette dug in her bag for her confirmation details and smiled in excitement when it was her turn. The clerk with the name tag Sandra found her on the system and gave her an information pack thick with leaflets.

"You must activate your details to use the university's online system," Sandra instructed briskly, "now, if you would please go to the next table to have your photo taken and your ID card produced, then you are all registered."

"That's brill thanks," Juliette did as she was instructed, with a happy grin. Once the picture had been taken, she fiddled with it, hooked it round her neck so it dangled down her chest. In the doorway were representatives from the Student Union. They thrust a bagful of freebies at her.

"Free shots in the Student Union bar tonight," one grinned cheekily.

"Erm…thanks," Juliette carried on walking, clutching her carrier of goodies close. Her throat was dry, so she decided to go to the canteen for a drink and a look around.

She was queuing again to pay and trying clumsily to extricate her purse with one hand, when her rucksack slipped, and fell to the floor with a thump. The contents scattered out across the vinyl floor. Juliette knelt down quickly and began gathering her possessions back up.

"Can I help you?" A deep male voice resonated. She looked up into warm, brown eyes and felt her stomach flip slightly.

"Yes, thank you," she said, taking the cat compact mirror out of his hands. A lipstick had rolled underneath the sandwich trolley. The man got on his knees to reach for it.

"Oh, it's okay," protested Juliette, "it's only a lipstick." She noticed he was wearing a navy suit and bright white shirt, "you'll get dirty!"

The man found it, pulled it out with a smile that showed white, even teeth. Juliette stared at his mouth for a moment, and withdrew slightly. He smelt of a light musk aftershave and was extremely attractive.

"Thank you," she gasped, stuffing the lipstick back in her bag. Thank god it wasn't a tampon, she thought with a shudder. His tie was slanted sideways, and she was tempted to straighten it for him. As she was staring, she noticed a staff sign clipped wonkily onto it. Maybe he's a lecturer, she thought with excitement. He appraised her for a moment, she felt herself blush, and hoped there was no lipstick on her teeth.

"Are you okay now?" He asked, breaking the silence.

"Yes erm…thanks again," she turned away reluctantly, but her skin tingled with the close proximity of him. Hastily she paid for her purchases, and hurried away to find an empty table. As she ate her warm buttered toast, her eyes followed him as he moved across the canteen. He sat with a large group of people, but as he greeted them, he glanced her way. Juliette quickly looked down at the table, pretending to be interested in a fleck of dust. The canteen was busy, and she noticed two women hovering in the doorway with trays in their hands.

"Would you like a seat?" She volunteered helpfully, pointing to the empty chairs around her.

"Yes, thank you," a sweet looking lady with grey hair pulled out a chair and sat down. Her companion flicked her hair and sat close beside her.

"I'm Evelyn Cooke."

"Juliette Harris – nice to meet you." She looked at the woman with the mega straight hair, it must have taken her ages to get it like that, thought Juliette. She despaired of her own unruly curls, couldn't do a thing with them.

"I'm Sophie *O'Neill*," Juliette wondered why she emphasised her last name.

"You've got them too!" She pointed to the bags of freebies they clutched in their hands.

"Yes," Evelyn replied, with a smile.

Sophie emptied her bag out on the table in front of her and began rifling through the contents. There were shop vouchers, household samples, leaflets, pens and a condom. Evelyn's eyebrows rose as she stared at the contraceptive in Sophie's hands.

"Oh," she remarked, blushing slightly.

Sophie laughed loudly, throwing back her head in a hearty fashion.

"I won't be needing this," she guffawed, "I've been done…don't have to worry about babies anymore. Here," she thrust the small packet towards Juliette, "you can have mine," she said magnanimously. Out of the corner of her eye, she noticed the man from the till observing them and felt herself redden.

"No thanks…I won't be needing it either."

Sophie shrugged, "oh well, I'll keep it as a souvenir then."

Juliette felt embarrassed and irked. As she listened to Sophie change the topic to rattle on about the cost of her designer handbag, she glanced across at Evelyn who smiled ruefully back. She stared down at her own battered rucksack. It had been a bargain at five pounds, but was sturdy and hardwearing. She watched Sophie flicking her long hair and one word sprang to mind: pretentious.

"Do you like football?" Sophie asked, bluntly changing the subject.

"No...but my son does."

"Who does he support?" Sophie enquired hastily.

"Erm...Liverpool."

Sophie's mouth curved into a sneer.

"Doesn't he support his local team?"

Juliette prickled and immediately went on the defensive, "well he is only ten, but no not really..."

Sophie interrupted, "only *my* hubby's a footballer. A professional footballer," she paused for effect, "he plays for Chattlesbury FC."

"Oh right," Juliette smiled politely, "we don't really play much football in our house."

"Don't you ever take him to the match?" Sophie's eyes were wide and incredulous. Juliette felt a surge of anger rise inside her, she wasn't about to divulge to a complete stranger that lack of finances did not enable her to do so.

She sipped her drink and smiled waspishly, "no, I prefer to take my children to the park." She turned her attention to Evelyn and began general chit chat with her.

Sophie, realising she had been snubbed, dug in her beloved Gucci bag, removed a file and haughtily began working on her little finger, whose nail looked worryingly as if it was about to split.

# Chapter Seven

Will was gelling his hair in the bathroom when there was a tentative knock on the door.

"Just a sec," he called, as he pulled on his t-shirt. His mom stood outside the door, a worried look on her face.

"You okay Mom?" he frowned.

"Yes," she nodded quickly, "can I talk to you son?"

He held open the door so she could enter.

"What's up?"

Flora swallowed nervously, perched on the edge of the bath.

"I overheard Fiona Bates talking in the petrol station earlier."

"Oh yeah," he replied, "who's the old witch moaning about now?"

"Well… you actually."

"What have I done?" He protested, squeezing mint toothpaste out of the tube.

"She seems to think that you're seeing the Kumar girl, you know, the family who run the newsagents."

Will froze, glanced at his mother and then spat into the sink.

"What made her think that?"

Flora looked embarrassed, "she said that she saw you erm... kissing."

Will didn't reply but wiped his mouth on a floral patterned towel.

"Will?"

He turned around with a determined look on his face.

"Yes, we *are* in a relationship."

Flora wrung her hands, "but Will, what about her family? I've heard about her father, he's a very strict man. What would he say if he found out?"

Will shook his head, "he's not going to find out."

"But people are gossiping about you! It won't be long until it gets back to him," protested Flora.

"And what about Dad? He's stressed enough as it is."

"He's not a racist is he?" He snapped irritably.

Flora shrank back looking shocked, "no of course not! I'm just worried about *you*. You don't need all the worry and upset, what with uni and everything."

Will placed his hands on her shoulders and smiled at Flora.

"Look, Mr Kumar won't find out and don't worry about uni, it's sorted."

Flora nodded uncertainly, "well if you're sure."

"I am, don't worry Mom." She turned to leave.

"Mom...you won't tell Dad will you."

Flora shook her head, "not if you don't want me to son." Then she was gone, back down the stairs, while Will was left muttering to himself, "Damn." He thought of texting Hema straight away to warn her, but was reluctant to worry her, so decided to leave it until he saw her later this evening.

* * *

It was a cold night, fog clung to the air and a full moon sparkled in the sky. As Will hurried across the housing estate, following the twisting roads, he thought about the lecture Dad would give him if he ever found out about Hema. It wasn't the fact that she was Hindu, although a catholic girlfriend would no doubt please his mom immensely. Girls in general were a taboo subject at the moment. Max Bentley often preached that he should secure a career before "having girlfriends." But Will enjoyed rebelling against his dad. Probably because he always thought he knew best. He was so condescending, Will thought with irritation. As for his poor Mom, well she didn't have a voice against her outspoken and overbearing husband.

Will turned the corner, crossed the road and then saw her standing there, beside the entrance to the park, a slim silhouette in black leather. She ran towards him, they clasped hands and kissed slowly. Boy she tasted good, thought Will, as he snaked a hand around her waist. As they waited for the bus to take them to the cinema complex, Will reluctantly told Hema what he had learnt from his mother. She was shocked and upset, shaking her head and frowning in dismay.

"What will I do if he finds out about us?" She wailed.

Will, a firm believer in living in the present, told her not to worry, "he won't find out," he soothed, "I'm just warning you, that's all."

Hema swallowed, looked down at the ground, the romantic moment forgotten. Will sighed, "how was uni?" he asked, swiftly changing the subject, "is your course any good?"

Hema's eyes sparkled as she smiled at him.

"Oh yes, the introduction was brilliant, I think I'm going to love it."

He felt a pang of envy, which he tried to disguise with an encouraging grin. He wished he felt that happy about being at university.

"Are you sure you want to be a social worker?" He asked. He was shocked by her career choice to be honest, he thought it sounded depressing and boring. Hema nodded as she wound her small fingers through his again.

"Since I was a little girl. It was either that or a teacher... and I've gone off the idea of working in education," she paused, her eyes bright, "I want to help people Will."

Will kissed her mouth and then her cute button nose.

"Very admirable," he commented, "but you already do...you helped me with my A levels loads."

She punched his arm playfully, "you don't need help! You are so brainy Will. I know you are going to do brilliantly at uni."

"Wish I could travel instead," he confessed. There! He had said it, told somebody at last of his real dream. She squinted at him in the darkness.

"Could you travel after? It's only three years."

"Suppose so," he replied a little moodily. He was disappointed, he hadn't expected Hema to sound like his mother. There was an awkward silence. Now it was her turn to change the subject.

"What are we watching anyway?"

"Die Hard of course," they embraced playfully as the bus trundled up to the stop. As Hema stepped aboard, Will thought about the five thousand sitting in his bank account. It was meant to buy a car, but he fantasised regularly of going to the travel agents and buying a one-way ticket around the world, then packing his bags, leaving his parents a short and succinct note and getting out of here.

But now there was also Hema to consider. He was pretty sure that he loved her. He didn't really want to leave her, but living here was so depressing. It felt like the life was being sucked out of him. Three years felt like a prison sentence to him. Maybe she could come with him he pondered. But tonight he wasn't going to dwell on that. Tonight he was going to have fun! He followed her down the swaying aisle, tweaking her curvy backside. She squealed, slapped his hands away, until they sank down onto hard seats. With their arms wrapped around each other, they laughed and chattered, peering out of the window at the traffic that flew by and watching the stars twinkling in the vast night sky.

\* \* \*

"I don't want a mentor and I don't need a mentor!" Ann was balancing a tray of macaroni cheese on her lap, watching X-Factor, when Jon had broached the subject again for the fifth time that evening. She was beginning to lose her patience and could feel her temper threatening to erupt.

"But the student enabling centre said that you're entitled to help…free help!"

Ann erupted, "I don't need their help," she shouted, almost flipping the tray, "I can manage perfectly fine myself thank you very much!"

Jon's mouth set in a grim line, "they.are.trying.to.help.you," he replied slowly.

"Well, I'll be fine!"

"Are you sure?" he raised a quizzical brow as he stood to his feet, takings Ann's tray. Ann sighed, "you're not going to give in are you? Ok…I'll see how I get on, if I need the extra help, I'll ask for it. Happy?"

"Good girl," her husband replied, stooping to kiss her forehead.

\* \* \*

It was the weekend; the weather had turned colder. The radiators pumped out heat, Ann was snugly and warm in her pink fleece pyjamas.

They had enjoyed a lovely day; shopping this morning then an afternoon outside at the nearby Woodland Walk. Autumn was Ann's favourite time of year, when the leaves turned golden, red and brown and fluttered down from the trees. She wished she could run through the leaves, twirl in the hazy autumn sunshine. But she couldn't and never would again. Ann pushed the thoughts away, sniffed and wiped her eyes, which had become wet with tears of anger and frustration. Life was so cruel and shitty, but at least she had her darling Jon: handsome, loyal, kind and stoic. He never let her down. She heard him whistling as he washed up and vowed that she would stop being such a bitch, just stop complaining and being generally difficult. She owed him that at least and she did love him, so very much. Resolutely, she wheeled herself over to the laundry and began folding it into neat piles.

"Want a vodka?" He asked, peering around the door.

"That would be lovely, thanks…but no ice."

They settled down for the evening, watched a grisly film on TV and then made their way to bed.

Once she was comfy under the warm, king-size duvet, they chatted about university.

"The other students seem nice."

Ann nodded, "they're okay."

Jon took her thin body in his strong arms, and pulled her to him.

"It will do you good to make friends," he commented between kisses. Ann sighed, found his lips with her own, warm and welcoming.

"I suppose so."

He murmured, "you sound like a moody teenager."

Ann gasped with delight as his mouth found her breasts and began their gentle assault. She gripped him, enjoying his groan of pleasure, then they were lost in each other's pleasure. Afterwards, they lay in each other's arms, hot and panting, watching the shadows moving across the ceiling.

"Love you," Ann whispered contentedly as sleep began to pull her under.

"Mmmm," Jon replied sleepily, shifting to mould his muscular body against hers and their limbs entwined as they dreamt.

* * *

Sophie's weekend consisted of a haircut followed by a spray tan. It was her mother's birthday and in celebration, the family were going to the 'Goose and Partridge' for a slap up meal. As she sat under the heat lamps, reading Cosmopolitan and drinking bitter coffee, the junior hairdressers rushed around sweeping up debris and making drinks. Alison, her favourite stylist was busy trimming another client's hair. Sophie watched the tresses falling softly to the floor and shuddered. No way would she ever go that short, she was having highlights; silver blonde this time, followed by a short trim. Then when she was all finished here, she was going next door to the beauty salon, for a jet of Bahama Bronze. She would have had her nails done too, but hadn't been able to fit it in. Heidi had to leave at lunchtime, which would leave the boys unattended, as Ryan was at footy practice. She had promised Josh and Jake she would take them up to their local farm for an afternoon of outdoor activities, so her nails would have to wait till later.

One of the junior stylists unwrapped a foil, checked the colour then moved the heat lamp away.

"All done Mrs O'Neill," she exclaimed brightly, "time for your wash." Sophie followed her to the sink, sank back in the chair and waited while the young girl unwrapped the foils then washed and conditioned her hair. Sophie had been coming to this salon for about six years now. It was a bit far to travel, but it was the best in the city and Sophie loved her hair. She spent a fortune on products to tame it and keep it looking perfect.

"Sorry," a splash of water caught her eye, making her blink. No tip for you! She thought sourly. Then, she was all finished and Sophie was waiting for Alison to move along her line of clients.

"Would you like another coffee?"

Sophie shook her head; too much caffeine gave her a headache.

"I'd love a water," she replied, smiling at her reflection in the mirror. Then she went back to her magazine, reading about the life of Katie Price, businesswoman and mother extraordinaire.

"Hello Mrs O'Neill," Alison stood behind her, petite with dark hair and a pair of scissors in her hand. "What are we having done today?"

Sophie snapped the glossy magazine shut, "just a trim please."

Alison nodded, and began tugging at Sophie's hair with her multi-function comb. They made general chit chat: the weather, holidays, shopping. Sophie informed her proudly of her new found status as a full time student.

Alison was impressed, "I'd love to go to uni," she gushed, snap, snap went the scissors.

Sophie beamed, "yes, I've always wanted to do an English degree."

"What are you going to do after?" Alison asked cheerfully.

Sophie paused, their eyes met in the mirror.

"I haven't thought that far ahead," she replied, with a cough.

"Oh," snip, snip, tendrils of hair floated to the floor. What was she going to do, she wondered, what could you do with an English degree?

"I'm just concentrating on my studying at the moment," she said breezily. Alison smirked, while applying straightening serum. In fact, Sophie hadn't thought about the course at all. She was too busy surfing the university forums, reading all the posts from faceless students. She had already found out that there was a prom in the final year. What could she wear to that? She thought, daydreaming of taffeta and silk.

The straighteners hissed and a plume of steam rose from them, to curl into the air, as a tired Alison finished off her hair.

"Beautiful," the hairdresser commented, squirting hairspray in a burst around her head. Sophie smiled gratifyingly.

"Thank you," she pressed a crisp twenty pound note in Alison's palm, who thanked her profusely. The actual cost of her hair came to triple figures, but it seemed churlish not to give a tip. And besides, they all knew she was married to wealthy Ryan O'Neill. It would seem selfish not to. By the time she had finished and paid for the spray tan, she had spent over four hundred quid. Feeling happy, Sophie reversed her four by four, almost banging into a parked mini, in the process. One last stop at the stationery mega store, then home. Sophie whizzed around the shop with a trolley, flinging in packets of pencils, pens, folders, paper, a pack of highlighters, two hole punches and even a few sharpeners. She was all ready for uni now, she thought with satisfaction. Another hundred was swiped on her credit card, then she made her way home, whistling along to the pop song on the radio. Now, what could she wear tonight?

Eight o'clock and the O'Neill household was in chaos. The twins, looking resplendent in navy trousers, shirts and waistcoats, tore around the house chasing Duke, their poor tormented Labrador. Upstairs, Ryan was flinging shirts from the rail.

"What *are* you doing?" Asked Sophie, as she eyed the pile of expensive shirts on the bed.

"Can't find my white Ralph Lauren…you know the one with the diamonds."

Sophie laughed, "they're not *real* diamonds you know honey."

"Might as well be…it cost enough."

Sophie sighed dramatically, "it's probably still in the ironing pile. Heidi's slacking. You know I caught her the other day squirting my Dior perfume." Ryan ran a harassed hand through his hair.

"Can you iron it for me love? It's my favourite and I've only worn it twice." Sophie nodded, thinking it was like living with another woman.

"Okay, but we need to hurry, we don't want to be late."

Half hour later they were ensconced in the four by four. Ryan had managed to talk Derek, their gardener, into driving them there. They would get a taxi back.

"Cheers Del," Ryan slipped him a tenna, as they pulled up outside the restaurant. Sophie clambered out of the vehicle, pulling her skirt down and snagging her tights in the process. She watched in dismay as a ladder ran up her very expensive hosiery.

"Damn," she cursed. Well at least her legs were brown, she could run to the toilet, whip off the offending tights and no one would know. Sophie ushered Josh and Jake out of the car, smoothing their hair down as they imitated a Spiderman pounce to the ground. Her mother was already there, propped against the bar, in a gold, silk dress, with a revealing split up the side and a low cut, tight bodice.

"I see your mom's dressed for the occasion again," Ryan noted drily. Sophie tutted in disapproval.

"Nan, Nan!" The boys tore into the pub. A few people looked around as they hugged her tight. Yvonne Fletcher shushed them,

"I've explained this boys. It's not Nan, not in public anyway, call me Yvonne, remember." She bent down to ruffle their hair, giving a man opposite unbridled view of her huge cleavage. He subsequently burst into a coughing fit and was patted heartily on the back by a passing Ryan.

"Hi Mother," Sophie greeted, air kissing both cheeks.

"Sophie darling. You look…nice."

"Mother, you look…cold," Sophie retaliated, "do you want to borrow my shawl?"

Yvonne waved her away, "that old thing? It's my birthday sweetheart, I'm allowed to reveal a bit of flesh."

"Course you are," Ryan said smoothly, as he kissed Yvonne's cheek.

"Ryan darling," she gushed, "you're looking dashing as usual." Sophie rolled her eyes, then followed the waiter as he showed them to their reserved table. She studied the menu, wondering what she could have that wasn't too fattening. She decided on salmon with new potatoes and vegetables.

"Do you want a wine honey?" Ryan asked, as he produced a wad of twenty pound notes out of his designer jeans pocket. Sophie nodded, licking her dry lips.

"Medium please darling."

The boisterous twins followed their father to the bar, where they perched precariously on stools, eating peanuts out of a complimentary bowl. Sophie looked across the table at her mom and new boyfriend...Roger, if she remembered correctly. They were whispering and laughing together, like a couple of school kids. Sophie felt a burst of irritation ignite inside her.

"Have you had a nice birthday?," she asked with a tight smile.

"Oh yes, wonderful darling," drawled Yvonne, as she ran her fingers up and down Roger's arm, "Roger bought me a weekend away to a luxury spa. Would you like to come with me? The package is for two people. I was going to take Ruth but she's developed an allergy to her cat of all things. Her face looks monstrous at the moment, all red and puffy." Yvonne's voice took on a whining sound, "say you'll come darling, you know how I hate being on my own."

Sophie hummed and ahhhed, trying to think of a plausible excuse, "well I can't really Mom, now I'm at uni, I have to study."

"Oh poo," Yvonne replied with a pout.

Roger took a large swig of his beer, leaving a froth of white bubbles across his upper lip. "My son's just finished uni, can't get a job, complete waste of time it was, has no idea what he wants to do with his life and it cost me thousands."

Sophie looked down at her starter, a medley of mushrooms. "Sorry to hear that," she said brightly, "but that's not going to happen to me."

Roger raised an eyebrow, "oh no?" He mocked, "what are you planning on doing then?"

Sophie had the sudden feeling she didn't like Roger very much. Quiet, laidback Mick had been much nicer and the same question, twice in one day, she was beginning to despair.

"I...I," she fished around for a suitable response.

"Yes darling?" Yvonne urged, stabbing at an olive.

"I want to go into teaching."

"Teaching!" The word reverberated around the table. Sophie smiled, kicking Ryan, who had slid into the seat next to her. She took a large swig of wine, then banged the glass down in defiance.

"Yes teaching."

A nervous waiter hovered nearby, "everything okay with the starter?" He asked politely.

"Yes mate, bostin," Ryan gave him the thumbs up as he speared a slippery prawn.

Yvonne nodded vigorously, "well yes dear, the little ones are so cute."

Sophie stuck her nose in the air, "that's not teaching, that's babysitting. No, I meant older kids, teenagers, secondary."

Ryan gawped at her while Roger whistled slowly.

"Wouldn't fancy that myself. Teenagers are bloody hard work, I remember being one myself," he guffawed, projecting bits of food onto the white tablecloth. Sophie shuddered with re-vulsion.

"You okay boys?" She turned her attention to Josh and Jake, who were playing aeroplanes with crusts of garlic bread.

"Mom, if you're a teacher, does that mean you can tell us the answers to all the tests?"

"Maybe Josh," she smiled and winked, crossing her knife and fork on the empty plate in front of her.

"It's very stressful you know, being a teacher," Yvonne said in a low voice, "Bertha Potts was one, had to take early retirement through stress. Ended up on anti-depressants." Yvonne shook her head sympathetically, "of course I tried to advise her against pumping her body full of horrid chemicals. She would have been much better by now if she would have taken up yoga. No one sees her anymore, she's almost a recluse, poor thing."

Sophie's head was beginning to throb, "it's a very rewarding career," she stated, folding her napkin in two.

"You don't need to work honey," Ryan commented, sounding just like her friend Amber.

"I want to. The twins are older now, they don't need me as much and there is only so much housework a girl can do."

Ryan grinned, "well you don't do much of that," he quipped cheekily, "that's why we got Heidi."

Roger guffawed again and high fived Ryan. Sophie felt irked, she had expected no support off her mother, but she thought she could have relied upon Ryan.

"What about shopping?" Yvonne said aghast.

"I'll still have time for that," Sophie responded quickly.

But Yvonne persisted, "and your friends, you'll never have time to see them."

"Mom," Sophie began patiently, in the voice she reserved for addressing the twins, "I'm only at uni during the week. I've got all weekend for shopping and partying."

"That's okay then," Yvonne replied grudgingly, "you have to consider Ryan as well though dear."

Sophie reached out to tweak her husband's cheek, "I always do."

As they ate their meal, Sophie thought fleetingly of her impulsive announcement that had surprised even herself. I'm not worried she thought as she swallowed a delicious piece of salmon. Teaching couldn't be that difficult. Right?

# Chapter Eight

Beep beep, the shrill alarm rang around Evelyn's bedroom, waking her from a fitful slumber. She pulled her glasses from their case and peered at the dusty clock. It was six thirty already and the first day of university lectures and seminars. A jolt of excitement drove her up, out of the warm bed and into the bathroom, where she splashed cold water on her face. It had the desired effect; the remains of sleep ebbed away and dreams were forgotten. Humming softly, she brushed her teeth, then wrapped herself in her old, fluffy dressing gown that hung on her bedroom door. She made her way down the creaking stairs and into the kitchen to prepare breakfast. As the milk sizzled away on the hob, Evelyn prepared sandwiches for lunch and popped two teabags into a plastic flask. Although the canteen sold an array of tempting food, it was expensive. Over the weekend the boiler had decided to pack up. An engineer had shook his head in sympathy as he revealed that it would cost two hundred pounds to fix. Evelyn had to delve into her emergency savings pot to pay for the parts and labour. But at least it was now in full working order again. As if on cue, she heard the timer click on and felt the radiator beginning to warm.

The large, old house was chilly now that Autumn had its grip, the outside temperature had dropped considerably cooler. Evelyn watched out of the window, as the fallen leaves from the apple tree danced and swirled in the gentle morning breeze. She drizzled a teaspoon of golden honey over her steaming porridge and sat at the kitchen table to eat. When she had finished, she stood to wash up the crockery, then slowly climbed the stairs to Mam's room. It was deathly quiet as she opened the door and peeked her head inside. Nora was fast asleep, lying on her back, chest rising and falling gently, with the duvet pulled tightly underneath her chin. Evelyn hated waking her, but knew she had to get her ready for their neighbour.

"Mam," she whispered gently, then more loudly, when there was no response. Nora's eyes fluttered open and she smiled when she saw her daughter hovering above her.

"Good morning dear," she greeted warmly.

"Morning Mam, are you ok?"

"Yes thank you. I had a very lovely dream about your dad, he was calling to me, he said he would see me soon."

Evelyn frowned, passed her a cup of tea and then sank onto the soft bed beside her.

"Did he tell you I need you here for a while longer?"

Nora smiled, patted Evelyn's hand.

"My time is nearly up my dear, I'm old and tired, but I've had a wonderful life."

"Ssssh Mam, don't talk so maudlin, you're bound to live till you're a hundred at least."

Nora laughed, "I've lived long enough, I'm not holding on for a telegram from the Queen you know."

Evelyn smiled, "I think you should, you might get your picture in the local newspaper." She stood, looking down at her dear Mam.

"I'm going to get dressed and then we'll get you up."

"Okay dear."

Evelyn went to her room, pulled on a comfortable pair of brown trousers and a cream angora sweater. She thought about Sophie, her new friend at uni, and wondered what she would be wearing today. A pair of clip on pearl earrings completed her attire and then she was ready.

"You look nice dear," Nora complimented her as she heaved her up out of the bed, "maybe you might meet a nice man at university," she added with a wink.

Evelyn blushed, "no, no I won't have the time or inclination for that." Then she changed the subject hastily, "I've finished my book."

"Oh well done Evelyn, can you read it to me this evening?"

Evelyn nodded with enthusiasm, "I will."

"Then you *must* send it off to a publisher my dear."

"I need to edit it first Mam, check the punctuation and grammar."

"You can do it," Nora encouraged, "oh it's exciting."

Evelyn huffed with uncertainty, "I doubt that it will be good enough for publication, but I've so enjoyed writing it."

"Of course it will," Nora admonished, as they made their way over an oriental rug to the bathroom, "my daughter, the author!"

By eight thirty, Nora was downstairs eating breakfast, while Evelyn peered out of the window, looking for signs of their neighbour. Judy was coming up the road, her face half hidden by a flowery brolly. Evelyn opened the door and looked up to a sky that was grey and stormy. She greeted Judy, inviting her into the warm hallway.

"Mam's just finishing breakfast," she said with a smile, "I should be back for fiveish, is that okay?" She bit her lip apprehensively, as she searched her kind neighbour's face.

"That's grand Evelyn, you get off and have a lovely day, don't worry a jot about Nora, I'll look after her."

Sighing with relief, Evelyn picked up her belongings, kissed Nora, then hurried off out to catch the number six bus to town.

Juliette was tired already and it was only eight o'clock. She stood in her kitchen, yawning, buttering sandwiches and ruminating over last night's shenanigans. The owner of the social club where she worked had put her down for an extra shift in preparation to deal with two teams of bawdy rugby players. For the first hour, everything had been fine and dandy. But soon the singing and back slapping had turned to shouting, the trading of verbal insults and the ensuing result of fisticuffs. Tables had been overturned, glasses had been thrown and grown men rolled on the floor, punching and kicking like babies. Without Mick's consent, Juliette had rung the police from her mobile, trembling fingers flying over the touch screen. As she spoke to an officer, she ducked to miss a flying bottle that shattered loudly against the optics. Ten minutes later, the riot van had screeched onto the car park, where an army of uniformed officers had burst through the doors yelling and wielding raised batons.

It had taken Juliette and the few other staff all evening to tidy up the debris. It was gone midnight when she had finally fallen into bed. Then no sooner had she closed her eyes, than the alarm clock was screeching her awake again. Now here she was, gulping hot coffee, standing in a pink fluffy onesie, while her children watched TV in the next room, munching breakfast. The clock ticked by as she rushed around, preparing for the day. She filled her rucksack with fruit. Her stomach was somersaulting in trepidation of the day's events. Breakfast had consisted of a soggy piece of toast, which she had forced down. Just lately her appetite had vanished. The waistband of her trousers hung loosely so she had to snap a belt into place. Curvaceous Marie had taken to buying her chocolate in an attempt to halt the weight loss, but at the moment it, seemed to be falling off her petite frame. Juliette ran an afro comb through her unruly curls, applied a blob of lip gloss and a few streaks of mascara, and then she was ready to face the day.

Harry and Molly walked next to her, up the busy street. They dodged around sniffing dogs and pushchairs, to reach the school gates with plenty of time to spare. As they waited, numerous cars pulled up on double yellow lines, to let out troupes of children. Juliette looked longingly at a revving silver Audi. She thought fleetingly of how much she would love her own car, but they were so expensive and running them would be a definite drain on her resources. No, it was the bus for her, especially now she was a struggling student. The headmistress of the large school was out patrolling the playground. She saw Juliette and made a beeline for her.

"Harry tells me you are off to university?" Mrs Morley's top lip quivered as she spoke, but her eyes were warm and bright.

"Yes, yes," Juliette replied, somewhat shocked that Harry would take the time to talk about his 'embarrassing' Mom. "It's my first lecture today."

"And what are you studying?"

"English," Juliette silenced her mobile which had just started ringing.

"How wonderful," Mrs Morley's smile widened, "I did history myself, but English is a terrific degree to do."

"Thanks," stammered Juliette, "I've always loved the subject."

As the bell rang loudly, there was a surge of children, pushing and shoving to get into line.

"Good luck my dear," Mrs Morley raised her hand in a salutatory wave then began yelling instructions to the unruly mob. Juliette watched impressed, as the playground fell silent and the juveniles trooped obediently inside. As she ran to catch the bus, she acknowledged a few of the other parents. That was the advantage of living in the heart of a big city: the buses were pretty regular, every ten minutes or so, especially during rush hour. It chugged into town, stopping to pick up passengers at each designated bus sign. Juliette disembarked at the town centre and weaved her way across the city, pausing to tinkle change into a busker's cap and to appreciate the old architecture that housed the many law firms and banks. Her brolly was no defence against the howling wind; it lifted her hair, whipping it around her face, driving rain against her small frame. By the time she reached the university entrance, she was thoroughly wet and bedraggled. The security guard chortled as she puffed up the winding steps and through the sliding doors.

"Miserable day," he commented, clutching his radio in one hand and a Mars bar in the other.

"Yes," Juliette nodded, smoothing wet tendrils back behind her ears, as she dug in her bag for her student identification.

"Have a nice day," he called as she strode off up the busy corridor. Juliette waved her hand in response, delved around for a tissue and wiped the smeared mascara off her rosy cheeks. Just ahead of her, a group of students were leaving the library, their arms laden with books. She recognised one of them from last week. An older lady, with a kind smile, what was her name? Juliette racked her brains – Evelyn, that was it!

"Evelyn," she called, quickening her pace. The lady spun around, and smiled as she recognised Juliette.

"Hello," she greeted warmly, balancing books on one hip.

"That's a lot of reading," Juliette commented breathlessly.

Evelyn looked down, laughed softly, "yes it is. I thought I'd get a head start."

"Good idea."

They walked companionably together, towards the canteen.

"Are you looking forward to our first lecture?" Evelyn asked.

"Yes I am. Introduction to Literature isn't it?"

"That's the one and then this afternoon, it's English Language Studies."

"Oh we're in the same lectures then."

Juliette smiled, "yes, they're core modules, we have to do them, they aren't optional like the others."

Evelyn tugged the door that led to the courtyard. Groups of students hung around, sheltering under trees, smoking and chatting.

"I really like the sound of the poetry module," Evelyn admitted, as they scurried through the wet weather.

"Me too!" Juliette replied, shaking raindrops from her hair, "and did you know that you can pick modules from other subjects to study?"

"Really?" Evelyn stared, wide eyed.

"Yes, like film studies and creative writing."

Evelyn's pulse quickened, "well I'll definitely look into that. Thanks."

They walked past the canteen, and headed for the lifts where a group of people had accumulated.

"Do you want to take the stairs?" Juliette asked, glancing at her watch.

"My back's not very good at the moment dear and the classroom's on the fourth floor isn't it, so I'll wait for the lift. But you go ahead if you want to."

Juliette shook her head, "I can wait with you. Here," she held out her hands, "let me take some books."

"That's very kind, thank you."

Evelyn handed a few over gratefully, her arms felt lighter and the niggling pain in her lower back began to dissipate.

They waited patiently for a second lift to ping into reception. It zoomed them up onto the fourth floor, then they found themselves wandering along corridors with clean, white washed walls and blue flecked carpets, following a line of noisy students, looking for room 432. It was a large room, blue like the corridor they had just wandered down. A row of tall windows looked down onto the twinkling city below. The darkness of the dreary day had triggered the lighting system and strips of fluorescent rays brightened the room. Warm air pumped out of static wall radiators, some students had draped coats over them to dry. At the front of the classroom a formidable looking projector hummed softly on standby, awaiting instruction. The room was already packed full of students, sprawled restlessly on cold, plastic chairs. There were many tables dotted around the room, seating up to ten people.

Juliette glanced around, feeling self-conscious in the doorway as inquisitive eyes stared her way. She spotted seats at the front and rear of the class. She hesitated, unsure where to go. Then a voice from a front table startled her.

"Hi Evelyn, come and sit here!" It squealed. Juliette moved aside so Evelyn could pass through the doorway.

"And you," Evelyn grabbed her hand, tugging Juliette with her. She felt a flicker of annoyance as she recognised the voice belonging to the pretentious footballer's wife from the canteen. There were a few seats left. Juliette pulled one out, shrugged her jacket off, hung it on the back of her chair and sat down. Opposite her, a lady in a wheelchair was reading a book on literary terms, head bent over, she did not look up.

"Hello," Juliette smiled across the table as she rummaged in her bag for a fluorescent pencil case. The lady sniffed, looked her way and frowned.

"Hi," she replied simply, then turned her attention back to her book.

Juliette got the distinct impression she did not want to engage in conversation, but introduced herself anyway.

"Ann Stokes," the blue eyed lady replied. She really was pretty thought Juliette, as she smiled in friendly encouragement.

Evelyn was chatting to Sophie about what had happened on the X-Factor on the weekend. Evelyn didn't like reality shows as a rule, but Mam seemed to enjoy it, so they watched it each week. She would sit in her high backed chair, with a small glass of sherry, toes tapping and singing along to the songs, while Evelyn would either read or work on her novel. As they were debating the singing abilities of one of the contestants, there appeared in the doorway a small chubby man with a head of curly grey hair, horn rimmed spectacles and a goatee beard which ended in a point. He was closely followed by a much taller, dark haired man who was carrying a hundred or so photocopies for the morning lecture. Juliette recognised the man from the canteen and felt her stomach flip with excitement. Her guess that he was a lecturer had been right! While the class descended into silence, he wrote his name on the board, in bright, red capitals: Ben Rivers.

He really was lovely looking thought Juliette as she chewed the end of her pencil. His jet black hair framed a face that was set out in perfect symmetry, there was a slight stubble shadowing his chin and cheeks, which accentuated his dark, good looks. Unfortunately, the rest of the class seemed to think so too. Juliette could almost hear the ripple of sighs that emanated from fifty or so females. Even a few males swooned. His clothes were also perfect; navy trousers, a smart shirt and tie covered by a trendy waistcoat. Juliette looked down at her own shabby attire of ripped jeans and sports sweater and felt her heart sink; *I have no chance* she thought, *he will never notice me!*

"He is gorgeous!" Sophie whispered, stating the obvious.

"Why, thank you!" The short man boomed, as he wrote his name underneath Ben's, signing it with a flourish: Brian Hodges. Sophie laughed nervously, while the rest of the class craned their necks, wondering what she had said to elicit such a response.

"First thing to tell you people: We all hate Ben Rivers."

The class descended into laughter. Ben leaned casually against the projector, rifling through his paperwork, with a faint smile.

"Welcome to English," Brian's loud voice reverberated around the room, "for the next three years, your ass is ours."

* * *

Just over an hour later, Brian informed the class there was going to be a half hour refreshment and comfort break. There was a sudden stampede for the door. Evelyn and Sophie scraped back their chairs and wandered off to find the ladies, while Juliette was left alone with Ann.

"Can I get anything for you?" She asked kindly.

Ann shook her head, "I'm fine thanks." Truthfully Ann wasn't fine. For the past hour she had been scribbling notes on medieval literature, her arm was now sore and aching. She was also tired and uncomfortable. The heat of the room had intensified. Ann was sweating in a woollen polo neck. She swigged her water, as she looked over her notes. A large portion was unreadable. A scrawled mess, she had been writing so quickly to keep up, that she had failed to notice that they were indecipherable. Ann felt her eyes well with sudden, frustrated tears.

"Are you okay?" Juliette asked, concerned. She looked towards Ben, who was watching them. He came to kneel beside Ann and said in a quiet voice.

"Would you like me to get you a note taker?" Ann nodded reluctantly.

Juliette watched as he went to speak quietly to Brian, who then disappeared from the room.

"Would you like me to take a copy of my notes?" Juliette asked, searching for ways to help and break the uncomfortable silence which had descended upon the table.

Ann looked up stiffly, "I should be okay."

Juliette shrugged, took a sip of her water, watched surreptitiously as Ben travelled around the classroom, giving out reading lists.

"Thank you," she mumbled, looking up to stare into un-nerving, dark eyes. He held her gaze for a moment before moving onto another student. Brian Hodges appeared back in the classroom puffing and panting, his asthma was playing up again and wasn't helped by the cigarette he had just enjoyed, while waiting for the enabling centre to organise an emergency note taker. A plump young lady with bright red piglets, Doctor Martin boots and striped leggings hovered at the table.

"Hello Melanie," Ben greeted, "nice to see you again." In response, she flung her arms around him, hugging him tight. The class watched with interest and a little bit of jealousy, wondering what their relationship was. He whispered something to her, she broke into peals of laughter, then he introduced her to Ann.

"Hi, I'm Melanie, lovely to meet you," she thrust a hand out and waited while Ann took it, shaking it slightly. "And you're Ann I believe." Ann nodded guardedly.

"Let me take a look at those notes and I'll see what I can do to help."

Melanie also asked to borrow Juliette's to look over, then set to work transcribing.

People were starting to filter back into the room, Sophie and Evelyn sat at the table and continued chatting about the weekend's TV. Evelyn poured lukewarm tea out of her blue flask, sipping it happily as she listened. She had managed to make a quick call home to check on Nora. Judy had assured her that Mam was just fine, drinking coffee and eating biscuits, while mooning over Jeremy Kyle. A relieved Evelyn had cut the call and was now ruminating on the mornings lecture. She had thoroughly enjoyed looking at 'The Wife of Bath's Prologue and Tale,' by Geoffrey

Chaucer. At first it had been extremely hard to decipher the language and the meanings behind the archaic words, but with the lecturer's gentle guidance, it had become clearer. Evelyn also loved hearing about the history of the time and the context it had been written in. An hour didn't seem quite long enough. It had been a very entertaining but succinct lecture with Brian and Ben sharing the limelight, bouncing ideas off each other. As she glanced over the reading list that had just been given out, she looked over the extra reading on medieval literature and wondered if they would all be available in the library. So many books to read, she sighed with pleasure.

As the class settled in their seats, pens poised and ready for round two, Brian cleared his throat, and stepped to the front of the class with a wide smile.

"For the seminar this week, we thought we would do something a bit different. An ice breaker if you like..." He was interrupted in mid flow by the sound of a loud mobile ringing. Mr Hodges slammed the book he was holding, down on the table, making Sophie, Juliette and Evelyn jump in surprise.

"Please, switch off your mobiles." For a little man, his voice could certainly carry. Sophie, recognising her chiming bells ring tone, delved in her bag, her face flaming. Ryan's grinning visage was flashing on the screen, like a demented leprechaun. As she snapped the phone off, a titter spread around the classroom.

"Right, where was I so…" The door squeaked open, a messy haired youth lounged in the entrance. Juliette smiled as she recognised Will, beckoning him towards their table.

"Nice of you to come," Brian commented, as Will slunk in and eased into the empty seat next to Juliette, "are there to be anymore interruptions?"

All eyes looked at him expectantly.

"Okay, I'll start again. Just for this week, we're going to do something a bit different. The seminar's not going to be related to the lecture. Although you can discuss medieval literature if you wish to do so." Glazed eyes brightened at this suggestion and yawns were stifled. "We thought we would go easy on you the first week, and let you get to know each other. It's all about communication folks."

So on their tables, they were to discuss their favourite literature. Ann brightened perceptibly, "I love anything by Angela Carter," she started off the conversation gruffly. Puzzled faces stared back at her.

"I've heard of her, but never read anything. Is she very good?" Evelyn asked with interest.

"Yes excellent. The Bloody Chamber? Nights at the Circus? She is fantastic at subverting femininity in her work."

Evelyn nodded, impressed, "I love Pride and Prejudice," she interjected, "it's so witty. I've read it five or six times."

"Emma is good too," Juliette piped up, "we did that on the access course. I've recently purchased a secondhand copy of Northanger Abbey, at a car boot sale, which I am determined to read."

Ann felt herself relax and enjoy herself.

"Yes, Jayne Austen was one of the great writers. Very clever, used humour brilliantly as a social critique."

Evelyn laughed, "I'd never thought of it like that."

"Have you read anything by George Elliot?" Ann asked, flipping her pen between her fingers.

Evelyn and Juliette shook their heads.

"Is he good?" Juliette asked, biting on a juicy, red apple.

"It's a she," Ann informed her, "she wrote a long book called Middlemarch, I've nearly finished it, brilliant piece of work."

Sophie, feeling left out, leant across the table, eager to contribute towards the conversation, "Jilly Cooper is absolutely fab. I'm currently reading 'Jump'. It's a monster of a book, but very entertaining."

"What's it about?" Ann asked.

"Rich people mainly and horses. I wanted one a few years ago. A horse I mean, but they are so expensive to keep and a huge amount of work." She shook her head wistfully, "I just haven't got the time, what with the kids, the house and now uni." Sophie sighed dramatically. Juliette thought about her own hectic life as a single parent and smiled at her ruefully.

"What about you Will?" She asked, wanting to include him in the conversation. "What books do you like?"

Will looked up from his phone, "Catcher in the Rye is cool and also 'A Clockwork Orange' "

"Oh yes," Ann nodded, "two classic novels of alienation and rebellion."

"A Clockwork Orange?" Juliette asked, "Isn't that the one with the strange language?"

"It's called Nadsat," a voice behind interjected. She spun round, gazed up at Ben Rivers, who was standing at the back of their table, his fingers pointed together in a steeple, as he listened. "There is a module you can take in the third year, which has 'A Clockwork Orange' on the reading list. It's called unpopular texts. Everyone on the table scribbled down the information.

"There are so many books I want to read," admitted Juliette, "it's just finding the time."

"Turn off your TV, turn off your phones. Read in bed, read in the bathroom, read on the bus. Find time," Ben smiled at her with encouragement, and she felt her stomach flip in response. He drifted away to the next table, leaving them to continue their discussion on books.

After a while, Brian called the class back together and they shared their ideas with the other students. Ann spoke mainly for their table, she was very knowledgeable and articulate. Evelyn found her opinions lively and entertaining, listening with interest. When Ben looked her way, Evelyn ducked her head, turned pink and stared down at the table. It was times like this that she hated her shyness, she was suddenly overwhelmed by a sense of crippling self-consciousness. Fortunately, Will came to her rescue, sparking a lively debate on the literary merits of 'A Clockwork Orange.' The seminar came to an end, with the lecturers explaining the essay which was due in week six. They bounded around the room, giving out copies of the essay question. Evelyn took hers nervously, speed reading over the criteria. It seemed straightforward enough; to compare and contrast two novels off the module's reading list. She folded it neatly, sliding it into a clear pocket in her folder. Students began filtering out of the classroom while the overhead lights flickered on and off. The rain had stopped and the day was brightening. They waited for the lift, chatting with ex-

citement about the afternoon's language module. On the ground floor, Ann wheeled outside
clutching her cigarettes and lighter, followed by
Sophie, while the rest of the group found a table
in the busy canteen.

# Chapter Nine

"And then I had a spray tan," Ann was listening to Sophie's vibrant rendition of her weekend, as they puffed on cigarettes in the courtyard. Blossom fluttered from the trees, lining the floor like a pretty carpet. Students of all ages milled around, mingling and chatting with staff. Cleaners and gardeners bent over, picking up debris and pruning plants. It was a hive of activity. Ann felt happy, adrenalin surged through her, making her feel determined and positive. Jon had been right; she was going to love uni. Rather out of character, she felt excited for the future. The next three years were going to be hard work, she acknowledged silently, but she knew she could do it.

As Sophie chattered on, Ann sent a quick text to her husband, telling him briefly of her morning, she even finished with a smiley face and kisses. He would be surprised, she thought with a grin. Sophie misunderstood her smile, taking it to mean interest in her topic of conversation, which had now moved onto Ryan. She gabbled on about his career as a professional football player.

"Do you like football?" She asked breathlessly.

Ann shook her head sighing, "do I look as if I enjoy sports?"

"Oh!" Sophie was stung by her forthright manner, "the disabled spectators have brilliant seats, right at pitch side."

"I'll remember that thanks," Ann shook her head in bemusement. She could see Melanie the note taker hovering in the doorway, a bright smile on her face.

"I'm with you this afternoon as well," she informed Ann, "if I go to lunch, will you be okay?"

Ann rolled her eyes, was about to retort sharply, when Sophie interjected, "Ann can sit with us, we'll make sure she's okay."

As they filed back inside, Melanie disappeared amongst the throng of people. Juliette had found them a table near the window, they had moved the chairs to accommodate Ann and were sitting eating their lunch. Sophie joined a long queue at the food station. Her stomach rumbled as she gazed at the array of foods on offer. There were pizzas, jacket potatoes, a help yourself salad station, various pasta dishes and piping hot meals with a choice of chips or vegetables. She picked up a dish, began stacking it with crisp cucumber and bright red cherry tomatoes, tuna drizzled with olive oil. When she had paid, she made her way back to the table, squeezing between Will and Evelyn. It was quiet around the table, everyone eating, lost in their thoughts. Sophie broke the silence,

"So, what did you all think about the lecture?" She asked, gazing at Will in particular. She wondered why he had been late. He really was lovely looking with his floppy hair and bright green eyes.

"Yeah, the seminar was ok," he began. His phone beeped an incoming text, he looked down furtively, fingers flying over the screen in response.

"It was very interesting, the lecturers were wonderful," Evelyn quipped, as she bit into an overflowing cheese sandwich.

Sophie grinned cheekily, "Ben Rivers is gorgeous," she replied, looking to Juliette for confirmation, who blushed and looked down at her plate.

"I hadn't noticed."

Sophie stared at her suspiciously, "well, me and Evelyn heard that he's gay, which is just typical really, a man that perfect couldn't be straight could he?"

Juliette felt her spirits deflate, "Is he?" She answered, nonchalantly, "how do you know that?"

"We overheard some third year students, talking about him in the toilet. Such a waste that he bats for the other side." Sophie sighed, swallowing a lump of gruyere cheese.

"It doesn't matter if he's gay or straight," snapped Ann, "what's important is that he's a good lecturer."

Evelyn quickly changed the conversation, opening a debate about the essay question. Will was listening distractedly. He was waiting for a message from Hema to say that she would meet him here for lunch. He yawned, looked across at Sophie, who was very pretty but annoyingly dizzy and seemed to him to be a bit of a chav, with her overdone make up, designer clothes and her bling. She was talking about her husband again, the rest of the group were nodding, but looking decidedly bored. His attention turned to Juliette. She was striking with her wild copper curls and expressive face, she appeared to have a really nice personality too and a dazzling smile to match. Next to her, Evelyn looked a bit dowdy, but was very warm and put people at ease with her gentle nature. Ann made Will laugh with her abrupt manner, air of no nonsense and permanent frown. He glanced at her wheelchair thinking she was brave to come to uni. It was hard enough as it was, without having a disability to boot as well. She seemed a bit touchy though, but wouldn't anyone who was permanently confined to a wheelchair?

Will began speed reading over Juliette's lecture notes, when his phone beeped an incoming text from Hema. It told him that she was on her way down to meet him. He grinned, excused himself from the table and went to wait for her at the bottom of the stairs. She appeared a few moments later, happy and beaming, chatting to a male student. Will felt a stab of jealousy, and tried to hide it with a welcoming smile. As she skipped into his arms, he felt gratified and pleased to see the other male had sloped off unannounced. Hema looked hot today and horny as hell. Her jeans and blouse were tight, emphasising tantalising curves.

"Was your lecture good?" She enquired, looking up at him with big, molten eyes. Will began telling her of the morning's activities, omitting that he had been over an hour late. He didn't really have a plausible excuse; just good, old fashioned laziness. Also, his mom had been out shopping so wasn't habitually yelling from the bottom of the stairs, to get him up.

"Come and sit with us," he pulled her by the hand towards their table. Juliette beamed at Hema as Will introduced her, then shuffled along, to make room for an extra seat. She noticed Ben Rivers strolling through the canteen doors and fidgeted in her chair, as her stomach flipped in slow circles. Accompanying him, was a tall, willowy blonde lady, dressed smartly in a camel coloured trouser suit, she placed a hand on his arm as she leant forward to talk to him. Juliette averted her eyes with resolution and began telling an interested Evelyn about her two children.

"Harry is ten and Molly has just turned seven," she informed Evelyn with a wide smile.

"Oh that's just lovely dear, but it must be hard work with two young children to care for, as well as studying. Do you find it a struggle?"

Juliette nodded, "it can be hard," she admitted," I'm on my own you see, but I do have a fantastic family that help out whenever they can."

Across the table, Sophie paused her hair combing, the brush wavered in her hand as she spoke, "I've got two young children as well," she informed the group, "Twins; Josh and Jake are eight. They are such a handful at the moment. It's so nice to come to uni for a break from family commitments and household chores," she sighed dramatically.

"Did I hear you say you keep a housekeeper," Ann asked sharply.

"Oh yes. Heidi," Sophie replied with a wave, impressed that Ann had remembered, "we have a gardener also," she boasted. "I did consider a nanny, but wanted to care for the children myself, while they were young."

Juliette stared at Sophie incredulously, "do you work?"

Sophie shook her glossy mane, laughing heartily, "of course not! No, no, I wouldn't have time for work and I think that children should have their mothers at home when they are young. I read an article the other day on the links of wayward children and working mothers…"

"Where was that? Perfect Parenting?" Ann cut in caustically.

"Erm no, I think it may have been Woman's Monthly," she supplied helpfully.

Ann shook her head in frustration, "I imagine it must be hard, shopping all day."

Juliette's lips lifted in a smile and she coughed to suppress the giggle that threatened to erupt. Ann was looking down at her lunch, jabbing her fork into a creamy Caesar salad.

"No, I love it," Sophie replied with satisfaction, completely unaware of Ann's hostility. Her mobile vibrated across the table and her attention was diverted by a text from Amber. Lunchtime was soon over. They cleared their table, returning trays and binning rubbish. There was a mass exodus from the canteen. Students filtered out, congregating around the lifts. As if by magic, Melanie appeared at Ann's side, clutching a pen and paper, in preparation for the afternoon lecture. Will and Hema canoodled in the foyer. Evelyn watched them surreptitiously as they kissed and held each other tenderly, she felt a flush creep into her cheeks and glanced away, before they caught her staring. The lift rumbled into reception, spewing out students at a furious rate. The group managed to squeeze in together, shuffling and clinging on, as they were whooshed up to the fourth floor.

They were in a different classroom this time, slightly smaller, but awash with the same decor and the odour of recently sprayed air freshener. More wall radiators hummed as they pumped out heat, the murmur of conversation growing, as the class waited for the arrival of the lecturer. She walked into the room gracefully, stooping to deposit an empty candy bar wrapper in the waste paper bin. Juliette looked in interest at the willowy blonde woman from the canteen, Ben Rivers circulated in her mind, distracting her again.

"This is the register." She held up a flimsy scrap of paper, then proceeded to circulate it around the room, for student signatures. Evelyn squinted at the name which had been scribed neatly on the board.

"Dr Helena Mulberry," Evelyn read aloud, "what a lovely name."

Ann scrawled her signature with a flourish, "yes," she commented, "it sounds like something out of a Jayne Austen novel."

"Well," the lecturer began with a small smile, "shall we begin?"

As the first language lecture proceeded, the fingers on the clock flew around. The class listened with interest, as the lecturer gave a very brief overview of the history of the English language. Dr Mulberry spoke with confidence, interspersing her informative speech with colourful slides that sparkled from the overhead projector. They stopped for a short comfort break, then ploughed through a lively seminar discussion on dialect.

Evelyn gazed up at the clock, wondering if Mam was ok. She had spoken to her at lunchtime and then again during the lecture break. Her laughing neighbour had assured her that Nora was absolutely fine; watching reality TV shows with copious amounts of tea. Evelyn sighed, she had enjoyed her first day at uni, but she now longed to get home to Mam and the comfortable familiarity of her terraced house. Just as Helena Mulberry was drawing the seminar to a close, a high pitched ringing shocked the room into silence. Helena strode to the door and peeked her head outside.

"Okay folks, that's the fire alarm. We need to evacuate the building now and meet in the courtyard." There was a scramble for the door as she continued issuing instructions, "please leave your belongings here, we just need to get out as fast and calmly as possible." Sophie, Juliette and Evelyn waited with Ann and Melanie for the lift, while Will burst through the double doors, following the rush for the stairs. On the ground floor it was chaos. Hundreds of students swarmed about, while panicked staff waved their arms, yelling instructions, in an attempt to instil calm and order.

Juliette was pushed roughly from behind, she stumbled forward, dropping to her knees, banging her elbows in a futile attempt to support her weight. Then she felt herself being lifted upwards by strong arms and stared into Ben River's eyes. A shove from behind pushed them closer together, she squashed against his chest. Her pulse quickened as she moved her hands upwards in an attempt to create distance between them.

He smiled down at her, "do you make a habit of falling to your knees?" He commented drily. Juliette gulped, grinning up at him, suddenly unable to form coherent words.

"Are you okay?" He continued.

"Yes," Juliette found her voice, nodding vigorously, mouth twitching. He was gripping her arms and it felt nice: warm and protective. A rising surge of attraction enveloped her, then he let her go and she felt suddenly bereft. Helena Mulberry appeared in her peripheral vision, staring at them quizzically.

"You need to make your way over there," he suggested helpfully, nodding towards the chill of the open door. Reluctantly she backed away, watching as he turned to help other students. She mouthed the word thanks as he was swallowed up in the crowd. Juliette left the building, searching around for her classmates. She found Evelyn underneath a gnarled oak tree, bent over talking to an annoyed looking Ann. Sophie stood at the back of them, yakking on her phone. She had no idea where Will was, he could be anywhere, she surmised.

"I think it's a hoax," Evelyn said wearily, as Juliette walked towards them breathlessly, "I heard one of the staff saying some students had set off the alarm as a prank." Plumes of cold air escaped from her lips as she spoke. Juliette shook her head in response, and folded her arms over her chest for warmth. They watched as the Dean of the university rushed from one member of staff to another, demanding to know what was going on. The congregation of people outside were cold and chuntering, growing impatient. A man next to them complained loudly to anyone who would listen, of the extortionate cost of tuition fees and the university's incompetence. Ann joined his conversation, regaling him with the missing application debacle.

Finally, after the security team had completed a full sweep of the building and another half hour had elapsed, the students were allowed to trickle back inside to fetch their possessions.

"I guess the seminar is over for today?" She heard Ann comment drily to a teeth chattering Dr Mulberry.

"Yes it most definitely is! Apologies, but as you can probably understand, people now just want to get home." After collecting her things, Juliette waited with Melanie the note taker, for Ann's husband to arrive. An exhausted looking Evelyn rushed past her, while Sophie dawdled behind, meticulously uploading the day's exciting events onto her Facebook status.

* * *

"And then we had to wait outside, while the security guards rushed around like a pack of blue arsed flies." Will was sitting at the oak veneer table, reliving the incident to an open mouthed Flora.

"Pass the salt Mom," he asked, reaching across the table. He sprinkled a large dose across his overcooked pork chop and mash dinner, in an attempt to improve the taste. The peas were rock hard he thought with a wince, as he shovelled a forkful into his mouth. Flora however, after years of exposure, seemed immune to her own culinary disasters. She cut her food into bite sized chunks then delicately popped them into her mouth with a happy smile on her face.

"But apart from that Will, how is uni going?" She tipped lumpy gravy out of a china gravy boat, looking at her son expectantly.

"It's okay," he said carefully, not meeting her eye.

"Just okay?" She asked in concern.

Will shook his head with exasperation, "no, it's good Mom – don't fret!"

A smile of relief filled Flora's face, "have you made some friends yet?"

Will grinned crookedly, "yes, they're mainly female," he ruminated, "but some of the students are pretty hot!"

"Will!" She admonished, with a soft chuckle. Then her eyes turned serious.

"And how are things going with your erm…girlfriend."

"You haven't told Dad have you?" He asked suspiciously.

"No, no, of course not," she replied hastily.

"Where is the old bugger anyway?"

Flora huffed in disapproval at his bad language, peering at the clock. It was gone six o'clock, he was usually home by now, her fingers fluttered to her throat in consternation.

"Still at school I presume."

"Ooohh that's a big word Mom, can you spell it?" He teased, coughing away a hard lump of potato.

"Don't be so silly," the uncharacteristic snap in her voice made Will's head lift in surprise. He peered at her through slanted eyes.

"Doesn't he text you to let you know where he is?" Will commented with irritation.

Flora crossed her cutlery, "he works very hard Will," she retaliated, "he doesn't have time for silly texts." Will shook his head, mumbling as he chewed his food. Just then a key could be heard turning in the lock, a few seconds later the front door rattled open. Ruby jumped up from underneath the table. Ears pricked southwards, she raced out of the room and down the hall to greet her master, tail wagging in an enthusiastic welcome. Max Bentley peeled off his winter coat, flinging it across the coat rack, then placed his sturdy briefcase in its habitual resting place next to the shoes. He strode into the dining room, pulling at a cherry red tie. Ruby yapped for attention at his feet, circling Max like prey. Flora jumped out of her chair, a bright welcoming smile on her face.

"Hello darling," she gushed, "How's your day been?"

She fussed around, fetching the warming dinner out of the oven, placing it at the head of the table and pouring ice cold water into a glass tumbler. Max sank heavily into his seat.

"Busy," he replied with a grimace. Will glanced at his father, noting the strained look on his face. Stress hung around him like a cloak.

"We had the call today," he rasped, jabbing a piece of pork. There was a pause and silence around the table, then Flora sat bolt upright.

"Oh my, do you mean Ofsted?"

Max nodded mutely in reply, "they're coming in two days' time."

"Oh gosh, are you all ready sweetheart?"

"No," Max retorted sharply, "I'll be in the study for the rest of the evening."

"Okay dear," Flora soothed, nodding hastily.

Max peered at his son, wagging a finger.

"When you're a Head, make sure you have a good management team to support you. Mine are absolute shite, a pack of backstabbing…" he bit back the expletive, taking a slug of water.

Will shrugged, "don't think I want to be a head teacher. Way too stressful." Flora shook her head at her son, then turned to smile kindly at her husband.

"It's a commendable career."

"What are you planning on doing then?" Max asked sharply.

"Not sure yet," the truth being, Will had absolutely no idea, but he knew for certain that he didn't want to go into teaching. Too much stress, responsibility and hassle. Although the long holidays were a bonus, Max seemed to spend them working in his study anyway. Will's nonchalant answer further incensed Max's foul mood.

"It's about time you set your mind on a career. Don't they have advisors at university?"

Will shrugged again, lounging back in his chair.

"Sit up Will, you'll have indigestion," Flora shrieked, sensing an argument threatening to erupt. Will wolfed the remains of his lukewarm dinner, eager to leave the table, so he could text Hema. Flora began jabbering on about some pretty material she had seen on the market, which would make a lovely pair of curtains.

"Don't you have any homework?" Max interrupted her brusquely, firing the question at his son.

"No," he lied.

"No reading? You must have tons of books to read surely?"

"Not yet," Will snapped back, "don't stress Dad, it's only the first day!"

Max shook his head, rising to his feet, knees creaking in protest.

"I'm going to work," he announced, disappearing into his study.

"I'll bring you a cuppa," Flora called after him. There was no response, just the sound of the grandfather clock ticking in the hall. Will helped her clear the table away, flinging scraps of meat at Ruby's upturned nose.

"He's such a shit to you," he fumed, dumping crockery in the sink.

"Will!" Flora retorted, "he's just stressed."

Will snorted in derision, "why don't you get a job Mom, it would do you good to get out of the house." He dried his hands on a flowery towel that matched the decor, "don't you get bored of housework?"

Flora shook her head, clutching a squeezy bottle of washing up liquid to her chest, "I wouldn't know what to do." She addressed her son with wide, troubled eyes, "I worked in a shop when I was younger, but I gave it up when I had you."

"It's not the 1970s mom," Will replied gently, "it's a big world out there, just think, you could make new friends, earn your own money. Let Dad cook his own bloomin tea for a change."

Flora sighed, "I like my life as it is, there's nothing wrong with being a housewife," she protested.

"Housewife? That word is so archaic! How about domestic goddess?" His eyes twinkled mischievously. Flora laughed, and pushed her son away affectionately.

"What could I do anyway, at my age?"

"Anything," Will answered, throwing his arms wide, "you could do whatever you bloody well like."

"Ahh, my idealistic son," she ruffled his hair with a grin.

"There's a lot of mature students on my course," he confided, "why don't you come to uni with me? We could party at the student union."

"Now you are being unrealistic," Flora scolded, "how would Dad afford that and anyway, I've never been the academic type. Exams scare me, uni doesn't interest me."

"Well whatever," Will grinned cheekily, "think about yourself for a change, go spend some of the miserable bugger's money." He bounded out of the kitchen and up the stairs energetically, while Flora was left wondering about the future, ruminating over her dear, sensitive son's words.

# Chapter Ten

When Evelyn finally struggled home with her load of books, Nora was napping in the chair. The room was hot, she tugged at her scarf, gazing down at Mam.

"Everything ok?" She asked Judy fretfully.

"Your mam is an angel," Judy smiled her way as she picked up her bag and coat. Evelyn sighed with relief.

"Do you need me again this week?"

"Well, she's at the daycentre Wednesday, but I do have to go in Friday morning, would that be ok with you?"

Judy nodded, "yes, that's fine." She gave Evelyn a brief rendition of the day. Judy laughed as she confided that they had found the playing cards and enjoyed a game of poker. She followed her neighbour to the door, giving her a grateful hug, then locked up for the night, pulling the brown, velvet curtains across with a swish.

"Mam," she whispered, kneeling beside the chair. Nora opened one sleepy eye, smiling at her daughter with delight.

"Hello dear, how was your day?"

"Oh Mam, it was great!" Evelyn beamed, "I'll tell you all about it over tea. Would you like fish fingers?"

"Yes, that would be lovely dear." As Nora flicked through the TV channels, Evelyn busied herself in the kitchen; warming up the grill and turning the fryer on. They ate their tea on plastic trays, while Evelyn gave Nora a rendition of the day's events.

"So there was no fire?"

"No, no." Evelyn assured her, folding over a piece of bread and butter, "it was just some students fooling around. Very irresponsible, and the Dean of the university, well he was livid. By the time we had the all clear to return inside, the seminar was over."

"That's a shame." Nora shook her head, biting into a fish finger, "what are the other students like? Are there many men?"

"Mostly female," Evelyn replied, swallowing, "although there is a nice, young lad, who sits with us called Will. He's a lovely chap, his girl-friend is studying to be a social worker you know. Then there's Sophie, the footballer's wife. I've told you about her, haven't I?"

"Yes, you have dear. How glamorous!"

"She is. Perfect hair and make-up." Evelyn conceded with a frown, "she does seem to have a nice personality, although she can be insensitive at times."

Nora chuckled, "must be all that money. Foot-ballers do get paid an awful amount. It's criminal really, compared to what a doctor or a nurse is paid."

"Soldiers too," Evelyn nodded in agreement, "but as long as people keep buying the tickets, nothing will change, will it Mam."

"That's right. Achh well, let's not worry about it. Tell me about the other students."

"There's a really beautiful girl called Juliette. Her hair is so red and wild; I've never seen any-thing like it. She is lovely, a single parent, very hardworking and strong, but there's something vulnerable about her too. I don't know how she copes with university as well." Evelyn shook her head in wonder, rounding up the errant peas on her plate. "Ann is a disabled student."

"In what way my dear?" Nora asked, looking up with interest.

"She's in a wheelchair. I haven't spoken to her much. She seems okay, very articulate and bright, but definitely has a temper and can be really abrupt. A note taker has been assigned to help her. Her name's Melanie, she's lovely though, very bubbly and friendly."

"You've met lots of new people then," Nora commented, as she crossed her cutlery together, to signify that she had finished eating.

"I have," Evelyn stood to take Nora's tray, "how about some jam roly poly?"

"Oh yes, with custard please, if we have any."

Evelyn searched the chilly pantry, while the dessert bubbled and hissed in the oven.

After they had finished eating, Evelyn cleared away, then trudged up the stairs to fetch her manuscript. She blew the dust off the box, as an excited Nora clapped her hands, jigging in her seat. The fire crackled, as Evelyn read her final chapter.

"The end," she said, voice shaking with emotion. She glanced at Mam, whose face looked transfixed with emotion.

"Did you like it?" Evelyn enquired nervously.

"Oh my," Nora began, reaching for her daughter's hands, "it really is wonderful. I know that I'm probably biased, but you are so talented. I love the ending, it's so happy and heartwarming."

Evelyn grinned with delight, "I'm so happy to finish it," she admitted, "although I've loved writing it, there have been many times when I've despaired, doubted myself and nearly given up. I'm just relieved to finish it. It's taken me over a year."

Nora nodded in agreement, "You have worked hard. Now you must send it off."

She pointed to the bookcase, where a recent Writers' & Artists' Yearbook nestled, amongst Catherine Cookson novels.

Evelyn looked across with trepidation, "I need to check it thoroughly first Mam. I could really do with another person to read it. You know, someone unbiased, who will give me an honest opinion."

Nora nodded, "Very wise dear, how about someone at university? A lecturer maybe?"

Evelyn chewed her lip uncertainly, "what would I do if they hated it? They might laugh at it!"

Nora tutted, "they wouldn't dare. Now Evelyn, you have to be prepared for criticism. As long as it's constructive, of course."

"Yes you're right," she nodded decisively, shuffled the pages back into place, bound them tightly with an elastic band then placed them carefully into the box.

"I'm going to work on it this weekend," she decided crisply, wondering how she would fit it around the many chores that required completing. "Right now I'm going to run a bath and have a relax."

With that, she took herself out of the room and up the creaking stairs, leaving Nora humming softly along to the radio below.

* * *

Sophie was lying propped up in the queen sized bed, surrounded by plump pillows and velvet cushions. The lamp cast an eerie light across the room, bouncing prisms of light off expensive bedroom furniture. It was gone ten o'clock, the twins had been sleeping for an hour now, the house was quiet, shrouded in darkness. Sophie snuggled down deeper into the bed, pulling the duvet up around her chin. She had just kicked Ryan out, to let the whining dogs into the garden for their nightly reprieve before they settled onto the downstairs settee. She could hear him, whistling them back into the house. Five minutes later, he was bounding up the stairs, propelling himself back onto the bed. Sophie laughed, slapping his cold hands away.

"Come here darling," he leered, rooting under the covers. She shrieked, as cold fingers wrapped around her naked waist. They wrestled briefly, before he lay vertically atop of her. Ryan showered her neck with kisses, cupping her breast eagerly. She stifled a sigh, she really wasn't in the mood for lovemaking tonight. 'A Clockwork Orange' lay at the side of her, beckoning and enticing. After finishing uni earlier, she had been to the book store, where she had spent ages in the classics section, filling her hand basket. Now she had a pile of books balancing precariously on her corner table, just waiting to be read. 'Riders' had been placed haphazardly back on the book shelf, three quarters of it read, folded over where she had been interrupted. Finishing it now would take too much time.

"I'm reading honey," she warned, wriggling from underneath him, rolling him back onto his own side of the bed. Ryan groaned, burying his head in the feather pillows in frustration.

"What are you reading anyway?" He asked, with a note of irritation. Sophie flicked the cover towards his face, "one of the students recommended it. It's very strange, but good in an interesting sort of way." Ryan pulled himself upwards, wincing as his back pressed against the cool headboard. He reached for his copy of 'The Sun', rustling the pages in defiance. Sophie watched him as he squinted to read the smaller headlines.

"You really should get glasses," she advised, in response he pulled a face. "They've got fab designer one's," she continued, "David Beckham wears them too, did you know?"

"Does he?" Ryan asked shocked.

"Yes, they're trendy now," she nodded, delving back into her book.

"Your mom rang earlier, was asking about you going to that spa weekend again."

Sophie sighed, closed the novel, dropping it onto the floor.

"I told her I haven't got time…What about Josh and Jake? How would you cope?"

"I could manage!" Ryan replied, glancing over the page three model with wide eyes, "and I could always ask Heidi to do some overtime and work that weekend."

Sophie hesitated, feeling tempted, she loved the indulgence and relaxation of a spa weekend. It had been years since she had been to one.

"Maybe," she answered.

Ryan looked sideways at her, "did I tell you I've been invited on a stag weekend the end of the month?"

"No!" Sophie said in outrage, glaring at her husband.

"It's Mickey's brother honey, I couldn't really say no."

Sophie pursed her lips in anger at the thought of her husband's wild and wayward friend. Although he was a brilliant and skilled defender and adored by the fans, Mickey's personal life left a lot to be desired. There were so many women, fast cars, gambling, paparazzi. Trouble seemed to follow him everywhere and usually made front page headlines.

"Well I'm definitely going to the spa now!" She sniffed. Ryan smiled happily in response.

"What's it like at uni?" He asked, swiftly changing the subject, "I bet it's full of purple haired people, demonstrating over everything," he chuckled, rustling the newspaper to the sports section.

"It's not like that at all. In the 70s maybe, now everybody seems to wear jeans and trainers."

Ryan glanced up in surprise, "aren't there any spaced out hippies?"

"No! Everyone just seems…normal"

"Really?"

"Yes," she nodded. She had been a little disappointed to be truthful. She had yet to meet any revolutionaries, although Ann seemed to be a tad rebellious.

"Well, I've done just fine, without going to uni," Ryan remarked, "not many ex-students earn as much as me," he boasted.

Sophie smiled, patted his hand, "that's true hun," she conceded.

"Do you really want to go into teaching?" He asked, an eyebrow raised. Thoughts raced through Sophie's mind, what could she say? She couldn't back out now.

"Yes," she decided crisply. He shrugged, his attention caught by an enlarged shot of a ball flying through Manchester United's net. Sophie reached down to retrieve her discarded book and lost herself once again, in the strange world of Anthony Burgess.

* * *

Juliette strode down the corridor of Huntingdon Primary School, glancing at her watch nervously. Parents evening had rolled around once again; another evening of looking over school books and chatting with tired, overworked teachers. She was heading for Molly's teacher first; Miss Daisy, her daughter's favourite so far. Juliette had been volunteering in her class for over twelve months now and had loved the experience. The young NQT had been like a breath of fresh air; bright, happy and enthusiastic. Harry's teacher, Mrs Foxley, in comparison was rather strict and formidable, steely eyed and waspishly direct. Parents gossiped at the school gates about her, that she was part of the furniture and had been at the school far too long. Juliette always remained tight lipped, refusing to get involved in idle chit chat. Harry seemed to like her anyway, so that's all that she cared about. Overall, Juliette was very pleased with her children's teachers and the progress they had made. It was a lovely school. Years ago, it had been in special measures, but with a new management team and assistance from the local authority, it had gradually progressed to outstanding. Juliette passed a cleaning lady, bent over scowling, as she sucked up embedded crisps. The classroom was quiet, its windows were covered with laminated letters, numbers and learning objectives. The doorway was strung with beads that tinkled as she slowly pushed the door open.

A set of parents sat at a table with the teacher, talking in hushed tones. Juliette tiptoed in, taking a seat at the back of the classroom and glanced around the familiar room. It was bright, colourful and busy with displays of children's work. Only last week, Juliette had hovered on plastic chairs to create an eye catching World War II display, utilising art materials, interspersed with children's work. Tuesdays were her day to volunteer. There was no uni that day, no work on the evening. Juliette enjoyed the camaraderie of being in a classroom. The children were so lovely, even the badly behaved ones. Miss Daisy taught with enthusiasm, passion and innovation. She believed in a holistic, child centred approach to teaching, encouraging the pupils to express themselves imaginatively both verbally and through their work. During lunch break, Juliette and Miss Daisy sat together in the hot, overcrowded staff room, chatting and laughing. Juliette thought Miss Daisy could have been an actress, she had such an expressive face and hands that gesticulated wildly when she spoke. Her hair was snipped into a severe, claret coloured bob. When she spoke, her tongue stud clicked across her teeth. She was young, straight off a PGCE, at twenty-two years old, enjoyed partying on a Saturday night, but she was also savvy, street smart and extremely hard working.

Juliette helped her as much as possible, but now she had started uni, she had dropped her two days volunteering, down to one. As she looked across the room, she noticed that Molly's teacher looked tired this evening and wondered how she would cope as a primary school teacher. By the time she had finished studying, her children would be older and more independent, but Juliette was realistic about the job and what it entailed. The workload was intense, the stress and pressure could be overwhelming at times. I must be crazy, she thought, picking at a cotton thread on her jacket. Despite all of the negatives however, Juliette viewed teaching as a worthy, fulfilling career; to shape young minds would be a privilege. She was excited and happy about the future. When she was younger she had dreamed of being a teacher; as a child she had played teachers with her dolls and teddies, acting out wild scenarios of school life. It was all she had ever really aspired to do. Now she grinned as she looked over Molly's art folder. They were really very good, she thought proudly, holding up a charcoal picture towards the light. Miss Daisy was shaking hands with the parents, bidding them good bye. She looked across at Juliette, beckoning her over.

"Have you had chance to look through Molly's work?" The teacher asked, as Juliette sank down gingerly on the miniature plastic seat.

"Oh yes, her work looks amazing," Juliette gushed happily. Miss Daisy nodded, grinning widely, to reveal a set of perfect white teeth, "she is very bright, she is also a lovely young girl and a pleasure to teach."

"I am so pleased to hear that!" Juliette exclaimed, feeling extremely relieved.

"I have no issues at all with Molly," continued the teacher with a beam, "she really is a delight and doing fantastically in all areas of learning. But she does seem to have a particular talent for art."

Juliette nodded proudly, "yes her art work looks excellent and she does spend time at home with crayons and paints."

Miss Daisy stood to wander over to her desk, pulling a carrier bag from behind her chair.

"I have something for you," Juliette peered into the bag which had been thrust into her hands.

"They're crayons and a sketch pad for Molly and a book on essay writing for you."

"Oh thank you so much," beamed Juliette, "but you really shouldn't have."

Miss Daisy waved away Juliette's protests.

"It's a thank you. For all the unpaid work you do in my class. You help me so much; I can't thank you enough."

Juliette smiled gratefully, cheeks dimpling in happiness, feeling suddenly overwhelmed by emotions and close to tears.

"Right, well," Miss Daisy flipped through the scattered books, "let's discuss her attainment levels."

An hour later, Juliette was pushing through the double doors and heading for home in Marie's silver Metro. Her older sister cursed as the traffic lights flashed red, just in front of her. The car shuddered to a halt and Juliette was flung forwards in the seat, she clutched at her belt, watching a man weaving through the line of traffic on his push bike.

"Sorry sis," Marie chortled, as she shoved the accelerator into neutral, "so, how are the kids getting on?"

Juliette gave a brief recap of the evening's outcomes.

"Wow! They are clever little things, wonder where they get it from."

Juliette threw a barbed look at her sister.

"Ha, ha, ha," laughed Marie, as she pushed down on the pedal and shot forward.

"How's Dave?" Juliette asked, as she rubbed lipstick off her teeth in the front view mirror. Marie pondered on the subject of her husband, before replying.

"He's okay. Still working too much, but hey ho, it pays the bills."

Juliette hummed in sympathy, longing to ask if their second IVF attempt had been successful. They had been trying for a baby for years now, with no luck. In desperation, they had taken out a large loan to pay for fertility treatment. The first attempt had sadly been unsuccessful, now they were just undergoing their second batch of treatment.

"I'm a bit worried about Harry," she commented, changing the subject.

"Why?" Marie glanced her way as she changed gear, "I thought he was doing well."

"He is, academically," Juliette insisted, "it's just that his teacher has noticed he's been quiet of late and he had a fight in the playground. Another boy had been teasing him about his dad."

Marie tutted crossly, "ugh, that toe rag. I knew he'd be involved somehow."

Juliette sighed sadly, "it's affected him badly Marie. The break up, prison, Marty disappearing then reappearing with no explanation. He's just a little boy, he needs stability."

Marie nodded in agreement, "it's not your fault you do know that?" She soothed, "you do a fantastic job. Harry will be okay, he's made of tough stuff like his mom and anyway, he's got loads of people who love and care for him. Don't stress sis." Juliette nodded, chewing her lip doubtfully, as she gazed out the window, watching the rain beating against the glass.

"Anyway," Marie said, a glint in her eye, "what about uni. Any hot men?"

Juliette broke into peals of laughter, "I haven't noticed!" She fibbed, blushing a deep shade of crimson.

"What? There must be a few surely and why are you blushing?" Marie sniffed suspiciously.

"Okay," Juliette admitted, "there is one. He's a lecturer."

"Oh," Marie teased, "bet you don't get much work done, ha. What does he look like?"

An image of Ben Rivers flashed into her mind, warming the pit of her stomach.

"He's dark haired," she gulped, "extremely handsome, well spoken, intelligent and he has the blackest eyes I have ever seen." She jolted out of her reverie to find her sister staring at her open mouthed.

"He sounds bloody perfect!"

Juliette felt her spirits sink as she replied quietly, "he's gay."

"What!" Marie shouted as she slammed on her brakes and the car shuddered to a sudden halt.

Juliette leant forward, clutching the dashboard, a look of consternation on her face. She checked the mirrors, thankfully there was no one behind, the road lay empty.

"It's really none of my business," she snapped grumpily.

"Well hell, okay girl, but you talking like you love the dude!"

"Don't be ridiculous," Juliette scrabbled at her feet to retrieve her fallen belongings, "all I said was that he was good looking." Marie pulled up the handbrake, shaking her head in disbelief.

"Uh-huh, okay sister. You are so barking up the wrong tree there. Forget about that guy."

"He's forgotten," Juliette replied hastily, "anyway, are you coming in for a night cap?"

* * *

Saturday morning dawned bright and chilly. Ann was snuggled up in her warm bed, reading 'Robinson Crusoe.' It was still early, just gone six am. Jon was downstairs, clacking cups in the kitchen. She could hear the kettle whistling cheerfully and the sounds of birds chirruping through the open window. That was one good thing about being a paraplegic, she surmised, since the accident had happened, all her other senses had been heightened. Her hearing seemed to have its very own radar; picking up the minutest sound. Ann's vision had always been excellent, 20/20 at her last eye test and her sense of smell was like a dogs, picking up any unsavoury scents. There was a sudden movement from the doorway, then Snowy, their three-year-old tom cat sprang onto the bed, stretching his claws and arching his back laboriously.

"Hi boy," Ann held out her hand for the cat to pad towards and sniff gently. He spun around in a succession of lazy circles then settled in the warm crook of her arm. She turned her attention back to her book.

"Any good?" Jon enquired, as he appeared in the doorway, carrying a tray of tea and biscuits.

"It's okay," Ann began, "they were so God fearing in those days, it's kinda strange you know."

Jon nodded, "and we all know how you feel about that subject," he winked, passing her a magical wife mug.

"No, no, I wouldn't laugh at anyone's beliefs, it's all down to personal preference," she argued, "just not for me. Religion's a crutch for people who…"

"Can't cope with the real world," Jon finished, hopping back into the warm bed, "I agree honey, one hundred per cent."

"I can't deny the book is a masterpiece though, the concept is absolutely brilliant and extremely original for its time."

"Ooohhh, hark at you," he teased, shooing the cat away, "that mog makes me sneeze."

"You love him!" Ann retorted, cooing at Snowy's retreating figure.

"Not as much as I'd love a baby."

"What?" Ann gasped, squealing in pain, as she bit down on her tongue. Jon slowly dipped his biscuit, "just saying," he replied.

"You want a baby?" Ann asked faintly, staring at him with incredulous eyes.

"Well heck yes, or maybe some kind of small person would do."

Ann gulped, "I'm shocked Jon, how would we…what…"

"Adoption?" He offered, grinning across at her.

"Are.you.serious?" She exclaimed.

"Deadly," he placed his drink down on the bedside table, took her free hand in his, twining his fingers through hers.

Ann sighed, "how could I possibly look after a baby or a child? I'm disabled Jon, it just wouldn't be possible and not fair on the child."

"Why not?" Jon asked defiantly, "it's only your legs that don't work, everything else is just perfect," he raised her hand to his lips to kiss it softly, "anyway, there would be two of us, remember."

"But you do so much already Jon," she protested shaking her head, "no, no I couldn't cope with a baby. Not a possibility."

"An older child then," he suggested, "I want this Ann, I've been thinking about it for a while now. There's so many kids out there who need love and a good, stable home. We could offer them that. Just an idea, think about it okay."

Ann nodded, for once speechless, watching as Jon slurped his tea then bounded out of the room to run the shower. On his return, he scooped up their cat, wrapping him in a blue fluffy hand towel.

"Just think, our very own bubba," he cradled the cat close to his chest, who in return let out a frightened miaow.

"Yes, just think," Ann replied in wonder, as a happy exasperated grin spread from ear to ear.

# Chapter Eleven

The first semester at university flew by. The leaves turned golden brown, crispy and curly, as they fluttered down from the trees. The students were busy, racing from one lecture to another, scribbling notes and debating topics, as the weeks rolled by. Reading lists were widely distributed, and this ensued in a stampede to the library as students grappled over the few free copies available. Personal tutors had been allocated to first year students. Juliette had gasped as she read the name Brian Hodges, flashing at her, while she was logged in at the Cyber Cafe. She wasn't sure she was happy about this, she whispered to Evelyn, who was sat at the next terminal. Evelyn eyed the group of suited lecturers at the nearby table and leant closer.

"He is a little bit scary," she agreed quietly, as her fingers flew over her keyboard, "oh, I've got Ben Rivers."

Juliette's head snapped up, her face lighting at the mention of his name.

Evelyn was smiling at her computer screen, "I'm happy, he seems really lovely."

"Who does?" Sophie asked loudly, plonking her bag down in front of them and spilling Juliette's hot chocolate.

"We were just discussing our personal tutors," Evelyn explained patiently, "who have you got?"

"Helena Mulberry," Sophie replied, as she rooted in her bag for her Chanel purse.

"Oh, she's nice," Evelyn smiled.

"She's okay, very well spoken," she imitated a posh accent, "and have you noticed how her and Ben Rivers are *always* together? Look," she pointed furtively towards the cafe entrance, where both lecturers stood, surrounded by a small flurry of students. Ann, who was seated at the opposite end of the desk, looked up from her screen to glare Sophie's way.

"I'm not sure about that dude being gay. Maybe he likes a bit of both," she speculated, oblivious to Ann's growing anger.

"Why are you so interested in his sexuality?" Snapped Ann, flinging her book down, "I've got friends who are gay."

Sophie held up her hands, "Whoa, I don't mind gay people at all," she gabbled, "but don't you think it's a bit erm…unnatural?"

"No. I don't. If two people love each other it really isn't *unnatural* and definitely is no one else's business," Ann's eyes slanted, "are you homophobic?"

"What??!!" Sophie shrieked, "of course I'm not…whatever you said. Anyway, I'm going to get a cappuccino, before the queue grows too long."

Ann watched Sophie flounce up to the coffee station, hair tossing wildly, "that woman makes my blood boil."

"She is entitled to her opinion," Evelyn defended her, "although she can be a little tactless at times, she has a good heart."

"I don't think she means to offend anyone either," agreed Juliette, "there's certainly no malice intended. In fact, she seems to be a little naive."

"Well yes, definitely naive, certainly thoughtless and maybe also bigoted," Ann snapped, "her whole attitude is just so ostentatious."

"She lives in a different world," Evelyn nodded, "but her and her husband do give an awful lot to charity you know."

"Do they?" Ann asked doubtfully. They watched Sophie laughing with the cashier, before she wandered back to their table. Ann tried valiantly to quell the rising sense of antipathy, she had to admit grudgingly that Sophie *was* gorgeous. She had the most perfect figure and a really pretty face, just a stinking personality, she thought sourly.

"So, who have you got as a tutor Ann?" Sophie asked, with a guilty smile, as she perched on the edge of the table.

"Celeste Feret," Ann replied, stony faced. All eyes looked at her quizzically, "we haven't had her for a lecture as yet. She's part of the language department," Ann continued, thawing a little as she spied a picture of Sophie's children hanging out of her purse. Jon had spent the weekend convincing Ann that adopting a child would be a brilliant idea. As a result, on Sunday night they had downloaded some literature off the internet and read through it together. Unable to sleep, she had lain awake, a seed of hope and happiness growing inside her. Their own child, she thought with a happy smile.

"Like a potato chip?" Sophie offered the bag towards her.

"No," Ann replied stiffly, "thank you, I've just eaten."

Juliette was watching Ben Rivers as he strode across the room, arms full of books and papers. Helena Mulberry trailed behind, a vision of elegance in a pale pink dress. He was waiting for the machine to dispense with his coffee, when he suddenly gazed her way. She felt like a rabbit caught in a bright beaming headlight. A few moments ticked by as they appraised each other, then he began to head towards their table.

"Hello ladies," he greeted politely.

"Oh hi," Sophie gushed, toying with her hair. Juliette couldn't see him, for he was standing just to the rear of her, but she shivered as she felt the pressure of his fingers lay on the chair back, lightly brushing against the arch between her shoulders.

"How are you enjoying uni so far?" He enquired, clearing his throat. It sounded husky, sexy, deep and melodic. In response, arm hairs sprang upwards and goose bumps pimpled her arms, the others around her table chorused positive replies, but she sat silent and flushed. What is wrong with me? She wondered. Feeling suddenly irate, she turned around to stare up at him coolly.

"There isn't enough books to go around from the reading list," she stated.

He smiled faintly, "I've put three day loans on them all, so hopefully that should be sufficient, but if you require any extra help, please come and see me." Juliette bristled with indignation, was he implying that she couldn't cope?

"I should be fine, thank you." She noticed Evelyn watching her, looking rather shocked and felt pangs of guilt, he is just being nice, her conscience wailed. She turned around to apologise, but it was too late, he had gone, with a friendly goodbye.

"Oh, isn't he just lovely," Sophie sighed, "what a waste!"

Ann banged down her flask of tea, Evelyn stifled a smile and changed the topic of conversation, while Juliette was left staring despondently at the door and his retreating figure.

* * *

Friday evening motorway traffic was a nightmare, Sophie decided, as she crawled up the middle lane, sandwiched between two huge haulage trucks. In the passenger seat, her mom Yvonne, snoozed, head tilted to one side, oblivious to the rush hour chaos which surrounded them; made worse by barricaded roadworks that stretched for over a mile. As darkness descended, hundreds of headlights snapped on, a slow moving twinkling line, that ploughed through the English countryside. Sophie flicked on the radio, wincing as the booming sounds of Calvin Harris blasted out of the surround system, reverberating around the car, shaking the windows and the gear stick.

"What, what?" Yvonne jumped in her seat, licking at a line of drool which was crusting over her foundation.

Sophie turned down the music, "hi Mom," she greeted cheerfully, "sweet dreams?"

"I wasn't asleep," Yvonne snapped, "just resting my eyes. Roger had me up most of the night with his sciatica!"

"Oh, shame," Sophie turned her head away with a small smile.

"Back pain is a terrible thing you know, especially when you are trying to abstain from traditional painkillers. Roger is so brave; he wouldn't even let me rub some of my homemade ointment in either. It's obvious you don't like him," Yvonne grumbled, "but you should give him a chance, he's trying really hard to fit in."

Pah! Thought Sophie, remaining silent.

"Anyway, are we nearly there yet?" Asked Yvonne, sounding rather like a petulant child.

Sophie checked her Sat-Nav, "about forty minutes left." She indicated, then swung sharply into the fast lane, in the hope of speeding up her journey.

"How will Ryan cope this weekend?" Yvonne asked, stuffing a toffee in her mouth.

"He's talked Heidi into staying," she sighed, "even though he has *no* footy training and *no* weekend match."

"I'm not sure I like your housekeeper," Yvonne disclosed edgily, "when I asked her to take my coat the other day, she looked at me as if I was dirt on her shoe."

"It's a foreign thing," Sophie replied, waving away the mention of her.

"You want to watch her with Ryan as well," she persisted, "she was positively drooling over him the other day when he had his shirt off."

*And you weren't?* Sophie thought with a shake of her head.

"Mom, she's ancient," Sophie replied, a superior edge to her voice.

"Don't underestimate the power of an older woman," Yvonne coughed, "some men are attracted to maturity you know."

"What, like Roger?" Sophie laughed.

Yvonne smoothed down her hair with a wink, "exactly, have I told you what he likes me to dress up as?"

"No, no, I don't want to know, too much information!"

They laughed together, as the rain began pattering down on the window screen.

"It's the groupies that worry me," Sophie confessed with a frown.

"That's why spa weekends are so important honey," Yvonne patted her daughter's hand, "you have to keep yourself looking beautiful: there's always someone lurking, wanting to take your place. And when you go back, Ryan won't be able to keep his hands off you. He'll be begging for it." She smiled knowingly.

Sophie nodded reluctantly, suddenly aware that she hadn't made love with her husband for more than two weeks. I must make more effort, she thought nervously. She would start by sending him a soppy text message as soon as she arrived at the hotel, then when she got back home she would make a trip to Ann Summers and purchase goodies purely for pleasure. No more nagging or stropping she vowed, well at least for a while anyway.

"So, how are your erm, studies going?" Yvonne asked, flipping through a glossy magazine.

"Fine, fine," Sophie nodded happily, grateful for the change of subject, "university is awesome." In fact, she should really be at home studying, the essay was due next week and she hadn't even started it.

"Never appealed to me," Yvonne sniffed, "university...I was clever enough to go you know, I was just always too busy looking after you."

Sophie's face fell, her lip drawing into a tight line, "well luckily it's different now," she retorted, stung by her mother's disapproval, "there are more options for women now: other than housework and child rearing."

"Yes, well, you were a bit of a handful and I was on my own remember."

Sophie bristled with irritation, that's typical - blame the child. "One of my friends at uni is a single parent," she snapped, wondering for the first time how Juliette coped. *There* was someone who was truly alone; no husband, no staff. She always seemed broke as well. No wonder she was snappy. And that rucksack she carried around, ugh, well that should definitely go.

"There is more help for single parents now-a-days," Yvonne commented with a nod, "more money, more support. It was hard when you were young, single mothers had a stigma attached to them, people looked down on you, judged you. And all because your bloody father did a runner."

Sophie's lip quivered at the mention of her missing dad Anthony. Apparently, according to her mother, he had vanished when she was just six years old. Sophie vaguely remembered her mother explaining that he had gone away on business, but when she had pressed for further information, she had revealed more. Yvonne had explained to a confused Sophie how her dad had developed serious professional and medical problems. As a financial consultant, he had made a catastrophic error at work, which resulted in the loss of millions of client investments. After being subsequently sacked and narrowly avoiding a legal prosecution, he had spent six months or so lounging around the house, gambling whatever spare cash he could get his hands on. He had spiralled into a bout of dark depression, which he refused to seek medical help for. Then one day, he had suddenly vanished. No note, no message of explanation. Yvonne had cried bitterly for days, worrying herself sick. The police had been little help, stating that some people never wanted to be found. They filed a missing person's report and put Yvonne in touch with a support group, but admitted that there was little else they could do. Yvonne suspected that Anthony had fled to Hong Kong, as he had business connections there, but after a fruitless year of trying to trace him, she had admitted defeat, given up and resigned herself to the fact that he was never coming back.

Initially life had been a struggle. Sophie remembered many days of waking herself up for school, only to find her mother fast asleep on the couch, clutching an empty vodka bottle. Yvonne's parents and brothers had rallied around to help: cleaning the house, doing the school run, fetching the food shop, paying the never ending bills. Grandma and Grandpa Fletcher were wealthy; they were also snobs. Not wanting their daughter to shame the family, they had flung money at her and booked her the best private therapist they could find. Slowly, Yvonne had dragged herself back to reality and managed to forget her errant husband. So followed a succession of boyfriends, some okay, some unsavoury. Sophie resolutely refused to call any of them 'dad,' even with her mother's encouragement, she wouldn't even refer to them as 'uncle.' In her young, impressionable mind, there would only ever be one real 'dad' for her; absent though he was. He survived in her imagination, like a mythical character that she dreamt would return to claim her as his one and only beloved daughter, they would have a tearful reunion and live happily ever after.

As the years wore on however, Sophie's daydreams dwindled, until it was almost difficult to picture him anymore. She had memories of dark hair, twinkling light eyes and strong arms that had flung her up into the sky. He had always smelt of aftershave too and dressed well in expensive suits. It was embarrassing now, to remember how she had declared as a child how he was the most perfect, handsome man in the world. He had chuckled and ruffled her hair in response. This romantic image of him was the only thing that remained and even that was fading. She didn't even have one photograph of him. Yvonne had burnt them all in a drunken rage, even her exquisite wedding album. Sophie had been horrified and distraught, when she had found out years later. There was no extended family on her father's side to gain comfort from either. He had been an only child, his parents, her gran and grandpa had died years ago, when she was a young child. Sophie had felt completely alone and abandoned. Father's day cards were addressed to Grandpa Fletcher, who now resided in a care home and suffered terribly from Alzheimer's. He no longer remembered Sophie. On her last visit, he had turned violent, hurling a glass vase, which narrowly missed her head and shattered the communal lounge window. Suffice to say, she no longer went to visit. Yvonne had stopped years ago.

A few years ago, she had tried to persuade Ryan to part with his cash and employ a private investigator, but he stoutly refused, claiming it would be disloyal to her mother. Years of whining and manipulation by Yvonne, had turned Ryan firmly against his absent father-in-law.

"We've only heard one side of the story," Sophie would insist beseechingly, "can't we at least try to find him." The answer had been a resolute 'no'. No amount of cajoling or sexual bribery would convince him otherwise. So Sophie had tried her hand at a little detective work. She had spent hours surfing the worldwide web; Facebook, twitter and other social media sites. But there was no sign of him, it was so strange, it was like he had vanished into a puff of smoke. The only remnants of him were a legacy of crippling debts, bitterness and a heartbroken child. Yet still Sophie hoped that one day she would see him again and that some small part of him still cared about her. One could always dream, she thought longingly, as the Sat Nav instructed her loudly to move into the left hand lane. The roadworks had slowly dwindled out and three lanes opened up to free flowing traffic. Sophie whizzed up the road, foot down on the accelerator. She opened the window a fraction to allow her hair to fly vertically behind her, her nose wrinkling as she sniffed the bracing countryside air.

The mention of her father had sobered the atmosphere in the car: the rest of the journey passed in an uncomfortable silence, with both women lost in their own thoughts. Snap out of it, she berated herself, swinging her vehicle through the narrow gates of Riverside Lodge. Yvonne also perked up considerably, as they followed the lamp lit drive up to the main reception.

"Wow, it's posh," her mom cooed at the large, whitewashed countryside hotel, "isn't Roger a darling booking this for us?"

"Hmm," Sophie replied, pulling up the handbrake with a snap. She noticed a man in a navy blue uniform leaning against a stone pillar staring their way expectantly. As Sophie unfolded herself from the driver's seat, he rushed forward, arms outstretched to take their bags. Yvonne clattered into the reception: which was impressively large and opulent. Sophie followed her to the welcome desk, where she waved her gift voucher at a tired looking receptionist.

"Room 201," Yvonne read out, as they made their way to the lifts. At their door, Sophie fumbled in her bag for change to give to the smiling porter. The room was beautiful, decorated in cream and gold with two large, perfectly made up beds. An antique wooden dresser was wedged in one corner and sliding doors led to a luxurious bathroom that housed a state of the art power shower, super soft fluffy towels and carefully hung his and hers matching bathrobes. A huge flat screen TV hung on wall brackets over a full length oval mirror that sparkled and shone.

"What's this?" Yvonne asked, fumbling with a knob next to the bed she had claimed. Soft music filtered out of the overhead speaker system; a classical piece that swooned around the room. Nice, Sophie thought as she plonked her overnight bag down.

"Hope you've brought something suitable to wear honey. I read the restaurant is super posh," Yvonne confided, emptying her vanity case of numerous tubes and bottles.

Sophie nodded with a happy smile, "gold glitter and killer heels…"

"Let's party then my dear," Yvonne grinned at her as she began flinging clothes off at a furious rate.

* * *

It was known as the 'festival of lights.' Will had googled, what is Diwali? On his smart phone and briefly read up on the subject, picking out specific snippets of information which he thought was of interest. Like how the festival celebrated the victory of good over evil, light over darkness and knowledge over ignorance. He wanted to impress Hema, he didn't want her thinking he was a complete neanderthal. He vaguely remembered his primary school teacher discussing the Hindu festival. They had made colourful pots and had Indian sweets as a treat, that were delicious and extremely sugary. He liked the ideology behind the Hindu religion; especially the reincarnation and law of karma beliefs. He had listened with interest as Hema had chatted to him, explaining how her family prepared for the five-day festival.

He hadn't seen her for over a week and was surprised how much he missed her. She had been studying and helping her mother clean – ready for the Diwali party they were hosting this evening. Will had been amazed to be invited, along with six others from school. Hema had managed to wrangle invites from her father who, she had giggled, had been in a marvellous mood as their shop takings were up, thanks to the debilitating roadworks outside the supermarket.

"We're just good friends ok?" She had whispered over the echoing mobile.

"I can pretend for one night," he teased. Will knew that Hema's father liked his conservative, dull Dad and his fretful, polite Mom. Flora sometimes popped into their shop for convenience, when the local monstrosity of a supermarket closed for a few hours on a Sunday.

"They're very hardworking," Flora commented, "that shop is always busy."

Will had frowned, Flora had been prying over the last couple of weeks, attempting to elicit further information on their relationship.

"Are you serious about her?" She delved.

Will had nodded quickly, "of course," he replied with a wink, rapidly changing the subject to instigate a conversation on her next favourite subject: university.

"Essay is due next week," he revealed, bending over to tie the laces of his designer trainers. There was a sharp intake of breath as Flora gripped his arm, "how are you getting on?"

Will shrugged, "fine, I'm halfway through."

"Oh thank the Lord," she sighed with relief, picking up a tea towel with a happy smile, "you know the next three years will fly by son."

He nodded as he shrugged on his leather jacket, inwardly groaning *three whole long years.*

"Here," Flora crossed the kitchen to pull a battered navy blue purse from behind the fruit bowl.

"Is that your hiding place?" Will asked with a wide grin.

"Yes," she nodded quickly, laughing merrily, "I know that is one dish that you or your father will not go anywhere near." She pulled out a creased twenty-pound note, "have this son. You deserve it after all your hard work. I'm proud of you and I know dad is too, even though he might not always show it."

Will frowned at the mention of his father. Ofsted had been and gone, with good results, but still he spent almost every evening locked away in his study. Will glanced at his mom with sympathy, "you keep it Mom, buy yourself something nice. Treat yourself for a change."

Flora shook her head, "it's for you," she insisted, "my wardrobe is bursting with lovely things that I never get the chance to wear. You need a break from studying, go and enjoy yourself," she pressed the note firmly into his hand with a soft smile. He grinned gratefully, shoved the cash into his jeans pocket, then left the warm, centrally heated house, to jog breathlessly up the street. Jimmy was waiting on the corner, like they had arranged, his arm slung casually across his girlfriend Sadie's shoulder. Next to them, chewing gum and looking decidedly bored was Rachel, Sadie's best friend. There were also two other girls from their year, whose names Will couldn't remember, but who tittered as he approached.

"Yo bro," Jimmy greeted.

"Alright?" Will drawled, raking a hand through his messy hair.

"Hi Will," Rachel cooed, appraising him with fluttering eyelashes.

"Late aint ya?" Sadie grumbled, "Hema will be thinking we ain't coming."

"Chill babe!" Jimmy let go of the lamp post he was lounging against, falling in step at the front of the group with his best friend. The girls trailed behind giggling and gossiping, stumbling on high heels that clacked on the icy pavement.

As they paused to cross the road, Jimmy asked, "does your dad know about Hema yet?"

Will shook his head firmly, "no and he's not gonna."

"Only time bro…the truth will out."

Will laughed, "I'll worry about that when it happens." He dropped his voice, "In the meantime, you need to make sure your girlfriend keeps quiet!"

Jimmy raised an eyebrow but nodded, "you are going to be in so much shit when it all comes out."

Will ignored the warning, "anyway, how are you and the missus getting on?"

Jimmy's face cracked into a wide, beaming grin that revealed uneven, white teeth and dimples, "she's certainly energetic bro, All night last night!"

Will rolled his eyes, pushing his friend, "yeah right…in your dreams."

"Seriously," he whispered, "the girl is insatiable." They burst into laughter as they walked through the wrought iron park gates. Jimmy looked across with interest, "what about you mate? Is she still a virgin?"

Will coughed in embarrassment, "no comment. That stuff is private."

"She is then," Jimmy clucked in sympathy, ruffling his mate's hair, "you'll have to marry her first you know."

Will grimaced, punching his friend lightly on the arm, changing the subject to their shared interest of football. He told Jimmy about Sophie's husband playing for Chattlesbury FC.

"Wow, Ryan O'Neill?" Jimmy let out a low whistle, "can you ask her to get a signed football?"

Will nodded, hopping around a stray cat that hissed at them in the darkness. They passed The Pearly Gate pub where a group of drunken men stumbled around the entrance, grasping bottles of beer.

"Are we going to the off license?" Called Sadie, "I fancy some cider and it's your turn to pay Jimmy."

"Yeah babe," Jimmy replied, as they pushed the door, activating the bell above that tinkled softly. The shop assistant was slumped in the corner on a stool, reading the racing section of the local newspaper. He stared at them suspiciously as they trooped noisily inside. After purchasing a few bottles and a six pack, they left to dodge the traffic on the busy main road.

# Chapter Twelve

Hema's house was at the end of a long winding road called Jackson Street. Will squinted in the darkness and could just see Mr Kumar's black Volvo, jutting out of the driveway, surrounded by bulging refuse sacks. The garden was sparkling with lights that had been wrapped around the fir trees and lit up the gravel pathway. The house itself twinkled like a Christmas tree and wind chimes pinged lazily in the gentle breeze.

"Oohhh, that looks so pretty," Rachel sighed theatrically. Lanterns illuminated the doorway of number 54. Will raised the heavy knocker, letting it fall with a succession of loud raps, as he gazed down at the 'welcome' mat. They waited a few moments, then heard clunking steps, the door swung open to reveal Hema in all her glory.

Will was shocked into silence, a smile frozen on his face, as his gaze travelled the length of her – WOW! She was dressed in cream and chocolate brown silk that glittered with sequins and diamantes. Her hair was loose, curling down her back and her face had been carefully made up. She looked absolutely stunning. Will's mouth dropped open in surprise. She giggled at his reaction, pulling him firmly through the entrance.

"Hi folks," she waved at his friends lagging behind, "I'm so glad you're here," she whispered, standing on tip toe and squeezing his palms.

"Here," he replied, thrusting a box of posh Belgian chocolates towards her. He had read that it was traditional to give and receive gifts during Diwali, so had duly despatched Flora to the city centre on a shopping trip. His thoughtful Mom had also bought a silk scarf for Mrs Kumar and bright white, folded hankies for her dad.

"Oh thank you Will," Hema squealed happily, "that's so kind. Please come in, you are very welcome." She led the group of teenagers down the hall, into a modern kitchen full of gadgets. The house was packed full of guests, occupying every room. After pouring drinks into bright red plastic tumblers, Will and Jimmy found two spare chairs squashed next to the buffet table, while the girls trailed after Hema, cooing at all the bright decorations: the Rangoli patterns and the Diya's that flickered around the house.

Jimmy leant across Will to grab a couple of vegetable pakora's from an oblong silver platter, handing one to Will.

"I'm starving," he said, taking a large bite, "did Hema make these?"

"Yes I did," she appeared in the doorway, grinning, "and the onion bhajee's - they are delicious and come with a homemade mint dip.

"Cool," Jimmy's eyes widened as he appraised the table of plentiful food.

Hema bent over the CD player, turning down the spirited Indian music, "help yourself to food everyone." Will and Jimmy joined the queue while Hema busied herself removing foil and clingfilm. After filling their plates, the two lads pushed through the crowd of people to lounge against the kitchen wall as they ate. They discussed Jimmy's work; he was training to be a plumber like his father and was busy whizzing about the city fixing toilets and boilers.

"Do you like it?" Will asked, spooning mint sauce over a poppadum.

Jimmy grinned, "it's ace. College is a bit naff, but I'm digging the practical side of the trade, you know meeting different people each day, helping people out."

Will nodded, feeling envious. Jimmy was earning good money and had just bought his first car, while he was stuck at uni, accumulating thousands of debt and no idea what he wanted to do with his life.

"I need a job," Will confessed.

"What kind of job?"

"Dunno," he shrugged, "if you hear of anyone needing a student for a few hours per week, let me know mate."

Jimmy nodded, tearing into his keema nan, "uni must be a laugh though right?"

"It's not what I expected," Will admitted, "but it's okay."

"Don't tell me, you wanted all night raves and sleeping till noon."

Will laughed, "something like that."

"Must be nice to see Hema though," Jimmy winked, "she's a fantastic cook, you've done well there mate. Sadie doesn't know how to turn the cooker on."

"Shush," Will warned, nodding his head at two older Indian women who were washing up at a large stainless steel sink. There was a sudden high pitched squeal, then Sadie came rushing into the kitchen.

"You'll never guess what, Hema's only dancing!"

Will swallowed a mouthful of food then followed Sadie into the compact lounge. He coughed as the smell of incense hit his nostrils. A large, rotund man sat in a corner atop of a beanbag, playing a Sitar and warbling loudly. Guests were clapping, stamping their feet and in the middle of the room was Hema, hips swaying in time to the music, arms raised as her fingers danced in the air. God she was hot thought Will, as he felt Jimmy nudging him. Just then a man sprang up out of the audience and began dancing energetically around her. He was young, tall, dark and handsome. Will felt himself consumed with jealousy and anger. He watched for a minute or so, as the dancing couple laughed and twirled around the room, cheered on by the onlookers, before turning away from them, to push roughly past Jimmy. As he stood sulking in the kitchen, Sadie's friend Rachel sidled up to him, coyly twirling a curl of hair around her index finger.

"You alright Will?" She asked, bubble-gum pink lips pouting provocatively.

Will nodded furiously, "I'm fine."

Rachel placed a comforting hand upon his bicep, "I wouldn't treat ya like that! She doesn't deserve ya in a million years." Before Will could move away, her arms had snaked around his neck and she was gazing up at him adoringly. The door squeaked open. Hema stared at them, with shock and hurt written across her pretty features.

Immediately, Will pushed Rachel away, "Hema!" He called, as she spun on her heel with a strangled sob. He raced down the hallway, springing up the stairs after her, but she was too quick. The bedroom door slammed in his face, stubbing his toe in the process.

"Hema, let me in please," Will rapped urgently, pressing against the oak frame. There was no reply, just the sound of soft, shaky breaths, "I'll break down the door and you know I will," he warned.

Slowly the door clicked open. Will paused before entering the darkened, lilac bedroom. She stood with her back to him, gazing out of the window, arms clasped tightly across her chest.

"Sorry," he began, moving forward, "that was nothing in the kitchen, I mean nothing happened, there's nothing going on. I just saw red when you were dancing with that guy…he was all over you!"

Hema slowly turned around, a look of anger on her face, "that's my cousin! My lovely, engaged cousin."

"Oh!" Will's face dropped like a stone from a great height, "I'm so sorry. I just got jealous and mad. You make me mad," he whispered, pulling her resisting body into his arms, "I'm crazy about you," he murmured kissing her neck. Will felt the fight ebb slowly out of her, as his lips travelled across her chin, to cover her mouth softly and slowly. Hema sighed as her hands came up to rest in his tousled hair. The kiss intensified until they were both breathless and panting with passion. Will pushed her backwards, lowering her gently onto the soft, springy bed.

"I love you Will," she groaned, her hands flickered underneath his shirt, touching his cool, taut skin, making his jaw clench. She was pulling it upwards fervently, over his head, then small hands splayed across his chest, as she gazed up at him, eyes full of desire.

"What about your parents?" He mumbled, between her kisses, "are you sure?"

Hema looked at him steadily, "lock the door," she instructed, "now come here." She opened her arms and he raced into them. They became a frantic tangle, tugging at each other's clothes, until they both lay naked, bathed in the soft lamp light. Then he slowly slid inside her and they moved together, kissing, nibbling and groaning, as passion increased to a tumultuous crescendo, that made them both cry out with fevered release.

Will was kissing her forehead, murmuring endearments, when an irate voice shouted up from the bottom of the stairs.

"Hema, Hema are you up there?" It called.

"It's my dad," she mouthed nervously, a look of fear in her eyes.

"Stall him," Will whispered, as he rushed around, flinging on discarded clothes and falling clumsily as he pulled up his jeans.

Hema giggled, hand over her mouth, "yes Dad, I'm just coming," she hollered. There was a minute of silence, then footsteps climbed up the stairs, making them both freeze.

"What are you doing?" Her dad queried.

"Just doing my hair Dad, I'll be down in a bit," there was a pause while they waited, breath held in fright.

"Okay," came the suspicious reply, "your mom needs your help in the kitchen, so please hurry."

"Yes Dad," Hema called, leaping from the bed to embrace Will playfully. He groaned, as she batted her lashes coquettishly, then ran a line of feathery kisses along his jawline.

"Love you," she sighed.

"Love you back," he dipped his head, to tug gently at her lips, until they parted.

"I have to go," he whispered, reluctantly releasing her warm, naked body, then goggling as she quickly snapped on her lacy underwear. Will tiptoed across the room, listened at the door, until the footsteps subsided back down the stairs. He blew her a kiss before bolting from the room to barricade himself in the bathroom. His reflection stared back at him; face flushed, hair messy, but he was grinning widely, feeling stupidly happy. Minutes ticked by, before he tentatively unlocked the door then came face to face with a firm mouthed Mr Kumar.

"Oh h-hello," Will stammered, his happy confidence knocked out of him.

"Will," Mr Kumar acknowledged, with a nod of his head, "we have a bathroom downstairs as well you know."

"I didn't realise," Will replied smoothly, his equilibrium restored. He squeezed past Mr Kumar's bulky frame, "this is a terrific party," he commented politely, as he made way his way down the stairs.

"I'm glad you are enjoying yourself," Mr Kumar called, as he peered his head inside the bathroom for a quick inspection.

Will bounded down the stairs. You *wouldn't be so chatty if you knew what me and your daughter were just doing* he thought guiltily. At the bottom of the winding staircase he found Jimmy pacing, with a bewildered look on his face.

"Where have you been?" His friend hissed, passing him a pint of lukewarm lager, "her parents have been looking for her and I've been stuck with Rachel moaning that you've been leading her on."

Will scoffed, "I did no such thing." He took a large swig of his drink, wincing at the warm flat taste. Just then Hema appeared in the doorway, a shy smile on her face as she glanced his way.

"The fireworks are about to start," she began, "we're all to go out into the back garden."

*They already have,* Will thought with a cheeky grin in her direction. *God she was beautiful.* Her face was flushed, her hair cascading wildly, she looked dazzling, bathed in the flickering lamp light.

"What have you been up to?" Jimmy nudged him, a quizzical look on his face.

"Nothing! Shush," Will mouthed back, feeling hot as he glanced around.

"I don't believe you!" Jimmy stated, as realisation dawned, "in her *house*, with her parent's *downstairs*. Her strict, religious parents – do you have a death wish?"

"Shut up!" Will pushed him forward, they scuffled together laughing, following the large group of people outside to the large fenced off garden.

Friends and relatives milled around on the patio, waiting as Hema's brother and dad organised the fireworks at the end of the garden. Will could see her, bent over, talking to a couple of small children who were chomping enthusiastically on toffee apples. She caught him staring and smiled across at him, pouting provocatively. Will moved through the crowd, ignoring Jimmy's words of warning. He stood next to her, hopping from foot to foot and blowing his hands to keep warm.

"Are you okay?" He whispered. Hema nodded quickly, cheeks dimpling. A rocket exploded in the dark night sky; a colourful blaze of bright lights that popped and whistled. Will shuffled closer to her, drawn by something which he could only describe as pheromones. He pulled her small hand into his, stroking her palm with his long fingers. He felt her shiver in response and grinned at the effect he was having on her.

"Look, look, it's beautiful," the small boy gazed up, pointing in wonder at the popping fireworks.

"Yes, you are Hema," Will whispered. She was staring up at him with a look of dark desire, when he was startled by a hand pressing firmly on his shoulder. He spun round to stare down at penetrating golden eyes, that were so much like Hema's.

"What are you doing with my daughter?"

* * *

"Down in one,"

Sophie eyed the row of shots on the bar queasily. The wine had been finished a while ago, now Yvonne had decided to move onto the harder stuff.

"It's two shots for the price of one," she had chirruped with glee. The bar man had poured them quickly, then retreated to a safe distance, where he watched with amusement as the two women knocked them back. Sophie winced as the liquid burnt the back of her throat.

"What time is our full body detox tomorrow?" She asked, coughing away a sliver of alcohol.

"Not till eleven honey. We can have a lie in and grab some breakfast first."

"I hope I'm not sick," Sophie grimaced at the mention of food. She had just eaten a three course meal, courtesy of Roger. Soup, steak and chips and a sticky toffee pudding, with lashings of vanilla custard. She must have gained at least four pounds in a couple of hours. Thank god there was a pool here, she would have to do some serious lengths to swim all that off.

"Of course you won't be sick," Yvonne replied with a shake of her head, "you used to be able to take your alcohol. What's the matter with you?"

Sophie wiped her mouth in irritation, "life is what's the matter with me Mother. None of us is getting any younger."

"Speak for yourself," Yvonne mumbled, as she ordered another round of drinks.

Sophie's mobile pinged loudly, whizzing across the slippery bar. Yvonne caught it with one hand, "oh, it's from Ryan, bless," she noted, peering at the screen.

"Mom!" Sophie snatched the phone from her, "aww, Josh and Jake say goodnight and Ryan's just ordered a Chinese…what?" She shook her head at the screen, "we have a fridge full of food."

"Tell them Nan says sweet dreams," Yvonne slurred, happily gulping down the Jagerbomb.

Sophie watched her mother, tutting with disapproval, "you know I should be studying, my essay is due next week."

"Pah," Yvonne waved away Sophie's comment, "what will they do? Give you a detention," she snorted with laughter and Sophie found herself chuckling along.

"What's your name?" She quizzed the young barman, who looked decidedly nervous.

"Mark," he replied edgily.

Yvonne flung her hand away dismissively, "boring," she replied, then looked at Sophie, "do you know that your name means wise?"

Sophie looked up from her phone, "does it?" She asked, with interest, "Ooohh, I'll have to tell a few people that at uni, they'll be well jealous."

"Yeah," Yvonne continued, "you were born on a full moon too. You just couldn't wait to come out, two weeks early you were."

Sophie stared at her mom, surprised by her wistful reminiscence.

"Was it an easy birth?" Josh and Jake had been born by caesarean section four weeks early, after a painful attempt at traditional labour. Sophie still shuddered at the memory.

Yvonne nodded with a wide smile, "you just flew out, the midwife nearly dropped you and you cried and cried, then they put you on my belly, all tiny and naked and then Anthony," her voice cracked slightly, "he held you and you were just silent, stared up at him, with these amazing huge eyes, it was so beautiful," she sniffed, eyes glazed by the memory. Sophie stared open mouthed, feeling tears prick the back of her eyelids.

"Sophie, have you ever wanted someone so much that it made you physically cry?"

"Mom, are you okay?" Sophie asked with concern.

Yvonne appeared not to have heard her, "I have, I know what that feels like. It's just awful. Your dad...he...I loved him so much, he just didn't love me at the end," she pulled out a tissue and blew her nose loudly.

"I'm sure he did," Sophie began gently.

"No he didn't," Yvonne said with bitter emphasis, "and who would blame him. I...I..." she trailed off then, her face red and troubled, "sorry," she faltered, looking around her. The bar was empty, but next door the sound of disco music vibrated through the paper thin walls.

"Come on," Yvonne grabbed her daughter's hand, tugging her off the stool, "let's see if we can gate-crash."

They hovered outside the function room, waiting until the door swung open and an inebriated groom staggered out, pint in hand.

"Can we come in?" Yvonne asked, smiling brightly. Sophie placed a finger over her lips to try to shush her, but there was no stopping her mother on a dancing mission.

"We wish you a very long and happy marriage," Yvonne hiccupped loudly. The groom staggered to his left, clutching the wall for support and peered at them bleary eyed.

"Come in and enjoy yourselves ladies," he ushered them into the large function room, pushing the doors shut firmly behind him. Loud music boomed out of towering speakers and flashing lights spun round and round, bouncing prisms of light off the walls and ceiling. A group of children dressed in wedding finery chased each other across the deserted dance floor, slipping to their knees and gambolling merrily.

"Is this a wedding or a wake?" Yvonne drawled, heading for the bar at the back of the room. They passed numerous tables decorated with pink flowers and helium balloons, seating guests who looked either drunk or decidedly bored.

"Oh that's pretty," Sophie pointed to a tall pink and cream flowered cake with a pair of lopsided bride and groom figurines. Where is the bride? She wondered. The room was full of people in posh outfits, but she couldn't see any inkling of white lace or satin. Yvonne hitched up her skirt as she hopped onto a ribbon swathed bar stool.

"Ugh," she said in distaste, as she slapped her bag down onto a sodden beer tray.

"Two jagerbombs," she called to a red faced barmaid.

"I'd really love a lemonade," Sophie protested.

"Don't be daft, it's special offers on the shots! We may as well enjoy ourselves, especially as Roger is paying." She ferreted in her bag, "look he's given me a wad of cash to fritter away, this is his treat, isn't he a darling?"

Sophie grimaced at the mention of her mother's boyfriend. What she was interested in discussing was her dad.

"Mom," she began, yelling above the sound of the disco music, "it's not too late to try and find him."

"Who?" Yvonne asked, clicking impatient fingers at the bar staff.

Sophie sighed, "Dad of course."

"What?" Yvonne snapped, "why would I want to do that? He deserted us, remember."

Sophie swallowed, "Ryan would pay for a private investigator," she continued, "I'm sure that we could find him."

"He doesn't want to be found," Yvonne grumbled, knocking back her shot.

"Well then, even if we could find out if he's okay, wouldn't that help us move on?"

"No!" Shouted Yvonne, "it would make a bad situation even worse. No, he's a toe rag who doesn't care about anyone but himself. Ryan can save his money. Let that bastard stay lost." Yvonne swiped the back of her mouth with a bitter look set on her face, "we've got Roger now, he loves me Sophie and if you gave him a chance, he would love you too."

"But, but…" Sophie's lips flapped in dismay, tears stinging the back of her eyes.

"No buts!" Yvonne stared at her with cold, accusing eyes, "he's history. Now, I don't want to talk about him anymore. I want to dance, come on," she slipped off the stool, grabbed hold of Sophie's hand and tugged her towards the dance floor.

"Okay, okay!" Sophie acquiesced, swaying slightly, "but please Mom, no more shots, you'll be ill."

Yvonne tweaked Sophie's cheek, "my sensible daughter."

Sophie followed Yvonne as she wobbled to the dance floor, feeling overwhelmed by a sense of melancholy and sadness. Boy she missed Ryan. Why does it feel like I'm the mother and she's the daughter?, she thought sadly, as her mom leapt onto the dance floor, exuberantly waving her arms and shaking her hips in time to Kylie. Why couldn't I have been blessed with a simple, sensible, sweet grey haired lady like Evelyn. Someone who loved baking and devoted herself to her grandchildren. Instead, I've been lumbered with a neurotic, man eating, party animal with more layers then a Spanish onion.

\* \* \*

They stood in the kitchen, a semi-circle of tension, while outside the fireworks popped and fizzed in the night sky. Will could hear the sound of laughter and children's excited squeals, the smell of hot dogs, baked potatoes and smoking sparklers. Mrs Kumar had sent for her husband. She stood gripping the table, darting angry looks at Will and then her distraught looking daughter.

"Mom, I can explain," Hema began, eyes imploring.

"I saw you holding hands...why Hema?"

Will stepped forward, shielding his girlfriend behind him, "we're just friends," he said calmly. Her protection was paramount, she was shaking and looked terrified.

"Don't lie," Mrs Kumar's angry voice reverberated loudly around the room.

"It's okay Will," Hema interjected, a bold look on her face, as she stepped to the side of him, "he's my boyfriend, I love him and I don't see the problem."

"You...you don't have time for boyfriends!" Mrs Kumar retorted, "you should be concentrating on your studies. There will be plenty of time for romance when you finish university."

Hema stepped forward, "but if it was a Hindu boyfriend that would be just fine Mom, wouldn't it? Well actually no, I want Will *now*, I'm nineteen now and old enough to make my own decisions."

Will stared hard at his girlfriend, feeling a wave of pride rise inside him. God he loved her.

Just then Mr Kumar appeared in the doorway, "what's going on?" He asked, looking annoyed, "I've got the fireworks to attend to."

"Close the door," Mrs Kumar instructed her husband, "now you can explain to your Father."

Hema swallowed as she turned to her father, "I'm in a relationship, with Will," she informed him quietly.

"What? What did you say?" His thunderous looking face revealed that he had heard every word.

"We're in a relationship," Will echoed boldly.

Mr Kumar glanced from Hema to Will with furious disgust. There was a pause, then he strode across the kitchen, "oh no, I don't think so," he grabbed Hema's arm, pulling her roughly away from Will.

"Leave her alone," Will shouted, hands clenched by his side.

"How dare you," Mr Kumar spat furiously, "this is *my* house. You are not welcome here any longer," he pushed at Will's chest, "now get out!"

Will backed away from him, looking at Hema, whose eyes were brimming with tears.

"Just go Will," she said, a face a picture of wretchedness, "I need to speak to my parents alone."

"I'm not leaving you like this!" Will shook his head in disbelief.

"Please, please go," Hema implored, "I'll be fine."

"Yes, get out," Mr Kumar hissed.

"Everything okay mate?" Jimmy stuck his head around the door.

"We need to go," Will instructed, his eyes not leaving Hema's, "I'll text you okay?"

Mrs Kumar stepped forward, staring at his face, "I'll show you out," she said coldly.

"Is the party over?" Sadie asked, as she clattered into the kitchen, followed by her friends.

"We're leaving," Jimmy said, nudging her.

"Oh, but the fireworks," the girls chorused in dismay.

"Now," Jimmy said, ushering them into the empty hallway.

Mrs Kumar opened the front door, as they trailed in a line through it.

"I'm sorry," Will began, feeling remorse weighing heavily upon him, "it's not Hema's fault, it's mine, blame me."

"You are not welcome here again Will," Mrs Kumar snapped angrily, "leave my daughter alone."

With that the door slammed loudly and they were left outside, shivering in the cold night air.

# Chapter Thirteen

For some, Sunday was classed as a day of rest, but for Juliette it was the busiest day of the week, which consisted of working the lunchtime shift, food shopping, cleaning and ironing. To add to the stresses of the day, there was also an essay to be finished, ready to be handed in tomorrow. By the evening, Juliette had collapsed on the sofa and was proofreading her completed essay. Overall she was pleased with the content; the structure and the argument. It had certainly been a challenge cramming all her ideas into 2,000 words, the last hour had been spent editing, inserting relevant quotes to support her argument and cutting out any unnecessary verbiage. As the spell check finished flashing, Juliette glanced at Molly, who was perched on the breakfast bar, playing with two grubby looking Barbie dolls.

"What you doing Mom?" Molly asked, peering at the ancient laptop.

"Just homework honey," she divulged with a wink.

After saving the document, she sent it to the printer and waited. A minute or two later, Juliette heard chugging noises emanating from the sitting room, as the second hand machine burst into life.

"Want some toast and Nutella?" She asked Molly, ruffling her hair fondly.

"Ooooohhhhhh yes please Mom and drinking chocolate too?"

"Oh no, chocolate overload!" She tickled Molly, eliciting screams of delight, "but okay, as a Sunday evening treat and for being the most adorable daughter ever" Juliette hopped off the stool and began preparing the supper, "go ask your brother if he wants some."

Molly skipped out of the kitchen calling Harry's name.

As Juliette busied herself at the stove, watching the bubbling milk, she heard the sound of muffled, throbbing music coming from next door. Juliette silently cursed her new neighbour. Another half hour the kids would be winding down for sleep. How would they relax with that noise going on? The previous neighbour had been as quiet as a mouse; a sweet octogenarian who had taken a nasty tumble and subsequently left to live with her daughter. Please come back, thought Juliette with a shake of her curly head. She prised open the jar of Nutella and grinned down at the small fingerprints embedded in the swirly chocolate. The noise from next door had accelerated in tempo and volume, Juliette could hear shrieks of laughter and watched with a frown as her pot of steel kitchen utensils vibrated. She banged the saucepan of milk on the lit hob, thank goodness the neighbours on the other side were relatively quiet and the flat above them was empty, awaiting occupancy. As she tipped frothy milk into two mugs, she sent up a silent prayer that they would soon get bored of DJ Jazzy or whoever it was, settle down and watch the TV.

The kids were watching an old re-run of Tom and Jerry. Harry was chuckling merrily and

Molly was hiding behind her hands as the cat and mouse continued their humorous chase.

"Half hour kids, then bed for reading," she instructed, setting down the tray. Her children's eyes never left the screen as they nodded their assent. Oh but they were good kids she thought, her heart swelling with pride. Her mom had told her there was nothing like a mother's love. Teenage, know-it-all Juliette had scoffed, but now she knew, now she understood. She would do anything in the world to keep them safe and loved, they were her absolute world. Some days she felt lonely, it would be nice to have someone to share their milestones and achievements, someone to curl up on the sofa with, kiss and caress after a long, hard day. But no, her life was good. She had raised them practically alone and would continue to do so. As she stared at them, she longed to scoop them up with a few belongings. Take them somewhere safe and picturesque, away from the concrete stairs, where youths hung out, spraying graffiti and causing mischief. Away from the blaring sirens of ambulances and police cars, tearing along the road below.

One day I'll have a beautiful garden she vowed, dumping the dirty crockery in the bowl, as she gazed out of the window at the moonlit sky. With a water feature, yes one of those big fancy stone one's, that gushed bubbling water all day and a patio that housed fancy garden furniture. Her daydream was interrupted by the shrill ring of the telephone. Juliette bounded into the hallway, snatched it up and listened as a cold caller impressed on her the buy one get one free offer on carpets at the moment. After a curt goodbye, she remembered her essay and went through into the sitting room to fetch it. She scooped up the paper, feeling proud. Here was her first ever university essay, toiled over and completed. Her eyes scanned the pages, pages one and two looked great, but then as she inspected further, she noticed with dismay that the rest of the essay was an inky, blurry mess. Oh please no, she thought with a sinking heart. A quick glance at the flashing machine confirmed her suspicions, yes the damned thing was out of ink. Why hadn't she noticed? It normally warned her.

"Drat!" She said aloud, feeling stress bubbling inside of her. The deadline was tomorrow, and there was no way she was going to ask for an extension on her first piece of work.

"What's up mom?" Harry asked, as he chomped on his food.

"Just the printer Harry, it's out of ink," she said with dismay.

"Can't you get some more from the shop?" Molly supplied, with helpful, wide eyed innocence.

Juliette shook her head, wishing it was that easy, "the cartridges are expensive Molls, plus I have to order them over the internet which takes at least a week and my essay's due in tomorrow."

"Don't worry Mom," Molly patted her hand, Juliette smiled down at her. What could she do? She wondered fretfully.

"Why can't Aunty Maz print it on her printer?" Harry asked, as if the solution was obvious.

"Harry! You are a genius," Juliette exploded, racing across the room to plant a sloppy kiss on his forehead. He looked both embarrassed and happy. He was getting to that age now, where displays of affection were becoming rarer, so Juliette took every opportunity to instigate them. She snatched up the phone, dialled and waited for her sister to answer on the fifth ring, explaining everything in a gabble.

So ten minutes later she emailed Marie the full document, with a message thanking her for printing it on her much newer, trendier contraption. Her sister would run it over to her early next morning, before the school run. I'll be pleased if I get a 'C' she thought hopefully. She had no idea what the lecturers were actually looking for and she really hoped that the referencing side of things would be okay. An image of Ben Rivers appeared in her thoughts. She imagined him hunched over a table marking essays, dressed in nothing but pyjama bottoms, strong arms shifting through mountains of paper, his gorgeous dark eyes, tired and weary.

"You okay now Mom?" Harry asked, looking at her quizzically. Juliette felt her face flame. Caught lusting by my ten-year-old son, she cringed with embarrassment.

"Yes of course honey," she cleared her throat, sent the document to maz@hotmail.com then rolled up her sleeves ready to tackle the pile of washing up.

In the kitchen, she was annoyed to find that instead of quietening down, the noise in the flat next door had escalated to such a level, that Juliette was worried there was some sort of all night party going on. I don't mind being a killjoy, she thought with determination as she settled the kids in bed with their books. Leaving the front door ajar, she marched across, rapping loudly on the chipped, stained door of number six. No answer, Juliette waited one full minute before banging forcefully with her clenched fist. Both hands were raised for maximum effect to deliver a third blow when the door swung open with a squeak. An annoyed looking woman with grey, straggly hair lounged in the entrance, holding what looked like a joint. Yes, it definitely was some sort of recreational substance, the aroma it emitted was pungent and overpowering. Juliette coughed, feeling her eyes water.

"Yeah?" The nameless woman queried, casting a bored look over Juliette's petite frame.

"Hello," Juliette began brightly, "I live next door," she wafted a plume of smoke away from her nose, "I don't want to spoil your fun, but I have two young children who really need to sleep and the noise of your party is erm…keeping them awake."

The skinny woman grinned, revealing a set of stubby brown teeth, "you wanna come in?" She asked, opening the door a fraction.

Juliette shook her head hastily, "no…thank you, I just wondered if you could turn the music right down," she shouted over the electronic beat, "or preferably off would be good."

The woman stared for a moment then shouted over her shoulder, "Raymond turn that shit down." Seconds later the volume dipped to a dull thrumming. Juliette breathed in relief, she thought it may get nasty and had been preparing herself for a slanging match and a trading of verbal insults.

"I don't like dance music myself either," the woman confided with a grimace, "gives me a bloomin bad head. I'm a Motown freak, was brought up on it. Now that's proper music." She smiled another toothy grin, while flicking crumbling ash on the carpet. In the background, Juliette could see a young couple propped against the stairs in a passionate clinch, while a large German Shepherd dog revolved in slow circles, as it chased its own tail.

"Right, well, thank you," Juliette said gratefully, backing away, "bye then," she lifted her hand in a wave, then disappeared back inside the safety of her own clean, warm abode.

By nine o'clock, Molly was fast asleep, curled sideways on her pillow. While Harry had fallen into half propped somnolence, earphones still attached. Juliette gently extricated them, placing them onto his overflowing bedside table. His room was larger than Molly's, bright blue with a football border snaking around the walls. As she tiptoed across the floor, she stubbed her toe on a set of jazzy roller boots and clapped her hand over her mouth to stifle the surprised cry of pain from escaping. Harry sunk further into dream land, oblivious to his hopping mother and the door that creaked as it closed. Juliette yawned, she was so tired, even stepping into her warm woollen onesie took an effort. In the sitting room she flaked on the sofa, pressed the remote and watched as the screen sprang into multi-colour life. She flicked absently through the channels, stopping when she found a documentary on wildlife in the Arctic. She watched with a smile as Polar Bears frolicked in the snow, whales burst through dark waters and penguins waddled across the ice. Then she found herself drifting off.

She woke with a warm fuzzy feeling, a numb arm and a wetness on her cheek. The animals on the screen had vanished, replaced by a panel of highbrow intellectuals debating climate change. Her muscles felt stiff, they ached as she shuffled into a sitting position. Shaking her head, she threw off the remains of slumber. Then she heard a noise, a sharp rapping that seemed to be coming from the front door. A glance at the clock informed her that it was 11.15pm. Who on earth could that be at this time of night she wondered nervously? The knocking came again, more urgent. She sprang to her feet, worried that the children would wake and hurried to the door. The chain was fixed firmly across, Juliette peeked through the spy hole. A face swam into view. It was Marty, looking red, flustered, and panting breathlessly. Oh no, she thought leaning against the door, maybe if I didn't answer he would just go away. No such luck, he banged again, louder this time. A wave of irritation encompassed her as she fiddled with the chain, pulling it free and opening the door, a tiny fraction.

"Marty, it's very late!" She admonished.

"I need to speak to you Jules, can I come in?" he panted.

Juliette tensed at the shortened version of her name, it sounded too personal, inappropriate and wrong. That was her family's nickname. People she cared about and liked called her Jules, not selfish wasters.

"Can it wait until tomorrow?, it's late." She responded curtly, still smarting from the university jibe, "Harry and Molly are sleeping, you'll wake them."

He held up a pair of dirty hands, "I'll be quiet, I promise. I need to speak to you… please." His face took on an urgent, pleading look. She was annoyed by his sudden appearance, but knew his determination when he had something on his mind.

Juliette sighed, "okay, but five minutes only."

They stood in the kitchen facing each other. Juliette's arms were folded tightly across her chest, as she surveyed him. He looked terrible; scruffy and unkempt, with a greying stubble darkening his chin and red, bloodshot eyes. His clothes were creased and stained. There was a strange aroma to him: sweat and something else, the same kind of smell that had emanated from the neighbour. Cannabis? Oh god, why had she let him in. She glanced over to the phone lying on the worktop and wondered how quickly she could call for help. Marty was the first to break the uncomfortable silence.

"Can I have a cuppa?" He asked, staring at the kettle as if willing it to burst into life.

"No. What do you want Marty?" She replied icily. She was still furious at his behaviour at Molly's birthday party, his nonchalant attitude and sneering disapproval of her merits as a mother. A coldness settled inside her.

"Don't be like that Jules," he pleaded, "I know I've been a bit of a dick but I've been through some real shit just lately."

Haven't we all Juliette sniped silently, she took a step away from him.

"I just want to say I'm sorry," he pushed his hands inside his front trouser pockets, "I want to make it up to you and the kids."

Juliette swallowed, wishing he would just go, she had heard it all before, many times. He would show remorse, shower the kids with gifts, tell her he loved her and couldn't live without her, wheedle his way back into her heart, then boom, back to the old Marty. No way!

He took her silence as agreement and grinned widely.

"I want us to get back together. To be a proper family. I'm serious this time."

Juliette coughed, great spluttering barks of air. How dare he!

"The answer is no Marty," she said firmly, teeth clenched, "now, I think you should leave."

"But…but, I'm trying to get straight this time Jules. I mean it."

Juliette shook her head wearily, "it's too late. The kids and I are happy on our own. I'm not letting you upset them again."

His jaw clenched in anger, "kids need their dads too," he muttered, eyes flashing dangerously. Juliette almost laughed, feeling rage rising inside her.

"Yes they do but not Dads like you!"

"What d'you mean?" He shuffled forwards.

As if he didn't know, Juliette sniffed, was he so insensitive?

"Criminals," she blurted out, "dishonest, unreliable wasters. They need good role models in their lives: love, honesty, stability."

"I'm not a waster," Marty snapped, "I'm trying to turn my life around. I made mistakes, got caught up with the wrong crowd, forgot what was important in life: family, home, relationships. I've got a job now, working evenings in a factory, that's where I've been tonight."

Juliette almost clapped his speech, "very commendable," her voice dripped sarcasm.

"What?" He replied, "Miss high and mighty perfect, never made a mistake in her life."

"My mistake was hooking up with you," she said furiously, then immediately wished she had never said the words, she would never ever regret her beloved children.

"Everyone deserves a second chance," he replied, his voice rising.

"You have had more than that," Juliette cried bitterly, "four, five, six chances, how many more do you need? You won't change, you haven't got the will power."

"I have, I am," he shook his head sadly, "do you want me to beg?"

"No, I want you to leave – now," her eyes glinted resolutely. She looked away from him to stalk to the door.

Marty's shoulders slumped, "okay I'll go."

Juliette breathed shakily.

"But I'm not giving up on us," he continued, "I want us all back together…forever. I'm going to prove it to you." His face had a look of determination, but his gait held a defeated slouch as he passed her and let himself out, without a backward glance. Juliette snapped the chain across, exhaling heavily.

Oh no she thought with despair, I cannot and will not let him back into the kids' lives, I refuse to see them heartbroken all over again. Hackles of protection caused the hairs on her arm to stand upwards, as she recalled their sadness over the years, their tears of disappointment when he cancelled yet another outing, their fear and bewilderment as she had explained the police had taken him away for a while. A tear trickled down her cheek. He was self-centred and egotistical that was for sure, never stopping to consider how his actions would affect his children. Completely oblivious to the hardships that she had endured: the lack of money, the worry, the constant strain of life and the pressure to raise her children correctly. There was no way he was just going to sleaze his way back into their life, not this time, she thought with resolution. She could manage just fine on her own. Juliette clicked off the lights as she checked the children were still sleeping. Thank goodness they hadn't witnessed that altercation, she thought with a shudder. The bed was chilly as she slid into it, she curled into a ball, wrapping the duvet tightly around her. Sleep eluded her, she tossed and turned for over an hour, replaying the scene, ruminating over her words. Had she been too harsh?, she wondered. Finally, she fell into a fitful slumber, where she dreamt of the freezing Arctic and fluffy, white Polar Bears chasing Marty across oceans of snow.

* * *

On Monday morning the registry was full of students queuing to hand in essays and coursework. The long line grew, stretching out of the building and onto the city centre street, where consumers jostled to pass through with their bags and shopping carts. Evelyn glanced at the clock which read 9.15am. Her lecture was due to commence at 10.00 and for that she had to cross numerous busy main roads and weave through the market occupying the main central strip of the city centre. The university campus occupied various different buildings, some modern and others were old, listed buildings. This particular one was of the more archaic. It had interesting stone pillars flanking the entrance, internally the walls and ceilings stretched upwards, decorated by artistic marble swirls, where a beautiful chandelier swung gently from the centre. Evelyn slipped slightly on the polished, wooden floor, as a smiling young man beckoned her over to the reception desk. She exhaled shakily as she handed over her bound eight-page essay. Last night she had been up until gone midnight, editing and correcting. This morning, as she scanned it over a warm bowl of porridge, she had been pleased and quietly confident with her efforts. Overall she felt happy with the result. It had been rather strange to write an academic piece rather than a creative one. A few times she had to reign in her imagination and stop it from overflowing onto the page.

"Anything else Miss?" The spectacled man enquired, as he handed her over a receipt.

"No, no, thank you," Evelyn tucked the paper inside her bag, moving away from the desk. Then among the throng of students, she spied Ann being pushed by her husband towards the doorway. She swung her handbag on her shoulder and hurried after them, following them out of the registry, onto the busy city centre street.

"Ann!" Her voice emitted in a high pitched warble that caused a few heads to turn.

"Hi there," she called, one hand raised in greeting as Ann peered around. Jon stopped, spinning to face her with a grin, as she panted up to them.

"Hello," he greeted warmly, "how are you?"

Evelyn blushed, rosy pink flooding her cheeks, "very good th-thank you," she stammered, "at least I am now that I've handed in my essay." She stared at Jon for a moment, mesmerised by the twinkle of his eyes. Some people just exuded genuine kindness and he was definitely one of those. It shone in his wide smile and friendly posture.

"Ann was pleased to finish hers too," he quipped.

"I am here," she grumbled, looking warm and cosy in a grey knitted hat, scarf and gloves set.

Evelyn smiled down at her, "how did you find it?"

"Absolutely fine," Ann replied, "the referencing was a bit of a bitch, but apart from that, I enjoyed writing it. How 'bout you?"

Evelyn shrugged with uncertainty, "I think it was okay. It was certainly a challenge."

"Did you discuss any of the literary theories?" Ann asked, digging in her bag for a polo.

"No, I didn't, should I have?" Evelyn frowned with worry.

"It's not mandatory, not in the first year anyway, but it may help you gain extra marks if you apply maybe one or two when discussing a work."

Ann began a spiel of some of the literary theories. Evelyn was impressed. They hurried across the busy city centre, dodging cars, buses and pushbikes. At the university entrance, Jon bent to kiss his wife, "pick you up at five," he said brightly, "have a nice day." Evelyn waved goodbye and watched as he sprinted up the path. She noticed that he was dressed in some sort of uniform: dark navy tunic with matching trousers and asked Ann what he did for a living.

"He's a physiotherapist," she explained proudly, "helps people with physical problems like myself. That's how we met." They made their way into the university, heading for the canteen.

"How very interesting," Evelyn commented, as she rearranged the canteen chairs to accommodate Ann. They chatted as the canteen filled with students. Evelyn was surprised to find her companion to be more talkative then normal. Ann told her about Jon's career and little snippets about their relationship; how they had met and their wedding, she even asked about Evelyn's Mam, enquiring after her health. Previously, Evelyn had found Ann to be opinionated and confrontational, two characteristics which she disliked in a person and completely opposite to her own timid, gentle nature. Today however, the prickly edge to her seemed to be softening, she appeared happy and open, the guard seemed to be dropping slightly Evelyn thought, warming to her as they talked.

As she was pouring tea from her flask, she noticed Will hovering in the doorway, with a worried look on his face. He was continually checking his phone, while pacing the corridor. As he scanned the room, Evelyn caught his eye and waved. She watched as he weaved around the furniture, towards them.

"Hello Will," she greeted cheerfully.

"Hi," he nodded at them both as he perched one hip on the edge of the table.

"Have you given in your essay?" Ann asked, blowing her hot coffee.

"Oh that, yeah," he seemed distracted and anxious, not his usual laid back self. When his phone suddenly rang he jumped up instantly, jolting the table and Evelyn's tea.

"Where are you?" He jabbered, hurrying off out of the canteen. Evelyn raised an eyebrow but made no comment.

"Shall we head to class?" Ann suggested, glancing at her watch and the emptying canteen. She could see Melanie the note taker hovering in the doorway and sighed. She really wasn't happy about having to rely on assistance, but as Jon had commented, that's what they get paid for and if she was entitled to the help, why not take it if it made her life easier. Melanie greeted them cheerfully, then they headed up to the classroom on the fourth floor.

# Chapter Fourteen

Ben Rivers was already in there, fiddling with the projector. He looked extremely handsome today, in a white shirt and tight fitting combat trousers. His hair was mussed up, as if he, or someone else, had just ran their fingers through it. The class was almost full, with people settling in seats, when Juliette burst through the door, dropping books and folders at her feet. Evelyn noticed Ben staring her way for a moment, before he calmly strolled over to help her collect her belongings. He was smiling at Juliette, talking to her in low tones, while she gazed up at him with pink cheeks. Then a group of laughing women stumbled around them, "excuse us," one giggled. Juliette blinked as Ben held out his hand to help her to her feet.

"I'm so clumsy," she admitted, taking the numerous library books from him gratefully.

"I had noticed," he replied with a wide smile.

"Oh," Juliette felt her stomach flip as she stared at a line of dark hair jutting out of the top of his white shirt. He smelt delicious; musky, fresh and very male. I wonder if that went all the way down, she thought, her mouth suddenly dry.

"Ben, can you sign my timesheet?" Melanie's interruption broke the spell. Juliette backed away, tripping over the projector cable in her haste to put distance between them. Evelyn was watching her with a bemused expression.

"You okay?" She asked, as Juliette slipped into the empty seat next to her.

"Yes, yes," Juliette replied, feeling flustered as she pulled out her battered pencil case.

"All ready," she smiled at Evelyn brightly, "where's Sophie and Will?"

"I don't know about Sophie, but Will is here somewhere."

"Here she is," Ann commented drily, as Sophie tore into the room like a mini whirlwind.

"Oh my god," she exclaimed, tugging off a designer scarlet beret, "that registry need more staff! I was waiting there for like half an hour," she quickly ran a brush through her long, poker straight tresses, "I nearly didn't get here on time."

"You managed to give your essay in then?" Ann asked doubtfully.

"Just about," Sophie nodded, "although it has been a bit of a rush. I have been rather busy," she coughed, taking a sip of water out of a large plastic bottle, then dug in her pocket for a bag of Jelly Babies. "Hey, is Will okay?" She asked, offering the sweets round the table, "only I just saw him on the stairs, arguing with his girlfriend. She looked as if she'd been crying."

Everyone at the table shook their heads with curious puzzlement, except for Ann, who was reading over the module itinerary with interest.

"It's Victorian Fiction this week," she noted, "one of my favourite eras."

"Oh yes," Evelyn nodded in agreement, "that's Charles Dickens era – right? Such a fab writer. I loved Great Expectations, although it did take me a while to read it."

"Over rated," Ann surmised, "I personally don't like Dickens, he was quite the misogynist, but to be fair, his work did critique many of the social injustices of the time."

"I like his writing too Evelyn," Juliette commented, sticking her chin out defiantly, "and the most recent TV adaptation was excellent." Evelyn looked across at her, giving her a small smile of thanks.

"Right class," Ben spoke loudly, his voice carried to the back of the room, "we're going to be looking at a brief context of the Victorian era and its influence on some of the literature of the time. There are so many great Victorian writers, I do recommend that you do some background reading on the era and explore some of the great works produced during this time. There is a list of excellent books on the handout. I've placed three day loans on them all, but I have also uploaded web links on the HIVE computer system and also there are extra pamphlets on the topic available from my office. If anyone would like to do further research or maybe to give you an idea for your dissertation in year three, do please come along and see me, I would be most happy to help."

Juliette blushed as he stared directly at her. Was he mocking her she?, wondered, noting the upturned corners of his mouth and feeling rather mesmerised by his sultry, sparkling eyes. She tore her eyes away in confusion, staring down at her blank page, just waiting to be filled. The door opened then, Ben paused in mid sentence as Will sauntered into the room, directing a curt apology at the lecturer. He pulled out a chair next to her and sat down with a great sigh, as if he wanted to be anywhere but here.

She peered across at him. He looked upset and worried.

"Are you okay?" She whispered in concern.

"Not really," came his quiet reply, "just personal stuff."

"Oh," Juliette said no more, picking up her pen as the lecture began. An hour later her wrist was aching and four A4 pages were full of scribble. This would match my doctor's writing, she thought with a grin as she placed her biro down. Ben announced they were to have a quick break, followed by a seminar on Victorian poetry. He disappeared mouthing the words coffee to an amused class, who began chatting loudly amongst themselves.

"Oh this poem is just beautiful," Evelyn remarked, peering over her glasses at the black and white handout.

"Let me guess," Ann said, looking up, "how do I love thee? Let me count the ways. I love thee to the depth and breadth and height my soul can reach…?" She paused to glance at Evelyn who nodded quickly.

"Wow," Sophie gushed, "that is so romantic! I am so going to read this poetry to Ryan, it's just wonderful. Listen," all eyes turned to her expectantly, "the bluebell is the sweetest flower that waves in Summer air: Its blossoms have the mightiest power to soothe my spirits care."

"Who is that by?" Juliette asked with interest.

"Erm," Sophie peered at the small print, "Emily Jane Bronte."

"Really," Evelyn said in surprise, "I didn't know the Bronte sisters wrote poetry too."

"Oh yes," Ann supplied with a nod of her head, "they were published too: Poems of Currer, Ellis and Acton Bell?" The table looked puzzled.

"Wuthering Heights is my favourite classic novel," Juliette smiled, "I just love the characters of Cathy and Heathcliff, so wild and romantic!"

"Have you ever had chance to visit the Bronte house in Yorkshire?" A deep voice resonated, startling her, she spun around to gaze up at Ben Rivers, who was clutching a frothy cappuccino.

"Erm, no," Juliette confessed, gulping at the close proximity of his frame next to her chair.

"You should try and go one day, if you get the chance," he commented, clicking the projector back to life.

"Is it very far?" She asked, wanting to continue the conversation and also acknowledging that geography had never been her best subject.

"A couple of hours," he replied with a smile. Juliette grinned back, feeling bubbles of happiness popping in her stomach. Next to her, Melanie looked from one to the other with a suspicious look on her face.

"He's dreamy isn't he?" She commented casually, as Ben went to speak to a lady with her hand in the air.

"What?" Replied a flustered Juliette, "yes, he seems very nice." She smiled at Melanie brightly, then rustled her handout, hoping that the conversation would stop there.

"Very dishy too," Melanie persisted.

For once, Juliette was grateful for Sophie's interruption, "absolutely gorgeous," came her verdict.

When everyone was seated, Ben called the class back to attention and began reading through the extracts of Victorian poetry. Juliette found herself mesmerised by his hands, watching them surreptitiously. They were large, smooth, tanned and expressive. They moved in circles as he spoke. She found herself wondering what it would feel like to be held by them in a passionate clinch. With a shiver, she picked up her handout and read along to the sound of his sexy, dulcet tones.

* * *

For lunch they decided to walk into the city centre and dine at one of the many pubs that lined the High Street. Reilly's Bar stood next to a 1970s retro clothes shop which blared out Rolling Stones music and was decorated with psychedelic murals that made your eyes blurry if you stared for too long. Sophie paused to admire the window display: the flower power tie dyed t-shirts, the colourful hippy skirts and the smoke from burning incense sticks, which added to the 'yeah man' ambience.

"Wow," she exclaimed, "this shop would be amazing for fancy dress." She gripped Juliette's arm, "we should have a night out and dress up as hippies."

Juliette laughed, "definitely a night out, not sure about fancy dress though."

They trooped into the dimly lit pub. Tables and chairs were scattered around the room and a large bar snaked down the right hand side wall.

"I'll get these," Sophie insisted, pulling out a bulging purse. Juliette picked a nice table in the corner, with a vase of wilting roses as decoration. They waited for Sophie to return with a tray of soft drinks.

"Hope these are okay, I got lemonade, cola and squash."

"Thank you dear," Evelyn said, sipping her ice cold lemonade.

"Thanks," Ann said grudgingly, dipping her hand in a pot of Bombay mix, which had been abandoned on the table.

"Ewwww," Melanie chirped, "have you any idea how many bugs fester in those things."

"bugs don't bother a paraplegic," she answered blithely, tipping a handful into her mouth.

"Where's Will?" Evelyn asked, looking around.

"Oh I think he was waiting for Hema, said he would catch up with us," Sophie replied, peering at the beer splattered menu. Juliette was busy counting change out onto the table, she was worried that she may not have enough, but as the pile grew she managed to scrape twenty pound together. That should do it, she thought with a happy smile, which froze as she noticed Sophie staring her way.

"Can I pay?" Sophie asked, touching her arm. Normally Juliette would have bristled at such a suggestion – there was no way she was a charity case! But she was touched by the look of worried kindness in her companion's eyes.

"No, no," she insisted, "but thank you anyway."

* * *

As the ladies were contemplating the food menu, Will was striding through the city centre, trying to placate a frantic Hema.

"We need to get inside," she rasped, a worried urgency in her voice.

"Why? Hema slow down…just stop!" Will grabbed hold of his girlfriend's grey parka sleeve, pulling her to a halt.

"Will," she hissed, "someone might see us."

"Don't be ridiculous," Will snapped in frustration, raking a hand through his hair," you can't hide away. What are you so afraid of?"

"My family of course," Hema retorted hotly, "Dad has told my uncles and now I'm the talk of the family! I've become the black sheep and it's all your fault!" She slapped at his hand as tears welled in her eyes.

"Oh right," Will began, voice rising, "I get it, so what happened to standing up to your parents and sticking with me. I thought you loved me Hema."

"I do," Hema replied, feeling contrite, "but it's just so hard, all this pressure," she chewed her lip forlornly.

"Don't worry," Will soothed, taking her hands in his, "they will come round eventually, when they see that we're serious about each other."

Hema shook her head urgently, "no Will," she replied quietly, "they will never accept us."

"But they have to," Will cried, oblivious to the stares of passers-by, "you have to live your life for you Hema. Stand up to them."

There was a lengthy pause while they stared at each other, strangers shuffled past them, oblivious to their angst. Hema broke eye contact, looking down at her feet and swallowing, "maybe we should cool it for a while," she suggested.

"What? No!" Will replied, feeling anger rising inside him, "don't you give up on us."

"Just for a while," she gabbled, "we both need time to chill out and concentrate on our studies."

Will stared down at her incredulously, unable to speak, his voice felt frozen inside him.

"It's just a break Will," Hema continued with conviction, "just until everything calms down ok?"

Will sighed with frustration, longing to take her into his arms and hug her tight, "does that mean that we're over, no more nights out, no time together?"

Hema bit her lip, "no Will…sorry, it's for the best."

Will released her hands, while a tick throbbed in his cheek painfully. He looked away, sadness gripping him like a vice.

"Am I being dumped?"

Hema ignored the direct question, "look, I'm going back to uni. I need to study, but you go with your friends and enjoy yourself." She smiled slightly, but he saw fresh tears glistening in her eyes.

"Hema," he implored, arms outstretched.

She shook her head, moving away, "no, don't say anymore please."

He watched as she began walking rapidly in the opposite direction, her gait wobbly and uneven. Will was left alone, shaking from anger, sadness, heartbreak, the cold November air, from everything. He buried his chin under his coat collar then kicked a stone that lay in his path. Longing to run after her, instead he waited until she had disappeared from sight, then began trudging towards Reilly's bar.

Music blared from the propped open doors, a burly doorman leant against the frame chewing gum at a furious rate. He glanced over Will as he approached, gave him a curt nod as he entered.

"Pint of lager," he called towards no one in particular. He dug in his pockets for ID, but no one seemed concerned with the youthful appearance of the punter.

"How you doing?" A woman with bright red chewed lipstick asked, as she handed him his drink. Will mumbled a reply, taking a gulp of the frothy liquid. She leant across the bar, cleavage straining against tight black lycra. Her aroma was beer and cheap perfume, an innocuous combination that made him feel slightly nauseous.

"Nice looking lad ain't ya?" She commented, as she played coyly with a sodden beer mat. He was saved from responding by Sophie calling 'hello' from across the room. Will turned and lifted a hand in greeting.

"Come and sit down," she squealed, patting the seat next to her. As he ambled towards her, he felt cheered by her pretty, animated face. His sunken spirits lifted slightly as he sunk down. What was he going to do he wondered? How could he convince Hema that their relationship was worth fighting for. He was pondering different scenarios to win her back, when he realised that Sophie was speaking to him about Chattlesbury Football Club.

"Could your Ryan get me a signed football please Soph?" He asked, remembering Jimmy's request. Her face lit up as she nodded, pleased to be asked.

"Oh yes, for sure," she replied, "I'm always happy to do a favour for a friend."

The other side of Sophie, Juliette was listening to their conversation and smiled with surprise. When she had first met Sophie, there had been little friendliness and affection between the two of them. Well certainly from her point of view anyway. But over the past couple of months, Juliette had warmed to Sophie. On first acquaintance, she had been annoyed by her flamboyant exuberance and irked by her gushing personality. Juliette had judged her as being shallow and spoilt, now she felt guilty for having those feelings. She realised that in fact Sophie was warm and kind, chatty and bubbly. In fact, she classed her as a friend, they had swapped mobile numbers, emails and friended each other on Facebook. Juliette had grown to like her dizzy mannerisms and her vibrant zest for life, her sparkly optimism and amusing chatter. There was so much negativity in the world, it was refreshing to be in the company of happy positivism. Even if it did stem from having a disgustingly wealthy other half, she thought ruefully. She glanced around the table at her other friends. She liked them all; Will with his boyish good looks and charm, Evelyn and her shy sweetness, Ann intimidated her sometimes with her forthright manner and intelligent talk, but Juliette suspected that she had built a wall around herself, underneath that hard exterior lay a softness and vulnerability, it shone in her eyes as she spoke of her husband Jon. Then there was Melanie, Ann's assigned note taker and support worker, she was lovely – very bubbly and confident with a self-assured attitude to match. She was openly gay, often commenting on the attractiveness of the female lecturers. Juliette longed to ask her about Ben Rivers, he fascinated her, yet equally frustrated her. Whenever he was around she felt attraction bubbling inside her and on a few occasions, she could have sworn that he also felt the same. She could see something in his eyes when he looked at her, his hands lingered on hers more than seemed appropriate. Yet he was definitely gay, she had heard many of the students discussing the subject. Her sister Marie's words rung in her ears, *forget about him* they urged. Concentrate on your studies, Juliette berated herself with a smile.

"You look happy dear, penny for them," Evelyn commented, nodding at Juliette.

"Oh, I was just thinking about Harry and Molly," she replied hastily, colouring at the fib. Just then the waitress appeared with a bright smile, pen poised over her notepad. After they had ordered their food, they chatted for a while about the next upcoming language essay. Sophie yawned, the weekend was still taking its toll, she felt tired, fuzzy and lightheaded, but it had been a brilliant few days, she wondered when her next night out was. There was an organised player's dinner with Chattlesbury Football Club, she sneaked a peek in her diary, it was pencilled in and highlighted for after Christmas. *So long,* her inner party animal wailed.

"Hey guys," Sophie began, when there was a lull in conversation, "me and Jules were talking earlier about a night out at Christmas," she looked around the table expectantly. Will was staring at his phone, eyebrows crinkled in concentration. Evelyn's head was ducked, she looked suddenly nervous.

"You do know there's a staff / student Christmas party at the student union in December?" Ann replied, sipping her lemonade through a fluorescent orange, bendy straw.

"OMG," Melanie gushed, with a nod, "we should all go, it's a fab night, although I don't remember much of last years, I was on the vodka, had it lined up," she explained, shaking her red hair with mirth.

"Oh wow," Sophie said, mouth open and eyes wide, "that would be perfect."

She nudged Juliette, whose face had brightened perceptibly, then turned to question Ann and Melanie, "do you need tickets?"

"Yes probably," Ann continued, "it actually sounds quite good, a disco if I remember correctly."

"Right then," Sophie winked, "that's a definite night out." She looked across at Evelyn, who was looking undecided, "please come Evelyn. It will be fab."

Evelyn blushed, "I'll have to see if I can get someone to watch Mam," she explained, "but it shouldn't be a problem."

"Fab," Sophie replied, eyes twinkling as she wrote in her diary with a flourish.

After lunch, they made their way back through the city centre to the University. On the spur of the moment, Sophie dragged them into the Student Union, to purchase tickets for the Christmas night out.

"It won't be long," she surmised, stuffing the change back in her purse, "they may sell out. I'll get them now, so we're not disappointed." Ann sniffed as Sophie handed her a sparkly silver ticket.

"I'll give you the money on Wednesday…thank you," she said, with a curt nod of her head.

Sophie waved away the mention of money, "nearer the time would be just fine," she chattered with excitement, reliving the weekend's excesses, an amused Will announced that she was a "legend" and laughed boisterously when she admitted she had been sick in a bin of the hotel's lobby. Sophie was oblivious to the pursing of Ann's mouth and the frown as she too listened.

"But how did you drive home dear, after consuming all that alcohol?" Evelyn asked, eyes wide with shock at her revelations.

"Oh I was okay by mid-morning, after three coffees, in fact I was buzzing all the way home, my driving improved dramatically," she chuckled as Evelyn's face relaxed into a relieved smile.

"The alcohol would have still been in your system," Ann retorted, looking down at her numb legs. It had been a drunk driver that had taken her life away from her. "It's very dangerous and irresponsible!"

The grin slid from Sophie's face, "I was fine honestly," she assured Ann.

Sophie glanced at Juliette who appeared not to have heard Ann's harsh words. Juliette was clutching her ticket with a huge grin on her face. Sophie guessed that she was thinking about Ben Rivers. It was so obvious that she liked him, it was written all over her face when she looked at him. Even Sophie had noticed the flush to her cheeks and the doe eyed look she gave him. She could empathise, that guy was delectable, but also gay. His sexuality seemed common knowledge amongst the female dominated students on the English course. In fact, everywhere she went, there seemed to be people gossiping about him. Why was Juliette wasting her time, she wondered? Oh well, who was she to question the powers of attraction? Sophie handed over a ticket to Evelyn, who was chewing her lip and looking rather dubious.

"I'm just concerned about leaving Mam," she admitted.

"Hey," Sophie soothed, "it's on a Saturday. No uni that day, can you get a sitter for her just for the evening?"

Evelyn smiled, "I could ask my neighbour. She's lovely and very helpful."

"There you go then – sorted." They ambled up the corridor, past the busy library and out into the courtyard.

Evelyn chewed her lip before admitting, "I haven't been to a disco in more than twenty years."

"Really!" Sophie was shocked, "oh my gosh Evelyn, where have you been hiding?"

Evelyn blushed, "I'm happy at home to be honest. I have everything I need right there."

Sophie stared at her with incredulous eyes, "but don't you have girlfriends to go shopping with, or on a night out?"

Evelyn just looked bemused, "Mam's my best friend," she replied simply, "nights out don't really appeal to me Sophie. I'm happy at home with my books, gardening, TV and radio. Also I am quite a bit older than you, I think our interests are somewhat different."

"Yes Sophie," Ann cut in crisply, "not everyone measures life by material possessions and how many parties they can attend. Indeed, many people take pleasure in the small, everyday things and building a loving, family life."

Heat flooded into Sophie's cheeks, "sorry Evelyn," she touched her friends arm, "I didn't mean to offend you. Me and my big mouth huh?"

"It's fine really Sophie," Evelyn insisted, smiling the sweetest smile.

"No, it's not fine," Ann blustered, "you really should think about what you say Sophie."

"Ann!" Evelyn remonstrated, "please don't make a fuss, I'm not offended in the slightest."

"I would be," Ann grumbled, ignoring the shocked silence which had fallen on the group, "well someone needs to tell her."

"Tell me what?" Sophie asked quietly.

Ann threw her hands in the air, signalling for Melanie to stop pushing her, "to stop with the drama and the pretentious attitude. Some people have a shitty life you know and really struggle. Not everyone is lucky enough to have an unlimited supply of wealth and if anyone says money doesn't make you happy, then they're lying."

Juliette had been listening at the back, she noted Sophie's down turned mouth and Ann's red cheeks, flamed by anger. Deciding it was time to intervene, she stepped forward, "that's enough Ann," she said firmly. "Sophie apologised, she didn't mean to upset anyone."

"It's not enough," Ann said, gesticulating wildly, "I bet you could do with just a fraction of her wealth to improve your life considerably."

"How dare you," Juliette replied, trembling with sudden fury, "my finances are nothing to do with you and neither are Sophie's."

Oblivious to Juliette's words of warning, Ann continued her tirade. Other students had started to notice and were openly staring their way. Evelyn attempted to shush her with a few soothing words but she remained stoic in her desire to inform Sophie of her failings.

"What about health care Sophie," she rasped, lighting a cigarette, "do you use the NHS like us commoners, or do you have a fantastic medical package that ensures you are treated straight away? I guess it's the latter. Do you think I would be stuck in this hideous contraption if I had more money?" Ann blew out a plume of smoke and looked down at her wheelchair with disdain.

"Ann!" Evelyn said aghast, she stepped forward with the intention of protecting Sophie, whose eyes were overflowing with tears.

"You're right," Sophie said, wiping her wet cheeks, "I do take money for granted and maybe my husband is paid too much, but I can tell you one thing. Out of the millions of people in this country, not many can kick a ball like Ryan O'Neill. He has a gift, a natural ability, so why shouldn't he benefit from it? It seems to me that you Ann, are just jealous. I'm sorry you're stuck in a wheelchair, it must be absolutely terrible, but it's not my fault, so don't you take it out on me. As for my privileged life? You really do not have a clue what shit I've been through. You're not the only one who has suffered," and with a loud sob, Sophie ran out of the courtyard and through the double doors of the Humanities block. Evelyn stared at Ann for a moment, shook her head in surprise, then took off after her.

There was an awkward silence. Will was looking at his feet, while Melanie was flushed and embarrassed.

"That was mean and downright nasty," Juliette snapped, as Ann began wheeling herself inside.

Ann paused to glare at Juliette, "oh come on, you've never really liked her, have you?"

Juliette felt like a chided child, "yes I do," she replied, "maybe at first I had my reservations, but now I've got to know her, I've changed my mind. I do like her, Sophie's sweet and kind. Sure she can be a bit outspoken at times, but so can you Ann. I'm certain that Sophie would never intentionally upset anyone. You shouldn't have spoken to her like that. Evelyn wasn't offended, so I don't know why you are."

Juliette stood with her hands on her hips, feet parted, glaring back, "I wouldn't blame Sophie if she didn't speak to you again after that."

# Chapter Fifteen

Jon was also angry at her, after hearing what had happened.

"That poor girl," he remonstrated, "you really shouldn't have spoken to her like that Ann."

"Maybe not," Ann admitted, "her naive way of looking at life just infuriates me."

"How well do you know her Ann?" Jon shook his head, dumping bubbling potatoes into a colander, "maybe her life isn't all sweetness and roses like you think."

"Okay, okay, point taken," she raised her hands in surrender as guilt overwhelmed her. Truthfully she felt dreadful. Sophie had been so upset that she had left uni early and missed the afternoon lecture. Juliette and Evelyn had snubbed her, Will was unable to look her in the eyes. Even bubbly, chatty Melanie had been un-characteristically subdued. By break time, Ann was consumed with guilt and had asked Evelyn for Sophie's mobile number, so she could call and apologise. Evelyn had coolly refused and then so had Juliette.

"You've got to stop being so mean to people," Jon said wearily, as he set the plates down on the table.

Ann sighed, toying with her food, "I know, you're right, I don't know what comes over me sometimes."

"Think of your future," Jon continued, shaking the pepper pot over his sausages, "if you want to be a lecturer you need to be friendly Ann and what about the adoption? You need to stay calm!"

"I can do friendly," Ann retorted, "I'll have to practise the calm bit."

Jon shook his head as he munched his way through his dinner.

"Practise on me Ann," he said with a small smile, "remember there is an adoption meeting at the weekend, you need to be on your very best behaviour."

Ann placed her cutlery down. "Are you sure this is a good idea? They might hate me, find me totally unsuitable as a potential parent and what about this thing?," she pointed at her wheels.

"They can't discriminate," Jon explained patiently, "just be yourself, but a nice version." He laughed then, his eyes twinkled at her from across the table. Feeling mischievous, she stuck out her tongue then burst into giggles. Seconds later her eyes filled with tears.

"I am such a bitch," she cried.

Jon sauntered over to kneel down beside her, "you're a beautiful bitch though," he agreed. Ann sobbed even louder, burying her face in his warm, soft t-shirt.

"Just apologise," he soothed, holding her tight, "you want me to speak to her?"

Ann shook her head, rubbing her cheek against his firm chest muscle, "no, but thank you, this is one mess I need to sort out myself." She raised her head, looking up at him with watery eyes, "I do love you Mr Stokes."

"Do you?" He enquired, kissing her salty tears away, "maybe you need to show me how much." With that, he scooped her up in his strong arms, kissed her lips then carried her up the stairs, kicking the bedroom door shut behind him.

\* \* \*

Will was having the shittiest day ever, he decided, as a white van rumbled past him, soaking him with the remnants of the afternoon shower. He grimaced at his soaking wet jeans. Great, he thought sourly, hopping as a puddle of rainwater pooled in his trainers. At least uni was finished for another day, he thought with relief, and what a strange day that had been. First he had been dumped, then Ann had kicked off big time, resulting in Sophie running out the uni in tears. He felt kind of bad for her. She was cool and hadn't deserved to be treated like that. But while it made him forget his problems for a while, the afternoon had still dragged on. The language lecture had been boring as hell, at one point he had almost fallen asleep, until Juliette had nudged him back to reality. He wanted to get home, so he could text Hema in private and hopefully persuade her to meet him later, but so far his begging texts went unanswered.

The bus was on time for a change. Will waited patiently as an elderly couple hobbled on ahead of him. It was packed, most of the seats were taken, apart from a space next to a scruffy looking guy with matted hair and a greying beard. Will parked himself down on the seat, beer fumes wafted over him, making him cough and edge further away, so he was balancing precariously towards the aisle. He looked down at his phone. The screen remained blank, no messages flashing meant no voice mail. He logged onto his Facebook account, checking over his status and private messages. Hema was still there, on his friend list; she hadn't deleted him *yet*. Over the afternoon he had messaged her four maybe five times. Who was counting? He was desperate to know if she was okay and if she would reconsider her decision. Will considered her to be frightened and acting rashly, she wasn't thinking straight, he thought with a frown.

"Waiting for a girl to call are ya?" The man next to him asked in a friendly Midland drawl.
Will smiled, "erm, something like that."

"Nothing but trouble are women," the man chuckled, shaking his head, "don't waste your time mate."

Will smiled politely through gritted teeth, wishing he would shut up.

"I was married once," the stranger continued, oblivious to Wills hostility, "twelve years we lasted. Then she cheated on me, and traded me in for a newer model. Lost my kids, my house, my career. Kaboom! Everything gone. Now I'm living in a hostel. I'm a proper down and out like," he sniffed. Will glanced over him, his curiosity piqued. On closer inspection, the man was younger then he first appeared. Although he was dirty and dishevelled, his face was smooth and wrinkle free. Poor bloke, Will thought with compassion.

"Sorry to hear that," he supplied, moving his long legs out of the aisle to accommodate an elderly lady, who squeezed past with a huge, shopping trolley.

"Thanks son," the man stuck out a gloved hand, "I'm Luke by the way."

Will took it, shaking it firmly, "Will."

"Well Will, my stops coming up, hope everything works out for you."

Will was momentarily speechless. What could he say to someone who had lost everything and had nothing? For once he was grateful for his odd parents; the steady familiarity of everyday life in the suburbs. The man rose and ruffled his hair as he passed him. Beer bottles in his carrier bag clinked loudly.

"Take care son," he said knowingly, "you've got that heartbroken look about you. Don't lose yourself like I have." With that the man was off, shuffling down the aisle, ringing the bell to signal the bus driver to stop.

"Luke," Will called after him as the vehicle rumbled to an unsteady stop, "cheers."

The man lifted his thumb with a sad smile then disappeared.

Will sat back down, inching along the seat until he was pressed up against the grimy window. He felt his spirits sink even further as he passed the Kumar's family shop. He craned his neck, hoping to catch a glimpse of her, but the door was firmly shut, with just a couple of kids outside it, kicking a ball around. Will sighed with frustration then checked his Facebook account again. The last entry was a tag from Rachel who had commented on Hema's Diwali party and posted selfies of the group in dubious poses over the evening. He paused in mid scroll to admire a close up of Hema's pretty, smiling face and noted with embarrassment that in the photo, he was staring directly at her, completely smitten looking. Well the secret is definitely out now he thought with a shake of his head. His mind flickered back to their shared passion. It lifted his spirits for a while as he remembered her soft, naked warmth and the love in her eyes. He was so engrossed in reminiscing, that he almost missed his stop. Jumping up, he hastily fumbled for the bell, hopped down the aisle, then waited for the bus to shudder to a stop.

As he trudged up the main road towards home, he snapped off his phone with resolution and tried to clear his mind of thoughts of Hema. Maybe a lad's night out should be arranged to cheer him up. He wondered what Jimmy was up to and resolved to call him later. A night of pool, alcohol and blokey chatter would benefit him enormously he decided, pulling his coat tighter, his teeth chattering in the cold night air. Winter had its grip, a full moon shone down on the bushes and trees, bathing them in a silver light. He slipped a few times on the icy pavement, and as he neared home, a cry behind startled him. It sounded like an animal: a scrounging fox or an excited cat maybe, he passed a woman gripping a young child, who stared at him through spookily, wide eyes.

"Don't stare Timothy," she scolded, then carried on her way.

Will was surprised to see his dad's car pulled up on the sloping driveway. He peered through the darkness, wondering why *he* was home, it wasn't even five yet, he thought sourly. Thoughts turned to food, as he wondered with amusement what culinary masterpiece Flora would be serving up tonight. Lunch had consisted of a plain burger with wilting lettuce and curly fries. He was now ravenous and in desperate need of sustenance, his stomach rumbling in agreement, as he fumbled in his rucksack for his door key. As he walked up the path, he noticed that Flora was looking out of the window, the net pulled back to reveal a worried countenance. Ruby was scratching at the door, whining in excitement. As he entered she jumped up on two legs, depositing pockets of fur on his coat and jeans.

"Hello girl," he paused to ruffle her furry head, then dumped his rucksack on the stairs. Warmth enveloped him, he placed his cold hands over the radiator, rubbing them vigorously.

"Hi Mom," he greeted, noticing Flora's small frame hovering in the hallway, "what's up?"

Flora was wringing her hands, shoulders slouched. Will sighed at her habitual anxious pose, one which had been more noticeable since Ofsted had been in at Max's school. Will guessed that the cause of her worry could be St Mary's. That school controlled their lives and Mom didn't even work there.

"Will," she whispered, rushing forward, "there's been a commotion at the school between your dad and Mr Kumar."

"What?!" Will thundered, marching up the hall, "where is he?"

"In his study," Flora answered, hurrying after him and grabbing hold of his arm, "he's in a foul mood, be careful what you say to him."

"When isn't he?" Will replied tersely, "don't worry Mom, I'm glad it's all out in the open."

Will marched through the lounge, with Ruby yapping at his heels. At the door of his father's study, he paused to listen, but there was no sound coming from within. He raked a tense hand through his hair, then pushed the door firmly open and strode into the dimly lit room. Max Bentley was sitting at a broad oak desk, shoulders hunched, as he read over paperwork.

He raised his head to glance at Will, "ah, the prodigal son returns."

"Everything okay?" Will asked, his voice raspy.

"Yep, just a mountain of paperwork to plough through before bedtime, same as every night, I…"

"Mom's told me," Will interrupted, "about Mr Kumar coming to your school. What did he want?"

There was no reply, just the steady tick of the wall clock, permeating the tense atmosphere.

"Well?" Will queried, feeling puzzled by his father's calm facade.

"Do you love her?" The query reverberated around the room, shocking him. Will had expected a raging tirade, not this subdued questioning.

"Very much," Will sighed, "what did Mr Kumar say?"

Max slowly placed his pen down, shaking his head, "he didn't do much speaking, shouting yes." There was a pause, and Will held his breath in anticipation, "Will, what the hell are you doing?"

"What? Nothing. We haven't done anything wrong."

"You should be concentrating on university, on gaining a career," Max snapped, "this thing with Hema, it's just puppy love." He jumped to his feet, "Mr Kumar was furious Will. He doesn't want you having anything to do with his daughter."

"It's not just puppy love. We are both nineteen," Will replied through gritted teeth, "we can do whatever we want."

"No," Max shouted, "no you can't. Her parents are a different culture Will. To start, they are not as laid back as your mom and I."

Will snorted, "laid back, are you joking?"

Max began pacing the room, "listen to me, you need to forget about Hema, concentrate on your career. You are too young to have this much hassle over a relationship."

"What would you know?," Will yelled, "Mr perfect bloody Catholic."

"Watch your lip - this isn't about me," Max snapped, "your mom is beside herself with worry, do you really want to make her ill again?"

Will had a flashback of his mother, when she had suffered severe depression a few years ago, the tears and the unnerving silence that had surrounded her. He wanted to shout at his dad that it was his fault she had been ill, but worried that Flora might hear. He decided to leave it until another time. So instead, he hung his head in defeat, he could almost feel the fight draining out of him.

"It doesn't matter anyway," his voice was quiet again, tinged with bitterness, "Hema's ended the relationship."

His dad stopped pacing, "good." Max stepped forward to place a comforting hand upon his son's shoulder, "it's for the best Will. It may not feel like it now, but it really is."

Will shrugged his hand off, "nothing to do with her being Hindu then?" He asked suspiciously.

"Don't be ridiculous," Max retorted, "I'm a head teacher Will, I embrace diversity."

He grinned at his own attempt at humour then sank back in his chair, "go do some homework, or at least pretend you are, for your mother's sake."

Will wandered off bemused, wondering if his dad had been kidnapped in the night and replaced by a liberal, improved doppelganger. As Will opened the door, Flora stumbled against it, "sorry," she whispered, fingers fluttering to her throat.

"Stop apologising Mom," Will advised, with a shake of his head. He stalked through into the kitchen and began running the tap to fill a tumbler with cold water.

"Is everything o-okay?" She stuttered.

"Hema's finished with me," Will replied tersely, taking a large gulp of liquid, "so you and Dad don't need to worry about me shaming the family."

"Will, I…we would never think that," she protested, concern etched amongst the weary lines on her face, "are you okay?" She asked, touching his arm.

"Not really," Will admitted, "but I'm gonna get her back. I know she loves me."

"Well, if you think that's the right course of action."

"It is," Will snapped, rubbing his throbbing temple.

"You do know your dad told Mr Kumar to leave. He wouldn't let him say a bad word against you son." Flora hunted in the medicine cabinet for paracetamol. "Take one of these," she instructed, "it's just a stress headache."

"Did he?" Will said with surprise, swallowing down the pill.

"Of course," Flora nodded, "you are his only son, he will always protect you. He may not always show it, but he is a good man Will. St Mary's is such a huge responsibility, he's under a great amount of stress there."

"He should be nicer to you!" Will cried, "you don't deserve to be the butt of his anger and frustration."

Flora hurried across to him, "shush, I'm not. I have a lovely life Will. I'm very happy. Stop worrying about me and focus on your studies, your career, your future. Make me and your dad proud."

"I have no idea what I want to do," Will admitted.

"You've got three years to work it out," Flora soothed with a kind smile, "and if Hema really loves you, she won't let you go. You are a handsome lad, I bet there are loads of girls who like you. Let her do the chasing."

"Like you chased Dad?" Will laughed.

"No, no," Flora blushed, "your dad chased me, from what I can remember. I was quite a catch when I was younger you know."

Will pulled his mom into a warm embrace, "I can believe it," he agreed, speaking into a mouthful of soft, coconut smelling hair.

"Well I'd better get on with the tea." Flora squeezed Will briefly, before extricating herself, "it's your favourite tonight: meatballs."

Will winced, "great Mom," he replied, "I'll be upstairs reading." He sprinted up to his room, while Flora hummed along to the radio and set about making the onion gravy.

* * *

Evelyn had spent most of the evening worrying about Sophie. She had called her landline number a few times, which had rang out and then clicked to an exuberant message from Sophie asking her to leave a message if she dared to. Evelyn had spoken slowly as the machine recorded her voice. She hated the sound of her herself, feeling embarrassed by her broad Midland drawl. Her message was short; hoping that Sophie was okay and if she needed to talk, then she was here for her.

Nora had been shocked after hearing about the afternoon's escapades.

"That poor girl, surely she didn't deserve that."

"No, she didn't Mam," Evelyn replied, "Sophie's a nice person with a good heart."

Nora nodded, "all that over a night out. I think that your friend Ann has other issues which might be upsetting her dear."

"Yes," Evelyn agreed, "hopefully she will apologise and then we can all be friends again."

Nora sipped her tea thoughtfully, "well, you must go out with them now dear, after all that fuss."

Evelyn watched the credits of 'Coronation Street' roll up the screen and swallowed nervously, "I've nothing to wear," she replied lamely. Nora looked across at her in disbelief. "Besides, nights out and drinking don't interest me." She stared at the ticket propped up against a figurine ornament, wondering if it was too late to cancel.

"Tch," Nora tutted, "you should go and enjoy yourself. A night out with friends will be lovely and just what Doctor Dunn would prescribe I'm sure," she winked playfully. "Drink cordial if that's what you fancy, but Evelyn, I know you enjoy a glass or two of sherry on an evening." Evelyn laughed at the twinkle in Mam's eye.

"And as for clothing," Nora continued, "your wardrobe is bursting with beautiful items my dear. Wear a nice dress, but it will be chilly, so you could wear that lovely fur jacket."

Evelyn sighed, "I don't know, I feel too old and weary Mam. Did I tell you it's a disco, it will be full of young people, I'll be so out of place."

"Flumadiddle," Nora replied.

"What?" Evelyn said with a laugh, "what does that mean?"

"Utter nonsense my dear, I thought you would know that, you being an author."

Evelyn shook her head bemused, "I like that word Mam, I might incorporate that into my next novel. Flumadiddle," the word rolled off her tongue, sending them both into giggles.

"Anyway," Nora said as she took a bite of ginger cake, "you can't let Sophie down now, she will be upset dear."

"Yes, you're right," Evelyn acquiesced, "okay, I give in, I'll go." She rustled the TV magazine, looking to see what they could watch next, as Nora clapped in delight.

Just then the phone rang, spurring Evelyn to her feet, "hello," she said breathlessly into the phone.

"Hi Evelyn, it's Sophie, just returning your call."

"Oh Sophie, I've been worried about you."

"You didn't need to," Sophie sniffed and Evelyn could hear the wobble in her voice.

"Are you okay?" Evelyn asked softly.

"I am now," Sophie replied quietly, "it was probably silly to leave uni like that, but I was just so upset."

"You don't need to explain. I would have felt exactly the same. If it's any consolation, Ann did feel terrible afterwards, she wanted to call you." Evelyn gripped the phone, hoping that she had made Sophie feel a little better.

"Did she?" Sophie asked, her voice a faint tremble, "maybe she was right. About every-thing."

Evelyn bit back the word flumadiddle, "no," she emphasised, "what Ann said was unfair and unnecessary. She can be unkind sometimes, take no notice of her." There was no sound from the other end, "please don't take it personally dear, she is abrupt and outspoken with everyone. I've noticed that even her husband falls victim to her harsh tongue."

"Yes okay, I suppose so…" Sophie's voice tapered off, drowned out by the sudden crackle of the phone line.

"Anyway dear, I've photocopied the lecture notes. So please don't worry. Shall I see you Wednesday?"

"Yes," Sophie replied firmly, "and thank you Evelyn, you are kind, I'm so glad we're friends." Evelyn sighed with relief, operation cheer up Sophie appeared to have worked. After ringing off, she meandered into the kitchen to make another pot of tea.

"Have you spoken to a lecturer about your book yet?" Nora asked, as she set the tray of drinks down.

"No," Evelyn gulped, "I really don't think it's good enough to be published Mam. I was just thinking of keeping it between you and me."

Nora squinted over the rim of her spectacles, shaking her head at her daughter's downturned mouth. "You must let someone else read it Evelyn. Don't be so shy. You should be proud of your achievements."

"Well I, I, I'm not sure."

"Ask a lecturer ASAP," Nora decided, "there's no shame in asking for help and advice. What are you afraid of dear?"

Evelyn sighed, reaching across to mute the blare of the TV.

"Criticism Mam. I'm afraid of criticism, even the constructive kind." She let out a long shaky sigh, "I'm scared that strangers will hate it. That I'll be ridiculed. I spend all day analysing and critiquing literature. I don't know whether I like the thought that someone may do the same to my work. It's so personal to write Mam. You put yourself out there to a sharp, cynical world. What if I'm truly not good enough? What if all this time, work, emotion, has all been a complete waste? You of all people know how sensitive I am. Could I really cope with others picking apart my novel? Finding fault. Hating it."

"You are worrying too much!" Nora admonished, "stop aiming for perfection. This is your first novel, you're not Jayne Austen dear. Some people will love it and some might not, it's just different opinions."

"And some might utterly hate it," Evelyn said quietly.

"Well then dear, that's a risk you need to take," Nora replied in a firm tone. "You are strong Evelyn. Stronger then you think. Be confident, believe in yourself, or no one else ever will."

Curled up in bed later that evening, Evelyn was still consumed with feelings of self-doubt. Sleep eluded her, she tossed and turned, plumping the pillows in an attempt to fall under. As dawn broke, the sound of birds sang through her open window. The sun's rays peeped through gaps in the heavy velvet curtains. Evelyn pushed back the covers. Attracted by the light, she stood in the window and pulled the curtains open a fraction, to stare out at a new day dawning. A glorious, bright morning unfolded before her eyes, making her gasp in wonder. The world slowly awoke, rising from a wintery slumber. The milk cart trundled down the street, pausing at a few houses, including theirs. Two cats rolled like balls of fluff, across the silver encrusted garden, their whiskers moist from the soft dewy grass. It was beautiful to watch and standing there, she was filled with a renewed positivism. She was going to stop being afraid. For so long she had hidden away, scared by the world around her, maybe it was time to start living. What was it her dear Dad had said to her?: "step out of the shadows". Evelyn touched the frosty pane of glass and smiled, "yes Dad I will."

# Chapter Sixteen

It was a busy weekend for Ann. On Friday evening she went to watch her niece Summer play in her school orchestra, after a last minute call from her sister, who had "forgotten all about asking her." After sulking for a while, Ann had decided to let Jon talk her into going. The hall had been full, but as soon as they had seen her wheelchair, a flustered teacher had directed them to the front of the room, where her sister was already seated, eating jam sandwiches out of crumpled tin foil. Mom and Dad were also there. It had all been very cosy and enjoyable, although there had been one point when Ann felt like disappearing when Jon, her sister and parents, had embarrassed her by singing along to the finale in loud, out of tune warbles. She also noticed some of the school staff sniggering their way, when her mom Betsy had jumped to her feet and danced along to Summer's flute solo. Afterwards, amidst much clapping and cheering, Summer had skipped off the stage and ran into Ann's open arms, her flute dragging behind her.

"Was I good Aunty Ann?" She asked, wide eyed and breathless.

Ann hugged her tight, "you were marvellous." They had stayed for the raffle and tea and cake then made their way home, to watch a nice romantic weepy, that had Ann thinking once again of Sophie.

"Was Sophie okay?" Jon asked, sensing her melancholy mood, as he locked up for the evening.

Ann rolled her eyes, "I've told you once, I spoke to her and apologised."

"But was she okay?" Jon reiterated, keys jangling from his hand.

"Yes," Ann sighed, "I think so. She said it was fine and accepted my apology." Ann shrugged, looking down at the wooden floorboards.

"That's all you can do then," Jon patted her hand.

"She was quiet though, not her usual bubbly self. I still feel terrible; I don't know how I can make it up to her."

"Just be nice," Jon advised with a grin, "and remember you have to be on your best behaviour tomorrow okay?"

"I promise," Ann replied with a pout. Jon cleared away the empty plates. She could hear him singing in the kitchen and smiled. The evening dragged on, Ann lay in bed, thoughts whizzing through her head, while Jon slept next to her, snoring softly. At two o'clock she snapped on her bedside light and opened her book with a sigh, her bookmark fluttered onto the duvet. She snuggled down, immersing herself in a fictitious world. Reading always calmed her frazzled nerves and helped her sleep. She could feel her eyelids drooping, as the sound of rain pattered onto the window sill and a strong arm wound around her, pulling her close, warm and safe.

The adoption meeting was held in one of the sprawling, high rise council offices that overlooked the city centre. It was a plain brick 1970s building, that seemed out of sorts when compared with the older, fanciful architecture that was dotted around. Ann stared out at the cold, gloomy day, sipping lukewarm, sugary tea out of a polystyrene cup. There were about ten people in the room mingling, while they waited for a lady called Jenny Grey from the adoption services. Jon was leaning against the wall, chatting to two men about sport. She could hear their stilted conversation and laughter as they discussed the failings of the English football team.

A woman with short curly hair and a friendly smile approached her.

"Hi there, is this your first meeting?" She peered over purple rimmed glasses and Ann nodded, remembering Jon's plea to be friendly.

"Yes it is."

"I thought so, I haven't seen you here before. I'm Glenda by the way," she thrust out a plump hand, which Ann took and shook gently.

"Ann."

"Lovely to meet you Ann," Glenda said with enthusiasm, "we're a lovely bunch, so don't feel nervous."

"Thanks," Ann smiled, "erm…do you adopt already?"

"Yes, yes, I've adopted two children: a brother and sister. Mom's a drug addict, not able to look after herself, never mind two children. It's heartbreaking really, but they've settled in so well with me and Roger." She signalled to her husband, who was chomping on a biscuit.

"Do you have any adoptive children Ann?"

"No, no, I mean not yet. We're just here to find out a bit more about the process and what the realities are."

"Good idea," Glenda nodded her head, "it's a huge step to undertake, but adopting a child is so worthy. There are so many children out there waiting for a good home."

Ann smiled, swallowing nervously, "well, it's very early days yet."

The door opened with a squeak, and a tall lady backed into the room, balancing a large box on one hip. She hurried over to the drinks station, dumping her belongings, then proceeded to make herself a strong coffee.

"That's Jenny," Glenda whispered, as Ann looked over with interest, "extremely nice lady, but forthright, speaks her mind, if you know what I mean." Ann nodded, a bit like me, she thought as she watched Jenny mingle. Jon called her over and they joined the others at a long table that smelt of potpourri. It reminded Ann of being at a high flying board meeting. She expected Alan Sugar to burst through the door any moment and start pointing a finger.

"Hi folks," Jenny greeted them with a wide sweep of her arm, "it's great to see familiar and some new faces. You are all very welcome." She beamed a broad smile and Ann felt slightly dazzled by the whiteness of her teeth. Jenny cleared her throat then began a run through of the afternoon's itinerary. Ann offered a sweet to Jon as the lights were snapped off and a DVD burst to life.

It was a short documentary on how adoption in the UK had evolved over the years. It interviewed various adoptive parents and concluded with a montage of children, speaking of their personal experience of being in the care system. Ann's eyes were brimming with tears and a lump of emotion had lodged in her throat.

"You okay?" Jon asked, as he gripped her hand. His own eyes were watering and there was a distinct break in his voice as he spoke. Ann nodded and looked around. Emotional faces stared back at her, watching as Jenny stooped to pause the DVD and relight the room.

"Now," she beamed, clasping her hands together, "let's have a discussion."

The afternoon flew by. Ann listened intently as the others spoke about their life as adoptive parents. When it was their turn to speak, she felt uncharacteristically self-conscious and unsure of what to divulge. She looked at Jon in the hope that he would speak for her. Thankfully he took the hint, cleared his throat and began a spiel of why they wanted to adopt. Underneath the table, she felt him grip her hand and she smiled at him with encouragement. When he had finished and was scratching his head, feeling rather flummoxed and unsure of what to say next, Jenny leant forward in her seat.

"And what could you offer a child?" She asked, with a bright smile.

"Erm, a loving stable home," he replied, glancing around the table. The others nodded their agreement, "a patient and caring couple, who want to offer a child in need, a happy, secure future."

"That's lovely," Jenny said with a nod, "and what about you Ann, what are your thoughts on the matter?"

Ann felt beads of sweat collect on her upper lip as she pondered on a response.

"Well, reiterating Jon's sentiments," she began, "we both love children and can't have any of our own, for obvious reasons, you may have guessed." She pointed at her wheels. "I was disabled following a road traffic accident, and before then, I hadn't considered having children. They seemed too draining, too messy..." she felt Jon grip her hand tighter as a few chuckles spread around the room, "but when you're faced with the certainty of a childless future, it makes you realise what a gift having children really is."

"We tried years to conceive," Glenda disclosed, "spent a fortune on fertility treatment. Then a colleague suggested adoption and we've never looked back. It's the most rewarding decision we have ever made."

"Amen to that," Glenda's husband said, looking heavenward, "our babies are a blessing."

"Oh we would prefer an older child," Ann cut in hastily, "I mean for practical reasons. It really wouldn't be feasible for me to chase around after a crawling baby, or an energetic toddler."

"Of course," Jenny nodded, "that's very astute Ann, the older children are often the hardest to place."

A lady with a severe bob and pursed lips nodded, "yes, we fostered a teenage boy, but unfortunately, we were unable to offer a more permanent home. He became involved in drugs, gangs. We couldn't cope, so had to let him go."

"It must work for both the child and the adult," Jenny said sympathetically, "I do understand how difficult it must have been for you. What we are trying to do with these meetings is offer support and guidance for a hard and often thankless undertaking. There are many positives to adoption, but also negatives too. What we *can* guarantee is that you will never be on your own," she directed her gaze at Jon and Ann in particular.

"And I do think that the positives far outweigh the negatives."

"Hear, hear," Glenda spoke up with a smile and a small clap of her hands.

After the discussion had petered out, Jenny told them they were free to leave, or to grab another drink and mingle a bit more, if they wished to do so. Glenda slipped a scrap of paper into Ann's hand, with her telephone number on.

"If you need any advice, or just someone to chat to, please call me anytime."

Ann was touched by her kindness, "thanks," she replied, "I will, if we erm…go ahead with it."

Glenda winked, "you would be terrific, I hope to see you again," she waved, then hurried over to her husband, who was halfway out of the door. Jon was chatting to Jenny; she could hear him telling her about Ann's university degree.

"Her aim is to be a lecturer," he finished proudly, making Ann blush as Jenny looked her way with interest.

"How fantastic," Jenny replied, "you must be so clever. I only managed to scrape a 'C' pass in English, books aren't really my thing. I'm much better with numbers."

Ann laughed, "I find some areas of maths completely baffling, especially algebra; who had the idea to put numbers and letters together anyway?" Jenny's peals of laughter echoed around the room.

"You know how to work off 25% discount in a sale though Ann," Jon quipped cheekily.

"Of course!" Ann replied, socking her husband playfully on the arm.

"Thank you so much for coming today," Jenny said with a warm smile, "I hope you are still interested in adoption and that we haven't scared you off too much."

"Of course not," Jon replied smoothly, looking at Ann, who shook her head vigorously.

"No, not at all," Ann confirmed, "I'm just wondering what happens now."

"Well," Jenny delved into her brown leather satchel, "here's an application form, if you want to go ahead with the process. Please think carefully and discuss it together and if you would like any further advice, my telephone number is on there too."

"Fab," said Jon, "We'll fill it in over the weekend then," he beamed a charming smile but Ann could feel her lips trembling slightly. This was going way too fast. Jenny seemed to sense the air of uncertainty and patted her hand reassuringly.

"It must be a joint decision and you are in no rush, so please take whatever time you need before making a final decision."

On the way home, Jon took a detour through leafy suburban streets, until they reached a park. They wandered along twisty lanes, passing a large lake, where elegant snow white swans floated on murky water, like beautiful granite statues. There were children everywhere; chasing balls, swinging from climbing frames, laughing and shouting, enjoying the lull in the rain. Parked vans touted for business; selling ice cream, toffee apples and hot dogs, tea and afternoon scones. It reminded Ann of her youth, when she could walk. She sniffed, pulling her scarf tight around her and listened to Jon, as he talked with excitement of the meeting.

"I think we have a strong possibility of adopting a child," he said, as he skimmed a pebble across the surface of the lake. It left ripples on the calm surface and circles that grew progressively larger. Ann nodded, gazing at the beauty of nature around her.

"Are you happy?" He enquired, his voice tinged with worry.

"Yes of course, don't pester," she replied with irritation, "I just need some time to get my head around it all."

"We can talk to other adoptive parents if you want, might help to make your mind up." He squatted next to her, moving a strand of unruly hair, which had escaped from its clip. Ann was silent, lost in her thoughts. Yes, she definitely needed more time to consider the prospect of being an adoptive parent but as she stared at Jon, all she could see was the warmth and love in his eyes, his never ending patience. He was such a good man, he deserved to be happy.

"No I'm sure," she replied, tucking her hand into his, "let's have a family."

\* \* \*

Sophie was watching Derek sweeping dead leaves up off their huge back garden when the phone rang for the third time that morning. The first call had been from her hysterical Mother, who was in a total panic over Roger's sciatica. Sophie held the receiver away from her ear, as Yvonne screeched how the condition had worsened over the week and how he was now unable to even get up out of bed. Sophie held back a snigger as she envisioned Yvonne dressed in a nurse's outfit, slapping poor Roger and telling him to stop making a fuss. Her Mother had never been the caring, compassionate kind. Her bedside manner was definitely on the hard side and that was putting it mildly.

"What shall I do?" Yvonne wailed. Sophie sighed theatrically, before proceeding to advise her Mother to make an urgent call to the Doctor, followed by a dose of strong anti-inflammatories. It was time Mom gave up on the alternative therapy and settled on a more conventional medical formula. This opinion did not go down well with Feng Sui mad Yvonne, who informed her daughter that drugs were the product of evil conglomerates who secretly strived for addiction and continued ill health. Sophie had told her mom she was insane.

"How did he hurt his back anyway?"

"We were practising tantric sex if you must know."

Sophie had fell about the kitchen with laughter, then CLICK the line had gone dead.

The second call had been from a solicitor with a broad cockney accent, enquiring if she wanted to claim for the accident she had sustained. Sophie had thought of Ann, stuck in her wheelchair and her eyes had filled with sudden tears. In anger and upset she had ranted down the phone. He had subsequently put the phone down too. Now she felt totally miserable and shuffled over to the cabinet to down one of her anti-depressants, then immediately felt disgusted with herself, as she was trying to wean herself off them. Now the phone was ringing yet again. She hovered in the doorway, waiting for the call to click to the answer machine. A lady with a husky voice introduced herself as Jayne, the Business Manager from Allhallows Secondary School. Sophie raced across the room, fell awkwardly on the sofa, then snatched the phone off its cradle.

"Hi, this is Sophie," she jabbered into the mouth piece.

"Oh hello," the Business Manager began speaking at a furious rate, explaining the reason for her call.

"I believe you requested to do some voluntary at our school?"

"Yes, yes that's right."

"Just remind me Mrs O'Neill, what department do you wish to gain experience in?"

"Please call me Sophie, erm… English. I'm at University at the moment, in my first year, studying for English and I'm considering teaching as a career option."

"Very good," replied Jayne briskly, "and how many hours would you like to volunteer?"

"Just the two mornings at the moment. I'm at uni the other days."

"Good, good. I will slot you in with Miss Brown, a fantastic English teacher, who has been at the school for years."

Sophie thanked her profusely and the arrangements were made. She was to go in next week with her most up to date police check. Luckily, she had paid for a CRB herself a month ago, so she could help at her children's art club in the local church.

"That will show everyone I'm serious," she decided with a firm smile.

"Mom can I have a drink?" Josh tore into the kitchen, mud splattering from his trainers. He was closely followed by Jake and their panting Labrador. Sophie grimaced at the muddy footprints imprinted on the tiles.

"Take your shoes off boys," she shrieked, as she searched in the fridge for the orange squash. A shoe was flung in the air, narrowly missing her arm and ending upside down in the dog's water bowl. The boys thought it was hysterical, bent over with laughter and despite her bad mood, Sophie laughed along with them.

"What would you like for dinner?" She asked them with a wide grin, feeling happy again.

"Spaghetti hoops," Jake shouted, as he slurped his drink.

"Beans on toast," Josh cried, after thinking about it for a full minute.

Sophie set about making lunch. While she stirred the beans she thought about the Language essay which was due in next week. All the books she needed for secondary reading had already been loaned out of the library. So in a panic she had ordered a few from Amazon and paid extra for next day delivery. Her folders were strewn across the table, paper and pens balancing precariously. She had intended on spending the afternoon working on her essay. She had plotted a plan out on white cards, she now had to re-read over her lecture notes to remind herself of the topic, then she just had to start writing.

It sounded simple enough but Sophie was tired and suffering from writer's block, which wasn't helped by the anxious thoughts tumbling around in her head. She still kept thinking about the argument with Ann. Her apology had seemed heartfelt enough, but Sophie was still smarting at Ann's tirade. Did she flash her money around too much? She wondered. Yes, a voice inside her snapped.

"Mrs O'Neill. Mrs O'Neil," Sophie spun around at the sound of her name. Derek was standing in the doorway, clutching the rake and a black bag bulging with leaves.

"That's me done for the day," he said with a puzzled look on his face, "are you okay?"

"Yes," Sophie nodded, she pushed the intrusive thoughts of Ann away, "thank you. The garden looks much tidier." She smiled his way, wondering why he was staring at her expectantly.

"Erm..." he began, clearing his throat, "Ryan, I mean Mr O'Neill hasn't paid me for two months."

"Hasn't he?" She replied, shocked at her lackadaisical husband, "I'm sorry," she murmured, cheeks tinging pink, "can you take a cheque Derek? I don't think I have that much cash in the house." She fumbled in the drawers, "here's a hundred and I'll do you a cheque now for the rest."

"That's fine," he said gruffly. Sophie quickly dished the boys lunch up, then rummaged around for the battered cheque book.

"It's here somewhere," she said, pulling the contents of the drawer out.

"I need paying too Mrs O'Neill," Heidi the housekeeper strode into the room with an armful of washing. Sophie glanced her way, nodding uneasily. Ann's words revolved around her mind and she swallowed, feeling suddenly uncomfortable at the extravagance of having two household staff. Maybe she should look after the house herself and make Ryan do the gardening. Did they really need staff for menial, everyday jobs, that other people like the lovely Juliette had to do alone? The thought of having to clean the house every day and cope with uni work made Sophie shudder. She was sure she could do it if she *had* to, but did she really *want* to? She realised then, just how lucky she was.

"Thank you," Sophie said, as she scribbled her signature, "both of you, for all your hard work."

Heidi was staring at her in surprise, while Derek just looked bored. Sophie acknowledged that she knew very little of her staff's personal life. She had always been afraid of being too friendly, so had kept a cool distance. Ryan however, was the opposite, he frequently hugged Heidi, asked about her granddaughter and had dropped her home a few times. Derek was like an old buddy, lots of back slapping, watching footy over crates of beer; they even went to the gym together. Sophie vowed she would chill out with her staff more, starting from today.

After they had left, Sophie made herself a strong coffee and sat down at the table, pen in hand, waiting for inspiration to strike. This was hard, she decided, maybe she should leave it till tomorrow when Ryan would be home and could entertain the boys. No, no she should persevere. She began reading through a chapter on Diversity in the English Language with determination. The clock ticked by, Sophie felt her eyelids droop and laid her head on her arms, with the intention of just having five minutes' rest. Then the doorbell chimed so loudly that she shot bolt upright in the chair, cricking her neck in the process.

"Don't answer that boys," she called, fearing it was Jehovah Witnesses. She had spotted them prowling the streets earlier and had pulled the blind slats down in preparation. She hurried into the lounge, where Josh and Jake were transfixed by Spiderman. "Have you been messing with the doorbell again?" she hissed, trying to peer unnoticed through a gap in the blinds. A bright gleaming Mercedes was parked up against her row of garden statues. Amber, she thought with relief.

The dogs were going wild at the door. Sophie shooed them away then grappled with the numerous locks.

"Your gates were open babe," Amber commented, as she flounced into the hallway. Sophie stared down with dismay at a chocolate smeared Angel.

"Don't mind her babe," Amber continued, "just plonk her in front of the tele and she's happy."

"Oh okay, hello Angel," Sophie ushered the child through to Josh and Jake, who sighed when they spotted her.

"Shush," Sophie remonstrated, "Angel's come to play for a bit, so be nice boys, okay?"

Sophie watched with amusement as Angel plonked herself on the sofa, squashing inbetween Josh and Jake, who looked as if they wanted to run away.

"I want to watch Dora the Explorer," she complained loudly. Josh picked up the remote and passed it to her with a resigned sigh. Sophie gave him the thumbs up, pleased that her boys were so kind and accommodating, even to Angel.

Amber had escaped to the kitchen and was seated at the table, looking at her books with a confused expression on her face.

"What is this?" She asked, without looking up.

"Just uni work," Sophie replied crisply, "coffee, tea?"

"Have you got decaf darling? I'm detoxing at the moment."

*Again* thought Sophie, but remained silent. She rooted through the cupboards. There it was, right at the back. It was out of date, but only by a few months. Sophie opened the jar, surreptitiously sniffing the contents. It smelt fine, she decided, tipping a spoonful into a large, daisy painted mug.

"All these books give me a headache just looking at them," Amber pulled a face, "where's your Ryan anyway?"

"Footy practice," Sophie replied, "he should be back soon."

"When are we going shopping darling? I need a new wardrobe desperately."

Amber was off to Dubai for two weeks. Her fourth holiday this year. Each time she went, she splashed out on a pile of new clothes. A few months ago it had been skiing. Sophie had followed her around the department stores, giving her advice on suitable attire and watching as she flung overpriced designer jeans, jumpers and exquisite underwear into her trolley. Her bills were always staggering. Normally it would not phase Sophie in the slightest, after all she always left with an armful of goodies for herself, Ryan and the boys. But the last shopping excursion had left a bad taste in her mouth. She had not enjoyed it and had felt uneasy when she thought of Juliette and that awful battered rucksack. On a scale of one to ten, she wondered how ostentatious Amber was.

"I'm really busy at the moment," Sophie replied, attempting to sound assertive, "I've got an essay due and a huge reading list."

"Oh," Amber's face fell in surprise and disappointment and Sophie felt a pang of guilt, "why don't you come round here for a girlie evening instead? I'll get some of those cucumber face masks you like and we can share a bottle of wine and maybe watch a DVD."

Her friends nose wrinkled in distaste, "I'm on a strict sugar diet honey. No alcohol. Remember, wine contains buckets of sugar and calories."

"Oh, erm okay," Sophie poured bubbling hot water, adding a dash of skimmed milk to each mug.

Amber was eyeing the twin's chocolate chip cookies and Sophie felt sympathy for her diet mad friend. She must be starving, she thought, as she gazed at her friend's skinny frame.

"So," Amber said, "how is Ryan?"

"Ryan?" Sophie replied, "he's fine thanks, same as usual."

Sophie was surprised by the question. She knew that Amber had always liked him, every woman did, for goodness sake, but she had never shown this much interest in him before.

"I mean, does he mind you going to uni every day?"

Sophie bristled, shaking her head, "it's not every day," she explained, "a lot of the course study is independent and has to be completed out of uni hours. I'm only actually there a few days per week."

Amber sniffed, "still, how do you manage to balance everything?"

Sophie stared at her, feeling a flicker of annoyance. She had the distinct impression that Amber disapproved, a bit like her mother and all her other so called friends. Does she think I'm neglecting Ryan and the boys? Sophie wondered.

"I'm lucky," she replied coolly, "to have household help, other students have to cope on their own."

Amber sneered, "you mean single parents? People on benefits? Scroungers who sponge off hard working folk like Ryan and Martin?"

Sophie winced at Amber's vitriolic rant. "I'm sure no one intends to be a single parent or on benefits," Sophie answered gently, "it must be difficult."

Amber snorted, "Are you joking? Have you seen the parents at Oakridge Juniors?" She was referring to the large Primary school that was positioned right in the middle of the neighbouring council estate, "they all seem to smoke, drive cars, dress in designer gear – albeit totally chavvy and soooooo outdated. How is that poverty? And why should we, the taxpayer, have to subsidise them, while they create more and more offspring? No wonder this country is going to the dogs."

"Here, here," a voice boomed from the doorway, making Sophie jump in fright. She turned to see Ryan stood in the doorway, clapping with gusto, "Amber for Prime Minister."

Sophie watched as a pink blush spread across her friend's face and neck.

"Hi Ryan," she purred, flicking her hair playfully, "how are you?"

"Awesome as ever," he replied with a cheeky grin, crossing the kitchen to playfully slap his wife's backside. "Has Del gone?"

"Hello, yes he finished at lunchtime, he's made a terrific job of the garden."

Ryan's face fell, "I wanted him to drop me and a few friends off for drinks later."

Sophie shook her head with disapproval, "he's the gardener Ryan, not the chauffeur. Where are you going anyway? I thought we were having a family night in," she sniffed suspiciously, watching as he opened the fridge and gulped down orange juice straight from the carton.

"Just the casino," he replied nonchalantly, wiping his mouth with the back of his hand.

Sophie felt her spirits deflate, "with Mickey?"

"Yeah, he'll be there, why?"

Sophie shook her head, biting her lip in annoyance. Acutely aware of Amber's presence, she bit back the expletive, instead stating, "well, I've got uni work to do anyway."

A glazed look crossed Ryan's face, "there we go then babes, sorted. I'm off for a shower, can you drop us instead?" He waved at Amber who blew him a kiss, while Sophie mumbled an affirmative reply. There was a flurry of activity from the dogs as they chased him up the stairs, barking playfully. Sophie sighed, stirring her coffee thoughtfully.

"Problems?" Amber enquired, eyes bright after surveying the almost domestic.

"Just the usual," Sophie replied, "that's marriage huh?"

Amber took her empty cup to the sink, looking at Sophie with sympathy.

"Listen honey," she began, "men are basically overgrown, hairy babies, who want attention twenty-four seven. Forget about this," she signalled to the books on the table, "your marriage is more important. Give him some attention; dress up for him, have spontaneous sex. Then he won't want to go out with the lads."

Sophie chewed her lip, "I don't know," she said uncertainly.

"It always works for Martin," insisted Amber, as she nodded enthusiastically. Sophie didn't know whether she agreed with her friend's unique brand of marriage counselling, but she was willing to give it a go. Things hadn't been right between them since, well, since she had started uni.

"Maybe we're both having a mid-life crisis," she said aloud.

"Could be," Amber replied, "don't stress about it babes, Martin went through it too."

"Did he?" Sophie asked, wide eyed.

"Yes. He became obsessed with golf weekends, dyed his hair and started wearing Levi's. I tell you babes, it was hard for a while, I thought divorce was on the cards."

"What did you do?" Sophie asked with a worried frown.

"Gave him an ultimatum. It was either me or the golf clubs. He must have realised how lucky he was 'cause he soon dropped his golf buddies. Now he only goes once a month. He still wears Levi's mind." Amber pulled a face of disgust and Sophie burst into laughter. Everything would be okay, she thought adamantly, her spirits lifting. Maybe she could book a meal, just the two of them, where they could have a proper chat, sort things out and get back on track. Sophie smiled gratefully at her friend, "thanks for the advice, maybe I could squeeze in a day of shopping." She winked across at Amber, whose face erupted into a huge grin.

"Yeah baby, Gucci here we come!" They raised their mugs, clinking them together and giggling with excitement.

# Chapter Seventeen

Across the other side of the city, Juliette was leaning against the bar scribbling notes on a pink fluorescent covered A4 pad. Her forehead was crinkled with concentration as she wrote. The overhead TV was a distraction, blaring out sports commentator's ramblings and advert music that was cheesy enough to make a child wince.

"Pint down here love when you're ready," an elderly man in a trilby hat shouted over the din. Juliette muted the sound, before hurrying down to the other end of the bar with a happy smile on her face.

"Here you are Malcolm," she said, passing her favourite regular a pint of creamy bitter. He licked his lips and winked at Juliette in gratitude.

"You are an angel," he noted, taking a swig of white froth, "how's school going by the way?"

Juliette laughed, he made it sound like she was a dizzy teenager.

"It is fabulous," she gushed, wiping the bar clean of sticky beer residue, "I'm just working on my essay at the moment."

"Good girl," came his approval, "you'll make us all proud, but we'll be sorry to lose you wench."

"Ahh thanks, but I'll still be here for a few years, I'm not going anywhere yet."

"You are going to go far my dear, there's good things in store for you, mark my words."

Juliette grinned, pulled a bag of pork scratching down and passed it to Malcom. "Here, on the house." He tipped his hat and she left him to munch on them in peace.

Juliette soon became engrossed in her books again. This essay is flowing nicely, she thought with satisfaction. She was three quarters of the way through, with just a conclusion and referencing to tackle. Her thoughts drifted to the Literature essay, they were due to receive them back next week. She had been mulling over it for days; would the content be good enough? Would the grammar and punctuation be to university standard? Her college essays had all passed, but she had no idea what the criteria of the marking was like at university. Juliette wondered if Ben had marked hers, or that funny little lecturer Brian Hodges. What if the referencing let her down? She had found *that* totally complicated and had stayed up late one night, surfing the study aid website, trying to decipher the format that was required. Juliette was striving for perfection, she was determined to do well, so she could take one step further towards her dreams.

Yesterday, she had been in the dentist's waiting room, flicking through a Home and Garden magazine, while Harry and Molly had their teeth checked. A photograph had mesmerised her, so she had torn the page clean out, then stuck it on the fridge at home. A beautiful picture to gaze at and fantasise over. It was a colourful piece on English gardens. One in particular had caught her eye; an abundance of flowers, a lazily swung garden hammock, majestic marble ornaments and a path that wound through blooming roses and beautiful, butterfly covered Buddleia's.

"That's what I want," she had divulged to Marie, who had chuckled softly and called her a 'romantic fool'.

"Mom and Dad have a perfectly nice garden," she had stated in her no nonsense manner, "why don't you move back in with them. You know they would love to have you and the kids."

"No!" Juliette had replied, aghast, "I need to stay independent Maz. I need my own space and the kids do too. Besides, Mom and Dad don't want us under their feet, they're not getting any younger. They need peace and quiet at their age."

Aunty Maz was with her kids now, spoiling them rotten no doubt with sweets and fizzy pop. Juliette tapped her phone until a recent snap of the kids appeared on the screen. Harry was grinning widely, his arm slung protectively around a beaming Molly. Aww they looked so gorgeous, she still couldn't believe that she had grown and nurtured them into the lovely children they were today. Juliette sighed, brushed aside a curl that had escaped and set about tackling the conclusion.

She was engrossed in her writing, when a shadow fell across the bar, blocking out the small sliver of sunlight.

"Hi Jules," a male voice greeted. She glanced up and was shocked to see Marty slouched opposite her, a five pound note in his hand and a cheeky grin on his face.

"Marty," she said, hackles rising, "what are you doing here?"

"A pint of your finest ale please Bar Maid," he replied cockily.

"You're not a member," she hissed, backing away slightly.

"I only want one," he retaliated, his grin drooping, "I needed to see you Jules, you never seem to be at home these days."

"I'm busy," she snapped, flinging her pen down, "earning money to keep *our* children."

Marty held his hands up, "I don't want to argue with you. I just need a quick chat."

"You have five minutes," she replied tetchily, gravitating towards the Guinness pump and pulling a pint. It had always been his favourite tipple. She used to buy a box of the famous Irish drink for Christmas; a stocking filler from the kids. That was when she still loved him of course. Funny how the little things stuck in your mind, as a constant reminder of happier times.

"Here," she slid it across the bar, watching as he caught it with one hand. Malcolm was staring his way with a frown. *Yes, he annoys me too,* she thought sourly.

"Bostin," he commented after draining half of the glass, "just what you need after a day's hard work."

Juliette raised her eyebrows, choosing to remain silent, waiting for him to tell her the real reason behind his visit.

"I want to take the kids ice skating," he announced, wiping froth from his lips.

"Ice skating?" Juliette was surprised, tension mounting inside her.

"Why not? It should be fun, I'll take them for a burger afterwards too, so you don't have to cook."

"That's very altruistic of you," she answered.

"What?" He shook his head, staring defiantly, "I've got rights Jules. I want to see my kids!"

Juliette felt her stomach clench into a tight knot of anxiety. She didn't want Harry and Molls to go ice skating with their Dad, she didn't want them going anywhere with him. Was she being selfish, too over protective? He was quiet as a mouse as he waited for an answer.

"I'll think about it," she murmured, feeling miserable. The happiness from earlier had vanished, now replaced by a gloomy cloud of responsibility, decision making and fear. Yes, she was afraid, scared that they would be let down yet again; they were young and fragile, needed protecting. But they also had a right to see their Dad, she knew that much to be true.

"I want to take them next weekend Jules. Why don't you come too?" His hand hovered next to hers.

Uh-oh, was this all part of his little plan to get them back together; operation family reunion. NO WAY!

"I won't be coming," she said crisply, pulling away from him, "I'll speak to Harry and Molly and let you know, okay?"

"Okay," he seemed happy with that. As she served Malcolm again, he scribbled his telephone number down on a beer mat. "This is my new mobile," he said, thrusting it at her, "give me a call babes."

She bristled at his term of endearment. I'm not your 'babe', she wanted to shout at his departing figure. At the door he turned to throw her a provocative wink, then he was gone, banging the door behind him.

"Bad penny that one," Malcolm commented, tipping his hat.

"I know Malcolm, I know," she shook her head sadly, "but he was good once." She shuffled back towards her stool and immersed herself once more in her perfect world of books.

\* \* \*

Will had even surprised himself, by rising at seven o'clock Monday morning. His normal ten hour sleep had been interrupted by thoughts of Hema and university. After tossing and turning, he had snapped off his alarm, had breakfast with his stunned parents, taken Ruby for a stroll then cadged a lift off his mom into the city centre. Flora was on the way to purchase her big monthly shop. Will recited a list of foods he needed in his life: Dorito's, pizza, curly fries and Dime bars – his all time favourite.

"You really should have some fruit," Flora berated, as she peered up with uncertainty at the blue and white road traffic signs.

"Is it left or right?" She wondered aloud.

"That way," Will pointed to a fork in the road. Flora was ambidextrous; left meant right and right meant left. It was easier to show her, especially when there was a huge haulage truck on their tail lights, beeping impatiently.

"What are you up to today?" He asked, wincing as she slammed on the brakes.

"Erm, shopping, housework, then I'm volunteering at the day centre."

"Oh," Will yawned and stretched his legs, "sounds exciting."

Flora cast him a sideways glance, "I've told you Will, I'm very happy. You'll realise when you're older and have a family of your own."

"No thanks," he spluttered, "no kids for me! I want to enjoy life."

Flora sighed, but remained silent.

"You can drop me here Mom, I'll walk the rest of the way." He unfolded himself from the car and watched as Flora chugged off up the road. How had she managed to pass her test? He thought, with a bemused shake of his head.

He swung his bag over his shoulder and trudged through the early morning mist. His rucksack was heavy, full of library books that needed returning. He had completed the Language essay over the weekend. Jimmy had been out with Sadie, Will had been stuck at home. It was either watch weepy black and white movies with Flora, or help his dad with a spot of DIY. So Will had escaped to his bedroom and worked like a Trojan, plugging in his iPod, with his phone on standby – just in case he heard from Hema. She remained elusive, not even active on Facebook. Jimmy had text him, asking if he fancied a double date with Sadie and Rachel.

"No way," had been Will's emphatic reply. The only girl he was interested in was Hema. She was still refusing to answer his texts however. Maybe he should cool it, he thought as he crossed the busy city centre street. Give her some space, yes he decided, that's exactly what he would do. Play it cool, then hopefully she would miss him, and realise that what they had was special. As he neared the university, he found himself looking for her, searching through the hordes of females, for a girl with beautiful, long, dark hair and golden eyes.

In the library he saw Evelyn, she was at a self-service machine, clumsily scanning a pile of books back in. He liked Evelyn, she reminded him a lot of his mom: sweet, shy and nervous.

"Hi Evelyn," he greeted.

She spun around with a shocked look on her face, "oh hello Will, how are you?"

He noticed the pink blush creeping into her cheeks and felt an overwhelming urge to protect her.

"I'm good thanks, are you heading to the canteen?"

Evelyn nodded, "yes, I haven't had breakfast this morning. Mam didn't sleep well; she's got a chest infection. I didn't like leaving her today."

"You look tired," Will noted her pale face and heavy eyes.

"I'll be okay," she shrugged, smiling at him brightly, "and where's your lady friend this morning?"

"We're not together anymore," he mumbled, shifting from foot to foot.

"Oh no," Evelyn replied, sympathy etched amongst the lines on her face, "do you want to talk about it. I'm a good listener, I mean, only if you want to of course."

"It's okay, I'm cool," he squashed the pang of longing he felt for Hema and held out his arm, "let's go get you some breakfast."

Juliette and Ann were seated at a corner table. Ann was engrossed in 'Moby Dick', while Juliette was eating croissants, crumbs flying everywhere. While Evelyn queued for food, Will sauntered over, flinging his rucksack down on an empty chair.

"Morning folks," he greeted cheerfully, eyes scanning the canteen. Juliette grinned, waved up at him, while Ann nodded and mumbled 'hello.'

"Have you finished your language essay?" Juliette asked, licking residues of butter from her fingertips.

Will nodded, "two days early too," he patted his folder, a proud look on his face.

Ann looked up, "I'm still tidying mine up," she admitted, "my weekend has been rather busy."

"We should get our essays back today," Juliette said, with a nervous smirk, "hope it's good news for everyone." They watched across the canteen, as a large table of lecturers laughed and chatted. Ben Rivers was sitting beside Helena Mulberry, their heads bent close together as they conversed. Juliette swallowed as her eyes raked over him. He was wearing dark brown today, teamed with a sparkling white shirt. His hair was sticking up again and there was a line of dark stubble covering his jaw. The messy look suited him. It was ridiculous how attractive he was, thought Juliette. She sipped at her coffee, then spluttered when she noticed Melanie the note taker appear at the side of him, chattering away, while she glanced mischievously across at Juliette.

"Er, shall we go to class?" Juliette said nervously, averting her eyes. They waited for Evelyn to finish her bacon sandwich then filed out of the canteen. A flustered Sophie was waiting at the lift, jabbing the button impatiently.

"Hi guys," she beamed, tossing her hair to one side.

Ann moved forward, "hello Sophie, how was your weekend?"

"Oh, erm fine... thanks."

Juliette watched the awkward exchange as tension crackled like electricity in the air.

Sophie began chattering, telling them about her voluntary position at the secondary school.

"I'm so excited," she gushed, "It's going to be so totally cool to help with the English lessons."

"That sounds interesting dear," Evelyn backed out of the lift, "is that what you definitely want to do?"

"I think so," Sophie replied, "I'm just going for the experience really, before I apply for any teacher training courses."

"Have you considered primary teaching?" Ann asked casually.

Sophie held the door open for Ann to enter the classroom, "no, not really. I thought a degree in English would be more beneficial to the older children."

"It's a major part of the primary curriculum too," Juliette said with a smile, "and the nice part of Primary teaching is, that you get to cover other subjects too."

"Yes, you're right. I hadn't thought about it to be honest," Sophie replied.

"My dad's a primary head teacher," Will supplied, as they took seats in the classroom, "always stressed now he's management, but he used to love the teaching side of the job, you know, being with the kids."

"I love being with the children," Juliette admitted happily, "every day is different. Teaching is such an exciting, rewarding, career – but I definitely want to work in the Primary sector. Teenagers, ughh, no way." She pulled a face and shook her shoulders, making Sophie laugh.

Evelyn was arranging her folder and listening with interest, "why not do some voluntary in a primary school as well Sophie. It would give you further experience, which would look good on your CV and also help make your mind up." She punched holes through last week's lecture notes, before organising them neatly.

"Oh, I'm not sure," Sophie replied, chewing her lip with uncertainty.

"I could arrange it for you," Will cut in helpfully, "Dad's school is nearby. They have students and volunteers there all the time. Want me to ask for you?"

"Would you Will?" Sophie asked, beaming widely, "that would be wonderful if you could."

"No problem, I'll sort it this evening." He snapped off his phone as Brian Hodges strode into the classroom.

"Hi folks," the lecturer boomed, plonking down reams of handouts and grabbing the Smartboard pen. The whole class craned their neck to see what he was writing.

"Modernism," his voice reverberated as he underlined the word with a flourish and a smiley face. "Did you good people know, that there is an awesome module on this specific literary movement which is led by non-other than yours truly? And I'm on commission, so make sure you sign up for it!" A titter spread around the room. "For now we are going to skim over it super fast and try to cram the basics into three hours."

Juliette glanced at the door.

"He'll be in soon," Melanie whispered, with a wink.

"Oh, erm…I," Juliette felt heat infuse her cheeks and neck, but was saved from answering by the interruption of Ann.

"Excuse me Dr Hodges, before you begin, are our essays due back today?"

Fifty pairs of eyes looked his way with expectation and relief that someone had broached the subject.

"What essays?" He spun around, a puzzled look on his face.

"Do you mean these?" A different voice replied, deep melodic, sending shivers down Juliette's back. Acutely aware of Melanie sitting close by and no doubt watching her every move, Juliette continued to stare at Brian Hodges. Damn it, Juliette thought, how could I be so stupid? Who else had noticed this ridiculous crush? How totally hilarious; a grown woman with two young children, besotted by a gorgeous, gay heart throb. Ha ha, very funny – time to get over this, she berated herself.

"What those old things?" Brian Hodges was playing along with his friend, teasing the students unmercifully, "forget about those, Modernism is much more interesting, don't you all agree? Now where was I?" He fiddled with the tip of his beard while murmurs of discontent spread around the class.

"Please, put them out of their misery," Melanie pleaded, with a soft chuckle.

"What, so you want them now?" Dr Hodges asked in surprise. There was a loud chorus of 'yes please' and a few irritated shouts of 'come on, get it over with.'

Ben Rivers casually strolled forward, "shall we have a vote Brian?" He asked. Juliette could hear the laughter in his voice and gulped – does he know too? Has he had a good laugh over her with Melanie and the other lecturers? She could just imagine it; Juliette Harris, one of many students who fancied the pants off him. How very boring, how very predictable!

"Hands up who wants their essay," Ben folded his arms and watched as a sea of arms shot upwards. All apart from Juliette's, who was too busy simmering with embarrassment to pay full attention to the comedic sparring that was going on.

Ben walked over, catching her eye with his penetrative gaze.

"Would you rather go straight to Modernism?" He asked gently, his eyes twinkling merrily, "I will if you want me to."

"No... I mean, I'd like my essay back too," Juliette fiddled with her pen as a distraction. He gazed down at her and she stared back at him defiantly. *What do you want?* She longed to yell. *Why are you always staring at me?* A hush had descended on the room and Juliette could see Brian Hodges from the corner of her eye, staring their way. She really didn't care.

"What is your name?" Ben asked quietly.

"Juliette," she whispered. He placed the pile of essays in front of her and leafed through them, until he found hers, a quarter of the way down.

He glanced over it with a smile, "you did well," he commented, handing over the bound paper.

"Thanks," she replied, pulling the essay. It remained steadfast in his hands and she gazed at him with puzzlement.

Then he was leaning forward, so his mouth was a few inches from her ear. "Your name is beautiful."

Juliette's stomach lurched in surprise and raw emotion. She fidgeted in her seat, bringing her face closer to his. Oh God she wanted him, she had never experienced this level of attraction for anyone, it was overwhelming. Just as she was seriously close to losing all inhibitions; yanking his tie and kissing him ardently, he had gone, leaving her feeling bereft and frustrated.

Juliette closed her eyes for a moment, breathing deeply until she felt herself relax, then she looked down at her marked essay and it was though a thousand stars had burst around her. Wow! She had been awarded a B12, how fantastic! She stared with glee at the pages in front of her, flicking through them to speed read the comments scribbled in green biro, dotted around the margins. Evelyn had been marked marginally better – a B13, top in the category. She clutched Juliette's arm, beaming with happy delight.

"Oh my," she exclaimed, "we have done so well Juliette."

Ann was next, ecstatic to have an 'A' emblazoned across the top of her essay. Melanie threw her arms around her, hugging her tightly.

Will was surprised but pleased to be marked a top 'C'. With all the turmoil and distraction, his first essay had been completed hastily over two evenings, he thought that he would fail it for sure. Mom will be overjoyed, he thought with a happy grin. Only Sophie looked downcast.

"I only got a 'D'," she lamented, clutching her essay to her bosom, away from prying eyes, "where have I gone wrong?" Brian Hodges peered at her over horn rimmed spectacles.

"We will be happy to discuss it with you," he said, in a sympathetic, friendly manner. Sophie looked sad and dubious.

"Or alternatively," he continued quickly, "you can discuss it with your personal tutor. Who have you got?"

Sophie mumbled her name.

"Oh yes, Doctor Mulberry is a real gem and will give you great advice. Isn't that right Ben?" He glanced at Ben for affirmation, who was busy distributing the rest of the essays and appeared not to have heard him. Sophie swallowed and looked Ann's way despondently.

"Don't worry," Ann said bluntly, "this is your first essay, you can learn from it and apply it to your next work."

"Yeah, don't stress Soph," Will piped up, "I'm only a few points ahead of you. Everything's cool though, this *is* only the first year."

"I suppose so," Sophie began flicking through the paper, wincing at the spelling and grammar marks and the inky slashes, "what am I doing here?" She whispered. Maybe Ryan had been right to have reservations. Maybe Mom's disapproval had been warranted. Could she really do three more years of this? Ann was watching her, "speak to your personal tutor," she urged, "they are there to help and guide you."

Evelyn rubbed Sophie's arm in consolation, "they also run an essay writing workshop you know dear, for first year students." Sophie blinked away the tears and thanked her friends.

After the excitement had abated and all the students had received their first grades, the lecture started. Ben and Brian took it in turns to speak on the subject of Modernism, it was a lively and engaging lecture. The minutes ticked by, soon it was time for a quick break, then they carried on for another hour before finishing with a quick seminar where they discussed some of the great Modernist writers: Virginia Woolf, T.S Eliot and Ezra Pound. Ann had enjoyed the lecture immensely and was buzzing after receiving such a good grade. As Melanie scribbled the notes down, her eyes were constantly drawn to her marked work. At break time she had text Jon to inform him of the good news. He had replied with an enlarged YIPEE – WELL DONE! And lots of celebratory icons. During the seminar, Ann had sparked a lively debate on Woolf and feminism which even had the lecturers impressed.

"Excellent debate," Brian Hodges commented as they were packing their belongings away, "your argument was informative, knowledgeable and articulate. I look forward to hearing more from you Ann."

Evelyn had hung back slightly as the students streamed out of the classroom. She wanted to approach Ben Rivers about her novel but felt overwhelmed by a crippling shyness and insecurity. As she was pondering what to do, he looked her way and smiled. She was just about to speak, when a plump lady with curly, blonde hair, bustled past her to commandeer his attention. *Another time*, Evelyn thought, *there was no rush*. She joined the others as they made their way to the canteen, where they enjoyed a lovely lunch.

Will was chomping on a baguette when he saw her. Hemi had entered the room, surrounded by her student buddies. She hadn't noticed him, but he saw her checking her phone a few times. He peered at her and noticed that she looked pale and tired and her frame seemed to have shrunk slightly. He gulped down a mouthful of soda, then rushed to intercept her at the Pizza Station.

"Hi," he greeted casually. Hema spun around, her face lighting when she saw him.

"Hello Will, how are you?" They exchanged polite pleasantries, when all he wanted to do was grab her and hold her tight against his firm chest.

"Why haven't you returned my messages?" He asked, his voice raspy.

"I've been…busy…with uni work, sorry."

"Oh," he stuffed his hands in his pockets and let out a frustrated sigh, "are you going to the staff/student Christmas party?"

"Yes," Hema nodded, looking up at him with wide, unfathomable eyes, "it sounds good."

"You mean your parents are letting you go?" There was a twang of incredulous bitterness in his voice, which made Hema wince.

"Yes," she snapped, pulling her folders tight against her, "it really isn't your concern any- more."

Will felt as if he had been slapped, boy that hurt.

"Fine," he replied, voice rising, "hope you have a great time."

"You too," she replied angrily, flouncing off across the canteen. He shook his head, *no more texts* he decided with determination.

Back at the table they were discussing the Christmas night out.

"So then," Ann asked, "it's a Chinese first, then the disco?" Everyone agreed. Evelyn looked a lit- tle nervous, but she was still smiling. Will's eyes darted to where Hema was seated. He was irked to see her next to that sleazy guy who always seemed to be following her around. They were chatting and laughing, which fuelled the anger inside of him. He clenched his fists with fury, then sprang to his feet.

"Excuse me," he scraped the chair back and stormed to the exit. The toilets were down a flight of stairs, not far from the Student Union bar. As he stood at the chalk coloured urinal, he noticed a flyer stuck lopsided to the mirror.

'Looking for part time work??

Job opportunities in the Student Union bar.

Variety of shifts available.

Recruiting NOW!

Don't delay, call in today.'

*Don't delay indeed*, he thought, as he washed his hands and flattened his quiffed hair. This job sounded ideal for extra money, he thought with excitement and he would also have the opportunity to socialise; meet new people. The bar was down another long flight of steps that led to a large room decorated in purple and blacks, with music memorabilia dotted on the walls. There was a lady jabbing a hoover underneath two pool tables, and as he walked further in, he noticed small groups of people lounging across the settees and over the tables. It was much quieter then the busy canteen, but there was a cool, welcoming ambience to it. Will stood at the bar and waited for a guy with green hair and facial piercings to finish serving drinks to an enamoured couple.

"Can I help you mate?" He had a distinct Australian twang to his voice. Will told him the reason for his visit.

"Yeah, we need someone straight away mate. Have you ever worked a bar before?"

"No," Will replied, "But I'm a fast learner."

That was it then, he was offered the job on a trial run. His career as a bar man had begun. Will would work a standard sixteen-hour week with overtime thrown in during the busy periods. He helped Wayne the barman, pull a crate of alcopops to the fridge.

"See you Wednesday," Wayne said with a shake of Will's hand, "we'll break you in gently, ready for the weekend rush." Will grinned and took the stairs two at a time, feeling optimistic about the future. It would take his mind off Hema and maybe he could start saving now for his one-way ticket around the world.

I am never coming back, he thought with determination.

# Chapter Eighteen

The morning at Allhallows had been a complete disaster from start to finish. First of all, Sophie had got lost, taken the wrong turn and ended up at a further education college instead of a secondary school. When she finally arrived, half an hour late, the receptionist had snootily informed her that registration had begun, so she would have to wait now until Mrs Brown was free. Once in the classroom, thirty pairs of bored, rebellious eyes had stared her way, studying her like she was prey. By attempting to ingratiate herself with the students, or young adults as they liked to be called, Sophie had dropped a clanger. A year ten, pleasant looking girl, had struck up a conversation. Although she seemed to have little interest in the subject of English.

"What's your name Miss?" She asked, popping bubble gum loudly, "where do you live? How old are you?" Sophie answered the questions with a bright smile until Mrs Brown had drawn her to one side, "don't give out any personal information," she had advised with a shake of her head. Sophie had taken note and attempted to instigate a conversation on the comprehension which they should be studying. A paper plane had flown her way, hitting her on the cheek and eliciting sniggers from the table.

After break, the pupils were even worse. A leather clad youth had asked her if she knew what an expletive was.

"Er...no," Sophie had replied nervously.

"Fuck you Miss."

The class had erupted into raucous laughter. Mrs Brown had slammed her book down on the table and given everyone detention. Bad manners and insolence, she had written on the Smartboard, "this is why," she had shrieked. This punishment did little to endear her to the 'young adults,' who spent the rest of the morning darting daggers at her and using various parts of their anatomy to convey rude gestures. By lunchtime, Sophie felt mentally exhausted and followed the English teacher to the sanctuary of the staffroom, thankful that she could go home shortly.

"Would you like a coffee?" Mrs Brown asked, as she tipped a huge heap into a 'Best Teacher' mug. Sophie eyed the frothy, dark liquid with a queasy, hot feeling. Her blood pressure was high; she was sure of it. She could feel a throb pulsing in her neck and she felt lightheaded and woozy.

"No, thank you... I've got water," she tugged a bottle from the depths of her handbag and took a large swig. Sophie looked around, searching for somewhere to sit. The staffroom was full, but she managed to squeeze onto a rickety chair, which was wedged into the corner.

"You're still alive then?" A tall man, dressed in a flamboyant tweed suit approached her.

Sophie laughed nervously, "oh yes, just about."

"I thought you might have run screaming by now," he chuckled, taking a large bite of Victoria Sponge. The smell of coffee in the room was acrid. They must all be totally hyper thought Sophie with disapproval. Although she acknowledged that she herself loved a cup of coffee upon rising, there was a limit which seemed to be lacking at Allhallows Secondary School. There was definitely a caffeine overload going on in here, thought Sophie as she watched the chatting staff members. Almost everyone in the staffroom was clutching Costa Coffee cups or flasks of bitter smelling liquid.

Sophie was just formulating a suitable, witty reply, when the tweed clad man abruptly turned his back on her to begin conversing with a striking brunette lady. *How rude* Sophie thought, tutting with annoyance. She listened as they began talking loudly of learning objectives and the National Curriculum.

Just then Mrs Brown appeared at her side and began reciting an outline of what the class would be learning the next time she was due in. Apparently, they were studying Doctor Jekyll and Mr Hyde.

"I can loan you my copy if you would like to read up on it," her tone was generous and conciliatory, after the torment of the unruly teenagers. Sophie paused, *was I even coming back?* she thought indignantly.

"It's okay, I can grab a copy out of the uni library. Er... I'll be off now then," she rose hastily, smoothing down her pencil skirt. As she did, a suited trainee teacher darted behind her, nabbing her seat. As they walked down to reception, Mrs Brown talked animatedly of her time at university. Sophie tried to convey interest, but the noise around her was distracting, the corridors were full of yelling teenagers and harassed looking teaching staff. She felt herself being shoved from behind and dropped her designer bag with a loud clatter, the contents spreading on the floor in a heap.

"Detention Kevin Dickson," Mrs Brown screeched, as Sophie shoved keys and makeup back inside.

"I have to go Mrs..."

"O'Neill," Sophie supplied.

"Yes, please excuse me, I have a lunchtime art club I assist with and I'm late already. Shall I see you Thursday?" She stared at Sophie keenly, who didn't have the heart to refuse her.

Once outside, Sophie breathed in the fresh air with large gasps. *Thank goodness for that*, she thought with relief, any longer and she may have had a panic attack. Maybe she needed to rethink her career plans. Suddenly there was a noise from one of the windows directly above her. Sophie looked up to see what the commotion was. Seconds later a cricket ball burst into the air, shattering the glass, narrowly missing her head and rolling at her feet.

A young lad tore out of nowhere, "thanks Miss," he hollered, snatching up the ball with a cheeky grin. Sophie's hands flew to her throat in consternation, while the receptionist appeared and began yelling "suspension."

Was this school really only ten miles away from her home? The behaviour was appalling, or was that endemic now throughout all Secondary's? Sophie thought back to when she was a teenager, she was pretty certain that it hadn't been this bad when *she* was at school. Now she was growing concerned for Josh and Jake's future. They won't be coming here, that's for sure, she mumbled to herself.

Feeling thoroughly drained, Sophie dug in her bag for her car keys and jabbed the alarm release button. Her four by four was gleaming in the afternoon sunshine. She had asked Ryan to clean it for her, who in turn had persuaded Derek to take it to the garage for a full valet. Whatever, it was looking good. As she neared it, she could almost see her slim silhouette, reflecting off the shiny paintwork. Then she happened to look down and was flabbergasted to see that her tyre was completely flat. *What the hell*, she thought with dismay, *I have to get out of this awful place.* She snapped on her phone; great, no signal. Feeling panicky she stalked back into reception, to ask for assistance. A kind, PE teacher came to her rescue, peering gravely down, then declaring that the tyre had in fact been slashed.

"Slashed?" Sophie had spluttered, overcome with rage, "how dare they vandalise my car!" The head teacher had been called out of an important meeting. He took one look at the damage and had begun bellowing how this unlawful incident would be dealt with most severely in the next whole school assembly.

"We'll find the villain," he had ranted, citing suspension and even permanent exclusion.

"Do you know who I am?" Sophie asked, still smarting with anger. When she revealed she was married to one of the top Midland football strikers, the head teacher looked as if he were going to keel over in shock. His main concern changed from outrage on her behalf, to anxiety that the school would be prosecuted and its failing reputation totally annihilated by the Press. He ushered her into his office, where she could "use his phone in privacy."

"The RAC will be here in half an hour," she informed him reprovingly. An overworked looking PA brought her tea, biscuits and a handful of glossy magazines.

"So you want to be a secondary school teacher?" Mr Jameson was clearing his throat, searching for ways to placate his reluctant guest.

"Not anymore," Sophie decided crisply, "of that I'm sure."

When the recovery man arrived, Sophie addressed the head teacher haughtily.

"I won't be coming back, but I will be forwarding you the bill." With that she flounced out of his office, down the litter strewn path and headed for home.

* * *

Evelyn was administering antibiotics to Nora the following day. It was wet and miserable. The wind howled outside, rattling the windows, whipping up mounds of leaves and tossing them high in the air. Evelyn had risen early to see to Mam, teeth chattering as the heating had broken *again.* She had a polo neck *and* a pullover on, to try to combat the cold. Mam looked tiny in the bed underneath two thick duvets. The house was freezing, the windows clogged with mist and rainwater. Mam coughed, her whole body shaking, while Evelyn patted her back and leant her forward. She was worried about Nora, the chest infection had a nasty grip on her, she had subsequently been coughing throughout the night and Evelyn had been in and out of bed, fetching water, taking her to the toilet and worrying over her. By four o'clock Evelyn had decided to sleep in the chair. Now her back was aching and her arms were numb, eyelids drooping from the exertion of staying awake all night. But Mam looked even worse. This morning she looked frail and exhausted, her eyes were sunken and her pallor was grey. Evelyn checked her temperature, the same as last night, slightly raised but not an emergency. Hopefully the medicine would soon start working and Nora would be fit as a fiddle again.

There was no uni today, which was a relief to Evelyn, she could stay home and fuss over Mam and if there was no improvement by tomorrow, then she would be on the telephone to Doctor Dunn, insisting on a home visit. That thought reminded her to call a boiler engineer. She was leafing through the business directory when the doorbell chimed loudly throughout the house. Evelyn hurried down the stairs, smoothing her hair, realising that she hadn't had a chance to comb it yet. She was surprised to see Jacob on the doorstep, with his council bus, rumbling behind him.

"Oh gosh Jacob! Mam won't be coming to the day centre today, she's not well. Sorry, I didn't think to ring and let you know." Evelyn was flustered and embarrassed that he had wasted a journey. He removed his cap, gazing her way with kind eyes.

"It's okay Evelyn. I hope Nora feels better soon. Can I do anything to help?"

Evelyn blushed, "are you any good at fixing heating boilers?" She asked hopefully.

"I used to be a heating engineer," he disclosed gently, "let me take a look at it."

Jacob worked quickly and with expertise, his fingers flying over the protruding pipes and switches. The boiler burst into life with a bang and Evelyn felt her shoulders droop with relief. She thanked him profusely.

"Anytime," he said warmly, "happy to help and Evelyn, please let me know if you need help with anything else."

Evelyn felt her cheeks burn like molten lava, "th-thank you Jacob," she stuttered. I'm sure everything will be okay now."

"I hope your Mam feels better very soon," he said with a chivalrous bow.

"Yes, hopefully," Evelyn replied, "it's a nasty infection, but the changeable weather doesn't help either does it?"

"You're right there," he agreed.

They stood in the doorway. Evelyn really felt she should offer him something in way of payment, but he refused to accept any money from her. On the spur of the moment, she asked him for lunch. Jacob was surprised but pleased to be asked and agreed graciously.

"See you later then Evelyn," her name felt like a soft whisper in the air and Evelyn trembled slightly.

Evelyn spent the rest of the morning on housework; hovering, dusting, emptying bins, the chores seemed never ending. She was nervous of Jacob's impending visit and berated herself for acting so impulsively. It was too late for reservations now, a voice inside argued, best just make the most of it and Jacob had been so very kind. So for lunch she made a delectable cold buffet: sandwiches, quiche, pasta salad and pork pie. Then dug in the freezer to defrost a lemon cheesecake. A pretty checked tablecloth lit up the table, with a bowl of sweet smelling potpourri sprinkled in the middle. When Mam heard that Jacob was coming for lunch, she struggled to sit up, with a happy smile on her face.

"How lovely dear, have you put the best table-cloth out?"

"Yes, yes," Evelyn soothed, passing her a glass of fresh water.

"Is this a date Evelyn?" Nora asked, with a cheeky wink.

Her daughter laughed, "no Mam, it's just a thank you."

Nora chuckled, which led to a coughing fit, "rest now Mam, I'll leave the door ajar and keep checking on you – okay?"

The doorbell chimed again, for the second time today. Evelyn hurried down the creaking stairs, pausing at the mirror to apply a line of lipstick. He was there, exactly on time, looking smart and carrying a large bouquet of pretty flowers.

"You didn't need to get those," Evelyn remonstrated, "it should be me buying you things."

"Nonsense," Jacob replied warmly, "you deserve them Evelyn."

"Thank you!" She took them from him with a wide grin, "I'm so grateful that you could fix my boiler." She led him through to the kitchen, hurrying to deposit the flowers in a lavender painted vase.

"It was my pleasure Evelyn. Here," he thrust a scrap of paper at her awkwardly, "this is my number. If you ever need any help, advice or just someone to chat to, please call me."

Evelyn blushed, but took it with a grateful smile.

They enjoyed a lovely lunch, chatting and laughing, washed down with copious amounts of tea. Jacob even popped up to say hello to Mam, who was thrilled to see him. After a hearty piece of cheesecake, Jacob reluctantly declared he should be leaving.

"I have to take the bus in for a service," he explained, "but thank you for a lovely lunch." At the foot of the stairs, he shouted a cheery goodbye to Mam, who responded in kind. Then his voice dipped to a whisper.

"Evelyn," he began, fiddling with his cap, "would you care to accompany me for a meal one evening?"

"Oh," Evelyn was shocked, unsure of how to respond.

Jacob stared at her intently, "just a nice get to-gether, between two friends."

Evelyn breathed shakily, "o-okay Jacob, I think that would be lovely."

The arrangements were made for some time over Christmas. Evelyn would contact him with a suitable date. Jacob walked up the path, with a broad smile on his face and a spring to his step. Evelyn watched him go, then closed the door, leant against it and wondered again if she had acted wisely. Yet he had stressed it was just friendship. She shook the reservations aside, as she climbed the stairs, to tell Mam the good news.

* * *

The weeks rolled by and Christmas loomed nearer. The city burst into colour; thousands of twinkling lights and flashing seasonal figurines that warmed the cockles of even the hardest of hearts. The shops flooded with consumers, late night shopping kicked in, with crowds of people visiting the Christmas outdoor market. Hot pork sandwiches, mulled wine and gift stores vied for attention. Ann and Jon had completed and sent off their adoption application form and now waited for the New Year, so they could proceed with police checks, medical examinations and reference testimonials. Juliette was busy with reading lists, taking care of the children, working and trying to fit it all in. Yet she was happy; trooping on with the support of family. Marty was still pestering her, he had taken the children ice-skating, but had to return them home early, as Molly had slipped on the ice and sustained a nasty gash to her knee. He was taking them to the cinema soon and had endeavoured to include Juliette in his plans. She had stoutly refused, keeping him at arm's length was the best course of action for both herself and the children. Harry was still antagonistic towards his dad, but reluctantly agreed to trail along with an exuberant Molly.

Sophie had been to see her personal tutor. Helena Mulberry had proceeded to lecture her of the importance of essay planning, time management and organisational skills. The next essays were due in January. Sophie dutifully began them early; making notes, reading extensively, undertaking research. She even turned down a Katy Perry tribute night at the Golf Club with Amber. Sophie had been mortified to receive another 'D' in her language essay and had hidden the results from Mom and Ryan in shame. Her husband had been livid after the debacle at Allhallows Secondary and even more enraged at the damage to his car. Sophie just wanted to forget the whole sorry incident and decided that secondary school teaching was definitely not for her. She was grateful to Will for finding a place for her at his father's school and made plans for a successful experience this time; reading up on behaviour management and the KS2 curriculum. She was off there this morning, with a feeling of excited trepidation. Teaching was a hard job! Anyone who thought otherwise must be foolish indeed. Yes, the holidays were great, but the stress was phenomenal! The thought crossed her mind that she should attempt to root out another career, but Evelyn had been so kind and encouraging, telling her not to blame herself, that she had decided to give it one more go with primary teaching. So here she was, indicating off the main road, with butterflies twirling around in her stomach and a tight knot of anxiety in her chest. *Please let this school be nice*, she thought with a sigh.

Sophie slowly crawled up the drive, carefully swinging her car around tubs of winter pansies that led to the front of the school. She smiled in delight at the huge welcome sign that hung over the doorway of St Mary's. It really was pretty, she thought, as she peered out of her window at vibrant hanging baskets and golden honeysuckle that weaved up a trellis. The sun was shining high in the sky, it bathed the building in luminous light. Sophie rubbed the glass, peering up at the huge cross on top of the building. Wow! She thought, as a feeling of awe overtook her, this is perfect. Suddenly, there was a loud rap on her door which made Sophie jump in surprise. A tired looking man with a dirty, annoyed face stood by the side of her car.

Sophie pressed the button, gulping as the window slid downwards.

"Hiya," she beamed, "you okay?"

"You can't park here," he snapped, "this space is reserved for Mr Bentley."

"Oh right Will's Dad yeah? Erm... isn't he here? I think he should be expecting me."

"How should I know?" The man shrugged impatiently, "he's probably off on one of his head teacher conferences; drinking tea and eating tuna sandwiches."

"And you are?" Sophie asked, wrinkling her nose as she caught sight of his long, black, fingernails.

"Caretaker," he replied brusquely, "you can park there," he pointed towards a patch of driveway, sheltered by a Weeping Willow.

"Will do, thanks er... Mr Caretaker," Sophie smiled as the electric window slid upwards. The burly looking man grimaced then stalked off. *Jeez* Sophie thought, *what was that about*?

After careful manipulation of her four by four, Sophie managed to squeeze into the tight space. She clambered out, smoothing down her woollen dress, then tottered forward on her killer heels, passing the caretaker, who was bent over a patch of soil, tugging at a group of wilting dandelions.

As she clacked up the drive, she could hear the sound of children shouting, screaming, laughing and guessed it must be break time. The doors slid open with a hiss, allowing her to step forward and wait at a glass fronted reception.

"Good morning," she inclined her head towards an attentive receptionist, "I'm here to see Mr Bentley."

"He's out at the moment, can anyone else help you?"

"Oh, well he was expecting me," she replied, feeling rather annoyed, "I'm Sophie O'Neill, Will, I mean Mr Bentley's son, has arranged for me to do some voluntary here."

The receptionist cocked her head to one side, then her face lit up in recognition.

"Yes, yes, he told me all about it. I'm afraid he is indisposed at the moment, but Mrs Bent the deputy is going to see you instead, please sit down," she motioned to a row of chairs behind her. Sophie perched on the seat, looking around her with interest. On the wall hung staff pictures, inside a huge papier-mache heart and a montage of children's artwork decorated the doorway. A laminated slogan stated, "we love our school and everybody in it." How lovely, Sophie thought, even the miserable caretaker was in there. Sophie noticed a beautiful porcelain figurine and guessed it was Mary, it really was striking, with fresh flowers laid around her feet. A nearby table held photo frames of various accolades and a signed plaque from an eminent clergy man, who had opened the school a while back. Sophie was impressed and stooped to lift a rose to her face. The fragrance was sweet, intoxicating. She noticed the receptionist watching her with a wary smile and dropped the flower in embarrassment.

"Mrs O'Neill I presume?" A head framed by tight, grey curls peeped around the door. Sophie spun around, hand outstretched, "that's me," she said with a grin.

"Come with me," the lady said breezily, as the door swung towards her. Sophie found herself almost running to keep up with the tall, trouser suited lady. The corridor was packed with children, hanging coats onto pegs. Sophie jigged around two boys who were play fighting with their scarves.

"Do you like Pokémon?" One asked, holding up a yellow Pikachu for her inspection. Sophie was just about to reply in the affirmative, when a formidable looking woman in knee high boots, appeared in the doorway and began bellowing. The children scattered to form a wobbly line, that snaked down the hallway.

"Mrs O'Neill!" Sophie jumped at the sound of her name. Mrs Bent stood in the doorway pointing, "this way please."

Sophie stumbled down the corridor and into the Deputy's office. She was sitting at a table, staring her way, with cold, grey eyes.

"Sit down," she said icily, motioning towards an empty chair opposite.

Sophie slid into the seat with a gulp, *why am I here*? She thought nervously.

"So, you're going to be doing some voluntary here, is that right?"

"Yes," Sophie began, feeling as if she were addressing a judge, "Mr Bentley's son Will has arranged it for me."

"Very well, may I see your CRB please?"

Sophie fumbled in her bag, pulled out the sheet and handed it over.

"Everything seems to be in order," Mrs Bent sniffed and handed the paper back, "however, I believe that you requested to go in year six?"

"Yes, that's right," Sophie confirmed.

"Not possible I'm afraid, the children and the teacher are preparing for Christmas plays, SATS, as well as a very important assembly. They really can't be distracted by a helper."

"Oh," Sophie's face fell.

"We do however have a space in the nursery, they would very much benefit from the extra help."

"Nursery!" Sophie exclaimed in dismay, lips flapping, "but I...I want to teach older children and my degree is in English. How is that going to benefit them or me?"

Mrs Bent leant across the table, "Mrs O'Neill, literacy is one of the most important areas of a child's learning, irrespective of age. Indeed, it could be argued that in the Early Years, it is even more important. It is then that literacy is formulated within a child's psyche you know and it is fair to say that language and communication is rather challenging at times for our younger pupils. I am sure that you would be an asset to our nursery," she smiled faintly, "now, now, come, let us go and I shall introduce you to the staff." She clapped her hands, spurring Sophie to her feet.

When they pushed open the door to the Nursery, Sophie felt as if she had wandered into Aladdin's Cave by mistake. The room was dazzling.

"Wow!" Sophie exclaimed, as she turned around, staring at the colourful walls, bright carpets and the beautiful glass wind chimes that hung from the ceiling.

"Oh, they're all outside," Mrs Bent remarked, as she peered out of the window, "we do encourage outdoor activities here as much as possible. The younger children thrive on it. It's just a pity this government doesn't seem inclined to extend it to the older children."

"Don't they get cold?" Sophie asked doubtfully.

"Nonsense. They have coats! Wind and fresh air kills the bugs you know." Mrs Bent paused to straighten a book which had fallen lopsided, "although I do admit that the wind can make the children a little, how can I phrase it, unruly."

Sophie thought of her own two children racing around the garden after falling leaves and nodded in agreement.

"Here they come now." They both turned to look out of the open doorway, as a long line of young children marched across the playground, led by a small dark haired lady.

"Ten green bottles sitting on the wall, ten green bottles sitting on the wall," she sang loudly, a chorus of out of pitch warbling accompanied her. Sophie took a step back, as children surged in, then proceeded to stomp into the coat room.

"Hello, I'm Cara, the nursery teacher." Now she was nearer, Sophie noticed how tiny she was. She had kind eyes and a beaming smile.

"This is erm… Mrs O'Neill, our new volunteer," Mrs Bent supplied helpfully.

Sophie took Cara's hand, shaking it warmly.

"Lovely to meet you! We sure need the help in here, my assistants are extremely overworked and underpaid, so an extra pair of hands is very much appreciated."

Mrs Bent stiffened, "of course the benefits of working in the Early Years is the very little marking. Key stage two is a challenging phase to teach by all accounts."

"Yes," Cara nodded, with a glint in her eye, "but then they don't have the observations to contend with."

Sophie smiled uncertainly, not entirely clear on the topic of conversation. There were vibes in the air too; awkward and hostile. She felt a layer of ice descend around her, but told Cara that she was happy to give it a go.

"Good, good," Mrs Bent smiled graciously, "I shall leave you in the nursery's capable hands," and with a nod, she turned on her heels and stalked out.

"Take no notice of her," Cara whispered, as soon as the door was closed, "she thinks she's perfect."

Once the children were settled on the carpet, Cara called their attention, "one, two, three, eyes on me." A hush descended across the room, tiny faces turned upwards towards their teacher.

"Well children, I am so pleased that you were so well behaved outside, I'm going to give you each a twinkly star, so give yourselves a pat on the back." A minute of chaos descended, as enthusiastic back slapping ensued. One child in particular was hitting others with exuberance.

"Now Betty, we don't hurt our friend's back do we?" Sophie smiled at the three-year-old, who obediently dropped her hand and folded them into her lap. Sophie sat gingerly down on the carpet, crossing her legs and pulling her skirt over her knees.

"We have a visitor today, she's going to be coming to help us in the nursery with our learning, so we must show her how special and well behaved we are." Lots of children nodded with wide eyes, while some looked bored and others picked their nose. "This lovely lady is called Mrs O'Neill, turn around children and say hello." The class turned to gaze her way. Sophie grinned widely, waving at them, feeling rather happy.

"Hello," she said hesitantly.

A chorus of greetings welcomed her.

"Are you a superstar?" A blond girl with pigtails asked, gazing up at her with wonder.

"No, but I wish I was," Sophie replied with a chuckle.

"I like your hair," another girl commented.

"Thank you," Sophie beamed, looking across at Cara with delight.

Now, now children," the nursery teacher clapped her hands, "we're going to do a little bit of art and a little bit of reading and some children can have the playdough and oh how lovely, Mrs King is making beautiful, twinkling stars in the corner and maybe, we can have the fairy castle and the cars out. Won't that be wonderful?"

"Yes, yes, yes," the children nodded and shouted with excitement. Cara called their names as she affixed stars to their jumpers, then sent them off to various activities.

"What would you like to do?" Cara asked, as she tugged at the construction mat.

"Erm," Sophie glanced around the room, eyes falling on the book corner, "can I read with the children?"

"Wonderful idea, if you can get them to sit still," the nursery teacher winked.

An hour passed quickly. Sophie had so much fun reading and playing with the children, they were absolutely adorable she thought, as they sat in a circle for fruit time. They ate juicy red apples and tomatoes that splattered over their clothes, most of the children drank milk, with Mrs King pouring pots of water for the others.

"Would you like a drink?" The teaching assistant asked. She disappeared into a tiny kitchen to brew two milky teas, then they sat and chatted with the children about what they would like off Father Christmas.

"Have you enjoyed it?" Cara asked with a kind smile, after all the children had left with parents and carers.

"Yes," Sophie replied in surprise, "I have. Would you like me to help two mornings per week, I'm free from uni then and have nothing else planned."

"That would be wonderful. Thank you so much," she began pegging the children's decorated stars to dry on a line.

Sophie watched with a puzzled frown, "can I just ask – are the head teacher and the deputy married?" She queried.

"Good heavens no! And don't let them hear you saying that," Cara replied, shaking off glitter with a laugh, "why do you ask?"

"Oh, erm," Sophie explained falteringly, "only I thought they had the same surname?"

Cara chuckled, looking at her fondly, "no, no, the head is Bentley, the deputy is Bent. Two different surnames."

Sophie blushed, "sorry, I didn't realise."

"That's okay, you don't need to apologise. I think we've all thought the same about those two."

"Oh," Sophie laughed, "well thank you for making me feel so welcome, I'm definitely going to be coming back."

She shook hands with the nursery staff, then headed for the door, while texting Amber to see if she was free for a shopping spree, before picking up the twins later.

# Chapter Nineteen

December blew in, bringing all sorts of weather: rain, sun, foggy mornings and biting cold. Juliette struggled through the crowds in the city centre wrapped in her old winter coat and furry boots. The carrier bags pinched her hands uncomfortably as she squeezed off the bus and walked quickly up the street towards home. Her feet were sore and her lips were cold. She licked them, expecting to feel icicles attached, her breath billowing out in clouds. A full moon hung in the sky and frost covered the ground in a silver sheen. She was thankful for the sturdy grip on her boots that prevented her from falling. A morning of cleaning and ironing, then followed by an afternoon of Christmas shopping had exhausted Juliette and she was due out tonight. It was the university staff / student Christmas party. She should be excited, but she felt flustered and a little bit queasy. It had been years since she had been on a night out without family. She knew Harry and Molly would be fine with their Aunty Maz, but she hated leaving them, especially when she could be warm and toasty inside with the TV on and presents to wrap. After hours of trawling the shops for suitable gifts, she longed to flop on the sofa with a cup of strong tea and to relax.

She couldn't quite believe that Christmas was only a few weeks away. She had allowed herself to be carried along by Sophie's exuberance over the impending night out. Now it was here she felt uneasy, nervous as hell and worried about who she may bump into tonight. A couple of evenings ago she had dreamt of Ben Rivers in glorious technicolour. He had been with his boyfriend; another gorgeous specimen and they had both been laughing at her. Oh the shame of possessing a crush on a lecturer. Sophie had to remind herself that she was an adult; a strong, independent woman, who didn't have time to be distracted by hot, gay, men. It was difficult though, especially when he stared at her with those un-nerving dark eyes and mesmerised her with his sexy voice. It left her feeling totally confused; maybe she was going out of her mind she thought with a gulp. Yes that was it, years of celibacy had finally made her crazy. She batted away thoughts of hot sex with Ben Rivers and pondered on the outfit she was going to wear this evening. That had been another worry. The idea of glamming herself up had crossed her mind, but then she thought about today's fashion. Everybody seemed to live in jeans for work and pleasure now, she didn't want to look old fashioned or even worse, desperate for male attention. So this morning, she had ironed her favourite denim, matching it with a sparkly top and hung it in her bedroom, ready to fling on.

Her maisonette was lit up, like a towering beacon in the night sky. Christmas lights twinkled in windows, neon signs wishing season's greetings flashed intermittently. Juliette smiled, tucking her chin underneath the warm, furry fabric. She loved this time of year, irrespective of the huge financial cost, the jostling crowds and the cheesy adverts. Christmas was magical. Most importantly it made Harry and Molly happy, she would worry about the financial fallout in January, along with millions of other families no doubt. Her children had been in hyper moods since December 1st, excitement coursing through them which would increase in the lead up to Christmas Day. This year, she was being more organised; shopping earlier and budgeting better. Today she had spent hours trawling around the shops, picking presents that hopefully they would love. She had even managed to find some gorgeous material, which she planned to transform into a diaphanous princess gown for Molly. But then thoughts of fairy-tale castles and balls disappeared as she neared the entrance to the maisonette. A group of youths slouched on bikes and scooters. She stepped around them, wincing at the sound of bubble gum popping and ignoring the pleas for her to buy them alcohol.

It was times like this she hated where she lived. She wondered what Sophie's house was like and if she had problems with the local hooligans. The concrete steps wound upwards, cold and grey. Juliette frowned at the garish graffiti splashed on the walls, the stench of urine and the cigarette butts littering the ground. The key was ready in her hand, but before she reached the door, it swung inwards and Marie stood blocking the light.

"Hi Maz," Juliette panted, as she passed her sister a few of the heavier shopping bags, "in my bedroom," she beckoned with her head and together they stuffed the carriers behind the wardrobe.

"Me and you need to have a chat sister,"

Juliette looked up in surprise at Maz, who was surveying her with hands on her hips.

"What have I done now?" She asked sheepishly.

"What's this?" Marie pointed an accusing finger at her outfit hanging precariously from the curtain pole.

"I'm wearing it tonight, why?" Juliette was puzzled by the look of distaste on her sister's face.

"That old thing?" Marie wrinkled her nose, "you're going to a party Jules. Your first party in years. You need to dress up a bit."

"But I…" Juliette protested.

"No buts," Marie decided crisply, "let's get you dolled up. It is Christmas after all, only comes once a year and all that."

Juliette protested, but her sister was adamant that she needed to make an effort.

"You might get lucky Jules. How long has it been since you've had sex?"

"What?" Spluttered Juliette, "I couldn't possibly pick some stranger up Maz! Besides the kids are here."

"Oh, didn't I tell you," Marie commented, as she searched the cupboards for different toiletries, "Harry and Molls are staying at mine for the night, so you can get drunk, fall over and have a proper lie in. Hubby is going to be picking you up too, so you don't have to come home alone. That's if you don't get lucky," she winked salaciously.

Juliette chose to ignore the innuendo, allowing herself to be ushered into the bathroom, arms full with an assortment of beauty products. There was shower crème to make your skin luxuriously smooth. A hair mask that guaranteed strength and shine. Moisturiser with added shimmer and of course a razor to defuzz. She sniffed the products, wondering how long they had been stacked in her dresser. Most of them were presents; she lacked the finances and motivation to indulge a beauty regime.

"And don't just use soap!" Marie snapped from outside the door.

It was all very time consuming, Juliette thought with irritation, as she exfoliated and cleansed, shampooed and conditioned. Once done, she wrapped herself in a Disney bath sheet, then padded into the bedroom, leaving a trail of wet footprints behind. Marie had tipped the contents of her meagre make up bag out and was bent over, rooting through the contents.

"How old is this mascara?" She asked, pulling the clumpy brush out for inspection.

"A few years," Juliette squeaked.

"Your eyelashes will fall out!" Marie said in outrage, "thank goodness I brought mine."

"I don't have time for make up," Juliette complained, as she sank gingerly down on the bed.

Marie shook her head, "comb your hair out, then we'll get started on your transformation."

The straighteners hissed for the final time, as Marie gently pulled them through the last section of hair.

"Oh wow, your hair is so beautiful," Marie stood back to survey her handiwork.

"Can I look?" Juliette asked, touching the smooth tresses that hung down her back.

"No! I'm doing your make up first." Marie plonked down on a stool, "close your eyes," she instructed. The minutes ticked by and she was almost finished.

"Have you got any darker lipstick then *candyfloss pink*?"

Juliette eyed her sister warily, "siren red, on the dresser."

She was applying it carefully, when Molly burst through the door, a ball of excitement, after watching 'Beauty and the Beast' for the tenth time. She was singing spiritedly, but stopped when she saw Juliette.

"Oh Mommy, you look so pretty!"

"Doesn't she just."

"Can I look yet?" Juliette asked, feeling impatient. The time was ticking by and she did not want to be late.

"I just need to add a few final touches." Marie was studying her sister, with her tongue dipped out of the corner of her mouth. She sent Molly back into the lounge to fetch her handbag.

"Luckily for you, I brought some body shimmer." She dabbed the brush in the glittery powder, then applied it in sweeping stokes across Juliette's shoulders and breastbone.

"Ta-da," Marie was staring at her sister with wide eyes, "bloomin eck Jules, you scrub up really well."

Molly nodded vigorously, "you look like a princess Mommy."

Marie laughed as her niece began bouncing on the bed, "you *shall* go to the ball! Now, what about a dress?"

"A dress?" Spluttered Juliette, "nobody wears a dress on a night out now-a-days."

"Of course they do," soothed Marie, as she banged the wardrobe doors open.

"Princesses have to," Molly said, with a serious frown.

"They can wear jeans too Molly," Juliette whispered with a wink.

Marie was rustling through her rail of clothes, "jeans, jeans, red t-shirt, blue t-shirt, purple t-shirt, jeez sister, maybe you are taking this student status a bit *too* far."

"I like to be comfortable," Juliette objected.

"Now you sound like a geriatric, you'll have your slippers warming by the fire next," Marie laughed. "Ah, here we are," she slipped her hand towards the back of the wardrobe, pulling out an exquisite black lace dress.

"Where was this from?" Demanded Marie.

"I...I bought it last year in the sales, if you must know, with my Christmas money."

"You don't need to justify spending money on yourself Jules. You deserve a treat. But wow, this is gorgeous." She held the lace, running her fingers across the soft material, "why haven't you worn it before now?"

Juliette pulled a face, "I haven't been anywhere that warranted it."

"Well now, tonight is the night. You are definitely going to pull with this on!" Marie laughed, "let's get you in it."

Juliette bit her lip, "I really don't think it's suitable."

"Please, try it on at least," Marie pleaded. She swung Molly up in her arms and waited outside the door, while Juliette reluctantly slipped it on.

"I'm wearing a warm shawl," Juliette warned. Marie rolled her eyes and playfully tweaked Molly's nose.

A few minutes passed before the door slowly opened and Juliette stood there looking scared to death.

"Well?" She asked her big sister and her daughter, searching their faces for signs of dislike.

Marie let out a low whistle, "wit woo, you are one foxy lady!"

"Really?" Juliette said, tugging at the hem of her dress. She wobbled slightly on her high heels. Four inches of pure pain, but they were the only suitable footwear on her shoe rack. It was either killer heels, scruffy trainers or toe freezing flip flops and she had to admit that they went so well with her glossy stockings.

Marie ushered her into Molly's room, forcing her to stand in front of her full length mirror. Juliette blinked in surprise, she had to admit that the dress was beautiful and rather revealing in all the right places. It clung to her like a second skin, accentuating her slim hips and revealing shapely thighs. Juliette touched her hair gingerly. It hung glossy and smooth down her back, smelling of raspberry and hibiscus.

"Do you like it straight?" Marie asked, with an eager smile and a nodding head.

"Yes," Juliette decided, "I do, it looks very different and long."

"You look sick Mom," Harry said simply, as he passed them on his knees, skidding cars along the hallway.

"Thanks honey," she called.

"Please keep it on," Marie said giving her a soft hug, "you look stunning."

Juliette nodded her assent. Then before she could change her mind, her purse, keys and shawl were thrust towards her and she was clattering outside to the waiting taxi.

* * *

When Juliette arrived at the restaurant, she was relieved to see that her friends had also made the effort and she was not the only person to be wearing a dress. Evelyn was looking sophisticated in a ruby red satin number and black fur jacket. Ann looked feminine and romantic in a flowing purple tunic and skirt, with her hair piled high in an elegant chignon that revealed striking cheekbones. Jon was accompanying her this evening and looked dashing in a smart suit and tie. He was chatting to a trendy looking Will as they ordered drinks at a tinsel draped bar. After much hugging and cooing over each other's outfits, they were shown to a posh table, decorated with candles, crackers and Christmas confetti. It all looked very sparkly and festive. As Jon passed her a glass of red wine, she felt herself relax.

Evelyn was sipping sherry out of a crystal goblet and peering out of a frosted window. "I wonder where Sophie is?" She rubbed at the glass, "Oh here she is now."

The door rattled open, a gust of wind lifted the tablecloths, while the crackers slid sideways. Sophie banged the door shut, "Brrr," she said loudly, "it's freezing out there." Then she squealed, rushing over to hug them individually. A hovering waiter took her leather coat to reveal a stunning, silver diamante dress. Crystal studded stilettos sparkled on her feet and matching earrings twinkled from her ears.

"OMG Jules, you look sooooo pretty," she hugged her friend tight, before taking a seat next to Evelyn.

"I've ordered you a wine dear, is that okay?" Evelyn had finished her sherry and was attempting to catch the eye of one of the fresh faced waiters.

"Sherry here please," Sophie yelled, over the din of the busy restaurant.

At the end of the table, Ann and Jon were prematurely pulling crackers. Jon laughed at his gift of nail clippers, while Ann feigned exuberance at her cheap, plastic ring. She plonked the paper hat on, then slugged back her vodka and coke.

"Steady," Jon said with a chuckle, as he unravelled and read a cheesy joke.

Ann huffed, "I'm celebrating two A grade essays," she explained.

"Cool," Will laughed, raising his pint, "cheers everyone."

They clinked glasses, "merry Christmas!"

Sophie leant forward to catch Ann's eye, "you've done so well," she gushed, giving her a thumbs up.

"Is she being patronising?" Ann's voice dipped lower as she addressed Jon and Will with a frown.

"Leave it love," Jon replied gruffly, "she's just being nice."

"Yeah," Will cut in, "Sophie's cool."

Ann gave them a thumbs up with a smirk, then pulled open the colourful menu.

* * *

The food was ordered and presented on delicate Chinese plates and bowls; starters of sweetcorn soup, prawn crackers and spring rolls. Then an abundance of dishes arrived for their main meals: curries, chow meins, sweet and sour and egg fried rice. It was washed down by copious amounts of alcohol. Evelyn excused herself, wobbling across the floor to the toilet, cheeks flushed and feeling hot. Although she loved her sherry, she had never drunk three quarters of a bottle in one evening before. She leant against the wash basin as she text Judy to enquire after Mam. Sophie banged into the lavatories, clutching a party popper and a glass full of Prosecco.

"You okay Evelyn?" She squinted across at her friend.

"Yes dear, I think I may have had too much sherry though."

"Aww," Sophie enveloped her in a warm hug, "we'll get you some water. Not going to be sick are you?" She wrinkled her nose as she surveyed Evelyn's perspiring countenance.

"Erm, I don't think so."

"Best to go on the soft drinks now," Sophie decided, feeling her forehead.

Evelyn nodded, bending to splash her face with cold water, as Sophie reapplied shocking red lipstick. They wandered back to the table, where the rest of the group were finishing their meals. Will was scooping rice into a large prawn cracker. He looked up with interest at Sophie as she took her seat.

"Hey Soph, how did you get on at Dad's school?"

"Oh St Mary's is wonderful," she nodded enthusiastically, "I love being in the nursery. I thought I would hate it, but the children are so sweet and the staff are lovely."

"Are you going to be there every week?" Juliette asked, as she dabbed her mouth with a napkin.

Sophie nodded, "yes, I love it in the early years. The secondary placement was totally awful; you were right about teenagers Jules. I don't know how the teachers do it."

"I'm still a teenager," Will interjected, "we're not all bad."

"I keep forgetting how young you are Will," Sophie said with a laugh.

"How was my dad? Hope he looked after you," Will commented with a scowl.

Sophie shook her head, "he wasn't there. I had to see the deputy. She was a bit scary, but the nursery teacher is awesome, she made me feel so welcome. They all work so hard."

"So you're happy to be in the nursery then?"

"Oh yes," Sophie replied, "I wasn't sure at first, but I think I'm going to love it. Next week I've been invited to the staff meeting, which should be interesting."

"Cool," Will nodded and underneath the table he surreptitiously checked Hema's Facebook page on his mobile. Her last status had been a photograph of her with friends, on the way to the staff / student Christmas party. Will was itching to leave, so he could see her.

"How is your job going Will?" Ann asked.

"Yeah it's great thanks. Hard work and late nights, but its good fun and the tips are cool."

Will had settled in well at the bar. Wayne was a great boss: patient, funny and laid back. The other staff were friendly enough; even the elderly cleaner and the stony faced bouncers had taken a shine to Will. It felt good to be earning his own money and he enjoyed socialising with the punters. Max and Flora had been surprised but happy with the news that he had a job. Flora had concerns that it may interfere with his uni work, but Max had been uncharacteristically pleased and if Will was not mistaken, he appeared almost proud of his only son. Over breakfast this morning, he had slapped his back heartily and chuckled as he reminisced on his own Saturday job at Woolworths, when he was a student.

"Will you be able to cope though love?" Flora had asked nervously.

"Don't fuss woman," Max had stated, "it will do him good to be contributing financially and meeting *new* people." Will had noticed the emphasis on new and the implications. Both of his parents were relieved that his relationship with Hema was over. They believed that he would just move on, meet someone else and that angered him. They seemed oblivious to the strong feelings he still felt for her. Although Will had stopped messaging now after seeing her around uni. She had been cordially polite but distinctly stand offish. He still wanted her, but he refused to beg. He had been out with Jimmy and a few of his school pals; playing pool, bowling, pub crawls. Laughing along with the lads had been a huge pretence, he had not enjoyed himself. He missed her a lot, it didn't feel right without her by his side. Will was pulled from his reverie by a sudden back slap from Jon. He was chatting about his student days; the wild parties, the late nights, the missed lectures. He made Will and the others laugh with his amusing tales, even Ann chortled along next to him.

"Penny for them mate," Jon enquired, looking at Will with raised eyebrows, "girl trouble?"

Will nodded, a resigned movement, "I love her Jon. Hema's everything to me, I just want her back."

Jon nodded, "I can tell, but don't stress. Trust me, if it's meant to be you'll work it out."

"I know," Will agreed, "it's just difficult seeing her around but not being able to be with her."

"Family eh?" Jon shook his head, taking a swig of lager.

Will liked Jon, he was a top bloke and easy to talk too. Will had never been able to speak to his own father about personal issues. Max Bentley was so stiff upper lip, quintessential English, caught up in work, everything else came second, which included his son and his wife. It made Will sad and resentful. He looked at Ann, noticing the way she was looking at Jon, her face all lit up like a Christmas tree. He noticed they were very tactile; holding hands, kissing, touching each other as if they could not bear to be apart. It was definitely true love between those two, he thought with a smile. He looked thoughtfully down the table at Sophie who was fussing over an inebriated Evelyn. Sophie was always talking about Ryan O'Neill, the big Chattlesbury FC striker. Will had heard about his reputation, read about his wild shenanigans in the papers. He appeared to be a bit of a dick, but she was so obviously into him. He felt kind of sorry for her, there was a loneliness and vulnerability about Sophie. He guessed the old saying was true: money really could not buy happiness.

* * *

The meals were finished and the drinks were dry. A friendly waiter cleared the table, and then with a 'merry Christmas', laid a complimentary tray of shots down. There was a clamour to grab a glass, which was then downed greedily. Apart from Evelyn who sniffed hers and then sipped at it in a ladylike manner, one little finger raised in the air.

"What are those?" She asked suspiciously, pointing at half a dozen wrappers.

"Oh they're fortune cookies hun," Sophie replied, beaming with happiness. She had just received a text from Ryan who was having an x-box competition with the boys. "I'll open one."

She grappled with the paper, pulling out a curled up looking object, that reminded Evelyn of an overbaked biscuit.

"Do we have to eat those dear? I'm quite full."

Sophie laughed, "no sweet, it's more about the message in the cookie. Let's see what mine says. Listen everybody!"

The chatter ceased and all heads turned to look her way.

"Follow your dreams," she read thoughtfully, "I have a good idea what *my* dreams are, but what are yours?" Flummoxed eyes stared her way.

"Look," she began, utilising the voice she reserved for the twins, "let's speak up about our dreams, share them with each other. Pretend we're in class. I'll go first, and why don't we make a recording of it, so we can look back on it in the future."

"Oh, I'm not sure," Evelyn said apprehensively, "and how shall we record it dear?"

"On my phone of course hun, look it's easy, you just press this button and aim the lens at me."

Evelyn fumbled clumsily with the phone while Sophie cleared her throat and smoothed her hair down.

"Ready?"

Evelyn gave her the thumbs up.

"Okay, hello everyone, I'm Sophie," she began brightly, "I'm a first year student at Chattlesbury University. I have met some awesome people," she took the phone and swept it around the table before passing it back to Evelyn. "I'm studying for an English degree which I am enjoying *immensely*. Although my grades so far haven't been too good, but I'm working on that." She coughed slightly, "My dream is to successfully pass my degree and embark on a career in teaching. Erm, I think I would like to be an Early Years teacher, so watch this space," she laughed merrily. "So, for years I have put my family first. I'm blessed to have a wonderful husband and children who I adore. Now it's time to look after me and sort out my future. So in a nutshell, what I'm trying to say is that I just dream of being happy and successful...and that's about it folks." There was a chorus of approval around the table, "now, whose turn is it next?" She peered expectantly at Evelyn who shook her head.

"I'll go next," Ann piped up. Sophie took the phone, walked to the end of the table and clicked the record button.

"I'm Ann," she began, grinning broadly, "and this," she pulled at Jon's sleeve, "is my amazing husband Jon. He is my rock, my soulmate, my lover and my best friend. In fact, he is absolutely perfect," Jon nodded playfully in agreement. "I'm only at university because of his encouragement, his support, his uplifting belief that having a disability is not a barrier to learning, improving, succeeding and that life is not all bleak. You know I am an English student like Sophie. I would also like to work in education, but my dream is to be a university lecturer – eventually. It's going to be hard work and will take years, but I think I have the potential and am determined to do it. So there, that's my dream," she paused, "and on a personal note, Jon and I are just in the process of applying to adopt a child to complete

460

our family, so hopefully that will also be successful for us." There was a round of applause before the camera zoomed in on Will's boyishly handsome face.

He raked a hand through his hair and smiled, "Hi Sophie, I'm Will the cheeky teenager; nineteen-year-old English student with no idea what he wants to do with his life. Oh but it must be exciting, interesting and fun. My dream is to travel. I want to see the world and experience life to the fullest. I would like to go scuba diving in Australia, snow-boarding in Austria, bungee jumping in Mexico," he paused to stretch his arms wide, "and money would be good, so I could retire a rich, international playboy with a harem of women at my beck and call." There were peals of laughter around the table, "Oh and I'd give some to my mom of course, buy her a house with a swimming pool and a cleaner so she could relax."

Sophie giggled, "maybe you should become a footballer," she commented, "is that *all* you want?"

"For now," Will chuckled with a wink. Sophie backed away, carefully turning her phone on Juliette, who was sipping her drink thoughtfully.

"How can I follow that?" She laughed, "well my dream is to be a primary school teacher. It's what I've always wanted from when I was a young girl, playing teachers with my teddies. Before now, life got in the way. I wasn't ready, lacked the belief and confidence to do it, but now, well let's just say like Ann, as a mature student, I'm determined to make something of my life and to guide others with theirs. I'm so very passionate about teaching and children's education. I want to make that difference, to me it's more than a career, it's a lifelong vocation. The pay isn't too bad, although I do think that all teachers work a ridiculous amount of hours for what they receive. I just want enough money to live comfortably, to give my children a decent life, where I constantly don't have to worry how I'm going to pay the next bill." Sophie swallowed, her hands shook slightly as she looked at Juliette's wistful countenance, "I would love a garden to sit in and sip tea, with roses and a hammock, where

I could read and relax." Evelyn reached across to place a comforting hand on her arm.

"Aww, that's a lovely dream, "Sophie sniffed, wiping at her eye.

"Now, last but definitely not least, is my lovely friend Evelyn. What about you Evelyn? What's your dream?" Evelyn swallowed, the heat of the restaurant and the effects of the sherry infused her cheeks, tinging them pink. She stared at the camera, the flashing light momentarily blinded her, what could she say? Suddenly she felt brave enough to speak out, no more hiding. "Well," she cleared her throat, "I'm Evelyn and my dream is to be an author." Interested eyes looked her way. "You see, I've written a rather long novel and I think I might send it off to a few publishers." There were a few gasps, "hopefully they will like it, but if not, at least I have tried."

"Well done Evelyn," Ann called in encouragement.

"And," continued Evelyn, "I would like to be happy and healthy. That's all I want."

"Thank you everyone," Sophie said, her voice breaking, "I feel truly humbled and blessed to have such wonderful friends." She placed her phone down on the table, "come on, let's go party!"

# Chapter Twenty

When they arrived at the Student Union bar, there was already a long line of people queuing down the street. Sophie slipped on the icy pavement, clinging onto Juliette and Evelyn for fear of falling and twisting her ankle. This had happened once before, when she had worn an even higher pair of stilettoes and had resulted in a rather exaggerated trip to Accident and Emergency.

"Women and heels," Jon shook his head and laughed with Will, who was eager to get inside. He caught the eye of the security guard, who beckoned him forward.

"Tickets everyone!" Sophie took charge, collecting them to pass to the red faced doorman.

"Yo Alex," Will high fived him with gratitude as they filed through the entrance. They paused to deposit coats at a paint peeling cloakroom that reeked of leather and stale beer. The main room was full of students mingling. A few people were on the dancefloor, throwing staccato limb movements in time to the loud music. The staff had made an effort to instil an ambience of festivity in the room. There were gaudy strips of tinsel and paper chains festooned around the bar. Colourful decorations hung from the ceiling and next to the enthusiastic DJ, swayed a smiling inflatable snowman.

"What *are* they playing?" Sophie complained, as she eyed the crowd of people waving money at harassed looking bar staff.

"Rock music," Ann replied, tapping her fingers in time to the energetic drum beat.

"It is rather loud," Evelyn acknowledged, looking around with astonishment at the smooching couples dotted around the room, "Doesn't working here give you a headache dear?"

Will laughed, "it's cool, you get used to it," he assured Evelyn, "but I am so glad I'm not working tonight. Wait here." He bounded off behind the bar to serve himself and the others, twirling glasses from hand to hand with expertise. Wayne the bar manager grinned at his confidence and threw him a complimentary bag of peanuts.

"Shall we find a table?" Juliette asked, as her eyes scanned the room. They found one next to two black painted toilets and a wilting pot plant.

"Here we are guys," Will laid the drinks down.

Evelyn gulped her lemonade thirstily, watching as Sophie unscrewed the wine bottle cap with her teeth and splashed it generously into plastic cups.

"Cheers!" She raised her cup, waiting for the others to clink them together in a toast.

"Merry Christmas!" They cheered, as the music changed to a fast pop tune.

"Oh I love this song, come on Jules," she grabbed Juliette's hand, pulling her to her feet, "you too Evelyn."

A protesting Evelyn was ushered onto the dancefloor, where they formed a circle and began jigging in time to the tempo. Will was checking out the room, his eyes searching for Hema, while Ann and Jon gulped their drinks, people watching.

"This is fab," Jon said, a happy glint in his eyes, "it takes me back to my student years."

"Here we go," mocked Ann, pretending to play an invisible violin with her arms, "the good old days eh?"

"They sure were," he replied, "but none as good as the day that I met you." He leant forward to rub her cold nose with his own.

"I love you," she beamed, "I'm so happy."

"Ditto," he whispered.

Just then there was a loud squeal and Melanie appeared at Ann's side, "hi lovely people," she greeted, hugging them both, then Will. "This is my girlfriend Tasha," she pulled a beautiful, girl with cascading black curls to her side with a proud look on her face.

"Sit down, sit down," Jon welcomed, pulling over two more chairs.

"This is Ann, one of the students I support," Tasha waved Ann's way.

"Where are the others?" Melanie asked, looking around, "oh," she laughed, as she spotted them throwing mean moves on the dance floor.

As the song finished, the DJ began chatting, welcoming all to the staff / student Christmas party.

"Get your request in folks," he shouted, above the sound of inebriated singing, "let's make this a night to remember." There were loud cheers from around the room. Evelyn used the lull in the music as an excuse to back off the dancefloor.

"Where are you going?" Sophie yelled, beckoning her back with a curled finger.

"Toilet break dear," Evelyn replied before rushing off.

"Actually I need to sit down too. I'm not used to wearing such high shoes," Juliette admitted, wincing as her shoes pinched her toes painfully. She hobbled off the dancefloor, pausing to hug Melanie.

"Wow! Look at you Juliette, you look gorgeous," Melanie commented, eyes wide. Juliette grinned, smoothing her mega straight hair, "I know a certain lecturer is going to be impressed," she continued with a cheeky wink.

"Is this the one who is love with Ben Rivers?" Tasha asked, taking Juliette's hand, "It's lovely to meet you."

Juliette's smile wobbled, "actually I'm…"

"What was that?" Ann interrupted, looking confused, while Sophie nodded knowingly.

"Er nothing," Juliette replied quickly, "they're just fooling around," she nudged Melanie surreptitiously.

"He's coming you know," Melanie whispered in her ear, "they'll all be here, the lecturers I mean."

"Oh that's nice," Juliette said, heart hammering, "anyway, what type of music do you like Tasha?"

* * *

Will noticed her straight away; walking through the entrance, hair fanning behind her in the cool breeze. She was surrounded by a group of giggling girls and looked breath-taking in a magenta cocktail dress studded with sequins that glittered and sparkled. He jumped to his feet, caught her eye through the crowds, pleased that a seductive smile slowly formed on her mouth. Impulsively he scraped back his chair and bounded over to her, taking her dainty hands in his own.

"Hi," she greeted, her lips a shy pout.

"Merry Christmas," he replied, leaning forward to envelope her in a gentle embrace, "are you okay?"

"I am," she nodded, "how are you? I hear that you are working here now."

"Yeah," Will replied, thrusting his hands inside his front trouser pocket, "just a few evenings, but it's cool." He was pushed from behind by a group of girls heading for the bar, "look, why don't you come and join us?" He motioned towards the back of the room, where Sophie and Juliette were singing and swaying to 'Teenage Dream.'

"They look like they're having fun," laughed Hema.

"Come on," Will flashed her a heart-breaking smile.

As they crossed the dancefloor, the pop song faded out and a slow, sultry number swooned around the room. He spun her around before taking her in his arms and drawing her close.

"God you're beautiful," he said huskily. The smell of her perfume intoxicated him; the scent of jasmine and a bouquet of myriad flowers began a slow assault on his senses. Her arms wound around him and then they were kissing fervently, oblivious to the other jostling couples on the dance floor.

"I've missed you," Will murmured against her warm mouth.

"Me too," Hema replied, standing on tiptoes to push her fingers into his hair.

Will groaned, "what are we going to do Hema?"

"Ssshh," came her soft reply, "let's just enjoy tonight okay?" She snuggled against his chest and together they revolved, underneath the glitter ball, warm and happy.

* * *

Evelyn was feeling slightly better. The flush had almost abated from her hot cheeks and her stomach had stopped churning. The soft drinks appeared to have counteracted the effects of the strong alcohol, so she had decided to stick with the lemonade for the remainder of the evening. She regretted drinking the sherry so quickly, but she had been so nervous that she had forgotten how potent it could be. Although the others seemed to have no problem holding their liquor and the drinks were still being consumed eagerly. Evelyn noticed Will on the dancefloor, locked in a tight embrace with Hema. She hoped that they could work out their differences. He had seemed so down the last few weeks. His happy go lucky character seemed hidden beneath an exterior of melancholy and distracted bravado. He really was a lovely lad she thought with a smile: kind, polite and thoughtful, she only hoped that Hema saw those traits in him also. Jon and Ann were laughing loudly, popping party poppers, scattering reams of coloured paper high into the air. Evelyn moved along the empty chairs until she was seated next to Ann.

"I think it's wonderful that you are adopting a child," she said, her voice rising to be heard over the loud music.

"Well thank you Evelyn," Ann's jovial reply threw her for a moment, she was so used to her brusqueness, it was a nice surprise to see her with her guard down.

"How long will you have to wait dear?"

"We haven't been accepted yet, but I think it's normal for an application to take six months or so to complete."

"Fingers crossed for you," Evelyn sipped her drink, "and you are doing so well with your essays. You will make a terrific lecturer."

Ann was touched by her friend's enthusiasm and sincerity. She herself had been delighted with her A grades and Jon had been even more so. He had hugged her tight, face beaming with pride as he skimmed over Ben River's comments. Then he had proceeded to ring around the entire family, to share her success.

"Let's request a song," she yelled impulsively across to her husband, "what do you reckon Evelyn?"

"Oh whatever you think dear. I'm afraid I'm not an expert on contemporary music."

"Neither am I," Ann replied with a chuckle, "what do you think Jon – 1970s?"

"Leave it with me," he jumped to his feet with a wink, scribbled down an idea and shimmied past an enamoured and oblivious Will and Hema.

"Juliette looks stunning," Ann commented, "how on earth is she still single?"

Evelyn shrugged, "yes she is beautiful and a lovely person too. Maybe she hasn't met the right person yet."

"What about you Evelyn, how is your love life?" Melanie interjected, staring straight at her with a serious expression.

Thoughts of Jacob flew through her mind, his number remained on the mantelpiece, but she hadn't yet contacted him. Sometimes she thought it might be nice to have a girlfriend to confide in and ask for advice, would it be a good idea to go for dinner with him?

An image of them holding hands in a secluded corner reddened her cheeks, "I...I haven't really time for romance, I'm too busy with Mam."

"Everyone needs love! It keeps the world spinning," Melanie threw her arms in the air, then placed an exuberant kiss on Tasha's cheek.

"So Evelyn," Ann said with a roll of her eyes, "you've written a novel? How exciting, what genre is it?"

"It's mainly a romance, but there are elements of adventure in it too."

"I would love to read it, when it's published of course," Ann said, "God I love books. They've helped me through some dark times."

"Oh, I haven't sent it off yet, but I do intend to," a flustered Evelyn replied, "and I think I know how you feel about books, they take you to a different world don't they."

"Books schmucks," Melanie interrupted, "let's get this PARTY STARTED!"

Just then the music ground to an abrupt halt. The excitable DJ began jabbering into the microphone, "attention please. I've had my first request and I must say it's a cool choice, if not a little different. This song is dedicated to Ann, a person who is bloody beautiful, brave and perfect in every way." He pointed across to an open mouthed Ann, "this babe, is for you!"

The strains of 'Rebel Rebel' by David Bowie reverberated around the room; guitar riffs and drum beats accompanied by a smoky sounding, distinctive voice. Feeling ridiculously happy, Ann wheeled herself onto the dance floor to meet Jon, who began whizzing her around.

\* \* \*

Juliette's eyes scanned the dance floor. The unusual song request had driven many of the diehard dance enthusiasts off. People were congregating at the sides and queuing for more drinks at the bar. Will was leaning against the wall, supporting a smitten looking Hema, all looking good in the amorous world of teenage life. Sophie was sprawled across two chairs, lost in her phone, while Evelyn was chatting animatedly away to Melanie and Tasha, shyness and inhibitions forgotten for the evening. Ann was bending her arms into the most peculiar shapes and singing along with gusto. Great, big, belly notes of sound that had Jon clapping along and high kicking with approval. Everything was good. In fact, she was having a blast, why on earth had she been so worried? And to think she had been tempted to cancel. Now all she needed to complete the night was Ben Rivers. Just a little look and maybe a shy hello would do, she thought with a giggle. There were a few of the lecturers here already, she recognised them from around the uni, but as yet she hadn't spotted anyone from the English department.

A few of the Registry staff were drinking shots in the corner, the canteen ladies were bopping in a tight circle around a pile of handbags. Even the jolly security guard who ate Mars Bars for breakfast was here, supping a pint, as he surveyed the evenings goings on. It was all quite lovely she thought, as she slipped clumsily on a stray pork scratching. A group of other English students were milling around nearby. One of the women raised a hand in recognition and then made a beeline for her. Inwardly Juliette groaned, it was Carol whats-her-name, the class arse licker, as Ann so eloquently had labelled her. She was a tall, striking, platinum blonde, with sly eyes, razor sharp incisors and a deathly pale countenance. She reminded Juliette of a vampire, one of those erotic ones that beguiled men then tore them to shreds. But instead of blood, her real thirst was for gossip. She was definitely the go-to person for all the up to date news on the university social scene.

"No English lecturers here yet?" She had drawled to Juliette.

Juliette shook her head, skin prickling uncomfortably, "I haven't seen any."

"I wonder if Dr Rivers will bring his boyfriend?" She threw back her head and chortled. A nasty sound, that had the hairs on Juliette's arms standing immediately on the defensive.

Juliette took a large slug of wine and noticed over the rim of her glass that Carol's eyebrows were lopsided. Yes, definitely out of proportion she thought. Maybe she had upset her beautician? Yes, KARMA!! she wanted to shriek. Uncontrollable giggles erupted from her lips. Carol stared at her, slightly puzzled for a moment then joined in the cackling.

"Anyway," Carol air kissed the sky, "see ya later babes."

Juliette shuddered as she walked away to join her circle of superior looking buddies. Then the door opened, light shone through and he was there. Oh my God! He's like a heavenly being thought Juliette in her drunken state. Brian Hodges was leaning on his shoulder and Helena Mulberry had her arm draped around his back. They looked like something out of a posy art film.

For a few moments Juliette felt stuck to the spot, then shook herself out of the sudden stupor by announcing cheerfully, "more drinks anyone?" She pulled a few crisp notes from her purse then wobbled across the dance floor. From the corner of her eye she watched him as he greeted some of the other university staff. Boy he looked good, she decided, licking her dry lips in appreciation. He was dressed even more impeccably than usual, in a tuxedo and dickie bow that hung precariously from starched white lapels. She almost jumped out of her skin as he looked her way, embarrassed to be caught ogling, yet again. His eyes lit in recognition and she stood transfixed as his gaze swept over her. Happiness fizzed inside her like champagne bubbles, she was so glad he was here. Helena Mulberry was tugging his arm, but he stood perfectly still staring her way. Juliette allowed a small, seductive smile to form on her lips, before breaking eye contact to strut provocatively towards the bar. She managed to squeeze in next to a pony tailed man and a woman with electric blue hair. The bar staff were rushed off their feet, pouring liquid into tumblers, cracking the tops off exotic sounding alcopops and colliding as they hurriedly scanned purchases into the till.

"Hello darling," the pony tailed man next to her drawled.

"Er, hello," Juliette smiled slightly, throwing him a sideways glance.

"Are you a student?"

"Yes I am."

The man thrust out a calloused hand, "I'm Chris, Spanish student and budding entrepreneur."

Juliette took it gingerly, he smelt of cigarette smoke, garlic and beer. Her nose wrinkled in distaste.

"I've never seen *you* around uni," he leered, "pretty thing ain't ya."

Juliette smiled politely, she attempted to edge away, but was trapped by the people at the side and squashed behind her.

"Fancy a dance later?" He asked, winking her way.

"No," she replied firmly, "but thank you."

He looked outraged at her decision. She gulped, turned away, waving her money high in the air, to try to attract the bar staff's attention. The blue haired lady disappeared with a tray of beer, allowing Juliette room to edge away from her unwanted admirer.

"Are you a lesbian?" The undeterred man sneered.

Juliette felt a little intimidated by his forceful tone and his mean eyes. She was in two minds whether to direct a sharp knee in his crotch or to just ignore him. Deciding on the latter, she hoped he would get the hint and just leave her alone.

"You don't know what you're missing," he chuckled nastily with a forceful tap to her shoulder, "I could make you squeal all night baby."

"That's enough," a firm voice interjected, "I think the lady told you she isn't interested."

Juliette watched with relief as Ben Rivers positioned himself between them. The man looked murderously indignant for a moment, but then turned away with a disgruntled 'whatever.'

"Are you okay Juliette?" Ben asked gently, eyes warm like melted chocolate.

"You remembered my name," Juliette replied, the incident forgotten already.

"Of course," he grinned, "although I nearly didn't recognise you with straight hair."

"Oh," she touched her scalp, "it was my sister, she's too blame."

"It looks beautiful," his eyes raked over her face, "you are beautiful."

"Thank you," she beamed, transfixed by the close proximity of his handsome visage. He smelt divine; musky maleness and minty breath. She was so close to him she could see a tiny scar above his left eyebrow and could feel the fabric of his shirt brushing against her arm. A heady combination of warmth and sexiness exuded from him, spinning Juliette's head and making her suddenly shy and flustered.

"What do you think of the staff/student Christmas party? He leant against the bar and appraised her with searching eyes.

"Oh it's great," she replied, "we've been for a meal as well, but yes, yes I'm enjoying it."

"And how are you finding the course?"

"Good. I mean it's fantastic, the university is brilliant and the lectures have been excellent, erm…" she trailed off, not wanting him to consider her a creep.

"I'm pleased that you are enjoying it. So, when you fill in your student satisfaction questionnaire it will be positive, hmm?" His dark eyes danced with amusement. Juliette grinned up at him, nodding happily.

"Can I buy you a drink?"

"Oh no, it's okay, I'm buying a round for my friends but thank you for offering."

"Maybe later then?" He replied, with a soft smile.

Juliette was distracted by the harassed bar man, asking what she would like to order.

"Ben darling where is my wine?" A husky, female voice whined from behind them. Helena Mulberry draped an arm around his shoulders. "Oh hello," she said as she noticed Juliette, "you're studying English right?"

"Right," Juliette replied, "I'm in your first year class."

"How lovely," she drawled, turning her attention back to Ben, "come on darling, let me help you with the drinks, we are all completely parched."

Juliette picked up her tray of bottles, "bye," she said in his direction.

"Enjoy the night," he mouthed, as she backed away from him.

Juliette felt her spirits sink as she struggled back to the table, liquid sloshing across her hands.

"Here you go," she chirped, passing the alcohol around, "and lemonade especially for you Evelyn."

Sophie beckoned her over, a frown on her face. "I saw you talking to Ben Rivers."

"Er, yes that's right."

"You do know he's gay Jules."

"Are you sure about that?" Juliette asked fretfully, pulling strips off the beer mat.

"Well that's the rumour," she whispered, leaning closer, "I've heard that he has Kylie posters in his office too, which pretty much confirms it, don't you think?"

"What?" Juliette stared at Sophie blankly, "I have no idea what you are talking about."

Sophie sighed with impatience, "she has a huge gay following apparently. Do you get it now?"

Juliette laughed, "if you say so. Oh listen, *this* is Kylie, let's go dance." She pulled Sophie onto the dancefloor as 'Love at First Sight' thrummed from the speakers. A ponytailed man appeared opposite them, jigging their way with a pint in his hand and a leer on his face.

"Is this your girlfriend then?" He sneered, looking Sophie up and down. "Nice."

"Piss off," Sophie shouted, turning her back on him and pulling an angry Juliette away. They shimmied around the dancefloor, revolving in circles, laughing and singing along. Juliette glanced over Sophie's shoulder, craning her neck for a glimpse of him. He was standing on the edge of the dance floor, talking to Brian Hodges, with that pesky Helena Mulberry hanging onto his every word. Bah! thought Juliette, as a twinge of jealousy took her by surprise. What am I doing? She wondered. Her brain was in total meltdown, too much alcohol had made leave of her senses. All she could think about was him, her eyes constantly searching for him. She forgot all about keeping her crush hidden, discretion had left the room about an hour ago.

"Should I ask him?" She shouted in her friend's ear.

Sophie clamped a hand over her deafened lobe, "ask him what?"

"If he's gay of course!"

"No!" Sophie replied, aghast, "you need to be tactful Jules, he could take offence. Think of your grades."

Juliette shrugged, laughing merrily, spinning Sophie round in circles.

"I need to know Soph, he's driving me nuts."

"Okay, okay," she held her hand up, "you stay here. I'll interrogate Melanie, she should know."

Sophie bopped off the dance floor, leaving Juliette to twirl alone. She noticed the ponytailed man making a beeline for her again and sighed with irritation. Then suddenly Ben Rivers was beside him, pushing him backwards with a firm hand. Juliette watched with shock as he spoke calmly into his ear. Whatever he said appeared to have worked, for he sloped off with a shamed expression on his face.

"Hey," Juliette called to thank him, but he pushed through the crowds and went to confer with the DJ. She turned away in confusion, maybe I should sit down, she thought shakily, then I should forget all about gorgeous lecturers. I really have no chance, she thought with misery, who am I kidding? Even if there was a slim chance that he wasn't gay, how on earth could she compete with the intelligence, class and beauty of Helena Mulberry?

"Hey folks," the DJ looked as if he were about to combust with excitement, "I've just had *the most* romantic song request. Apparently there's a woman alone on the dance floor who is smart, funny and gorgeous."

Juliette was amazed to see the crowd cheering and clapping in her direction.

"This is for you sweetheart."

The lights dazzled her as she gazed wide-eyed at Dr Rivers as he hopped down off the stage. He strolled slowly in her direction and she looked around in confusion, expecting Helena Mulberry to pop up and glide into his arms. There was no one there, except for her.

"May I have this dance?" He asked, holding out his hand.

"Yes," Juliette almost choked on the word as he pulled her close. The music swooned around the room. It was a slower number but beautiful.

"What is this?" She asked, peering up at him.

"It's called 'If You Ask Me To' by Patti La Belle," his reply was muffled against her hair.

"Really?" She said, as she wrapped her arms across his back. He felt strong, muscular. A feeling of safety overwhelmed her, emitting a sigh from her parted mouth.

"You sound surprised?"

"Er, I thought you might like Kylie."

Ben laughed, looking down at her with a quizzical look, "far too frivolous for me. I love eighties music."

Juliette sighed with relief, "me too," she grinned up at him.

They revolved on the spot. Juliette leant against his chest, feeling his heartbeat strong and regular, beating against her cheek.

"You are tall," she commented.

"Six foot three. I often bang my head, but it helps with dealing with unwanted suitors."

"Oh yes," she smirked, "thank you for that, he just wouldn't get the message."

"Do you always attract unwanted male attention?"

"No," Juliette blushed, thankful that the dim lights hid the redness, "it must be a one off."

"I don't believe that." There was a pause, "how are you still single?"

"I must be fussy I guess," she flirted.

"You're gorgeous," he said, smiling down at her.

"And you are very charming!"

His hands slid down to rest at the small of her back where he began a gentle caress, slow circular movements that left her weak kneed and gasping.

"How long have you been a lecturer?" She asked, coughing slightly.

Ben thought for a moment, "ten years or so. Before that I was a primary school teacher, specialising in English of course."

"Oh wow, did you not enjoy teaching that age range?"

"I did, but I wanted more of a challenge and didn't want to go into management, lecturing seemed ideal."

Juliette nodded, "I want to be a primary school teacher eventually, it's all I've ever aspired to be."

"A commendable career, extremely rewarding. Will you be applying for the PGCE? They run one here at Chattlesbury."

"I haven't thought that far," Juliette replied truthfully, "but that would be ideal and convenient for my children."

"You have children?" His surprise brought a wince to Juleitte's face, was this when he backed off, made his excuses and fled?

"Yes two," she replied brightly, "Harry is ten and Molly is seven."

"And you're on your own with them?"

"I am," she nodded, "but I'm lucky to have a wonderful family who help out all the time."

"That's good," he stared down at her, "your hair is very red."

"Your eyes are very brown," she replied breathlessly.

He dipped his head, their noses bumped and she could feel his cool breath fanning her lips as they met briefly, slowly. Jolts of electricity shot through her. Then impulsively she was reaching up to pull his head down, as she met his kiss hungrily: wanting, needing, longing. Suddenly he pulled away.

"Wait," he murmured, breaking the spell.

"What's wrong?" She cried, frustration welling inside her. Ben stepped back a fraction, releasing her from his warm embrace.

"Are you gay?" She asked loudly. The music had stopped, and people were staring their way with interest. Carol the gossip was whispering with her cronies, pointing and shaking her head with disapproval. At that moment Juliette couldn't care less what anyone else thought. All she was concerned about was him and finding out the truth. Ben's face was set in a grim line, he didn't look happy, his gaze was dark and stormy.

# Chapter Twenty-One

"I'm sorry," Juliette muttered, feeling mortified, how could I have asked him such an impertinent question!? Her hands slid down his arms, then she took two shaky steps backwards, before fleeing from the dancefloor. Head down, she bolted to the toilets and thankfully they were empty. Juliette leant against the porcelain basin, her breathing terse and ragged. Her reflection in the mirror showed a wild eyed woman, whose rebellious hair was starting to kink. What have I done? She groaned. At this moment she felt like curling up in a cubicle, until the feeling of guilt had assuaged. As a distraction she spun the taps, watching the water gush out before sticking her sweating palms underneath. The cool liquid offered a temporary relief but then the door banged open with some force and Melanie stood with an irritated look upon her face.

"Juliette, what are you doing?"

"I don't know," she wailed in response, "I am so embarrassed. I kissed him and he's gay."

Her wet hands flew to her face and she peeped at Melanie with discomfiture.

Melanie frowned, "what makes you think that?"

"It's common knowledge amongst the students," Juliette cried, "everyone says so, I just presumed it must be true."

Melanie stepped forward, softly shaking Juliette's shoulders, "you shouldn't listen to rumours."

"But I, I thought…then he isn't?" Hope flickered across her face.

"Sometimes I hate working here," disclosed Melanie with a hard edge to her voice, "the rumours and gossip get you down after a while. So you really like him huh?"

"I can't stop thinking about him," she beseeched. "I can assure you Melanie, that I have tried to deny the feelings that I have for him, but to me he is perfect and that isn't realistic is it, to feel that way for someone that I hardly know."

Melanie sighed, "I can see how much you admire him and he is pretty close to perfect, I mean for a guy. I feel protective of Ben to be honest, he's like my big brother. We've worked together years and I don't want to see him getting hurt."

"Ben, hurt?" Now Juliette felt completely confused, "do you know how much I like him?"

"Okay, okay," Melanie held her hand up as a truce, "firstly, he is *not* gay. Never has been, never will be."

A huge smile erupted over Juliette's face. She felt like jigging and shouting from the rooftops, but managed to remain outwardly calm as Melanie continued.

"Believe me, I should know!"

"Then why all the rumours?" Juliette shook her head with bewilderment.

"Truthfully? That's what he wants people to think, especially the students. Of course his close friends know the truth though."

"What?" Juliette laughed nervously, "Why would he pretend to be gay?"

"It started as a rumour," Melanie disclosed angrily, "he'd been having a *lot* of female attention. One woman in particular, a real ego maniac was a bit too persistent, so when he turned her down, she concluded that the reason was obvious – he *must* be gay. She set about telling anyone who would listen. The rumour spread and Ben never denied it."

"Oh that's awful. He shouldn't have to justify his sexuality to anybody," Juliette was outraged on his behalf.

"Yes well what can I say, he's a nice guy. A definitely great, completely straight bloke, who probably just hasn't found the right person. He's a bachelor Juliette. Well he was until now." Melanie smirked lasciviously, "he likes you! I can tell. He has *never* danced with a student before. I've seen the way he looks at you in class too. It is soooooo obvious that he's into you. Surely you've noticed it?"

"I...I did think there was an attraction be-tween us."

"Of course there is. Any fool could see that. He kissed you Jules, what more proof do you need?"

Juliette felt excitement coursing through her, "but I've blown it. I listened to stupid rumours, instead of following my gut instinct and now I've offended him. On an epic scale."

"Go and explain how you feel about him," urged Melanie, "it's not too late."

Juliette shook her head, "he's way out of my league!"

"Are you crazy?" Melanie was looking at her as if she were, "you are beautiful, intelligent, a lovely person and smoking bloody hot. He is too, you're just perfect. For one another."

Thoughts were running wildly through Juliette's mind – what could she say to him to make it right? As she paused to consider the best way to deal with the situation, Melanie was already ushering her towards the door.

"Come on girl, go and get him," She shoved her out onto the dancefloor, which was now heaving with people getting their groove on to cheesy party music. Juliette peered around her, there was no sign of him, but she could see a worried looking Sophie staring her way.

"Where is he?" She muttered, "I've scared him away. Maybe I should leave it till another time."

Melanie shook her head, "Uh-oh that will be like never! Girl you definitely need a lecture on confidence and self-belief. He'll be with the other

English staff of course, probably being bored to death as we speak. Let's go find them."

Juliette followed her through the crowds, eyes scanning the room. Then she spotted Brian Hodges, swigging from a Newcastle Brown Ale bottle, while thrumming his fingers on the table, in time to the beat.

"Hi Brian," Melanie greeted cheerfully, "where's Ben?"

"He's gone," he replied, casting a cool glance at Juliette, "had to be up early, so called it a night."

"Oh," Melanie looked across at Juliette with sympathy, "when did he leave?"

"Not long, a few minutes ago actually."

Juliette noticed Helena Mulberry staring at her and flushed uncomfortably.

"Can I pass on a message?" Dr Mulberry interjected, "I'll be seeing him tomorrow."

Juliette's skin prickled with jealousy, she turned to Melanie with a defeated look upon her face.

"Forget it," she sighed, "let's go get a drink."

Melanie was undeterred and stood her ground as she squared up to Helena, "No thanks, I can pass the message onto him myself." She guided

Juliette away from the table of intellectuals. "You might be able to catch him," she urged, "it's not too late. Don't give him up. Find him!"

Juliette nodded, springing into action, rushing through the exit doors, down the winding corridor. She paused to tug her shoes off, clasping them tightly as she bounded up a long flight of steps. Then she was outside, shivering in the cold night air. Oh my it was snowing! Flakes of white dropped around her, landing at her feet, clinging to her eyelashes and dampening her face and hair.

"Ben," she shouted into the darkness, "Ben."

There was no reply, just the muffled sound of distant traffic. She walked gingerly across the courtyard, calling him again. Then she perched on a bench, not caring that it was wet and seeping liquid through her flimsy dress. The freezing temperature made her teeth chatter and her hands shake.

"Juliette! Come back inside," Sophie and Melanie stood in the doorway, peering at her through the darkness.

"I've lost him," she yelled, "I've only just found him and already I've lost him." The words echoed back to her. Sophie rushed forward, grabbing hold of her.

"You'll catch your death!" She remonstrated, "look you're freezing."

Melanie wrapped her shawl around her and hugging her tight, they led her back into the warmth and the light.

* * *

It was almost mid-day before Will surfaced from dream land. His head was throbbing painfully and his mouth felt furry and dry. Bile rose in his throat as he swung his legs from the bed, driving him to the lavatory at a furious pace. Drinking with Jon Stokes had not been a good idea he decided, as he surveyed his red eyed reflection. How many pints had they downed before they had started on the shots? Too many he decided, as he bent to rinse his mouth out with ice cold water. Ann could hold her liquor too he acknowledged, remembering the speed that she had drank her wine. After an enormous yawn and a stretch that had him almost touching the ceiling, Will padded down the stairs. He could hear Flora banging cutlery in the kitchen as she laid the table for the Sunday roast. She tutted as she spotted him lounging in the doorway, rubbing his head wearing just his underpants.

"Will," she admonished, "you'll freeze to death."

He waved away her concern, pulling the fridge open to gulp cranberry juice straight from the carton. The light shone on a mouth-watering chocolate gateaux, which had Will's stomach grumbling loudly. How long had it been since he had eaten? He wondered, glancing at the clock.

"It's snowed," Flora informed him, a happy smile on her face, "the garden looks so pretty."

Will wiped his mouth, "good. I might get next week off uni."

"It is your last week," Flora berated, "how long will you have off? Two, three weeks? Anyway, how was last night? I heard the dog barking late and Will did you knock over my Royal Doulton figurine? It was lying on the hall floor with an arm missing."

Will looked blank, "I really can't remember," he admitted.

Flora sighed as she bustled about the kitchen, "well never mind, I'm sure it was an accident. It was a good night then?"

"It was cool! Pretty awesome in fact."

"I'm so glad to hear that son," she shook ice off a bag of vegetables, "your first semester is nearly over and Christmas is just a cat's whiskers away. Both you and Dad will be able to have a well earned rest."

"Rest?" Max Bentley strode into the kitchen, "he'll need the time off to read books and prepare for his next essays."

Will grimaced, "whatever. I'm off out in a bit."

"In this weather?" Flora shook her head.

"I love the snow," Will replied smoothly, "I'll take the dog with me."

"Ah thank you son, she's due for a walk. I haven't had chance to get out today."

"Chill Mom," Will squeezed her shoulders gently.

"Your friend is doing well at St Mary's," Max commented, as he tugged off his snow encrusted boots, "Sarah? Is that her name?"

"Sophie," Will corrected, his interest piqued, "yeah, she mentioned she had been placed in the nursery."

"The nursery teacher speaks highly of her. Apparently she has a natural ability with the young children."

"She'll be pleased you said that," Will replied, as he checked his phone for new messages, "She's been pissed 'cause her essay grades so far haven't been too good.

Flora deposited a handful of salt into the bubbling potatoes, "Is Sophie the footballer's wife?"

Will looked up from the screen, "yeah, she's married to Ryan O'Neill."

"Oh goodness," Flora replied, "I'm sure he's the one whose picture is always in the newspapers."

"Just watch what you disclose to her Will," Max said in a serious tone, peering over the rim of his spectacles, "I like my home life to stay private. The staff love a good gossip, don't add any fuel to their fire."

Will sighed, rolling his eyes, "I doubt she'd be that interested in St. Mary's compared with the scandals that go on in the footballing world."

Max coughed, "you'd be surprised with what goes on in a catholic school! But seriously, I'm a professional Will, my livelihood depends on my good character and morals. I've no doubt that there are some at St Mary's who would love to see me ousted. Don't embarrass me with idle chit chat."

"Is the lecture over for the day?" Will queried, yawning theatrically.

Flora stepped in between them, "I'm sure he won't darling, he understands how difficult it is being a head teacher – don't you Will." She stared meaningfully at him.

"I suppose so," Will acquiesced, "anyway, I'm jumping in the shower." He darted out of the room, chuffed to receive a text from Hema. Today was going to be a good day, he decided.

\* \* \*

The following week, Sophie arrived early at St Marys, before the parents could descend on the car park. She had been late on her last visit and had been shocked by the ferocity that a parking space could elicit. One man had actually jumped from his shiny car and had begun verbally abusing a svelte Mini that had nipped in his intended parking spot. At one point he had raised his fist, shaking it at the window screen in outrage. She had thought for a moment that she may have to fetch the head teacher, but then a good natured lolly pop lady had appeared, waving her stick and telling both drivers to grow up. The situation had been diffused, but Sophie was still alarmed. It was shocking how they parked; on grass verges, along double yellow lines, in clearly defined staff spaces. Sophie was reminded of all the times that she had stressed over a spot to drop her children, now she would be making more effort to walk with them, irrespective of the weather. Thank goodness the snow had cleared though, she thought as she wrapped her scarf tightly around her, although it was still chilly and the ground was covered in a twinkling sheen of ice. She turned off the throbbing engine, checked in the mirror to make sure her make-up was still in place, then stepped gingerly down onto the frosty path.

The strange caretaker was out shovelling grit onto the walkway, his face tucked under a fluorescent beanie hat.

"Good morning," Sophie called cheerfully as she passed him.

"What's good about it?" He grumbled, "Mr Bentley's had me up since seven, scared that one of the parents will slip on ice and sue the school."

"Oh," Sophie paused, "well you're doing a grand job."

He mumbled a caustic reply, then turned his back on her to resume his gritting.

Sophie shrugged and carried on walking, fumbling in her bag for her gate fob. Max Bentley was out patrolling the school grounds, she could see him in the distance, arms behind his back as he inspected the playground apparatus. A click of her security fob allowed her to enter the building, where she found the corridor warm, flushing her cheeks pink.

"Hi Sophie," Andrea called from her classroom, as she passed by. Sophie paused, peeking her head around the door.

"Morning," she called. Andrea was a lovely year one teacher: funny, kind and welcoming.

She was writing simple sums on the Smartboard, underneath an emblazoned learning objective. "How are you?"

"Tired," Andrea turned, revealing a face lined with weariness, "the kids had me up most of last night and I really do feel shattered."

"Oh no," Sophie replied, her heart strings pulled by the teacher's down turned mouth, "can I do anything to help?"

"Can you take my class for me," she laughed, "no, no thank you Sophie, I'll manage somehow," she waved and Sophie continued on her way.

At the end of the corridor, Cara the nursery teacher hovered next to the photocopier, cursing as the paper jammed for the fourth time this morning.

"Hi Sophie," she greeted, a harassed look on her face, "go and get a coffee in the staffroom, the teaching assistants aren't in yet."

"Um okay," Sophie paused at the foot of the staircase, then bounded up. The kettle was already bubbling away. A dark haired lady stood in the corner with her back to Sophie, she was reading a board that was signed staff notices.

"Hello," Sophie greeted amiably, "I don't think we've met, I'm Sophie O'Neill."

"Hi," the lady spun round, a smile on her face, "I'm Gina, very pleased to meet you."

"Are you a teacher?" Sophie asked, as she squeezed past to grab a mug off the chrome rack.

"God no!" Gina replied, "I'm a learning support assistant, or an LSA for short. I work with the older children in key stage two."

"Cool," Sophie nodded her way in a friendly manner, "what kind of work does that entail?"

"Oh it's group work mainly, intervention for literacy and numeracy but I'm a jack-of-all trades really – displays, admin for the teachers, I even do PPA class cover, although I've never been offered any more money for that particular job, not even a thank you." Her lip curled downwards and she looked thoroughly fed up as she continued, "I was just reading about this damn single status."

"What's that?" Sophie asked politely.

"It's a pretence by the council to make pay fairer and equal, but really it's just an excuse to take money off old, loyal staff. They're trying to do it to me! I've been here years and they are dropping my pay."

"Well that's terrible, can they do that?" Sophie thought of the ruckus if they were to drop the footballer's wages. The fans were always chanting about it, if they played a bad game.

"It looks that way," Gina confirmed, crumpling the paper in her fist with disgust, "well I've had enough, I'm outta this place as soon as I can find another job."

Sophie tipped a large teaspoon of sugar, swirled it around the frothy liquid, "well yes, if you're not happy."

Gina surged forward to grasp her arm, "don't trust anyone here," she mouthed, "it's a viper's nest and there's some here will do anything to get ahead."

Sophie baulked in surprise, "okay," she replied slowly, "I'm just here doing voluntary. I'm at uni studying English, but I'm in the nursery and they all seem lovely."

"Yes, well maybe I've spoken out of turn. I've been here far too long of course. Just watch your back, jealousy and bitchiness is rife here."

"In a catholic school?" Sophie asked doubtfully.

Gina nodded, "it used to be nice here, staff
supported each other. Now it's full of young,
pretty girls all competing with each other and
management encourage it!"

"That's not good," Sophie said sympathetically.

Gina released her arm, smiling apologetically,
"sorry, I don't mean to be negative. Shush, I think
someone's coming."

A voice called up from the bottom of the stairs,
"Gina are you up there? There's a child that
needs changing please." Sophie recognised Mrs
Bent's authoritative tone. They smiled at one another, then Gina smoothed down her pencil skirt
and proceeded to clatter down the stairs, leaving
a bewildered Sophie, wondering what she had let
herself in for.

* * *

Sophie spent the morning making props for
the Christmas play: hats, crowns, halos, stars.
She also pinned costumes, adding sparkly bits

and clipping on wings. It was quiet in the nursery, the children were in the hall with Cara, practising for the nativity. Sophie could hear their singing and Cara's firm tones, telling them to stand still and concentrate. The other nursery staff were busy; stapling children's work to the walls, preparing resources, tidying up the toys. It was a hive of activity and Sophie felt happy.

"I'm going to the staff meeting today," she divulged to Mrs King.

The nursery nurse laughed, "oh my, you're in for a treat there."

"Will Mr Bentley be there? Only I haven't had chance to meet him yet."

"Yes he'll be there, along with the rest of the management team and all of the teachers. They tried to make it compulsory for the teaching assistants to attend, but there was a revolt and lots of complaining. In the end they gave up on us." Mrs King chuckled, "The meetings aren't too bad if Mr Bentley leads it, but if it's Mrs Bent, it can drag on."

"What's Mr Bentley like?" Sophie asked with interest, as she shook glitter liberally over a table full of halos.

Mrs King paused to consider the question, "very ambitious," she decided, "he's a nice enough man, but at times can be ruthless. You wouldn't want to cross him."

"Really," Sophie exclaimed with surprise, "his son Will is lovely, so laid back and funny."

"I've never seen his son," Mrs King revealed. "He never discusses his family, keeps himself professional at all times."

"Oh," Sophie replied, "doesn't he have friends here?"

Mrs King snorted, "no way! Although when he was a teacher here, he was friendly with Mr Moore. A lovely man who has left now," she leant closer and dropped her voice to a whisper. "When the head teacher vacancy came up, Mr Moore asked Mr Bentley if he was going to go for it. He wouldn't have applied for it if he had known. Max Bentley told him he wasn't, then applied for it on the sly. He's very pally with the chair of governors, had the job before he walked in the interview. Stitched his friend up good and proper."

Sophie gasped, "ambition is not always a good thing is it. But what happened to Mr Moore?"

"He left shortly afterwards. Got a head teacher position at a community school, not far from here. They're still friends apparently, goodness knows why."

Sophie shook her head then smiled as she spied Cara leading the children back into the nursery for milk time and then home.

* * *

The staffroom was packed, all seats taken in anticipation for the meeting. It was warm and stifling, Sophie pulled at her polo neck sweater as she slid into a seat next to Cara. Some teachers were marking books, heads bent over, red pens poised as they slashed the pages. There was more than one conversation going on and Sophie was surprised to see the caretaker laughing with Winnie, the other year one teacher, as they looked at their phones.

"They're an item," whispered Cara, "thick as thieves, the pair of them."

Next to Cara, Rob the tousle haired year six teacher, was pontificating on his World War 2 display.

"I despise teaching history. Why spend time raking over the past? It's gone, finished, over. As educators, surely we should be looking at the here and now and the future. Animal welfare, conservationism and the environment. Teaching our children to have respect for the planet instead of outdated ideologies. Why isn't environmental studies part of the primary curriculum for goodness sake?"

There were a few nods and murmurs of assent.

"Get off your soapbox Rob," Cara said, "take it up with the unions." Laughter spread around the staffroom.

"Pfftt, the unions are about as useful as a chocolate teapot."

A very nervous looking lady in a tartan pinafore cleared her throat, "they were good when I had my depression, very supportive to be fair."

"That's because almost every teacher in the land is suffering with, or has previously had depression. They've become experts in dealing with the encumbrance of mental illness."

There was a sudden flurry of activity from the stairs. Silence descended as the Head and Deputy burst into the room.

Sophie gazed at the head teacher, looking for the resemblance between father and son. They looked nothing alike she concluded, apart from sharing the same hair colour. Will was trendy and cute with his floppy hair and soft faced good looks. Max Bentley was indeed handsome, but he had a conservative aura around him, dressed in a smart, expensive looking suit with perfect hair and teeth that sparkled as he smiled. He nodded her way as he entered the room, moving aside for Marcia Bent to stride into the centre.

"Well people," Marcia began, as an uneasy fidgeting spread, "there's a few things on today's agenda that need addressing."

"Bad combination those two," Cara whispered, sending the year six teacher into a bout of hearty coughing.

"First of all people," Marcia began, eyes darting around the staffroom, "let's talk Facebook."

A groan emitted from the younger teacher's lips, Sophie stifled a giggle.

"Let me remind you," Marcia began, slamming her folder down on the rickety table, "we are professionals and therefore have to be very careful indeed what we write on social media. Parents are everywhere and if it's not them, it's their children. They could be friends with your friends and so could inadvertently be seeing everything you like and every post you share." Her voice rose to a shriek, "think very carefully what you write. They will take any opportunity to sue our school. I personally think social media should be banned from the teaching profession." She sniffed with disapproval and Sophie noticed a few of the teachers shaking their heads, "but anyway, in preparation of this serious matter, I have compiled a new social media policy, which you must all read and sign."

Max Bentley adjusted his tie, "thank you Marcia," he motioned for her to sit down. "Now onto league tables, we're slacking folks," he shook his head in annoyance. "There's local schools that are beating us and we really can't have that can we," he glared at the key stage two group, "lower league status means less pupils and then that results in school cuts." He slashed his throat with his fingers, "so what I need from the key stage managers is an effective and successful strategy to combat this and to raise our attainment levels pronto!"

Paper rustled as ideas were jotted down, "not now!" He cried, "we're failing in maths, boys are outshining the girls. The council will be accusing us of sexism next. Think people!"

"More maths workshops, lunchtime and after school?" A year four teacher held up her hand.

"Yes, yes," Max strode around the room, "we need to inspire them with numbers, encourage them to enjoy maths. Get the dinner ladies involved, they can play number games right?"

A murmur of approval ricocheted around the room.

"Maybe the numeracy leader has some ideas?" Marcia leant forward in her chair, eyes focussed on the year six teacher.

"The children are already under enough pressure with the SATS," Rob commented with a defiant look, "maybe we could get the parents involved."

"Yes," Max nodded curtly, "send more numeracy work home, talk to the parents and impress on them the importance of the subject. Okay, next on the agenda," he paused to glance over his notes, "there's a residential trip coming up. Who is going to volunteer?"

There was a hushed silence then Marcia sprang up. "I have a form here requesting signatures for it. We need to get organised people and the teaching assistants need to get involved too, so encourage them." She growled the words, looking round with slanted eyes, "and there is to be no alcohol whatsoever. I'm sure that as professionals we can all abstain for a few nights."

Cara laughed, "that might be difficult," she commented, hands held in the air.

"It's no laughing matter," Marcia frowned, "the children are in our care, so we need to be on the ball. No alcohol! Chocolate of course is acceptable." Peals of laughter spread around the room to Marcia's fury.

"Okay," Max cleared his throat and stepped forward, "I know I nag you, but we are a brilliant school and you work extremely hard. Ofsted were hounding us not long ago, but we got a good and you should all be extremely proud of yourselves. Now we need to consider how we can make our school outstanding. It will take hard work, but I know we can do it as a team together."

Wow, thought Sophie, he certainly knows how to motivate.

"So," Max continued with a smile, "the next teacher training day, you can all stay at home and prepare reports, but get the teaching assistants in to do cleaning or other admin tasks."

"And that doesn't mean they do your displays for you," warned Marcia, "only last week I was at a school around the corner and the teaching assistants were pinning up children's work. Unbelievable while literacy is going on! Let me remind you that *I* have the key to the stationery cupboard. Sending teaching assistants for sugar paper during lesson times will not wash with me. We need to tighten our belts people; our funding will only stretch so far you know."

"Displays are important to be fair," Max snipped, "the parents seem to like them when I walk them round the school and the Ofsted woman was impressed with the dining room collage. What was it she called it? – 'pleasingly aesthetic.' Maybe we could designate one of the support staff as a display co-ordinator. I've seen that done at other schools with success."

"Gina's good at art," a year two teacher quipped. "she studied it at 'A' level."

"Good," Max nodded with a thoughtful smile, "utilise her then and maybe she will stop ranting about getting another job. It's not good for the school's ethos for staff to keep leaving. Parents like to see familiar faces and the governors start asking difficult questions if there is a quick turn round of staff," he pulled at his tie, as beads of sweat formed on his upper lip.

"The PTA want to hold a bake-a-cake stall for charity in the nursery at the end of term," Cara interrupted, "is that okay?"

"Yes, yes," Marcia waved at the idea, "but make sure you supervise accordingly and that there are health and safety procedures in place."

Cara looked at her blankly, while Sophie wondered what could be dangerous about baking a cake.

Marcia leant forward, eyes flashing, "some members of the Parent Teacher Association are very meddlesome indeed and are out to cause trouble. They like nothing more than a good gossip at the school gates, so don't give them any excuses and be careful with hygiene," her voice rose an octave, "otherwise they'll be suing us for food poisoning next."

Max looked down at his agenda, "just one last thing before I let you go and have your lunch. Child protection. Make sure you are fully read up on the matter. The council are on the prowl again, asking tricky questions in schools, trying to catch people out."

"Here are two handbooks which are to be kept in the staffroom," Marcia interrupted, head bobbing, "we should all be proficient in this matter, no excuses."

"I've arranged for the teaching assistants to go on a refresher course in the near future, although whether it will fully register is doubtful."

"You need to remind them people," Marcia remonstrated, wagging a finger, "they spend far too much time gossiping in the corridors. Their working day is meticulously planned out. I've issued them all with timetables, ensure they stick to them! And if they have a few minutes to spare, send them up to the staffroom to read over the school policies."

"Right, well, I think that concludes this staff meeting. I'm sure you all have marking and resources to prepare, so I shall keep you no longer."

Marcia blocked the doorway, hands on hips, "just before we leave, can anyone remind me of the signs of abuse please."

"Verbal!" Shouted Winnie, looking smug.

"Sexual," supplied a weary looking key stage two teacher.

"Emotional," a sweet looking newly qualified teacher held up her hand.

Then there was silence.

Marcia tutted, shaking her head, "neglect maybe?" She said in a condescending tone. "This should be second nature to you people, thank God Ofsted asked me about it." She narrowed her eyes as she spied Cara, rooting through the communal Christmas sweet jar, "what about you Cara? Are you aware of any?"

"Erm…physical," Cara replied, after a slight hesitation, as she sucked on a sherbert lemon.

"Did you forget for a moment?" Marcia mocked gently.

"Nope of course not. Just checking that you hadn't." Cara winked at Sophie, who was trying to chew a rock hard toffee with sophistication.

"Okay that's enough," Max Bentley held up his hands, "back to work everyone." The management team filed down the stairs, leaving the rest of the staff to roll their eyes and mutter with resentment.

"So, how was your first ever staff meeting?" Cara asked, as they trooped down the stairs.

"It was certainly…interesting. Beats Eastenders any day." They broke into peals of laughter, as Marcia peeped her head out of her office and shook her head with disapproval at their gaiety.

# Chapter Twenty-Two

It was the last lecture before Christmas and Evelyn was looking forward to having some time off to rest and recuperate. The last couple of days she had been feeling tired and rundown with a sore throat that refused to budge and painful, muffled ears. Mam was all better though, apart from a lingering bout of the sneezes. Evelyn deduced that it was probably a culmination of late nights, long reading lists and sharing Mam's germs that had caused her to feel poorly.

"You've been overdoing it," Mam had berated this morning, as Evelyn fussed around her, "let's have a fish supper tonight and I'm paying, so no arguments. Then after, we'll stoke up the fire and snooze like ladies of leisure."

"Won't that be heaven," Evelyn had agreed. She moved to the window, to tug back the velvet drapes, "oh thank goodness the snow has cleared though." The traffic was trundling down the street as normal, which meant the bus service would be back to its regular timetable and uni would be open for business. "Our country certainly grinds to a halt after just a dusting of it." She bent to kiss Mam, then hurried out the door to collect her coat and folders.

They were all meeting in the cyber café at 9.00 am. Sophie had text her an hour ago to inform her. Evelyn thought back over the weekend, she had thoroughly enjoyed their night out, although she had been up at three in the morning with heartburn. She guessed her body was unused to eating so late and too much sherry had exacerbated the sharp, needle like pains in her chest. She had enjoyed the dancing though, it reminded her of when she was a teenager; the social clubs where travelling singers serenaded starstruck youngsters with love on their minds. The end of the evening was a bit of a blur. Will had disappeared with Hema without a goodbye and Sophie and Melanie had been fussing over a distraught Juliette. Evelyn didn't know the full reason, but she had heard Ben River's name mentioned a few times. She had seen them dancing, indeed the whole bar had been witness to it. So that was why Juliette acted so strangely whenever he was near. She liked him romantically. Evelyn could see that now, and it looked like the feelings might be reciprocated. They had looked so happy on the dancefloor and then Juliette had ran off and Ben had disappeared and the night had been pretty much over after that. Jon and Ann had insisted on seeing Evelyn home. Bundling her into the taxi and waiting until she had turned the key in the door, before speeding off up the street. Mam had been fast asleep as she had tiptoed into her room, but in the morning, she had enquired after the evening's events.

The bus rumbled to a stop in the city centre and almost all of the passengers flooded off. Evelyn tucked her scarf inside her coat and pulled on warm, furry mittens before setting off towards the university. There were patches of black ice dotted across the pavement, she skirted around them with care. The last time she had fallen, it had resulted in a fracture and a wrist encased in plaster for weeks. Just yards in front of her there was a group of youths whizzing along the pavements on skateboards. Evelyn smiled at their energy and recklessness. How nice it would be to go back in time for just one day to a day of youthful, carefree abandonment. Memories of her dear Dad flooded her senses – his warm smile and hearty chuckle, his quick wit and integrity. The smell of outdoors that followed him, earthy and fresh. Evelyn gulped down a lump of raw emotion, sometimes she missed him terribly. The grief was like a dull ache, ever present, bittersweet memories that engulfed her, how she would love to see him again.

But back in the present, she was relieved to see that there was plenty of vacant seats in the Cyber Café. It was still early and quiet, only the sound of the catering assistants working methodically, permeated the air. They chattered amongst themselves as they swept floors, wiped surfaces down and chinked the cutlery. Evelyn took a seat next to the window and stared out at a snapshot of another busy morning in the city. People hurried by, some looked in at her inquisitively, many others stared down at the ground or at their phones. The shops were just opening. Evelyn watched as a man grappled with a large board that advertised full English breakfast and hot pork baps. A council refuse truck chugged to a halt opposite her and she watched with amusement as the driver and passenger sang along to music she was unable to hear. Then she noticed Will in the doorway and she turned towards him, a welcoming smile and a raised hand had him bounding over like a playful puppy.

"Morning Evelyn," he greeted cheerfully, dumping a pile of books on the table.

"Morning Will." She noticed the twinkle in his eye and the bounce in his step and felt pleased that he was reunited with his girlfriend.

"Where is everyone?"

Evelyn shrugged, "we must be early."

"Did you enjoy our night out?" He appraised her with a knowing smile, "the sherry went down well?"

"Rather too well," Evelyn laughed, "but where did you go Will? I didn't get a chance to say goodbye."

"I took Hema home," he explained apologetically. His phone beeped an incoming text and he pulled it from a denim clad pocket, "that will be her now."

Evelyn watched his fingers fly over the screen, marvelling at the speed. Modern technology was overall a mystery to her although she was pretty proficient on Word after spending hours inputting her manuscript. Phones, however, were another matter. There were so many designs and some appeared so complicated with their touch-screen and predictive text. It was supposed to help make your life easier, but Evelyn found herself more confused. Sometimes days passed before she even turned her mobile on, as the trusty landline was her preferred method of communication.

"Here's Ann and Sophie," Will commented with a nod towards the door.

Evelyn watched them chatting at the counter and thought how glamorous Sophie looked this morning. Her hair was piled high in a perfectly twirled chignon, revealing a face that was stunningly made up. She was struggling with a bulging sack and as she crossed the café towards Evelyn, numerous eyes watched her.

"Morning," Sophie pulled her into a warm embrace, enveloping Evelyn in a cloud of Christian Dior perfume. Ann trailed behind her, balancing on her lap a bacon sandwich which oozed tomato sauce and a bottle of chilled spring water.

"Hi," Ann held up her hand in a greeting.

"Is Jules here yet?" Sophie asked, with a worried look.

"Haven't seen her yet," Evelyn replied, "is she okay?"

Sophie glanced around before leaning closer and replying in a whisper, "I haven't heard from her all weekend. Has anyone else?"

There was a chorus of 'no's' and shaking of heads.

"We've got Ben Rivers this morning, I'm just worried she won't turn up."

"What was going on with her and Dr Rivers?" Ann asked. "I saw them dancing, he disappeared and then she was upset."

"Er...I think they just had a fall out."

Will whistled, "Ben Rivers and Juliette? Dancing? Well that's a surprise."

"Not really," Sophie disclosed, "she's liked him for ages."

"Has she really?" Ann asked, "I thought he was gay."

"Seems not," Sophie replied, pulling out her teabag and depositing it with a splat on the table.

"Here she is now," Evelyn warned. They began discussing the weather, the chance of snow for Christmas.

Juliette paused at the counter to grab a pot of yoghurt and a drink before joining the queue. She was tired, lack of sleep had left her red eyed and pale, but she still looked ethereally beautiful. Her curls were back with a vengeance, bouncing around her face in a wild mass of ringlets.

"Thank you," she nodded to the cashier, then made her way across the café to join her friends. As she walked, her eyes darted left and right, on the lookout for any lecturers. She had almost stayed at home today. Part of her cringed at the thought of seeing Ben Rivers again, but part of her longed to be in his company. The staff / student party seemed an eternity ago and the weekend had dragged by with thoughts of it occupying her mind. Had kissing him been a dream? She wondered. All weekend she had thought of him. Their dance, their chat, revolving through her mind, stuck on repeat, tormenting her. And the reminder of his lips pressed against hers had kept her awake at night. She fretted over her behaviour towards him. Had her boldness and desire repulsed him? Is that why he had suddenly left? Or was it because she had asked him straight out if he was gay? Juliette cursed her rash manner of speaking, wishing that she could spin the clock backwards and approach the topic with more tact. But then why was she still worrying? Melanie had been adamant that he was heterosexual. The way he had held and kissed her proved that, but Juliette was embarrassed by her own forward behaviour. The alcohol had loosened her inhibitions, but the truth was that she wanted him. So very much.

"Hi Jules," Sophie greeted, "I've been texting you all weekend, where have you been?"

"Sorry," Juliette replied, blushing furiously, "I've been busy with work and the kids."

"Are you okay Juliette? You look exhausted." Ann looked her way with concern.

"Yes, yes, just not enough sleep," she laughed nervously, "so are we ready for our final lecture of the semester?"

"We sure are," Sophie replied, "but first I've got a little something for you all."

She hauled a big bag up onto the table and began rifling through it, "merry Christmas everyone!" She squealed, "I feel like Santa Claus."

Sophie pulled out a brightly wrapped present, glancing over the gift tag before passing it to Will with an enormous smile. He looked surprised, but took it gratefully.

"Wow, thanks Sophie, I didn't expect this. Can I open it?"

"Yes!" Replied Sophie with excitement, as she distributed the remaining presents.

Will tore off the princess Christmas paper.

"The paper is for my children's classmates," she apologised.

"I think it's adorable, Molly would love it," Juliette interjected, "but you really shouldn't have done this Soph, it's very kind of you."

"Yes thank you Sophie," Evelyn exclaimed as she prodded her gift.

"Awesome!" Will was staring down at the Calvin Klein aftershave, one of his favourite scents.

Evelyn grappled with a stubborn piece of sellotape. It refused to budge, she had to pass it over to Will, who tore it off with gusto.

As she pulled back the glittery paper, she was delighted to see a beautiful bound notebook and a fancy, designer pen.

"It's for your writing," Sophie revealed, "you'll be able to jot down all your ideas and inspirations."

"It's beautiful," Evelyn felt tears prick the back of her eyelids, "thank you so much, but Sophie I feel terrible, I haven't got you anything."

Sophie shook her head, "it doesn't matter, it's just a little token."

Juliette thought that the little token must have cost Sophie quite a bit of money. She gasped when she opened her own present to reveal a multi-coloured Benetton rucksack, "Sophie! This must have cost a fortune."

Sophie giggled, "I was fed up of looking at that old, battered bag of yours. Everyone needs a designer bag in their lives."

Juliette investigated inside the cool leather. It was large enough to fit books, pens and her lunch. It was just perfect.

"Thank you so much," she leaned across to hug her, "what have you got Ann?"

Ann was watching the others, the wrapped present on the table in front of her. She felt guilty for all the times she had been nasty to Sophie. The others were right, she was a lovely person, how had she been so blinkered?

"I can't accept this Sophie," she said gently, "it's very kind of you, but I really don't deserve it."

"What?" Sophie replied, lips flapping, "of course you do, we're friends aren't we?"

"I've been a bitch to you, you shouldn't be buying me gifts."

Sophie waved away the confession, "it's all forgotten Ann, we can start again from now. Please open it."

Ann looked at her with a rueful smile, "you're not going to take no for an answer are you?"

Sophie shook her head with a grin, "open it," she urged.

Ann tore off the shiny paper, gasping at what lay inside. The scarf and hat set was exquisite, soft, luxurious and expensive looking. As she picked them up, a pair of matching gloves fell from the lining. She touched the cobalt fabric gingerly, "thank you, this is gorgeous."

"It will keep you warm and cosy," Sophie said, "and the colour looks great on you. Now where is Melanie?"

The café was filling up, Juliette spotted Carol and her group of friends staring her way and whispering. The gossip had begun already, she thought with dismay, I should have been more discreet. She watched with an impending sense of nervousness as Carol got to her feet and walked towards them.

"Morning ladies and gentlemen," she greeted boldly, "I see Christmas has arrived early for some. How wonderful!"

Juliette scowled down at the table, wishing she would go away.

"Did you all enjoy the staff, student party?" Carol enquired with a glint in her eye.

Evelyn answered for the group, oblivious to Juliette's distress, "oh yes, it was a terrific night."

"Some more than others," she said, staring pointedly at Juliette, "I wonder if we'll have both lecturers this morning?"

Juliette felt a surge of anger and was about to retort sharply, when Ann intercepted her.

"I'm hoping that we do," Ann's face bore an overly sweet smile, "I'd love a Christmas kiss off Ben Rivers."

Carols smile faltered, "yes well, I'll see you all up there." Off she flounced, hair tossing wildly.

"Now that's a bitch," Sophie commented as she began packing her belongings away, "shall we go to class?"

* * *

Juliette sat quietly in the classroom, as the others chatted around her. There was much excitement for Christmas and the students were full of cheer and festivity. Evelyn was telling Sophie about her plans for the holidays. She had invited Jacob for Christmas lunch after he had dropped off presents for her and Mam. The kind neighbour Judy would also be dining with them. It seems that both Jacob and Judy were alone, with no family to visit. Evelyn's heart strings had been tugged as she had stared at the gifts in Jacob's hands. He was such a kind man and Judy had been such a help with Mam, so sweet and thoughtful. Evelyn hated the idea of them both alone on Christmas day, so with Mam's blessing she had insisted that they enjoy a festive banquet in her humble abode. Since then she had been poring over recipe books and purchasing little titbits to make the dinner perfect. She was aware that she had yet to organise a meal out with Jacob. He had looked at her expectantly the last few times she had seen him, but had remained silent on the matter. Evelyn had been relieved. The truth was she felt too embarrassed to broach the subject and was terrified by the idea of going alone on a night out with him. How would she cope if he had romantic intentions and heaven forbid, made a pass at her? The thought of it flamed her face and spun her head with worry. So then Christmas dinner seemed an ideal way to thank him, with the company of other people to save any awkwardness.

As they were chatting, Melanie burst into the room, encased in a reindeer jumper with bells attached, that tinkled as she moved. She accepted the present from Sophie with great enthusiasm, squealing with delight at the new Katie Perry perfume. "Love it," she exclaimed, spraying the scent in a burst around her neck and wrists, "this smells divine, thank you."

"You okay?" Melanie whispered in Juliette's ear.

"No," Juliette admitted with a gulp, "I'm nervous as hell and feel sick with embarrassment."

"Don't stress," soothed Melanie, "just see what happens."

"The other students are beginning to notice," hissed Juliette, "how could I have been so brazen? They're gossiping about me."

"Brazen?" Laughed Melanie, "this isn't the dark ages Juliette, let them gossip! They're all just jealous 'cause Ben asked you to dance." She perched on the edge of the table, swinging her legs up.

Juliette shook her head at Melanie's mirth, "he probably hates me now. I offended him and scared him off. The poor guy must be trauma-tised."

"Quit with the self-depreciation," warned Melanie, "if he mentions it, just tell him you were overcome with lust and alcohol. I'm sure that he'll understand."

Juliette laughed grudgingly.

"Hi Kids!" Brian Hodges shouted as he strode into the room, banging down handouts onto the desk, "welcome to twentieth century literature."

\* \* \*

The lecture passed quickly, but there was no sign of Ben Rivers. Juliette scribbled down notes, her eyes constantly darting towards the door.

"Where is he?" she fretted, her stomach felt like it was tied up in knots. Melanie winked her way before asking Brian of the missing lecturer's whereabouts.

"He had an appointment first thing. He should be here anytime now."

Ben strode through the doorway and Brian continued, "ah, speak of the devil."

"Morning," Ben nodded.

Juliette felt her heart hammering and slunk down in the seat, wishing that she was one of Harry's super heroes with the power of invisibility.

"Don't worry," soothed Melanie, as she touched her arm gently.

The students filed back into the room clutching snacks and beverages. Juliette stole a sneaky glance at Ben. He was fiddling with the projector, head bent, looking dashingly handsome as usual. Juliette recollected their kiss and her cheeks flushed with desire, as she imagined his lips pressed firmly on hers. He glanced up and she quickly averted her gaze to stare out of the window at the blue skies and the sunny morning. She loved this time of year, when the weather was cold but bright. Winter had always been her favourite season.

"Good morning Miss Harris," Ben was standing in front of her.

"Oh morning," Juliette exclaimed with nonchalance, avoiding his eyes. He passed her a handout and then moved onto the next table. Melanie gave her a thumbs up teamed with a large grin and Juliette felt ridiculously happy. This is madness, she thought, how is it possible that I like him so much when I don't know a thing about him?

Brian glanced at her briefly before calling the classes attention and commencing the seminar.

After an hour of heated discussion and debate, Juliette packed up her belongings feeling a little bit miffed. Ben hadn't looked her way once and when asking questions, it seemed that he was deliberately ignoring her. Her mood was further incensed when Carol strolled close by and remarked bitchily, "oh dear." She wondered if she had misread the situation and berated herself once again for the way she had acted at the party. Unrequited love stinks, she thought gloomily, stuffing her pens inside her new rucksack. Then as she was following the others to the door, her shoulders slouched with despondence, a warm hand touched her and a gentle voice wished her a merry Christmas.

"Here," Ben pressed a scrap of paper into her hand with a smile, "I'll wait to hear from you."

Juliette looked down in astonishment at the scrawled mobile number. Her mouth opened and closed a few times, but before she could utter a reply, he had moved away to answer another student's query.

"Merry Christmas," she whispered to his retreating back.

* * *

The cold and the snow vanished, heralding mild temperatures that surprised even the weather people. Christmas day arrived and the streets were full of dog walkers and children testing out their new toys; scooters, bikes, skateboards and roller skates whizzed up and down the pavements, eliciting whoops of delight from the children and gasps of fear from the grownups. Will endured a morning of mass, followed by Flora's dubious cooking. For one day of the year, his dad completely relaxed. His study was firmly closed, his computer unplugged and packed away in its case. They played Trivial Pursuit, then relaxed with a beer and a classic James Bond movie. Surreptitiously he messaged Hema, pleased to hear that she was okay and enjoying the time off uni. Things had been going well since their reconciliation at the party, although she still worried constantly about her family. They were back to the old sneaking about, but Will was okay with it at the moment, just to be spending time with her again was a joy. Everything was cool he decided, sliding down in the armchair, chuckling at the politically incorrect acting on the screen.

Sophie and her clan dined out with Yvonne and Roger. Although she wished she had stayed at home as the twins were a handful; tearing around the restaurant, blowing paper whistlers and annoying the other diners with their light sabres that flashed neon bright and played the 'Star Wars' theme tune. Sophie was constantly on her feet, shushing them and ushering them back to the table. Ryan and Roger polished off two bottles of red wine and then, to her embarrassment, began singing Christmas carols and fooling around with the star -struck waitresses.

"Oh men will be men darling," Yvonne said, batting their behaviour away. She herself had been drinking Jack Daniels for hours and was lounging in her seat, a drunken smile on her face, numb to the lecherous antics of her partner. Then it was back home for more alcohol and a rousing game of 'Let's Dance' on Josh and Jake's new Wii. Sophie watched Roger contort himself into the most undignified positions and wondered what had happened to his sciatica. Two weeks ago he had virtually been on death's door, but here he was now dancing and fooling around like a complete buffoon.

"It's a miracle," Yvonne had decided, "my herbal cream I mean. I rubbed it in three times a day and he's like a twenty-year old again."

Sophie had raised a sceptical eyebrow and remained silent. She knew for a fact that Roger had been taking strong anti-inflammatories and basically doing nothing but lie in bed for weeks. But it was Christmas, so Sophie let all the niggles wash over her. She refused to argue on the Lord's holy day. By four o'clock she was opening her second bottle of Prosecco and was giggling over 'Only Fools and Horses.'

Evelyn spent a busy morning preparing turkey and gammon, with an array of mixed vegetables then a mouth-watering choice of Christmas pudding or chocolate trifle for dessert. All the food was homemade, even the bread and apple sauce, the house was full of delicious scents that had everyone's stomach rumbling. Jacob arrived looking smart in a suit and tie and surprised Evelyn with a beautiful scarlet poinsettia. She took it gratefully, while chastising him gently to stop buying her gifts. She had placed him next to Judy at the dining table, but throughout the afternoon he gravitated towards Evelyn, instigating conversations and assisting her with the washing up. Overall it was a great success; scrumptious food, fine wine and excellent company. Mam was at the centre of it all, making their guests chuckle with her quick wit and humorous observations. It was well into the evening when Evelyn bade goodbye to her guests and pulled the chain across the door. She kicked off her best loafers, wriggled her toes inside warm slipper socks then flaked in the armchair next to Mam, snoozing with contentment as the TV blared.

Juliette's Christmas was a hectic one; Molly and Harry tore around the flat with excitement, not knowing which toys to play with first. Not only had they received two sackfuls from Juliette aka Santa, there were also numerous gifts from family; they were crammed underneath the tree and scattered over the carpet. The children had woken Juliette while it was still pitch black, she had peered at the alarm clock, bleary eyed, and managed to shoo them back to bed for another hour. After that she had given in, risen with a tired smile and vertically challenged hair, shrugging into her dressing gown, while Harry and Molly squealed with delight at the temporary grotto cum living room. She too had guests for Christmas lunch: Mom, Dad, Maz and Dave came to eat and generally help out. Dad carved the turkey, while Mom dished up the veg and Marie and Dave entertained the kids. Then after they had consumed the food, complaining of the shockingly high calorie content, Juliette added to it by presenting a huge, home-made Christmas pudding which they lit and ate with lashings of cream and brandy sauce. By the time they had finished, almost all of the kitchen's contents were piled around the sink.

"Bloomin 'eck, that's a lot of washing up," Dave commented as he cracked open a bottle of lager, "I think I'll go and put the batteries in the kids' electronics."

Marie waved him away with a swipe of the tea towel, "that was lovely Jules, you are such a fantastic cook."

Juliette filled the basin with soapy water, "it was my pleasure and it was a thank you for all the help that you give me all year round. Mom and Dad too. I do appreciate it; I don't know how I'd cope without you lot."

Marie enveloped her in a soft hug, "I knew I should have bought you a dishwasher for crimbo," she eyed the mountain of dirty crockery.

Juliette laughed, "I don't need one, I have a perfectly functional pair of hands. Besides, they eat up electricity and never clean the plates as good as a scrubbing brush can."

"Okay, okay, chuck us your marigolds then," her sister pulled them on with a resounding twang, "are you pleased to be broken up from uni?"

"I am, it's nice to have a rest, but I'm looking forward to the new semester too."

"And how was your night out? You hardly mentioned it Jules, did you not enjoy it?"

Juliette felt her cheeks flush and bit her lip with nervous remembrance.

"What's wrong?" Marie's ears pricked at the uncomfortable silence, "did something happen?"

She nodded slowly, "nothing bad," she disclosed, "in fact it was a pretty perfect night."

"You've met someone haven't you?" Marie cried with excitement, "tell me everything."

Juliette swallowed, there was no deceiving her big sister, "remember that lecturer I told you about months ago, the one I thought was gay."

Marie nodded, a puzzled look on her face, "don't tell me he's bisexual Jules."

"No, well I mean he's straight. We danced and now he's given me his number." She looked at Marie, waiting for the news to register.

"You mean you and a lecturer got it on?"

"It was just a kiss," Juliette gasped.

"He kissed you?! Isn't that like totally unprofessional of him?" Marie was shocked.

"We're not children Maz, I'm a fully grown consenting adult."

"Yes but he's your teacher, couldn't he get into trouble for that?"

"Of course not," Juliette replied, feeling her patience beginning to wear thin, "but obviously we're not going to be shouting it from the roof tops. It really is no one else's business."

Marie scrutinised her sister, "if you say so, just be careful okay? I don't want my sister's heart broken by some highbrow intellectual."

Juliette clattered the plates back into the dresser, feeling annoyed, "we only kissed! Can't you just be happy for me?"

"I'm just concerned for you Jules. These academic types don't live in the real world, well not in our gritty world anyway. They know how to talk the talk, but aren't able to walk the walk, if you get my drift."

Juliette sighed, "I have no idea what you are on about. Ben Rivers is lovely, he's super smart, absolutely gorgeous and funny. I like him a lot, so I'm going to text him and wish him a merry Christmas and see how things progress from there."

Marie held up her hands, "okay, okay fair enough. I just hope he isn't leading you up the garden path."

Juliette banged a mug down in annoyance, "how can he be? He's single."

"Well look, if you want to go on a date, Dave has some lovely friends he can introduce you to. We could go on a foursome." Marie nodded with eager expectation.

"No thank you," Juliette replied firmly, eager to change the subject, "I can choose my own dates. Anyway, show me this necklace that Dave bought you for Christmas."

After a lovely afternoon of eating far too much chocolate, playing with toys and snoozing on the settee, Juliette's family left. She stood in the kitchen, making hot chocolate, yawning and happy. Although she loved Christmas, it was a tiring day. Now she was looking forward to some me time; a soak in the bath and a chance to lose herself in a light hearted novel, where the word classic was just a brand of car or an expensive cigar.

"Is Daddy coming?" A small voice asked. Juliette looked down at a head of wild curls, so much like her own. A mini me, she thought with affection.

"Not today honey, but he did say that he would try and come tomorrow." She ruffled her daughter's hair and wondered where Marty was spending Christmas. Probably holed up in the boozer with his shady mates, she surmised. He had dropped off presents last night, with a promise to take the kids out over the holidays. Juliette poured the bubbling milk into two plastic Disney cups then took them through to the lounge.

"Brush your teeth afterwards," she said to Harry and Molly as they dunked their biscuits in.

The bathroom was chilly, she stooped to turn up the heating a notch before discarding her clothes and filling the bath with warm, bubbly water. She sank down in the tub with a groan, immersing her body in the fruity scent was heavenly, she could almost feel her aches and pains soothing away. A Lucy Diamond novel was resting on the shelf, but instead she picked up her phone and spent a few minutes scrolling through her Facebook news feed. Sophie and Will had posted Christmas messages. She laughed at a picture of Sophie holding two bottles of wine above a caption that read 'let's get this party started.' Will had posted a cryptic message with a grinning selfie wishing the special people in his life a great time and had tagged a quote from Bob Marley about the meaning of love. Then there was a shot of a plateful of sprouts from Melanie entitled, 'these things should be banned!' Juliette chuckled then went on a liking and commenting spree before logging out. She had decided when she started uni that she would limit the amount of time she spent on social media, it could be addictive and a waste of an evening. Her sister Marie was on other sites such as Twitter where she had thousands of followers. Juliette wondered what she had to tweet about, but as Maz patiently explained, social media was a good form of free advertisement for her flower shop.

Juliette wondered if Ben was on Facebook and typed his name into the search engine. A long list of dubious looking men with interesting hair styles popped up. No, she doubted that he was the type to bother with social media. He would be inundated by friend requests for a start, off hordes of nubile females no doubt. Juliette was secretly pleased that he lacked a Facebook account and even more pleased that she had his mobile number stored securely in her contacts list. Her finger hovered over the screen, then she quickly typed out a brief message wishing him a happy Christmas and hoping he was having a good time. Seconds later her mobile whistled, causing her to jerk upright, splashing water over her face. It was him, he had replied and super fast!

**Merry Christmas Juliette, it's good to hear from you. Currently being beaten at Monopoly by my niece and nephew. Have you had a good day?**

She loved that he used proper English, instead of shortened text talk. There wasn't a silly emoticon in sight, quickly her fingers flew over the screen.

**Had a fab day thank you. Ate far too much and now relaxing. I like your choice in board**

games, although my favourite has got to be Pictionary.

**Drawing is not my forte – you would definitely beat me at that.**

Juliette laughed with delight and thought for a moment of a suitable reply.

**You just need a good imagination – that's all.**

There was a delay for a few moments before Ben replied.

**Maybe you could teach me one day.**

**Maybe.** Juliette felt like an outrageous flirt and bit her lip as she awaited a reply.

**I will hold you to that. Enjoy your night, Ben.**

"Oh no, don't go," she said to the phone.

**Thank you. You too, Juliette.**

She snapped off her phone with a sigh, closed her eyes and sank back down to daydream about Ben's dark eyes, hypnotic voice and those amazing hands.

# Chapter Twenty-Three

For Ann this Christmas had been the best ever. Jon had seen to the turkey, while she had prepared all the trimmings. It had been a joint effort, with cheesy festive songs blaring and the wine flowing. Her parents Betsy and Charlie had joined them by late morning and were tangoing around the kitchen with paper hats and huge smiles. They were staying over for the night. Hence Ann had been busy changing bed sheets and cleaning and airing the room in preparation. So after enjoying a lavish, three course meal, they mucked in together to tidy away, then retired to the lounge to watch TV. The national anthem rang out and all raised their glass to celebrate. Ann watched the Queen's smiling face disappear from the screen and turned to look with exasperation at her mother Betsy, who was wiping a tear from her eye.

"Pur-lease," Ann drawled, with a shake of her head.

"I can't help it, the national anthem on Christmas day chokes me up every time."

Jon topped up her sherry with a chuckle, "you enjoy yourself Betsy."

"At least she's smiling for a change," Ann commented, with a point towards the screen.

"It's a very serious job being the Queen," Charlie said knowingly.

"Oh yes Dad, it must be so difficult having chestfuls of jewellery, an unlimited supply of money and servants at your beck and call."

"Ann," Betsy cried, "show some patriotism please."

"She's just a normal person like you and I," Ann replied, "no better, no worse. Nobility isn't a birth rite you know, it's the way you act and treat the people around you. Anyway, I much prefer the medieval times when Kings fought alongside their fellow man on the battle field – that to me is true royalty."

Betsy sniffed, "well I love our Royal Family. Say what you like Ann, you won't change my mind on this. They are an asset to our country, an institution to be proud of and I'm not ashamed to tell you I'll always be proud to be British."

"Me too," Shouted Charlie, raising his glass towards the ceiling, "God save the Queen and the United Kingdom."

Ann muttered into her fizzy wine, but decided to let the topic drop. The last thing she wanted to do was start a debate or even worse, an argument.

Betsy it seemed had the same idea. "Anyway sweetheart, how is the adoption going? Have you heard from them yet?"

"Not yet Mom, but it takes ages to process the paperwork."

"We're going to see another couple who have adopted children," Jon disclosed, "we met them at the adoption meeting and Ann's kept in touch with her."

"We're going to meet the children," Ann said happily.

"How exciting," Betsy grinned, "I'm so looking forward to having more grandchildren. Don't you agree Charlie?"

She looked towards her husband for confirmation. His eyes were closed and he was snoring gently, his chest rising and falling. Betsy tutted, "has your sister told you her good news?"

"No, why, how many pounds has she lost now?"

"Oh erm, maybe I shouldn't have said any-thing then." Betsy drummed her fingers, looking suddenly shifty.

"Just tell me Mom," sighed an exasperated Ann. Her mother could be so annoyingly dizzy at times. Maybe I take after pragmatic great uncle Bob thought Ann.

"Oh erm, well…She's pregnant!"

The smile slid off Ann's face and she was over-whelmed by a dull sad aching and a sharp stab of envy.

"She's only just found out," explained Betsy, "I suppose she hasn't had a chance to call you herself yet."

"Bullshit!" Ann bit out.

"Ann!" Betsy was shocked, "she probably didn't want to upset you."

"I'm not upset," Ann said brightly, "of course I'm happy for her – she's my sister. It's just so bloody unfair, life I mean."

Jon hoisted himself out of the chair and stooped to hug her gently, "Don't get upset love, not at Christmas. We'll have our own family one day."

Ann nodded and wiped away a tear that had pooled in the corner of one eye.

"Aww sweetheart," Betsy rushed over to smother her youngest daughter in a fierce embrace, "everything will work out for you. You're so brave and strong Ann, you put the rest of us to shame. Don't get down now love. We all adore you to bits."

"I know," Ann managed a watery smile, "besides, there are a lot of people worse off than me, so I do try and look on the positive. It just gets hard sometimes you know."

Jon nodded, feeling her emotional pain. He reached out to chuck her under the chin, "let's open the chocolate liqueur that you've been saving. We can all get merry and play charades."

"Great idea," Charlie opened his eyes wide, jumping upwards, "but I prefer whisky if there's any going."

A loud burst of laughter rang around the room, then Jon disappeared in search of more alcohol.

* * *

In no time at all, Christmas was over and the New Year hurtled towards them like an unmanned freight train. On the spur of the moment, Sophie decided to host a house party and proceeded to invite most of the village, stars from the footballing world, along with friends and family. Amongst those invited were all of the uni crowd. She had fired off texts, pleading with them to help her celebrate the New Year. She was pleased that nearly all of them were coming, except for Evelyn, who wouldn't leave her mam. Sophie revelled in writing lists: guest lists, food lists, to-do lists. There was so much to organise that she thought momentarily that maybe she had been a tad impulsive. Heidi had gone back to Germany for the holidays, so Sophie had to do all of it herself. She considered calling Amber, to ask if she could borrow her housekeeper for the day but shook her head firmly.

"I can manage," she told herself, "I am a strong, capable woman." Organisation was the key she decided, as she jotted down what housework chores needed doing. The house was actually clean enough she noticed, pulling a finger over the table, inspecting it for dust. It had been given a good blast before Christmas, with just a few of the main rooms needing a hoover round. Sophie bought fresh flowers for each room and sprayed air freshener liberally. The result was an abode which smelt like a wild country garden and which had the dogs sneezing continually. As she occupied herself with the more mundane chores, Ryan and Derek went beer shopping, returning with a boot full of alcohol. Sophie watched as they staggered with packs and bottles into the kitchen.

"What have you bought?" Cried Sophie, as the table and floor quickly filled with beverages.

"What haven't we bought eh Del?" Ryan laughed boisterously, "let's see, we've got wine, champagne, alcopops, spirits for the ladies. For the men there's a selection of ales, lager, whisky, you name it baby, we got it."

"This must have cost a fortune!" Sophie shook her head, "you do know that the guests will probably bring their own drink too."

"Good," Ryan replied, catching her in his arms for a playful embrace, "this is going to be the party of the century sweet cheeks, I can't wait."

He reminded Sophie of an over excited adolescent, but despite that, she still giggled at his wandering hands. "Remember our New Year's resolution – to stop boozing?"

"It aint New Years yet Mrs O," Derek said, as he heaved a slab of bitter across the slate tiles.

"Well my liver is certainly going to need a detox after consuming this," she pointed to the case of champagne, "mind you, Mom and Amber will be here, so they'll drink a lot of it."

Sophie left them to organise the alcohol and went off to do the food shop with a reluctant Josh and Jake.

"Why do we have to come?" Josh complained, as she strapped him into the back seat.

"Cause you do. Besides Mommy needs help getting the shopping."

The twins were no help at all. They skidded down the supermarket aisles in their super hero costumes, shouting 'Death to Dr Dread', acting completely loud and boisterous. Other shoppers stared her way, some blatantly tutting and shaking their heads. Sophie cringed in embarrassment, "boys calm down!" Then they proceeded to sneak unhealthy snacks into the huge trolley: chocolates, sweets, crisps, toffee popcorn, in it went.

"Where is the fruit? You love satsumas," Sophie said as she endeavoured to instil an appearance of a sensible, five a day mother. Josh and Jake zoomed off to the fruit section, leaving a momentarily relieved Sophie chance to browse the meat section without disturbance. She threw the food in: pork pies, sausage rolls, gammon, pizza, vol-au-vents. The trolley was almost full and she wasn't even half way round. Then she remembered that she had a few vegetarian guests, so back she trotted, retracing her steps to add more cheese, margherita pizza and vegetable pasties. The desserts were the last to be added. Sophie held onto the trifles and gateaux as she zoomed towards the checkout. Josh and Jake appeared, as she was unloading the trolley, with arms full of fruit.

"What is all this?" Sophie asked, taking the kiwis, the apples, raspberries and blueberries from them, "will you eat all of this?"

"Yes," shouted Josh exuberantly.

Sophie flung them onto the conveyor belt with a shake of her head, watching as a washed out, bored looking cashier quickly scanned them. Sophie winced as the total cost of her expenditure flashed on the till and made a mental note that another of her resolutions was to be more frugal.

Once the boot of the car was packed full, Sophie set off for home, following a long line of shoppers leaving the supermarket. As she waited for her turn to exit, there was a buzzing from her phone. Will had text her, asking if it would be okay if he bought two friends as well as himself and Hema. He was a lovely lad, she thought as she replied that it was fine with her. The thought of the impending party created bubbles of excitement in her stomach. What could she wear? She wondered – the red jewelled mini dress or the long purple satin number with the side split? A white van swerved in front of her suddenly and she slammed on the breaks, narrowly missing his tail end.

"What's happening Mom?" Jake asked from the back.

"Nothing sunshine, Mommy just needs to concentrate on driving." She replied with an apologetic smile.

Soon enough she was home, pulling onto the winding gravel driveway, surprised to see Amber's car parked up underneath the bay window.

Free from the restraints, the boys tore across the lawn, chasing the neighbour's poor cat, while Sophie swung open the boot and staggered through the side entrance, arms laden with bags.

In the kitchen, Amber was perched on a breakfast stool looking glamorous in leggings, a tight tunic and long boots that almost reached her knees. She was listening attentively to an excited Ryan, her head cocked to one side and her eyes wide.

"We're top of the league at the moment and determined to stay there. The club needs this promotion into the Premier League; more TV coverage, better sponsorship deals, increase in wages for everybody. It's a win, win situation."

"It must be so totally cool to be a footballer," Amber simpered, "oh hi Soph," she waved distractedly, her eyes back on Ryan

"It's hard work," Ryan replied with sombre satisfaction, "people think it's all fast cars and fancy bling, but you have to be like super, super fit. Isn't that right Soph?"

"If you say so dear," Sophie joked, "I could do with a hand, the cars full of shopping."

Ryan hopped down from his seat, "anything for you my love," he teased, catching her in a playful embrace.

Amber averted her eyes and reached for the kettle, "fancy a cuppa?" She asked.

"Yes!" Sophie answered, "I need caffeine *right now.*"

"Not for me," Ryan said, "I'm off training in a bit." He disappeared to fetch the shopping in, while Sophie organised the fridge, wondering where she was going to fit everything. By the time she had finished sorting and squeezing, every space was occupied. Last week's salad had been binned, along with some mouldy looking cheese and more cabbage water. A piece of sea bass which had expired its freshness date, was shared between the dog's bowls. They bounded into the kitchen, noses frantically sniffing out the food.

"Phew! I'm glad that's over."

"Now you just got to cook it," smirked Amber as she passed her a mug of frothy coffee.

They crossed through into the large conservatory, sinking down onto the soft seats. Josh and Jake were tearing around the garden like two whirlwinds.

"I wish I had a quarter of their energy," Sophie admitted, "I'm always tired just lately."

"Time of year hun. Maybe you've got a dose of that SAD. I get it most years hun, you just gotta keep looking forward to spring."

"Maybe," Sophie replied, blowing her drink.

"I am so looking forward to your party tomorrow," Amber squealed.

"It should be good," agreed Sophie, "did I tell you the vicar said he might pop in?"

"No way!" Replied a wide eyed Amber, "but what about the drinking games I had planned?"

Sophie laughed, "I don't think he'll be staying long. He probably just wants to come for a free feed."

"And will Ryan's footballer friends be coming?"

"Most of them," Sophie confirmed, "Ryan's set up a roulette wheel especially for them. Boys and their toys, you know what they're like."

"I can be their very own croupier for the evening."

"What about Martin?" Sophie laughed.

Amber waved away the mention of her husband, "he can keep the vicar occupied."

There was a silence as both women pondered on the impending party.

"How are you and Ryan getting on now?" Amber enquired, sipping her coffee.

Sophie considered the question, "We're getting there," she replied, "Christmas was good, although he's been training a lot. There's been quite a few matches over December."

Amber tutted in sympathy, "I know that feeling honey. Martin never stops working! He was even replying to emails while we were eating our Christmas lunch. Angel and I were stuck the whole of boxing day with his interfering mother. It hasn't been a nice Christmas for me to be honest. Hopefully the New Year will be different."

Sophie was suddenly struck by how unhappy her friend looked. As well as looking painfully thin, there was a melancholy air about her that she hadn't noticed before. Sympathy washed over her, she leant forward and rubbed Amber's arm.

"We'll have a good time tomorrow night I guarantee it and maybe we could have a spa weekend sometime in January, just the two of us – no kids, no men, pure girly indulgence."

Amber nodded gratefully and they relaxed back, to chat about fashion and celebrity gossip.

\* \* \*

New Year's Eve was a blustery one. Sophie was up early taking the dogs for their morning stroll. She was wrapped up well in a new designer coat with an eye catching fur trim. It was a present off Ryan. Although she had squealed with delight as she opened it, she couldn't help but think of the five winter jackets she already had, hanging in her wardrobe. Maybe a trip to the charity shop was required she thought, as she stuffed a pack of half eaten mints into the warm furry pocket. Sophie pulled on a warm, woolly hat and wriggled her fingers inside tight leather gloves before clipping on the dogs' leads. She strode up the country lane, head down against the buffeting wind, passing trees that bent and swayed in the strong gale. The path was deserted so she bent to release the dogs. They bounded up the embankment, yelping at darting squirrels and frantically sniffing the muddy earth. Her mom was due this morning, she had insisted on coming to help with the party preparations, even though Sophie had assured her that everything was under control. Last night she had been up late dressing the table, folding napkins into pretty shapes and sprinkling stars over the clean, bright table cloth. She had also bleached and cleaned the three toilets and hoovered around the furniture. She had fallen into bed exhausted but excited for the party. Now all she had to do today was cook and lay out the buffet food. She came to a fork in the road and decided impulsively to follow the signs for the village centre. Ryan and the boys would be in bed for another hour at least and she felt that she needed the exercise after the indulgence of Christmas. Sophie was on an elevated dirt track which overlooked the pretty village. As she squinted through the early morning mist, she could just decipher the Post Office and the newsagents, the pub sandwiched between a butchers and a delicatessen. Overhead, the Christmas lights twinkled, a colourful line that flipped and swayed. For the second year running, Ryan had been asked to turn them on. He was the village celebrity and very popular with the residents. Sometimes they walked down to the pub with the boys and enjoyed a meal and a chat with the regulars. That seemed ages ago though, Sophie thought with a sniff. Now he usually went down with Derek, calling her hours later to beg for a lift back. Sophie made another mental resolution; to spend more time as a family. As she neared the courtyard, she clicked the leads back onto the dogs, pulling them to heel. The butcher was just opening up, struggling with a board that advertised a buy one get one free offer on pork chops.

"Morning Mrs O'Neill," he called across the street, tipping his cap.

"Morning," Sophie called cheerfully, waving his way.

"Nice Christmas?" He enquired.

"Lovely thank you," she replied warmly, "did you?"

"Fabulous as always."

"Did you sell many turkeys?" She asked with a smile.

"I did, along with gammon, duck and pheasant. My meat freezer is bare so to speak."

Sophie held a hand up as she carried on past his shop towards the fountain in the centre of the village. She watched the whirling water for a few moments, before digging deep in her pockets for some coppers. After murmuring a wish for the New Year, she flung the small change into the icy depths. Across the road, the florist was just opening, bringing buckets of flowers out onto the pavement. Sophie decided impulsively to buy more roses. Pink one's this time, for the hall and the kitchen. Holding on tightly to her purchases, she waited while the dogs sniffed the ground. A milk cart trundled past, splashing dirty rainwater high into the air. Sophie shivered and looked to the sky. If she hurried, she might just get back before the rain started. The clouds were grey and bleak, rolling ominously, blocking out the warmth of the sun. She tugged at the dogs and began walking quickly towards the hill and home.

The rain started a few minutes later, small droplets that soon changed to a torrential downpour. She ran blindly, while the dogs yapped at her heels, thinking it was some sort of game. By the time she reached home she was thoroughly soaked, her hair dripping wet and plastered over her face. She shrugged out of her very trendy but totally impractical jacket, underneath, her jeans stuck to her skin. Hastily she pulled them off, along with squelching socks. Ryan was in the kitchen, reading the sports section of the local newspaper as he waited for the kettle to boil. He looked up with a grin as she plodded through.

"Hey babe," he teased, "raining is it?"

Sophie flung the towel at him, "make me a cuppa," she called, as she sprinted up the stairs, to turn on the shower. Soon she was warm and dry again, cocooned in a fluffy dressing gown as she pulled a comb through her freshly washed hair. Josh and Jake were still sleeping, as she tiptoed past their room. Although they had plenty of bedrooms to choose from, they insisted on sharing one. The landing was strewn with their dirty clothes, which they had flung off in haste. Sophie picked them up, plonking them in the laundry basket with a grimace. When was Heidi due back, she wondered? The washing was piling up and already she was bored of housework. As she passed the guest bedroom, she heard loud snores emanating. Derek had slept over again; he had been up late last night playing pool with Ryan. She had heard their raucous laughter coming from the games room. Sometimes it felt like Ryan was married to him – they spent so much time together. Sophie carried on down the stairs, padding softly back into the kitchen. Her tea was lukewarm, she popped it into the microwave, waiting for the timer to ping. Ryan appeared in the kitchen, muttering something about the wind knocking down one of the fence panels. He snaked an arm around her waist, "come back to bed," he said as he kissed her neck.

"Are you joking?" She cried, "have you forgot we have a party tonight. I'm just about to start the food. And you need to tidy the garden and the driveway."

Ryan sighed, letting her go. "Is Del up yet?"

"No and he shouldn't be staying over so much either. Doesn't his poor wife mind?"

"Sounds like they have an open relationship," he replied with a shrug. Sophie shook her head with disapproval and turned away to ignite the double oven. For the next hour she busied herself cooking the buffet food. As she was rolling up her sleeves to tackle a mountain of dirty plates and pans, Yvonne breezed through the doorway.

"Hi darling," she air kissed her daughter's cheeks, "why is Ryan playing golf in the garden?"

"What?!" Sophie rubbed at the misted window, "sometimes I really feel like I have three young boys."

Yvonne raised an eyebrow but remained silent.

"Here Mom," she threw her a tea towel, "get stuck in."

"Has the dishwasher broke?" Yvonne asked, wrinkling her nose.

"No it's full and this method is quicker." Sophie clicked on the radio, turning up the volume as a cheesy eighties song blasted around the kitchen.

"Erm, I'll be on my own tonight," Yvonne shouted over the music.

"No Roger?" Sophie asked, secretly rejoicing.

"He's in terrible pain with his back again and the doctor has advised that he have complete rest. I erm, wondered if I could sleep here for the night."

Sophie nodded, "yes no problem, you can help me with the tidying up tomorrow," she laughed at the look of horror on Yvonne's face. "Just kidding Mom."

They spent the remainder of the morning preparing buffet food. The table was soon full with trays of sandwiches, pork pie, sausage rolls, pasties, salads and a delectable selection of desserts.

"I'm done," Yvonne exclaimed, sinking down onto a kitchen stool. Josh tore into the room, munching on a family bag of Maltesers.

"Where's your brother?" Sophie asked.

"Watching tele," he replied, "Nan, Nan, come upstairs and look at my awesome Lego from Father Christmas." Yvonne sighed wearily before getting to her feet.

"Come on then buster," she chased her grandson out of the kitchen, leaving Sophie alone with her thoughts. Had she prepared enough food? She wondered. Was there enough alcohol? She eyed the crates and bottles stored in the chilly utility room and decided there was. After a bout of nagging, Ryan had set about tidying the garden, raking the leaves up and throwing the boys' outdoor toys into a dilapidated shed. Derek had surfaced at midday, mumbling something about getting home to the missus before he arrived back for the evening's celebrations. The afternoon passed quietly. Sophie watched TV with the twins, painting her nails a vixen red, as Yvonne snored gently in the chair next to her. At four o'clock she wrestled them into the bath, rubbing their hair vigorously with sweet smelling shampoo.

"I hate bath time," grumbled Jake, as Sophie swiped a soap bubble out of his eye.

"Me too." Piped up his mirror image. Sophie ignored their protests, supervising as they scrubbed at their teeth.

"There all done," she sat back on her haunches with a proud smile, "your clothes are on the bed, please don't get dirty." As she was coming out of their bedroom, she saw Yvonne disappearing into the bathroom. She would be in there for a good hour at least. Sophie made her way to her own room. Ryan was on the bed, face upwards, breathing heavily. He opened one eye as she shut the door.

"All done?"

"Yes, everything's ready," she replied, with a squeal of excitement, "now I just need to make myself beautiful."

"You already are," he patted the bed with a cheeky grin, "come here."

Sophie glanced at the clock, they had a couple of hours before the guests started to arrive. She tumbled down onto the mattress, into his open arms and eager kisses. Afterwards they dozed, tangled limbs wrapped around the warm duvet.

"I really must get ready," Sophie mumbled, extricating herself from underneath Ryan's heavy arm. She sat up, rubbing sleepily at her eyes, "did I tell you all my uni friends are coming this evening? Well everyone apart from Evelyn."

Ryan yawned, "does that mean we'll have purple haired, spaced out hippies here and indie music requests?"

Sophie tutted, "I've told you everyone is perfectly normal. Melanie has bright red hair though and she's a lesbian, so no homophobic jokes please."

Ryan grinned, "I'll be on my best behaviour, for sure."

"Who did you say is doing the music anyway?" Sophie changed the subject.

"Er, Derek's organised it, it's a mate of a mate, supposedly fantastic."

"Well I hope they're good. A lot of people are coming to help us celebrate tonight." Sophie sprang from the bed, "OMG, look at the time." She rushed into the en-suite, leaving Ryan room to spread out like a starfish on the bed.

\* \* \*

Oh my gosh, what a beautiful house!" Juliette stared in awe at the sprawling detached building, at the top of the winding driveway, "are you sure you have the right number Maz?"

Marie stuck the car into neutral, then spun in her seat, "yes, that's what it says on the wall plaque – Thistledown House, right?"

Juliette nodded, "that's the one. Well I'd better get a shifty on, thanks so much for the lift sis."

"Are you sure I can't pick you up?"

"No, I can call a cab" Juliette assured her, "help yourself to the booze, enjoy yourself. I won't be late."

"Don't stress Jules, we're sleeping over re-member. Just don't wake me up when you come in."

"I'll be as quiet as a mouse, but you and Dave can have my bed. I'll sleep on the fold up bed settee."

Marie nodded her assent, "have a great time and remember, if you can't be good, be careful."

Juliette laughed as she clambered from the car, happy that she had made the decision to wear jeans and flats. She felt so much more comfort-able in this attire. She waved until her sister had disappeared down the dimly lit street and then made her way towards the front door. The gravel crunched underneath her and from the nearby trees an owl hooted. Christmas decorations were dotted around the garden; a 'santa stop here' sign, brightly lit snowman figurines and a giant inflatable reindeer bobbed in the evening wind. The whole house was covered in lights, even the chimney stack. There were hundreds of them, twinkling and shining, all different colours. The heavy oak door was swathed with mistletoe, wreaths and musky smelling pine cones, and in the corner were stacked two brand new look-ing scooters and an upended pair of jazzy roller boots. Juliette stood on tiptoe to reach the bell, she could hear the chimes ringing throughout the house and hoped that Sophie had heard it over the thrum of the disco music. Seconds later the door swung open to reveal a smartly dressed young boy with neatly combed golden hair.

"Hello," Juliette said, as she knelt down to greet him.

"Hello," he replied, "are you one of Mommy's friends?"

"I am," Juliette confirmed, "may I come in?"

He held the door wide open for her to enter, then disappeared up the hall yelling 'Mom.'

Juliette shrugged off her coat and stood nervously, looking around at the stunning wall art and the full length ornate mirror.

"Jules," Sophie squealed, as she rushed forward to embrace her, "how are you? Have you had a good Christmas?"

"Yes, lovely thank you," Juliette was engulfed in a cloud of expensive smelling perfume and strong hairspray.

"Come in, come in," Sophie tugged at her arm, pulling her into a huge room, where music pulsed from towering speakers and spheres of light flashed across the walls and floors. She spotted Will and Hema canoodling in a corner, amidst a sea of faces that she didn't recognise.

"Ann and Jon are in the kitchen helping themselves to food, are you hungry?" Sophie shouted over the din of the music.

"No, not at the moment thanks," replied Juliette, "your house is absolutely gorgeous!"

"Would you like to see the rest of it?" Before Sophie could utter a reply, she tugged at her arm, pulling her out of the room and up a vast, winding staircase, to give her a whirlwind tour of the house. Numerous doors opened to reveal sumptuous bathrooms and luxuriously decorated bedrooms. Juliette thought of her tiny maisonette which she could just afford and sighed.

"This is amazing; do you have a nice garden too?"

Sophie looked around, as if she were seeing it for the first time, "it is a lovely house," she conceded, feeling tremendously guilty that she took it all for granted, "but compared to others on this estate, this is relatively small. As for the garden, come and see for yourself."

They passed couples smooching on the stairways and a large dog that was merrily chewing on a bone. Sophie led the way into an enormous kitchen that was easily the size of Juliette's entire flat. She waved open mouthed at Ann who was spearing pasta salad onto a posh dinner plate. "Hi Guys," she called, as Sophie whizzed her past and out of the back door. Juliette stumbled down a high step, onto a brightly lit patio, full of pot plants and mini fir trees. The garden stretched into the darkness, dotted with children's play equipment and two goal posts.

"Is this the size of a real life football pitch?" Juliette gasped.

"It's not far off," Sophie divulged, "that was one of the prerequisites when we were looking. A garden large enough for Ryan and his mates to practise in. Speaking of my charming husband…" she trailed off as a cheeky looking chap ambled across the garden towards them.

"Are you smoking again?" Sophie asked in a peculiar, high pitched fashion, "coach Jones will be fuming if he catches you."

Ryan O'Neill flicked ash on the beautiful lawn and rolled his eyes with indifference, "one won't hurt."

"This is Jules," Sophie said, "one of my friends from uni, I was telling you about."

Ryan lifted Juliette's hand to his mouth in a charming manoeuvre, "lovely to meet you."

Juliette squirmed with unease but smiled brightly, "hello, Sophie's just been giving me a tour of your home and I must say that it is pretty spectacular."

Ryan looked pleased at her words, "it is awesome," he agreed, "I'm thinking of adding an extension in the New Year."

Sophie looked aghast, "we don't need any more rooms."

"It will increase the value of the house," Ryan blew out a plume of smoke, "what do you think Amber?"

Juliette looked round to face a woman dripping with jewellery, staggering across the lawn.

"Soph, you really need some stepping stones. This grass is killing my heels. What are you three talking about?"

"Extensions," Ryan replied smoothly, slipping an arm around her waist, "a necessity or not?"

Amber giggled, "Oh definitely a must have," she decided, "our sun house has been such a great investment."

"We already have a conservatory, I really don't think the house needs to be any bigger." Sophie felt embarrassed and irked, she wondered what Juliette thought of her husband's comments. He was bragging, she thought angrily and Juliette did not look impressed. There was a fixed smile on her face and an aura of disapproval.

"Where property is concerned, you can never be too big," Amber replied with a snort. "Who are you?" She stared at Juliette, eyes coolly appraising her.

"Juliette is a student, on the same course as me," Sophie quickly explained to Amber.

"How super," Amber replied, as a glazed look crossed her face, "I'm Sophie's best friend, we're very close." The jealous vibes emanating from Amber were painfully obvious.

Sophie smiled brightly, taking Juliette's arm, "now would you like a drink?" She was relieved that Juliette nodded eagerly. She led her away, leaving Ryan and Amber giggling over a lewd joke.

"I'm sorry about that," Sophie began, "Amber can be possessive at times, but she does mean well."

Juliette assured her it was fine, inwardly deciding that she didn't like either of them.

"So, have you heard from a certain lecturer?" Sophie's eyes were wide and enquiring.

Juliette nodded with a wide grin, "I have. We're going for a meal next weekend."

"Oh my God!" Sophie grabbed hold of her arm, squeezing her tight, "this is so romantic."

"Hang on, don't get too excited, it's only food," Juliette laughed, "we're just sort of almost friends."

"Yeah right 'just sort of almost friends', for now," Sophie rolled her eyes as she led her back to the kitchen. "Now, what would you like to drink?"

Juliette eyed the bottles and cans lining the utility floor, "I'll have a babycham please."

As Sophie was cracking open the bottle, a group of men entered the kitchen, guffawing loudly.

"Excellent party Soph," a dark haired man commented as he stooped to help himself to a six pack of lager, "keep us going for half hour eh lads?"

"This is Mickey," Sophie introduced him with a rueful smile. Juliette listened with interest as Sophie explained that they were footballer friends of Ryan's. They were pleasant enough, friendly and chatty, but there was also an air of arrogance surrounding them, as if they were used to getting exactly whatever they wanted. Juliette noticed their designer clothing and the expensive looking jewellery and gulped as she wondered how much they earned per week. It did not bear thinking about, the notion that their monthly wage could purchase her entire flat and all its contents. She pushed the thoughts aside and concentrated on listening to Mickey. He was the most gregarious of the group, frequently laughing and winking Juliette's way, as he regaled her with wild stories of the footballing world.

"That man has no morals," Sophie disclosed after they had left to join the other lads at the roulette wheel. "He'll be in the paper again next week; boozing, gambling, wild parties and loose women. It all goes on at Chattlesbury FC."

Juliette shook her head, maybe having lots of money wasn't always a good thing and this house, although undeniably beautiful, lacked real warmth. There was something missing. Juliette's flat was cosy and warm, chaotic yet loving. This was like a show home; cream coloured carpets and lush furnishings. It felt empty, as if nobody truly lived here. Poor Sophie thought Juliette with a shake of her head. She should feel jealous of her luxurious lifestyle but instead, all she felt for her was sympathy. They chatted for a while about uni and the new modules which were due to start then made their way back into the disco room.

"I've got to go and mingle," Sophie yelled above the loud music, "the others are over there." She pointed to the uni crowd, waving her in their direction. Juliette hugged them all, before becoming embroiled in a conversation with Ann on the trappings and evils of wealth.

# Chapter Twenty-Four

Will was squashed onto a velvet stool with Hema perched on top of him. He nibbled her neck, wishing that they could be alone.

"Get a room you guys," Sadie squealed.

"So it's definitely back on with you two?" Jimmy asked, speaking between mouthfuls of buffet food.

Will squeezed Hema tight, "looks that way."

"Our families have no idea though," Hema disclosed, "and that's the way we want it to stay, total secrecy."

"You two are playing with fire," Jimmy said with a shake of his head.

Will shrugged, "Hema's worth it."

"Who is that?" Jimmy pointed to the makeshift dance floor, where an older lady was flinging her limbs around wildly.

"Sophie's mom," Will replied, "she's been on the vodka all night."

"Man, this house must have cost a fortune," Jimmy whistled, "tell me again why she's at uni?"

"She wants to be a teacher, God knows why," Will revealed.

"What about you mate? Don't ya want to follow your Dad's career?"

"No way!" Will shook his head furiously, "teaching would sap the soul outta me man. I have no idea what I want to do yet."

"Better make your mind up soon." Jimmy nudged him in the ribs.

Will scowled, "now you sound like my dad."

"Come on," interrupted Hema, "let's go dance." They stepped around Ann who was sipping a fruity alcopop through a bendy straw. Jon was telling Juliette loudly about his job and what it entailed.

"It sounds so interesting," she said.

"It doesn't pay as much as what these guys are on," he said with a sweep of his hand. The footballers and their wives had entered the room and were commandeering a position next to the DJ station.

Juliette glanced their way, "some people are overpaid. Is that Bobby Bishop?"

Jon confirmed it was indeed the famous striker.

"That's one footballer I do know," Juliette laughed.

"Did I see a vicar here earlier, or was I imagining it?" Ann piped up with a frown.

"I saw him too," Juliette confirmed, "what a strange mix of people."

"Sophie's twins are adorable though," Ann said with a smile, "I wonder if they'll play football when they're older too?"

"I must use the ladies," Juliette said, as she placed her drink down on an ornate table.

This house was a strange mix she thought, as she made her way out of the room and up the winding staircase. The kitchen was ultra-modern, with contemporary designed work stations and trendy, state of the art contraptions. Yet the other rooms were dotted with antique wooden pieces. And on the landing wall was a huge canvas painting of a stormy sea. Juliette squinted, trying to decipher the signature in the corner. It was magnificent she decided, the mix of colours was stunning, it must have taken months to complete.

"I hate that painting," a voice warbled. Juliette turned to face the dancing lady from earlier.

"Oh I think it's fantastic," Juliette replied with a smile, "I'm Juliette by the way, one of Sophie's uni friends." She held out her hand politely.

"Yvonne Fletcher, Sophie's Mom" came the reply. Juliette was struck by her dark mahogany hair and her bright make up. She looked nothing like Sophie.

"I prefer modern art myself," she sniffed, "but then Sophie has always had a quirky taste in home décor. She takes after her father."

"Oh is he here?"

Yvonne snorted, "he ran away a long time ago," she slurred, "left me to raise Sophie all alone."

Juliette was shocked but her face remained impassive, "I'm sorry to hear that." Inwardly she was thinking *poor Sophie*.

"That's what men do; let you down," she grabbed hold of Juliette's arm, "are you married?"

"Er, no," explained Juliette, "I'm a single parent of two children."

"Bravo!" Yvonne clapped lightly, "I feel like I've been on my own for years now. I do have a boyfriend, although he doesn't believe in marriage. So I guess I'm still waiting for my prince." She rested her head on Juliette's shoulder and she was overwhelmed by the strong fumes of alcohol. Juliette realised how drunk she was and eyed the winding staircase nervously.

"Look, I'll just pop to the toilet, you wait here, then we can talk some more." Yvonne nodded dejectedly and propped herself against the banister.

Juliette rushed into the toilet, which was an extravagant affair of gold taps and marble steps, leading to a Jacuzzi style bath. She quickly swilled her hands then unbolted the door. Yvonne was sitting cross legged on the floor, her whole body shaking from a bout of hiccups.

Juliette helped her to her feet, guiding her back down the stairs.

"Would you like a coffee?" She asked hopefully.

"Coffee?" Shrieked Yvonne, "it's New Year's Eve darling, don't mention that word again."

Juliette smiled but nodded.

"Has my daughter put you up to this – sent you to check up on me?"

"No, no," Juliette shook her head, "Sophie's a lovely person, you must be so proud of her."

"I am," slurred Yvonne, "but she was always a Daddy's girl, broke her heart when he ran away."

Juliette shook her head as she imagined a bewildered and hurt Sophie. She wanted to ask more but felt as if she would be prying.

"How about some food?" Juliette asked, anticipating the victuals would soak up some of the alcohol swirling in her system.

Yvonne nodded reluctantly and pointed the way to the kitchen. Ryan was leaning against the doorway chatting to a burly looking man.

"Mom!" He shouted, opening his arms wide. Yvonne pushed against Juliette, stumbling forward to be caught by her grinning son-in-law. "How about one of my legendary cocktails?"

"Oh yes please," Yvonne agreed, her eyes alight with the anticipation of more alcohol.

"Actually, I was going to brew a coffee," Juliette suggested, stepping forward as her eyes scanned the room for a kettle.

"Coffee?" Ryan mocked, "that's banned on New Year's Eve…save it for the morning eh Del?" He turned to nudge his accomplice who guffawed loudly and slapped his back in a cheesy attempt at male camaraderie. Yvonne was laughing along in agreement.

"If you're sure," Juliette said with a sigh.

"She is," Ryan snapped. Juliette's lips pursed into a thin line as she watched him pour shots of liquid into a chrome shaker. What a complete and utter twit she thought with a shake of her head. What on earth did Sophie see in him? Just then her phone beeped. It was a message from Ben, wishing her a happy New Year and hoping that she was having a good time this evening. Not sure about that one Juliette thought with a rueful smile, as her fingers tapped out a reply.

"Fancy a cocktail darling?" Ryan drawled in her direction.

"No thank you," Juliette replied, with a wrinkle of her nose. Yvonne had begun a slow smooch around the kitchen with the other guy, whoever he was. Ryan noticed her look of disapproval and tutted loudly.

"That's just Del," he explained, in a patronising tone, "gardener by trade but he's like family." He leant toward her, lowering his voice, "she's just lonely that's all."

"You must be proud of Sophie," she said, eager to change the subject.

He threw her a bewildered look, "er, of course. She's an ace wife and mother."

"I meant about her going to uni," she replied, her tone hard.

"Oh that," he rolled his eyes, "I'm a bit confused as to why she's doing it to be honest. Me and Del have had bets on whether she'll last the full three years." He chuckled as he threw a cherry in the glass with a plop.

"I'm sure she will," Juliette protested, "if she has a good support network at home that is. Excuse me," she pushed past him with a scowl and slammed out of the kitchen.

"Who are these people?" Ann shouted in her ear as she re-joined them, "you've just missed a huge cat fight. The men are blind drunk and the dog's been sick all over the fireplace."

"Oh my god," Juliette gasped, "poor Sophie!"

"Yes quite," Ann replied, "I can't believe that I envied her."

"All that glitters is not gold," Jon cut in, with a knowing look.

"Well, at least Will's enjoying himself," Ann rasped.

Juliette turned to watch him spinning Hema on the dancefloor.

"I need a cigarette and some fresh air, are you two coming?"

Jon and Juliette exchanged amused looks and weaved Ann around the bopping crowd.

The garden was as busy as the house. A crowd of men had gathered on the lawn and had formed a circle, where a ball was being kicked around. Glamorous looking women were draped across the garden furniture whooping and cackling.

"How the other half live eh?" Jon commented drily.

"I wish I'd stayed at home," Juliette said wistfully. At this moment she wanted nothing more than to curl up on the sofa with her children, cups of hot chocolate and a tray of Garibaldi biscuits.

"Do you want a lift back with us?" Ann asked with a sniff, "we're leaving as soon as it's polite to do so."

"That would be brilliant, thank you," Juliette let out a relieved sigh.

The remainder of the evening dragged on. Juliette stayed with Ann and Jon, continuously checking her watch, wishing the hours away. Ten minutes before midnight the entire houseful trooped into the garden to watch an impressive fireworks display. As rockets zoomed and banged overhead, the DJ leapt onto a table and counted down to the New Year.

"Happy New Year," Jon cheered, pulling her into a warm embrace.

Ann waved a sparkler, "let it be a good one."

"Can we go now?" Asked a weary Juliette.

Suddenly there was a high pitched yell. They watched in horror as a defunct firework whizzed sideways, hitting a beautiful gazebo straight on. It burst into flames, the wood buckling and crumbling underneath the fizzing rocket.

"Call a fire engine!" A woman shrieked. The crowd scrambled back into the house.

"Get some water!" Jon yelled, but no one was listening. The door to the kitchen was blocked with people panicking and pushing.

"Jesus," Ann said, as they watched the gazebo turn into a flaming ball.

Ten minutes later two fire engines roared up the driveway, narrowly missing the back end of a Porsche. The firemen jumped out, tugging hoses with them but it was too late. The gazebo was a crumbling, smouldering mess. Pockets of fire were soon extinguished and smoke curled high into the night air.

"I think it's time to go," commented Ann, as they searched around for Sophie. They found her slumped in a sumptuous chair, white with shock. "Everything's under control," soothed Juliette, as she crouched down in front of her, "can we do anything to help?"

"No, no thank you," came the bewildered reply, "and thank you for coming. I'm so sorry it's ended like this."

"It's not your fault," Jon said calmly, "just try and get some rest. If you need any help clearing stuff up, call us in the morning, Okay?"

Sophie nodded, her eyes swimming with sudden tears. She heaved herself up out of the chair, following them to the open doorway.

Juliette hugged her gently, "see you at uni?"

"Yes, bye," Sophie watched them disappear down the drive, then with a shaky sigh closed the door.

* * *

"Oh my goodness!" Evelyn was sipping tea in the canteen, the local newspaper spread out on the table in front of her.

"What is it?" Melanie asked, leaning closer.

"Were you not at Sophie's New Year's party dear?"

A blank look ensued then remembrance dawned, "oh we were invited but Tash had a bad stomach, we stayed in for the first time like ever."

"This is awful," Evelyn remarked with a shake of her head. She slid the newspaper across towards Melanie, so they were both able to read it.

'Wild celebrity party turns into inferno' screamed the headlines. Melanie gasped, "is that Sophie?"

"I think so dear," Evelyn slipped on her spectacles to inspect the black and white photo of a scared looking Sophie in a tight embrace with another lady.

"I think this may be her husband," she commented, peering at an emblazoned shot of a group of men piled into a Jacuzzi, holding cans of beer high in the air.

"That's Ryan O'Neill," Melanie confirmed, "what an absolute dick!"

There were further pictures on pages two and three. A rather incriminating shot of the local vicar swinging from a garden hammock was captioned, 'the real face of religion?' next to a close up of councillor Matilda Brunswick bent over a bush described as the 'sickness of politics.'

Melanie snickered, "this looks like an excellent party though."

"It really wasn't," said Juliette. She was standing behind them, looking down at the newspaper with dismay, "how on earth did the press get in?"

Sophie arrived thirty minutes later, her head covered in a woollen bobble hat and sunglasses shielding her eyes. Ann looked out at the dark, dreary day and frowned.

"You don't need to hide away Sophie. None of this is your fault." She said gruffly.

"Somebody sold their photos to the Press, can you believe it?" Sophie replied, wringing her hands. "I just can't trust anybody."

"Maybe the problem is that you trust the wrong people," suggested Ann.

"But they're my friends," cried Sophie.

"Are they?" Ann's eyebrows shot southwards, "how well do you really know these people?"

Juliette had to agree with Ann and nodded in sympathy, "how is your mom?"

Sophie rolled her eyes, sinking down into the seat with a sigh, "she slept with our gardener. Can you believe it? I almost feel sorry for her boyfriend, Roger Ramjet."

"Well she is an adult," Juliette replied, smirking at the childhood book character reference.

"I suppose so," grumbled Sophie. "I'm just so worried about the media intrusion. I'm sure that there were reporters following me here."

Evelyn patted her hand, "you'll be safe here dear, try not to worry."

Melanie sprang to her feet, grabbing hold of Sophie, "come on don't stress, let's go and enjoy Introduction to Poetry." She threw a wink Juliette's way, before ushering Ann forward, out of the canteen.

"Juliette," Evelyn's voice was a tremulous warble, "I wonder if I could ask your advice?"

Juliette looked her way with interest, "yes of course Evelyn, what's up?"

"Erm, I was thinking of asking one of the lecturers to read over my novel. Do you think that would be a good idea?"

Juliette's smile dazzled Evelyn momentarily, "yes, I think that would be an excellent idea Evelyn. Do you erm, have anyone in mind?"

Evelyn nodded, "I thought maybe Dr Rivers. He is my tutor after all and he has always been so friendly and approachable."

Juliette's face took on a luminous shine, like the sunshine beaming after the darkest of thunderstorms. Well, Evelyn thought, is this what it looks like? How had she not noticed before, it was written all over Juliette's face. Love in glorious technicolour.

"How beautiful," Evelyn murmured.

"Pardon?" Juliette laughed nervously, "but to answer your question, yes I think Dr Rivers would be the perfect one to ask." She cleared her throat and swiped her purse back inside her rucksack.

"But would you come with me?" Evelyn asked, her hand flying to her throat, "I could do with some moral support."

"I really think you got this Evelyn, you don't need me tagging along." The thought of seeing Ben Rivers in his office both petrified and exhilarated her.

"Still, I'd feel better if you were there with me," Evelyn persisted. Juliette was surprised, she had never seen Evelyn so determined before.

"Well if you really need me to."

\* \* \*

They climbed the stairs to Ben's office.

"I'm not sure this is a good idea; he must be so busy with essay marking." Evelyn paused at the top of the steps, catching her breath.

"No backing out now," Juliette decided firmly, "have you got your manuscript with you?"

Evelyn patted her bag, "I've brought half of it."

"Well then," Juliette smiled, "don't worry Evelyn. If he can't help, then I'm sure there will be somebody else in the university who can."

Juliette ushered Evelyn forward, "go on, he won't bite!"

Evelyn laughed nervously, her hand paused in a ball, ready to knock. Just then the door swung open and Brian Hodges burst through the gap, clutching a jam smeared piece of toast.

"Oh hi ladies," he said, surprise etched on his face, "are you after me?"

"Er... Dr Rivers actually. Please," A flustered Evelyn replied.

"Go on in," Doctor Hodges stepped aside allowing Evelyn to take a hesitant step forward.

"Shall I wait outside?" Juliette whispered.

"I'd like you with me," Evelyn replied.

They entered a small room crammed full of books. They were everywhere; on shelves, perched on desks, they were even piled precariously high on the floor. Evelyn stepped around them and waited for Ben to spin in his chair.

"Hello ladies," he greeted warmly, "what can I do for you?"

His eyes rested on Juliette and she felt a thrill as his face lit up.

"Evelyn wants to ask you something... I mean she'd like to speak to you, er..." Juliette nudged her friend, willing her out of silence.

Ben looked Evelyn's way, his eyebrows raised with expectation.

"Yes," Evelyn began, clearing her throat, "the thing is Dr Rivers, I wanted to ask your advice," she hesitantly began explaining the reason for her visit.

Juliette glanced round the room. It was small and rather cluttered, with a filing cabinet wedged in the corner and two desks crammed close together. There were mugs and pens strewn everywhere and the desks were covered with paper and odd looking bits of stationery. It smelt nice though, the aroma of coffee hung in the air, and the hint of aftershave, fresh and musky. There was an open laptop flashing from Dr

Hodges desk and then Juliette noticed a cork board on the wall directly above it. On it were pinned pictures of Kylie Minogue in various states of undress, lyrics to one of her best known songs and concert memorabilia. Juliette gasped, her hand flying to her mouth to stifle the giggle that threatened to erupt. So it was Dr Hodges who liked Kylie, not Ben. How had people got it so very wrong about him? She wondered.

As Evelyn chattered, Juliette looked past Ben at his own desk. She noticed a picture in a frame; a fresh faced looking lady with her arms around two laughing children. A sister maybe, Juliette deduced, remembering his text from Christmas. They did look alike – the same dark haired good looks and youthful complexions. The window was propped open, she could hear the sound of students conversing and the revving of vehicles. Morning mist curled through the gap like searching ghostly fingers. Juliette shivered, wondering how on earth Ben wasn't frozen to death, but then he did look rather snug in a warm looking cable sweater.

"So anyway," Evelyn was beginning to stutter with nerves, "I was hoping that yourself, or another member of the university staff would be willing to read over it for me and to give me some feedback."

Ben leant back in his chair, a broad grin on his face, "Firstly Evelyn let me congratulate you on writing and finishing your book. I've been trying for years. Not an easy task and I think it's highly commendable. So yes of course I would be happy to read over it for you. In fact, I feel honoured that you have asked me. Although it may take me a while as I have essays to mark and lectures to prepare for. Leave it with me okay?"

Juliette swooned slightly, damn he is dreamy she thought, feeling pleased for Evelyn.

"Okay," Evelyn nodded quickly, a wide smile on her face, "and thank you so much Dr Rivers. I do appreciate you giving up your time. You must be so busy, thank you."

Ben held up his hand, "it's fine really Evelyn and please call me Ben."

Evelyn blushed, "well this is half of it," she passed him a bulging carrier bag, "I can bring in the rest tomorrow if that's okay with you."

"Yes please do," he said warm and polite, "and if I'm not here, just leave it on my desk."

"Well then," Evelyn backed towards the door, "I'll be on my way to class."

Juliette moved to follow her out but was halted by Ben's gentle tones, "Miss Harris, may I have a quick word?"

She turned at the sound of her name, gulping at the self-assured smile and something in his eyes that looked like a mixture of mirth and desire. He waited until Evelyn had closed the door before rising to his feet. Long muscular legs that stretched him to his full height.

"So, you had a good Christmas then?" He moved slowly towards her.

"Yes," she whispered, acutely aware of the tension that hung between them.

"And are you still free the weekend then?"

Juliette backed away from him slightly and felt the cool feel of wood against her thighs. She leant backwards, placing her hands firmly on the desk behind her.

"I am," she assured him. There was a glint in his eyes and the chemistry between them was palpable. "Maybe I should go," she gabbled, feeling nervous and excited at the same time. Then in two strides he was standing right in front of her, gently touching her cheek, "I've been thinking about you."

"Have you?" Juliette's words came out flirty and playful, inside she was a ball of nerves. "I was worried I had scared you off."

His lips curled in amusement, "well Miss Harris, do you *still* think that I'm gay?"

"I haven't decided," she replied as his nose brushed hers, "maybe you need to convince me."

Juliette gazed at him boldly, her stomach was somersaulting like crazy and her skin tingled under his touch.

His lips hovered over hers, then slowly he kissed her and she was closing her eyes, lost in the sensation of his mouth on hers. As the kiss deepened, she felt him grip her hips and instinctively her hands went up to twine in his hair and to pull him closer. Juliette's knees were shaking with desire as he reluctantly pulled away from her mouth, to trail a line of fervent kisses down her throat.

"Oh," she murmured.

"Is that good?" Ben asked between kisses.

"Yes," she cried, as his mouth covered hers again.

Then there was a sudden bang as the door slammed and Brian Hodges stood staring at them, looking rather shocked.

"Erm, can I come in?" He asked tentatively.

Juliette sprang away from the desk as if it were scorching hot. Her cheeks blazed with embarrassment while Ben adjusted his tie and cleared the huskiness out of his throat.

Brian stood still, scratching his head as he surveyed the couple before him.

"I was just going," Juliette gabbled, snatching up her belongings and heading for the exit.

"Don't leave on my account," Dr Hodges said gruffly.

"Excuse me," Juliette murmured, worried that she had come across as being rude.

"See you in class Miss Harris," Ben called.

Juliette hurried up the corridor, mortified with shame. Now all the lecturers would know for sure, she fretted, as well as the students. They would be the talk of the university. Thoughts raced through her mind. Would Ben be in trouble, she wondered, would his role be compromised or worse in jeopardy? She ducked into the toilets, splashed her face with cold water and waited a few moments until she had composed herself. He was so hot though, she hadn't been able to resist him and Jesus, that kiss, she could almost feel the steam coming out of her ears, thinking about it. A group of chattering women bustled into the room and Juliette groaned as she spotted Carol the gossip in the centre. Juliette moved quickly to dry her hands, head tucked down, hoping she hadn't been recognised.

"Oh hello," a voice clipped with attitude spoke her way. Juliette smiled at Carol, as she squeezed past.

"Looking forward to Introduction to Poetry?" Carol's beady eyes surveyed her, watching for a reaction. The room had fallen uncomfortably silent and Juliette realised that they were all gawping her way, waiting for a response.

"Erm yes, I am," she smiled politely, though her teeth were gritted.

"I'm so glad we've got Ben Rivers again," Carol continued waspishly, "I'm sure that most of the class fancy the pants off him."

Juliette felt a surge of anger, do not retaliate, she told herself. A reprieve came in the form of a beeping text message. Juliette was thankful for the distraction and fumbled in her bag to fish out her phone. She pulled at the door with her other hand, desperate to escape Carol and her hangers on. Although Juliette was amazed at how she had accumulated so many friends. She really was a vile person. It was like being back at school, with the class bullies – jealousy, nastiness and pure spite. As the door closed behind her she heard one of the other women remark, "I wonder who that's off?"

When she stumbled into the classroom a few minutes later, the lecture had commenced and the room was silent. Juliette slunk into the seat next to Will, quickly opened her notebook and wrote today's date. Ben was standing at the projector, discussing poetic form. He glanced her way with a smile and despite her nervous, tumbling stomach, her lips lifted with happiness.

Until Carol and her friends noisily entered the room.

"Sorry Sir," she batted her lashes coquettishly then sniggered in Juliette's direction.

"Immature bitch," Ann said, deliberately loud.

Juliette gripped her pencil, but remained silent. Ben's mouth had set in a firm line, as he waited for them to take their seats. Then he recommenced his lecture and Juliette mirrored the rest of the class, scribbling away, heads bent in concentration. She was impressed with the lecture. He discussed sonnets and blank verse with confidence and clarity and used colourful slides to show examples. It was certainly succinct given the limited time frame, but was informative, interesting and lively. Juliette marvelled at his intellect, his expressive articulation and his lively wit that had the students laughing out loud. Although she did find it difficult to fully concentrate at times. Her mind repeatedly wandered back to their passionate kiss and the feel of his warm embrace. In no time at all the lecture was over and they had stopped for a break. Ben disappeared and the class became a hive of noisy chatter.

"Well I enjoyed that!" Sophie said happily, "I didn't know what to expect to be honest. I've always thought poetry dull, but that was just excellent."

"It *was* interesting," Evelyn agreed, "and Dr Rivers made it so easy to understand."

"Yes," Ann agreed, "but then I've always loved poetry."

Sophie sighed, "it's so romantic. Who on earth is Lord Alfred Tennyson? I've never heard of him, but his writing is exquisite. All I remember of poetry is reading depressing William Blake at school and not being impressed at all."

"He was Poet Laureate of Great Britain," Ann supplied, "born in the early 1800s if I remember correctly. Most prolific during the Victorian era. When I was at school, we studied Wilfred Owen. Fantastic poet. Anthem for Doomed Youth? A brilliant use of language, brings tears to my eyes now thinking about what the soldiers went through."

"What do you think Will?" Evelyn asked. She was going to ask Juliette too, but she was looking decidedly distracted, with a faraway look in her eyes and a pink blush staining her cheeks.

"I'm not really into love poetry," Will admitted, "all a bit arty farty fuss and nonsense to me. Although I do like limericks and Benjamin Zephaniah is pretty cool."

The seminar was soon under way. Sparky debates and personal interpretations bounced around the room. Evelyn even contributed her understanding of the imagery in a poem by William Morris. Although while speaking, she did blush furiously, afterwards she felt a sense of euphoria. It was the first time she had publically voiced an opinion during a seminar and she felt proud. Ben Rivers knew exactly how to coax the students into sharing their thoughts. He never laughed and always listened attentively. With his gentle guidance, the seminar was a great success. Full of passionate debate and enjoyment. As it was drawing to an end, Brian Hodges snuck in and sat in the corner taking notes.

"Well that's it for today, thank you for your very interesting feedback," Ben clicked off the projector. Then there was an almighty bang from the corridor and two men ran into the room.

"What the hell?" Dr Hodges exclaimed, jumping to his feet.

"Sophie, Sophie O'Neill?" One of the men boomed. He was rough looking, with a shock of grey curls and ruddy cheeks. He had a voice recorder gripped in his hand and was waving it above him. His smaller, flaxen haired companion had a posh looking camera raised and was scanning the room.

"Oh no, it's the press!" The words flew from Sophie's lips, causing the men to spin towards her, like carnivores after their prey.

"Sophie, is it true that Ryan has been suspended?"

"What?" Sophie gasped, "of course not!"

Click, click, click went the camera. Sophie raised her hands to shield her face from the glare of the Nikon.

"Hey! Stop that," Ann cried, "you pair of bozos, you shouldn't even be here."

There were gasps from around the room as students craned their necks to see what was going on.

"You need to leave now," Ben suggested in a firm tone.

The two men ignored the warnings, "Sophie, is it true that Ryan is having an affair?"

"What?" Sophie shook her head with bewilderment.

The camera was still flashing, catching every expression on Sophie's face.

"Right you pair that's enough – OUT!" Brian Hodges advanced towards them with a glare. The camera man dodged out of his way, banging into Will who had risen from his seat and was blocking him from making further progress towards Sophie.

"Leave her alone," Will said calmly.

"Get outta my way, boy," came the snarled reply, "the public have a right to know what's going on."

"I don't think so," Ben interjected smoothly, "you are trespassing on private property and her personal life is really none of your business. You should be ashamed," he pulled the camera from his hands.

"Hey, you can't do that. Give me my camera back," the photographer yelled. He lunged for Ben, who moved quickly out of his way. Then Will was rushing forward to grab him in a rugby tackle move that had them both rolling on the floor.

"Oh God," Sophie jumped to her feet, "just stop it. Leave me alone." Tears fell from her eyes as Evelyn held her back, trying to comfort her. Brian was frog marching the reporter from the class, while Ben was pulling the camera man to his feet.

"Get out of this university."

"I'm going," the man said with a scowl, as he readjusted his clothing, "but we'll see you around Sophie." He grabbed his camera back with a grunt, then followed his colleague out of the door.

"How did they get in?" Brian rasped, kicking the door shut. Ben shrugged, he was watching Juliette with her arms round a distraught Sophie.

"I'll zap them," Ben said angrily, shining the light of his projector pen at Sophie.

"Jesus Ben, quit shining that light at her – what are you trying to do, blind her? Everyone needs to stay calm," he lowered his voice, whispering an aside to Ben, "let's get security on the fuckers." Dr Hodges left to alert other members of staff of the incident.

"Oh for God's sake, can you believe that woman has been filming this," Melanie retorted, pointing at the back towards Carol, who was standing with her phone held high, "it will be all over Facebook next!"

"Why would you do that?" Ben said, taking strides towards Carol, "Please delete that footage, this is someone's personal business."

Carol pouted and muttered something unintelligible under her breath but reluctantly deleted the recording.

"Okay it's gone," she flung her phone down and sat back, arms crossed defensively. Ben ignored her feeble tirade and crouched down in front of Sophie, asking if she was okay.

"I should be used to the press by now," she admitted, "when I was younger I enjoyed the attention but I don't anymore. The lengths they will go to, to sell a story is sickening."

Ben nodded, "I would advise you to stay here until those unsavoury men have been escorted from the premises. Can I get you a drink? Vodka, Malibu? A shaken but not stirred martini?"

Sophie laughed, "no thank you Dr Rivers, I have water in my bag. Besides I'm supposed to be on a caffeine and alcohol detox at the moment. One cappuccino will have me on the ceiling."

"Fair enough," Ben said with a smile, "well I'll just be over there doing my marking. If you need anything, don't hesitate to ask." He ambled over to a desk and began sifting through a mountain of paperwork.

# Chapter Twenty-Five

The class had fallen silent, with most of the students dispersing for their lunch break.

"Are you going to be okay?" Will asked Sophie, "only I've arranged to meet Hema. I'm taking her out for dinner…" he trailed off, frowning at Sophie's pale countenance.

"Oh I'll be fine Will honestly," she replied, her voice wobbly, truthfully she was still shaken by the whole incident, but she didn't want to worry him further, "go and enjoy yourself." She was touched by his thoughtfulness and the brave way he had confronted the intrusive photographer, "Evelyn's going to stay with me anyway."

"And I'll nip downstairs with Ann and get you a sandwich," Juliette said, as she followed Will out of the room.

"Would you like me to call your husband?" Evelyn enquired, "maybe he could fetch you dear."

Sophie cast her mind back to her and Ryan's earlier conversation. He was training for most of the day, in preparation for a big cup match the weekend. His phone would probably be switched off and in his locker anyway, and she really didn't want to worry him.

"I'll speak to him this evening," Sophie decided wearily, "they've probably been pestering at the club too – the press I mean."

"How awful for you," Evelyn commented, pouring lukewarm, sugary tea from her flask.

Brian Hodges had re-entered the room and was conversing with Melanie. They looked Sophie's way a few times before Melanie nodded and made her way to where her and Evelyn were seated.

"Sophie, Tarquin Haverstock would like to speak to you," Melanie said, her mouth set in a firm line.

"The course leader?" Sophie gulped, eyes wide, "am I in trouble?"

"No, no of course not," Melanie winked down at her, "he just wants a quick chat that's all."

Sophie followed Melanie from the room, down the stairs and into a brightly painted office.

"Well, well, here comes our very own celebrity," he jumped to his feet, a small man with blonde spiky hair and a colourful shirt that hung out of the waistband of his trousers.

"Come in, come in," he said with a soft Irish lilt, "you are very welcome."

He pulled out a chair, motioning for her to sit.

"I'll be going then," Melanie said as she disappeared from view.

Dr Haverstock pushed the door closed just as the telephone rang.

"Excuse me," in a flash he had picked it up and was jabbering into the mouthpiece.

Sophie glanced round the room in surprise. The walls were covered with posters: Led Zeppelin, The Doors, Janis Joplin. There was even a Beatles mug tilted precariously on the radiator. Dotted around the windows were banners: save the whale, stop the ivory trade, protect the rainforests. Oh my gosh, Sophie thought, I've met my first hippy. A khaki parka was flung on a coat peg. This is so retro, Sophie thought with a gasp and what was that peculiar large white sign on the back of it – could it possibly be a CND symbol?

Tarquin had cut the call and was staring at Sophie. "Another essay extension request, that's my fifth today," he said with a shake of his head, "but why are the excuses so mundane, so unoriginal; busy with work, demanding children. Whatever happened to being disgustingly hungover or on a demonstration rally or even just plain knackered hmm?"

Sophie heard her own discordant, nervous laughter and wondered what she should tell him.

"Well now," he began, as if reading her thoughts, "what are we to do with *you?*"

"I'm so sorry to bring this trouble to your university," Sophie gabbled, "I had a party you see and some of the guests must have notified the press. I trusted the wrong people. You must think I am very naïve." Her lip trembled uncontrollably.

"For sure *bean alainn*," he replied with a wink, "but aren't we all?"

"What did you call me? My name's Sophie."

"Tch, just a bit of Irish to liven up the conversation. English can be so stuffy and boring, don't you think?"

Sophie looked confused, "er, I hadn't really thought about it." She wondered why they were having this conversation. Am I in a lecture? She thought with annoyance as she rose to her feet.

"Sit down," Dr Haverstock instructed, as he himself jumped up and began pacing the room. Sophie watched with astonishment, what a funny little man!

"Just look at those eejits," he ranted, pulling the blinds back with a swish, "like a pack of baying hyenas, after the blood of one woman."

"I think I need to explain," Sophie began nervously, "you see my husband has a love / hate relationship with the press. He likes the attention when it's good, but not so much when it's bad. Our relationship at the moment is…"

"Stop right there!" He held up a hand decorated with rings that glinted and sparkled.

His jewellery is nicer than mine, Sophie thought, looking down at the diamond rocks strapped to her fingers.

"Your personal life is your own affair missy. We're not in the business of judging anyone at *this* university."

Sophie opened her mouth to thank him, but he held up his hand, "but Sophie, maybe we could help you academically. If you need an essay extension, a mentor to help with your studies, even a counsellor to talk to? Hmm, yes, we have them all here." His eyes were kind and warm as they surveyed her.

Sophie gulped in surprise. She wasn't completely sure if this man was a raving lunatic or a really decent guy.

"Th-thank you," she stammered,

"And would you like an escort home? Make sure you get back safe and in one piece?"

"Oh no, it's fine. I mean I'll be fine, but thank you for offering."

"Well then *blade* you're free to go," he slammed the window shut with a bang that made her jump. She grabbed her bag, "thanks erm, bye…"

Just as her hand was on the door handle, Dr Haverstock called out, "and remember missy, 'mistakes are the portals of discovery'."

"Pardon?"

"James Joyce, famous Irish modernist writer. Stream of consciousness?"

Sophie stared blankly.

"Do the modernism module, it's bloody fantastic so it is."

"I'll bear it in mind, thank you again."

"Well now, you're our student, of course we will support you, you don't need to thank me." Dr Haverstock turned away from her with a wave and began typing at a furious pace and Sophie wandered back up to class feeling much calmer.

\* \* \*

The rest of the day passed uneventfully. The afternoon was taken up with European Literature, which promised to be an interesting but difficult subject. The module was led by a lady with a severe looking haircut. Her name was Dr Wilomena Symthe. Rumour was, that her surname had originally been Smith, but she had changed it by deed poll to the more uncommon sounding Smythe. She had a clipped posh accent and spoke slowly, rolling her r's and sounding out big, fancy words so the students could scribble them down correctly. The lecture therefore went on forever, there was no time for a seminar and it even ran over by thirty minutes.

"Talk about tumescent lecturing," Ann complained, yawning loudly.

"What was that dear?" Evelyn asked.

"Basically verbal diarrhoea."

"I think I may have missed my bus," Evelyn commented, as they crossed the courtyard.

"Get in with us," Ann decided, looking for Jon through the crowds of people. Here he was now, jogging up the path in his work uniform.

Sophie lingered behind, her sunglasses firmly in place, "do I look ridiculous?" She asked Juliette.

"Erm, well it is dark Soph," came the reply, "there's no one here, don't worry."

Sophie peered around her, feeling nervous.

"Let me walk you to your car," Juliette said, as she slid an arm through the crook of Sophie's.

"I'll be fine honestly," Sophie began to protest, "but hey, why don't I drop you home."

"You're not fine though, let me walk with you," Juliette insisted.

They walked in companionable silence, each lost in their own thoughts. It was busy, with people milling about and long lines of traffic building up on the main city centre roads.

"Here's me," Sophie said cheerfully, pointing her keys to unlock the doors. "Are you getting in?" She asked Juliette who was leaning against a lamppost looking uncertain.

Juliette slid in the passenger seat and sighed, "I live in a horrible area, you might not want to go there, er, just drop me by the bus stop."

"Don't be ridiculous," Sophie replied, "it can't be that bad, besides, I'm no snob Jules."

"I know you're not," Juliette smiled, "but believe me it is pretty bad. The police patrol the area all the time and only last week there was a drug raid on the flat below me. Teenagers hang about causing trouble, they've nicknamed it ASBO central."

"What's ASBO?" Asked a perplexed Sophie.

"Anti-social behaviour order, basically acting like a yob."

Sophie was shocked, but tried not to show it, "but you're okay in your flat though?"

"Well I just lock out the world and make sure the kids are supervised at all times." Juliette sighed wistfully, "but one day I'll be gone, to the middle class suburbs, with the tree lined avenues, gorgeous gardens and the wisteria around the doors."

"I'm sure of it," Sophie replied, with a firm, positive tone, "but before you do, just let me take you home for now, okay, and you can tell me all about your date on the weekend."

\* \* \*

As expected, Ryan was livid when he heard about what had happened at the university.

"Those bloody vultures," he ranted, "I had them at the club all day too, hanging around, trying to sniff out gossip like stray dogs. I even had to sneak out the back way like some common criminal and disappoint the fans." He paused to take a shuddering gasp of air, "who the hell sold those pictures anyway? It was a private party. I knew I should have paid for a couple of door-men."

"And what good would that have done? We can't frisk every guest that comes here!"

"Can't we prosecute?" Ryan yelled, his tone was getting louder by the minute.

"I doubt it," Sophie replied with a sigh, "there were so many people I didn't know there Ryan. We don't know who it was, it could have been anyone."

"They must be laughing," he snarled, "I bet they've made a few quid out of it. I'll kick their ass when I find out who it is."

"You're not going to find out, so you may as well drop it," Sophie began folding the laundry into a neat pile, "next time we'll just invite very close friends and family. People we trust."

Ryan was pacing the kitchen, "what about your student pals?" he retorted, "you're always saying how short of money that red headed girl is. Maybe she saw an opportunity to make some easy cash."

"Don't be horrible," Sophie was appalled, "Juli-ette was as disgusted as me by the reporter's behaviour today. There is no way she would plan and perpetrate something so devious. She's utterly lovely, a good friend and I trust her completely."

"Hmph," came his childlike reply, "it could have been that broad in the wheelchair. She was giving me daggers all night. Looking down her nose and disapproving. Maybe she wanted to get one over on an able bodied sports man."

"Or maybe it was one of your idiotic mates," shrieked Juliette, "or should I call them superficial hangers on? You're being totally paranoid Ryan, just quit picking on my friends!"

"I'd love to get hold of them." He balled his fist, thumping it down onto the table, "were you okay though, at university I mean?"

"Me? Oh yes fine, couldn't be better," the sarcasm dripped from her voice. She was angry, angry at the person who had betrayed their trust, angry at the press for their intrusion but most of all angry at Ryan for being so bullish and inconsiderate. He glanced her way, realising how upset she was.

"Come on Soph, don't be like that," he reached out to embrace her, "let's not fight about it."

Sophie sniffed, allowing his arms to encircle her waist. God she needed a hug right now.

"It was horrible Ryan. They burst in the class taking photos. I was totally embarrassed. All the other students were staring and gossiping. Then Will started fighting with one, it was just awful."

"I hope they rang the newspaper to complain," Ryan commented as he kissed her throat. Sophie stepped back slightly, "I'm not sure, Tarquin Haverstock had security throw them out."

"Who?" Ryan guffawed, "is that a man?"

"Yes," Sophie said tetchily, "and he was very kind and understanding so don't make fun!"

"Okay babe, let's forget it. Why don't we go upstairs and give each other some stress relief?" He raised his eyebrows in a cheeky attempt to make her laugh. It worked and she allowed herself to be pulled by the hand towards the staircase and the opulent balustrade. As they climbed the stairs, Sophie thought fleetingly of Juliette, her tiny flat and lack of garden, right in the middle of ASBO central.

\* \* \*

The week passed by without any further press intrusion. The university had increased security; the mars bar guard had been given the extra responsibility to 'keep any eye out for any suspicious activity.' He took it very seriously, following Sophie around the uni and assuring her that she was safe under his watch. Tarquin Haverstock was also attentive. He had stopped Sophie again on the way to class, to enquire after her welfare and to reiterate his offer of academic help. All the uni gang rallied around her, cheering her up and offering support and a listening ear if she needed to off load any worries. Sophie felt blessed and was touched by their concern and kindness. Her own mother and best friend were occupied with their own lives and dilemmas. In fact, Yvonne had been coolly indifferent when Sophie had confided in her.

"That's the price of fame," she had commented breezily, "you shouldn't take it so personally Sophie. It will be someone else under the press spotlight next week."

Her mother then went on to criticise how she, Sophie, had always been the same as a child: melodramatic and ungrateful. She made Sophie feel that the whole debacle was in fact her fault and the reporters were merely undertaking a thankless task.

"How's Roger?" Sophie had bit out with a hint of cattiness, "Derek sends you his love."

Then she immediately felt guilty, "sorry Mom, my nerves are completely frazzled at the moment."

"Ah yes, well I must dash darling," Yvonne had replied, her voice softer and brighter, "but call me if you need me."

Amber had given her little support either, deeming the whole incident as being hilarious.

"I would have enjoyed the attention," she divulged, "and at least *your* picture in the newspaper was flattering, unlike the poor vicars." There was that, conceded Sophie as she vowed to look on the bright side.

# Chapter Twenty-Six

So the weekend arrived and Juliette had worked herself into a complete fluster. She fretted over what to wear, how much money to take, what to do with the kids. In the end, Marie took charge, bundling them into her car with the promise of a late, fun filled night, movies, hot chocolate and toasted marshmallows.

"Enjoy yourself kiddo," she said, gripping her in a bear like hug, "and remember, if you're hating it, text me and Dave will come fetch you in a flash. Where are you going anyway?"

"I have no idea," Juliette replied with a nervous smile.

Marie shook her head, "well please put me out of my misery and let me know you're safe and happy."

With a promise to do just that, Juliette waved them off, then began preparing for the evening.

She soaked herself in the tub until her body resembled a prune, exfoliated and moisturised until her skin was smooth and flake free, she even cut her toenails and painted them a baby pink hue. Her practical and big pants were flung across the room. She rummaged to the depths of her underwear drawer until she found a black, satin bra and knicker set, with the labels still attached. Her hair was fluffed and back combed until it cascaded around her shoulders smelling of coconut, soft and gleaming. Then she squirted her most expensive perfume (a Christmas present off Maz) across her cleavage and the pulse spots at her wrists. She stepped into a new black dress, (purchased in the sales from Primark – a bargain at £12.00) it looked surprisingly chic when teamed with a pair of pretty pearls (a loan off Mom). Then finally, she rubbed vigorously at a pair of dusty black stilettoes until they shone and stepped into them with a nervous glance in the mirror. Ta-da! Ready or not Dr Rivers, here I am.

Another twenty minutes until he was picking her up. Juliette stuffed her money in her clutch bag, reapplied her lip gloss, then paced the living room, pausing to fluff a cushion, straighten the curtains, kick at the turned up edge of the floor rug. With an impatient sigh she picked up her keys, flung a shawl across her shoulders, then banged the door on the way out. She was meeting him at the end of the street, outside the Blue Badger pub. Despite telling herself that she shouldn't be ashamed of where she lived, she was. The thought of him pulling up outside the maisonette block made her wince with unease. So here she was, tottering down the street, swerving round the dog mess and the puddles pooling across the pavement. At least it had stopped raining, she surmised. All day it had lashed down and the wind was blowing a gale, lifting her hair and twisting it around like a whirly gig. Then she saw him, leaning against a big, blue posh looking car and none of it mattered.

"We're catching the train," he said with a smile, as they pulled into the multi storey car park.

"Oh," Juliette was surprised, "where are we going?"

"Just to the next town," he replied, "it's a surprise."

Juliette nodded, feeling happy. He looked so handsome in the evening light, dark hair and stubble and the most heart breaking smile. Juliette's stomach fluttered when he looked her way. She waited while he hopped out of the car, then opened the door for her so she could slide out. At least her heels gave her further height, her head was almost touching his chin, but she still felt tiny in stature compared to him.

He watched as she smoothed down her dress, "are you okay?"

"Yes…thank you, are you?"

"I am. I was just contemplating how you are going to walk in those heels."

They both laughed, "you might have to give me a piggy back later on."

He grinned, "with pleasure, come on," He took her hand tugging her gently towards the exit.

The sound of the trains was deafening as they entered the busy station.

"It's been years since I caught a train," yelled Juliette. There were crowds of people scattered about, purchasing newspapers and coffee, heading home after a busy day in the city.

"I love travelling this way," Ben admitted, "the scenery, no traffic jams, being able to read uninterrupted for a while."

"Sounds heavenly," Juliette's breath curled in the cold night air, she shivered, partly from the chill but also from his close proximity. The anticipation and possibility of what the evening would bring. She watched him surreptitiously, as he perused the locomotive timetable.

"Ours should be here soon," he said, as he joined a queue to purchase tickets.

Juliette stared at the glossy magazines on the news rack, the same predictable headlines, stick thin models on the front covers. Give me a book any day she thought with a sigh.

"The train is coming now," Ben said, "can you run?"

"Run?" Juliette stared aghast at her already throbbing feet.

"Jog then?" He ushered her towards the entrance to the platform and off they set, weaving through the crowds, up a flight of steel steps, over a graffiti covered bridge, down onto another platform where lines of strangers stood waiting patiently. Seconds later a train zoomed to a standstill in front of them. Doors whooshed open and they laughed as they jumped on with a crowd of jostling commuters. There were no seats left so they clung onto a rail as the train pulled away from the station. Juliette was sandwiched between Ben and a large man who was holding onto a shiny briefcase. The train sped up the track and Juliette lost her balance, bumping against Ben. This is nice she thought, as she placed one hand on his chest to stop herself jolting forward.

"Do you work out?" The words left her mouth as she felt his muscles.

"I have a work out room," he confirmed with a nod, "some cardio apparatus, weights, dumb bells, that kind of thing. I hate the gym, much prefer exercising in private, all those lines of people repeating the same movements on the same machines, like rats on a wheel."

Juliette nodded, "I wish I could afford the gym! I do love swimming, although I don't get much chance to actually swim as the kids coerce and bully me onto the slides, the wave machines and the rapids.

Ben laughed, "that sounds like fun."

They chatted as the grey, steel structures of the city dwindled out to be replaced by emerald green countryside, hedgerows and trees that flew by. The train slowed as they neared another station.

"Is this our stop?" Juliette asked, peering out at the darkness.

"Next one."

Commuters flooded off, leaving plenty of empty seats. Juliette sank down opposite Ben. They smiled at each other, then his gaze travelled lower down to her legs. I am so glad I wore a short dress thought Juliette with a blush, "so, er…what did you do New Year's Eve?"

"Family party," replied Ben, "music, food, party games. I even played my saxophone."

"Really? How long have you been playing?"

"Since a teenager, I've got a tenor and a soprano, I play in a local band at weekends mainly, pubs social clubs. Drive the dog mad practising at home. He sings along, would you like to see?"

He pulled out his phone and Juliette moved to squash close to him. The video clip of the dog (named Heathcliff) howling along to Ben's rendition of Valerie was hilarious. Juliette wiped the tears of laughter from her eyes.

"Your dog is a star."

"He's extremely mercurial, but cute I suppose."

She fished her phone out of a sparkly clutch bag, "this is Harry and Molly." She showed him a recent snapshot of them hugging and pouting at the camera.

"They take after you," Ben said, "lovely looking, you must be very proud."

"Thank you," Juliette reddened, "I am."

"You look beautiful this evening, have I told you?"

"Erm yes, twice now, but keep on, I could get used to it."

Ben moved a curl from her forehead and stared down at her with blazing eyes. She leant towards him, her lips parting instinctively. Then the whistle sounded loudly making her jump in fright.

"It's just the train slowing down. Look, we're nearing the station."

Juliette leant across him to look out at the approaching platform, it was small with a bright neon sign flashing a welcome to Castleford.

"I've heard of this place," Juliette exclaimed.

"Have you never been?"

"We passed through it once on the way to the seaside, but no, I've never actually looked around. I just thought it was a little village, with not much going on."

"You're in for a treat tonight then." Ben got to his feet holding out his hand, "come."

* * *

They left the station and walked uphill towards an archaic looking church which had light streaming through the stained glass windows.

"Oh my gosh, this is beautiful," Juliette gasped as she stared up at the gargoyles and intricate stonework.

"Are we going in?" She asked, as Ben led her up a winding path.

There were graves on either side of them, marble headstones shaded by gnarled trees. Flowers wilted in the cool breeze and eerie cries from nearby wild animals resonated in the stillness.

"Would you like to?"

Juliette nodded eagerly, following him towards a heavy oak door that opened into a dimly lit porch. They walked through, the air was heavy with a heady perfume of incense and flowers.

"Wow, this is stunning," there was a long nave bordered by tall, flickering candles and rows of wooden benches. At the end of each seat was tied a small spray of cream and yellow roses. Juliette touched them gently, bending to sniff their sweet scent.

"They're left over from a wedding earlier," Ben explained.

"But how do you…"

"Ben, Ben dear boy," a deep voice resounded. Juliette spun to see a man striding towards them, arm outstretched and face beaming.

Ben clasped it firmly, "uncle."

"How are you?" The bearded man asked.

"I'm good, no great thank you."

"This is your uncle?" Juliette exclaimed, eyes wide.

"Ron, please call me Ron. Lovely to meet you Miss…" he trailed off, looking at her enquiringly.

"Juliette," she found her voice after a lengthy pause.

"Miss Juliette, beautiful name for a beautiful lady."

"Thank you," Juliette smiled warmly.

"Uncle Ron is the parish vicar here," Ben supplied.

"Oh," Juliette looked towards his neck, searching for a white collar.

"I've taken off my uniform for the night," he said with a conspiratorial wink, "ach but it's been a smashing wedding today. Your Aunt Pat and I were invited to the reception. We both had a few too many whiskeys and now she's away to her bed." He chuckled, his complexion was ruddy and his eyes merry. Juliette liked him already.

"But she's left you a bottle of wine, she thought you might be thirsty after your journey. Do you like red dear?"

"I do," Juliette nodded enthusiastically.

"Well," Ron clasped his hands together, "I'll leave you to look around my humble church. Enjoy yourselves this evening and Ben, don't be a stranger."

Ben gripped him in a manly embrace, "give my love to Aunt Pat."

Uncle Ron kissed Juliette on the cheek before disappearing outside.

"Do all of your family live here?" Juliette asked, as Ben opened the wine.

"A few cousins."

She sipped at the wine, it was delicious: fruity and full bodied and tasted expensive.

"How about your parents?"

There was a pause, "both dead," Ben replied flatly.

Juliette put down her glass, "I'm so sorry. I didn't mean to pry."

Ben sat down at a pew, "it's okay, it was cancer, first Dad in his lungs, then eighteen months later, Mom had it too, in the pancreas and pretty much everywhere else."

"Oh Ben I'm sorry," Juliette covered his hand with her own warm fingers, sympathy and concern etched on her face. How dreadful to lose both parents in such a short space of time. She tried to envisage a world without her dear Mom and Dad and couldn't.

"Let's look around," Ben rose to his feet, "you know this church is hundreds of years old."

"It's stunning," Juliette stared in awe at the colours in the glass windows and the murals hanging from the stone pillars. There was a beautiful stone font and altar with golden cups and crosses resting on it.

"Doesn't your uncle worry these artefacts will be stolen?" Juliette asked as she ran her fingers over the cool metal.

"Not in Castleford. It's real olde worlde. Residents leave their doors unlocked, have credit accounts at the local shops, have village dances and fetes, where everyone participates."

"How lovely." Juliette felt a pang of sadness for her own maisonette and shady neighbours, where no one socialised and mistrust was rife. "This is amazing." She stopped to admire a majestic organ, "it must be so dreamy to be married here."

"Are you always such a romantic?" Ben teased.

"I guess so, isn't every female the same?"

"Not my sister," he shook his head emphatically, "she's a real tomboy, wouldn't catch her in a white frilly dress. But you, you're different,"

"Maybe I was a princess in a past life," Juliette grinned, "only a feisty, warrior type."

"Like an Amazonian?" Ben suggested.

"Yep, just like that," Juliette laughed as Ben caught her by the hand and spun her round.

"Well now Miss Harris, Amazonian princess, are you hungry yet?"

"Famished," Juliette replied with a nod. Ben pulled her closer so his arms were encircling her and their noses were touching.

"Are you having a good time so far?"

"I am," Juliette replied breathlessly. He kissed her lips lightly then spun her away from him, in a pirouette that left her head dizzy.

"Let's go get some food."

"Not much further now," they walked hand in hand through quaint cobbled streets, peering in tiny shop windows and stopping to admire a stunning marble lion.

"You're right, this is so olde worlde. The architecture is beautiful."

Juliette's feet were throbbing painfully and she was aware that she had been tottering ungracefully, although Ben seemed not to have noticed. He was chatting away, telling her about his youth, the carefree summer days spent here. Why oh why did I not wear flats? She thought with a grimace.

"The restaurant's just here," he led her to a door where the sounds of music emanated.

"It's a jazz club and a five star eaterie too."

Juliette was impressed as they entered and waited for a lady to take her shawl and Ben's jacket.

"Mr Rivers, so lovely to see you again," a trouser suited maître d' led them to a pretty window alcove, where candles lit the table and a pot of fresh flowers created a colourful display.

"Champagne?" Ben enquired with a glint in his eye.

"Oh er…if it's not too expensive."

"This is on me," he explained, "I want to spoil you."

Juliette quickly calculated how much money she had in her purse.

"Okay," she smiled, "but I do want to contribute towards the bill."

Ben ordered for them, a long, French sounding bottle that had the waitress nodding with approval.

"I have no idea what food to order," Juliette admitted, peering at the fancy menu.

"The beef is exquisite," he replied, "and maybe oysters to start?"

Juliette giggled as the champagne fizzed up her nostrils.

"Are you trying to seduce me Dr Rivers?"

"Who moi?" He grinned boyishly and she felt her heart racing in response.

She let him order for them both and they relaxed into an easy conversation. When the oysters were set down in front of them, Juliette eyed them dubiously.

"OMG," she began, "I can't believe I'm just about to eat oysters."

Ben smiled with encouragement, "go on, you go first."

Juliette picked up a shell, staring at the contents. It really didn't look that appetising, in fact it resembled a squidgy mess, but she was willing to give it a go. She sniffed it first, it didn't smell bad so what the hell, here goes. The contents came out easily enough in her fingers, quickly she stuffed it in her mouth. Urgh, it was slimy, cold and chewy. Juliette swallowed it down with a huge gulp of champagne. She looked across at Ben who was laughing behind clenched fists.

"Your turn," she said brightly.

He picked up a shell, tipped his head back and the oyster slid gracefully into his mouth.

"Mmmm," he said with a wipe of his lips.

Juliette stared wide eyed, "you've done this before haven't you," she said with a touch of envy.

"No, I just googled it."

Juliette burst out laughing, "you googled how to eat oysters?"

"I did," he confirmed, "I wanted to impress you."

Aww, Juliette was touched by his words, "did you like it?"

"Honestly no, it was vile."

"Totally gross," Juliette agreed, "let's skip to the main course."

The beef was just perfect, tender and mouth-watering, lightly flavoured with a sprinkling of herbs. Juliette dabbed her mouth with her napkin, "that was delicious," she said, "and this is a lovely restaurant."

Ben nodded, "it's not just the food that's great either, the musicians are talented guys, they add to the ambience."

"Yes," Juliette cocked her head to one side, listening to the gentle sounds of a piano and the low whistle of a clarinet.

"So you like jazz music as well as eighties?"

"I do and why on earth did you think I like bubble-gum pop, Kylie, was that the one?"

"Erm, I just overhead another student saying she thought you were a fan."

"I'm glad they think I'm that interesting to gossip about.

Juliette laughed, the champagne had relaxed her and she wanted to be truthful with him. "I think a *lot* of the students think you are interesting."

Ben leaned towards her, "I'm only interested in you."

Juliette swallowed, "are you really?"

"Of course I am," he insisted gently.

"But, well, I mean," now she was flustered, "do you do this often?"

"What?" He seemed genuinely puzzled.

"Take out students." There, she had said it, the thing that was worrying her.

"Never," his reply was firm and resolute, "you are the first, the only one."

Juliette grinned, feeling ridiculously happy, "I'm so glad," she sighed with relief.

"Enough talking, dance with me?"

"What here?"

"They have a dance floor," he led her up winding steps to a small square where the band played and a husky sounding man crooned, with a pint in his hand. Juliette felt suddenly shy and overcome with guilt for the way she had questioned him.

"I'm sorry," she babbled, "I didn't mean to grill you, I hope you're not offended…"

"Shush," he interrupted, "you talk far too much."

Juliette fell silent, allowing him to take her in his arms. They moved slowly, pressed close together, revolving on the dimly lit dance floor. She looked into his eyes and saw warmth, kindness and desire.

"I like you, a lot," she blurted out, "since the first day I saw you in the canteen. You're gorgeous, clever, funny and kind." She stopped as she was struck with a sudden self-realisation. She was falling for him, head over heels, hearts, flowers and cupid, the whole shebang. Marie's words of caution rang in her ears and she stepped back slightly. I've said too much, given too much away, I need to be cool and indifferent she silently wailed, now he's going to run a mile. But he didn't. He stood there smiling, his amazing, heart breaking, stomach clenching smile.

"And you. Are. Very. Honest and utterly lovely." Then he was kissing her tenderly, his arms were holding her, strong and protective and she was standing on tip-toes kissing him back and touching his face with wonder. It was passionate and overwhelming, it was just perfect.

* * *

While they waited for their desserts, Juliette perched on his knee, where they took a series of selfies, hugging, kissing and pulling stupid faces.

"I need the ladies," Juliette laughed, picking up her handbag. Once ensconced in a cubicle, she typed out a quick message to Maz asking if the kids were okay and assuring her that she was having a wonderful time.

**Kids cool, stuffed with chocolate. Enjoy! Xxx**

Juliette grinned at the response, swilled her hands, retouched her make up then rushed back outside to Ben. The pudding was there; plump strawberries on mounds of creamy vanilla ice cream. They finished off the champagne, wolfed down the desserts, then clattered back upstairs for another dance – a faster one this time, that had them both spinning and chuckling loudly.

Ben glanced at his watch, "we should be heading back to the train station," he said regretfully.

To Juliette's chagrin, he insisted on paying for everything and would not listen to her protests.

"Cook me a meal," he suggested, "as a repayment."

"It's a deal," Juliette agreed, with a twinkle in her eye, overjoyed at the thought of another date with the subliminal Dr Rivers.

They retraced their steps through the now deserted streets.

"Let's go this way," Ben swerved up a side alley.

"You really know your way around huh?" Juliette commented, nestling against his chest.

"It hasn't changed much since I was a child. I have a good memory."

They skidded down a steep embankment. Juliette tugged off her shoes, her throbbing feet sank into dewy grass, she sighed with relief.

"Piggyback?" He offered crouching down.

She hopped onto his back and he stumbled, almost tipping them both over.

"Am I too heavy?" She asked laughing.

"Not at all, too much champagne I think. Actually you are as light as a feather," he hitched her thighs up to rest on his waist.

"There's a river not far from here," he told her, as they set off.

"A river? How romantic," she kissed his stubbly neck, leaving a trail of faint lipstick marks.

Ben coughed, "watch out, I might drop you."

"I'm just getting my own back on you," she teased, breathing in the divine scent of him.

"You are very distracting Miss Harris. You constantly distract me in class."

"Oh do I Dr Rivers? Maybe you need to concentrate on your books more."

She heard him groan as she nipped at the tender skin behind his right ear.

"Maybe I need to give you detention."

"Oh yes please," she squirmed playfully, feeling his muscles tense.

"Right that's it," he swung her down and round to face him. They stumbled into a shop doorway and into each other's arms and fervent kisses.

\* \* \*

Juliette threw a pebble into the swirling river, watching as it disappeared beneath the bubbling froth. The gushing water was noisy, but strangely soothing, the moonlight shimmered on the surface casting a luminous silver sheen. Fish jumped from dark, murky ripples, their fins flapping wildly before they dived gracefully back underneath the torrent. The enamoured couple hung over a barrier watching the revelations of nature below them.

"Make a wish," Ben said, pressing a shiny penny into her palm.

Juliette smiled shyly then closed her eyes. *I wish, Harry, Molls and I could live here.* She lobbed the penny as high and far as she could.

"What was your wish?" Ben asked.

"I can't tell you!" She socked him playfully on the arm, "it won't come true."

"Do you believe in the tooth fairy too?" He asked with a rueful smile.

"Of course, I am she!" They laughed and cuddled closer.

"Are you warm enough?" Juliette nodded, her face was squashed against his chest and her arms were wrapped tightly round him. At this moment, she had never felt warmer.

"It's a full moon, look." She stared at the silver orb, peeking from behind dark, misty clouds. Stars twinkled, a net of diamonds in a pitch black void.

"Selenophilia," murmured Ben against her hair.

"What does that mean?" She peered up at him.

"It means to love the moon, to find it captivating."

"I like that word…selenophilia," it rolled off her tongue, melodic and smooth.

Juliette was silent while she pondered, "and you are cognoscenti."

"Tell me your definition."

"A person with superior knowledge. That's you Ben. You have a superior knowledge of literature, you're amazing."

"Thank you," he bowed his head, "you are extremely kind, but I really think there are other superior cognoscenti than me at Chattlesbury. Now we must go."

He moved away so she could slip on her shoes, "what time is it?"

"Almost twelve, and the last train is due any time now."

"Oh gosh," Juliette quickened her pace so they were almost running. Down the street they flew, passing a clock tower gathering momentum to chime the witching hour. Into the station they tumbled, the train was there at the platform, the driver rumbling the engine to life as he prepared to pull away. Ben lunged forward, thumping the door lock, allowing them to fall inside the carriage, panting breathlessly.

They fell onto seats, sitting opposite, they surveyed each other. Juliette thought how completely lovely this man was, how considerate, kind and knee trembling attractive. She hoped with all her heart that he would play a part in her future. While he was thinking of her and her beguiling smile, her endearing positivity and her energetic zest for life, she was sexy and warm and exciting and he was desperate to know her better. But they remained silent, appraising each other with lingering looks, happy smiles and untold words, while the train zoomed down the darkened track, shooting electric sparks into the night sky, as they headed home, back to familiarity, back to Chattlesbury and the beginnings of a new day.

To be continued…

Dear reader,

We hope you enjoyed reading *The School of Dreams*. Please take a moment to leave a review, even if it's a short one. Your opinion is important to us.

Discover more books by Julia Sutton at https://www.nextchapter.pub/authors/julia-sutton

Want to know when one of our books is free or discounted? Join the newsletter at http://eepurl.com/bqqB3H

Best regards,
Julia Sutton and the Next Chapter Team

The story continues in:
Visions of the Heart

To read the first chapter for free, please head to:
https://www.nextchapter.pub/books/visions-of-the-heart

The School of Dreams
ISBN: 978-4-86752-855-6 (Large Print)

Published by
Next Chapter
1-60-20 Minami-Otsuka
170-0005 Toshima-Ku, Tokyo
+818035793528
13th August 2021

9 784867 528